WHAT CAME WEST

ALSO BY JOSH WEIL

The New Valley
The Great Glass Sea
The Age of Perpetual Light

WHAT CAME WEST

A NOVEL

JOSH WEIL

DOUBLEDAY
NEW YORK

FIRST DOUBLEDAY HARDCOVER EDITION 2026

Published by Doubleday, a division of Penguin Random House LLC, 1745 Broadway, New York, NY 10019.

Doubleday and the portrayal of an anchor with a dolphin are registered trademarks of Penguin Random House LLC.

LIBRARY OF CONGRESS CATALOGING-IN-PUBLICATION DATA
Names: Weil, Josh author
Title: What came west : a novel / Josh Weil.
Description: First Doubleday hardcover edition. | New York : Doubleday, 2026.
Identifiers: LCCN 2025032088 (print) | LCCN 2025032089 (ebook) | ISBN 9780385550994 hardcover | ISBN 9780385551007 ebook
Subjects: LCGFT: Novels | Fiction | Historical fiction | Social problem fiction
Classification: LCC PS3623.E4273 W43 2025 (print) | LCC PS3623.E4273 (ebook)
LC record available at https://lccn.loc.gov/2025032088
LC ebook record available at https://lccn.loc.gov/2025032089

penguinrandomhouse.com | doubleday.com

Printed in the United States of America
1st Printing

The authorized representative in the EU for product safety and compliance is Penguin Random House Ireland, Morrison Chambers, 32 Nassau Street, Dublin D02 YH68, Ireland, https://eu-contact.penguin.ie.

for Jen

It is as if a man, whose back was broken or nearly so and who was compelled to go bent, should find a branch backbone sprouting straight up from below the break and should gradually develop new arms and shoulders and head, while the old damaged portion of his body died.

—JOHN MUIR, *MY FIRST SUMMER IN THE SIERRA*

AUTHOR'S NOTE

This is a work of fiction, in no way meant to make claims on history or speak for any community. But it is set amid an all-too-real past of genocide, extinction, and environmental destruction, the gravity of which was ever present throughout the writing of this book.

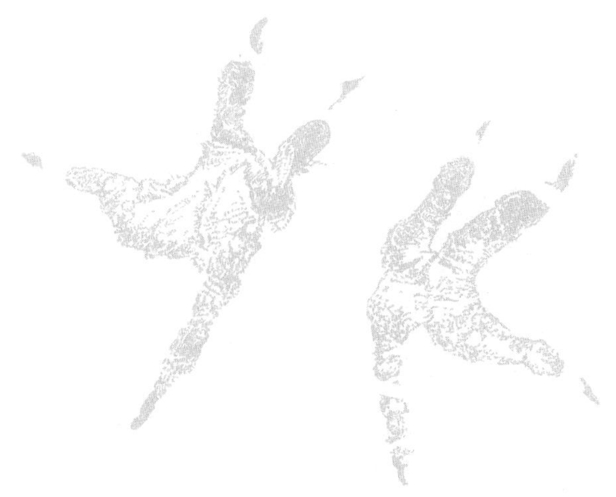

WHAT CAME WEST

AUTUMN, 1849

A man, or something worse.

In the black night, they hear it: a screaming breaking through the low and ceaseless roaring of the river, its ache or anger or fear or whatever desperate thing might make an animal or man make such a sound echoing around the canyon, off of the boulders, then sinking beneath the hush of rushing water, before coming again.

On the bank, listening, two men and a boy. The biggest man is white, bearded, balding, a rifle in his hands. The other is dark skinned beneath his black mustache, a kanaka, native to the Sandwich Islands, crouched beside his dog, fingers buried in its neck fur. The boy is still too young to shave, though within the year he won't be, his fuzz-soft face faintly lambent in the last reaches of the firelight. He grips a knife, slick and stinking from the gutting of fish. Behind them, the campfire is a red unsteadiness, a whiff of trout skin burning. Beyond it: the mules' uneasy shifting.

"Could be a catamount," the boy's father whispers.

The kanaka shakes his head. "Too low. Their sound more like a woman."

"You think it's a man?" the boy says.

Another scream. In the strip of sky above the canyon, there is no moon, just stars, their light too faint to show more than a riffling of rapids, the stillness of stones, the black mass of the far bank like some great weight the boy can feel tilting the earth beneath his feet toward whatever over there is screaming.

Then his father is shouting across the ravine. "Hey, you okay? You need help?" But each word seems to only push the screaming louder. And as the boy watches his own fire-thrown shadow shiver before him on the river's surface, the realization shoots through him: for all he cannot see, the same is not true for whatever over there is watching them. The dog's teeth flashing with each bark. The gleam of the blade at the boy's side. On his fingers, the fish slime has glued the handle to his fist, and as the stone-clatter crashes closer down the far bank, he grips it till it seems to fuse with his own skin. His father's rifle rises—its glinting streak—into a sudden silence: the stone-clatter stopped, the screaming stopped. As if whatever—*whoever*—had been rushing for them had recognized the glint, known the meaning of a gun.

Though later that night, the three of them back around the fire, the boy sits gouging with his fingers at a blackened shell of fish, listening to his father argue with the kanaka about whether the savages up here, so much higher in these unknown mountains than any other miner had ever been, could be acquainted with the weapons of whites. Whether there could even be a white come here before them. Or if it might have been a bear. Or some other creature as yet undiscovered, save by the Indians. Which is when the kanaka, ripping the crisped head off another charcoaled trout, tells them about the bohemkuleh. He is sucking out the insides when he says it, and through his mouthful they cannot make out the word, but this is why they partnered with him: his long-ago migration from his island home to here, his years lived in the lowlands, his marriage to a digger squaw, her valley language near enough that of the hill diggers higher up.

"Road women," he tells them now, flames shifting fish grease across his face. "They call them road women."

The boy's father reaches to the pan, pulls out another trout. "You said it didn't sound like a woman. Said it couldn't be a—"

"I said they *call* them that." With his nails, the kanaka scrapes away the charring. "But it ain't a woman. And it ain't a man."

"What is it?" the boy says, and his father turns that look on him, that mix of disappointment and tenderness that comes when the man remembers his son is still a kid.

The kanaka sits shaking clumps of charred fish off his hand for long enough that the dog, still by the river, gets off three barks. "Both," he says. "At the same time. Or able to switch back and forth. But always bad." A spirit, he tells them, or some kind of creature, he isn't sure, only knows his wife's tribe believes they haunt the woods at night, flitting through the darkness between trees, screaming so plaintively they lure you out.

"Why?" the boy says.

"To get inside. Your skin, your body. Get at your head. Make you go mad." Like a parasite, he explains, except it feeds off your mind, leaves you less than human, unfit to be with the tribe, unable to do anything but weep and cry, let loose that same plaintive screaming, lure another softhearted soul into the woods, so the bohemkuleh can exchange your body for the next.

"Well"—the boy's father smacks the small fish against a rock, a sudden spray of blackened bits—"I, for one, don't feel particularly *lured.*" He grins at his son, says, "How about you?" And the boy, his own jaw stiff as the frozen river stones, has to turn away. Behind him, he hears his father still talking, but he is listening to the dog. The echo of its barking coming back across the river. It *had* sounded sad. Something in the screaming stirred by more than rage or pain. Maybe that is why the picture he cannot shake is of the digger squaw he once saw grieving someone who'd died. She'd smeared soot and pitch over her face, so thick the tattoos on her cheeks and chin barely showed through, her hair stiff with it, her eyes stark white inside the crusty blackness. Remembering the screaming, he sees it coming from her mouth. The tears in her eyes. The moon has broken over the ridge, crept halfway down the other side. Soon he will see her, crouched there on that far bank, hunched and shaking in her silent grief, waiting for him to wade across and help her. Her face snaps up: teeth white as her eyes, tongue black as her throat.

A hand on his back. He turns to see his father's face, the big beard moving with his chewing.

"No, son." His father's smile is a slight brightening beneath his beard. "It was just a catamount." And turning back to the kanaka across the flames, he says, "Isn't that right?"

The kanaka spits a slurry of manducated fishbones, wipes his mustache with his wrist.

"Who's to say there ain't some kind of cougar up here sounds like a man?" the boy's father says. "Nobody. Nobody *been* up here. Nobody'd know. No." He stands. "It was a catamount. Smelled this." Gives his half-eaten fish a shake. "Simple as that. Big old cat out there wailing away 'cause it wants a bite."

This time he smiles a grin so big the boy can't help but smile back. His father gives the fish another flap, sends a quick-lipped kissing sound toward the river—*kiss-kiss-kiss*—and the boy can almost believe it *had* just been a cat. The longer it goes on—the flapping fish, the kiss-kiss-kissing—the more likely it seems. Stirred by his father, the dog barks faster, and it is a relief to remember the dog is a hunter, bred to go crazy at coons and cougars, a relief to think *that's* what got it worked up, to cast his fears away with the fish when his father at last rears back and throws it.

In the morning the fish-half is still there, lying blackly on a rock. But the dog is gone. They find it not far downriver, its spotted body swarming with flies. Closer, the boy can see it has bled out its throat, a disorienting feeling washing through him—revulsion at the claw-rent gash, relief his father had been right—until he looks at the kanaka. The man is crouched over the dog, face drained of anger, replaced with fear. And dropping beside him, the boy thrusts his hands into the blood-gunked neck fur, fingers searching for the punctures of incisors.

"Kid," the kanaka says. Says it again. And when the boy looks up: "That was done with a knife."

"Fellas?" His father, calling from the open jumble of stones outside the thicket.

The blood is spread across a rockface in ragged red lines not even fully dried.

Two letters: *GO.*

Written big enough they should have seen it from their camp. They'd left their only firearms back by their bedrolls—the boy's revolver; his father's rifle; an old half-patched, crack-barreled flintlock that is the kanaka's only gun—a half-minute run at least. That, as they stand there looking up and down the river, seems to grow longer, the ravine expanding with an even vaster emptiness, the water rushing louder, the rocks rising over the chasm's sides to an impossibly distant sky.

"Sonofabitch," the boy's father says. He is looking at the water. At something under the current. A dark round hole that the boy, looking closer, sees isn't a hole, but a pan.

"Someone's been here?" the boy says.

His father's gaze jerks to their camp. "Sonofabitch," he says again, louder. And then is splashing in.

It is their pan. Their shovel. There is another flash of something else—head of a pick, bit of a drill—and they are all three in the water, slipping onto their hands and knees, groping for their tools. The boy's father goes under, wading out after the spade, comes up sputtering and splashing, crashing back toward the shore. Even over the river's thunder the boy can hear the blade bash deeper and deeper into the gravel, his father's grunts as, hammering the handle with a rock, he drives it in as if to mark the bank. "Ours!" he shouts into the roar. "Our claim!" Bellowing it up and down the canyon, his voice swamped by the river's own.

They spend the rest of the morning wading into freezing rapids, plunging under icy pools to salvage what they can. A digging knife lost, the handle of a pan, but most they manage to save. No real damage done. Except for the feeling that has been stolen from the place itself. For the past six days, making their way up the Yuba's south fork, ever since leaving the other miners far down by the main branch, they'd been in awe of the river. Even the kanaka, used to such things, would whistle when, rounding a curve, they'd come upon a cascade so smooth and clear you could see the beveled stones beneath. Even the boy's father—who'd only risked this rush upriver out of a desperate wish to strike it rich enough to leave for home before another winter—seemed unable to stop saying, time and time again, *Some country*. To the boy it had appeared an endless necklace of viridescent jewels, deep emerald pools strung together by silver falls, draped across stones so smooth and warm with midday sun he could rest his cheek on one, as once he'd done upon his mother's breast, and shut his eyes, and feel again as serene as when he'd been a child.

No longer. Now the river's beauty seems some kind of trap, a lure to lull them out of alertness, the ease the boy had felt perched by a smooth-pooled stretch with pole and line just the past evening now a rawer loss than any of the things thrown in. Hunting the scattered tools, the men had kept an eye on their surroundings—rock shadows ready to spring, flashes of glare thrown by the rising sun—heads whipping around at sounds of squirrels, cocking to catch a woodpecker's pounding.

Now the kanaka wants to go back. They are by the water's edge, preparing the rocker cradle, the boy leveling a spot for the heavy wooden box to rest on its curved boards while his father sets the smaller mesh-screened hopper on its top, the kanaka standing beside their soaked clothes drying in the sun.

"What," his father says, checking the canvas apron beneath the screen, "and leave our claim to him?"

All week they have found traces, but nothing like the gold flakes they panned at this place in a mere hour the evening before. Which was why they'd planned to stay, unpacked, brought their equipment down by the river. The whole reason they were here at all. The only reason any man who could write a word in English would be.

"Don't you see?" the boy's father says. "He's *trying* to scare us."

"Well," the kanaka tells him, "it's worked."

"Why?"

"*Why?*"

"Why do you think he wants so bad for us to go away?" In the kanaka's silence the boy's father says, "Hand me that," and, seeing the other man refuse to move, the boy reaches for the plank at the kanaka's feet.

"And why wouldn't he stick *his* shovel in the ground?" the kanaka says. "Hmm? If he wants so bad to show us it's his—"

"'Cause he *don't* want." The boy's father bolts the handle onto the hopper. "Don't want to show no one. We see a claim up here, what we gonna do? Go upriver, stake our own. Back to the bar for more supplies. Within a week, the whole damn river's . . ." His chin juts out, hand sweeping swift erasion of the scene's solitude.

"Then let's do it," the kanaka says. Back when they'd started, they'd found a wide trail high on the ridge above but opted to pick their way along the bank instead, try their luck at each likely-looking bend, cut down on the chance of running into hostile Indians. A risk, the kanaka lays out now, that seems well worth it: just haul up to the ridge, take the open path back down, make the camp in a few days' fast ride, come back with a whole company of men, see what this sonofabitch does then.

Which, when he's done, the boy's father tells the kanaka he's welcome to do. While they stay here working the cradle the whole week it takes him to get down and back, find for themselves just what it is this fucker wants so much to hide. "Go on," he says. "Get your stuff packed. You can have a mule. Go on, get up the ridge." He jerks his bearded chin again, this time upward and behind, and the boy sees two buzzards have come, the big birds cutting slow arcs across the narrow swath of sky. "Just bury your damn dog first," his father adds. "Me and my boy got our own work."

By the time the kanaka has dumped the carcass farther downwind, packed one of the mules, they have set the rocker cradle up, one shoveling gravel into the hopper, the other pouring water on top. Over the rushing river, the boy can just hear the clacks of hooves on stones.

"Travel safe," his father calls, without so much as a glance.

Looking back, the boy can see the kanaka struggling to lead the mule up the slope, the man's ancient gun gripped in one hand, so cracked and patched it likely wouldn't even shoot, the companion the boy had traveled with for near a week now scrambling alone up some dusty trail broken by deer or bear or whatever—whoever—else.

"If you see something," his father shouts again, starting to work the handle as the boy begins shaking the cradle, "give a holler."

But it is their shouting—his father's exhilarated roaring, his own higher-pitched whooping—that brings the kanaka back.

By nightfall, with all three of them working the rocker, they have found more gold—some nuggets big as musket balls—than any of them had mined all season. They stop only when it gets too dark to see, celebrate that night with the last whiskey, the men passing the flask to the boy same as any other. And when he's drained it, he turns to the darkness beyond the fire and, shaking the flask in a fist so fatigued he almost drops it, lets loose a sound somewhere between a shout and scream. His voice breaks halfway through. The men bust up laughing.

"He showed him!" the kanaka says.

"You showed him!" his father says, and for a second the boy's elation sinks beneath a sense that they are mocking him, but then his father rises and roars out at the nighttime too. The kanaka throws his head back with a long, high howl. Together they fill the canyon, cover even the river's sound. And when they're done and the echoing is over, his father says, in the space beneath the rapids' returned roar, almost as if speaking to himself, "We sure did."

All day there's been no sign of whoever came the night before, but still they hobble the mules close, collect a woodpile big enough to last the night, set the order for the watch: the boy first, for as long as he can stay awake, then his father till the moon has crossed the sky and dropped behind the western ridge, when he'll shake the kanaka.

Waking, the boy isn't sure if he'd heard the Sandwich Islander's name in his head. Then it is there again in his father's gruff shout. His father is standing, pant legs red in the embers' light, upper half lost to the dark. The river snuffs his echo, leaves only the thuds and whimpers of the spooked mules.

The boy: "What is it?"

His father: "Get up."

When he does, he sees, in the low glow, the third bedroll—the kanaka's—empty. "Maybe he's—"

"Give me your gun."

For a second, the boy doesn't understand. Then—the rifle: the kanaka had it—the boy hands over his revolver. A gift his mother gave to him the last day he saw her. It is a six-shot pepperbox, its short barrel a single heavy cylinder drilled with half a dozen holes, designed so the entire drum rotates from round to round and, even with its small bore and bad accuracy, he knows it's better than the kanaka's cracked musketoon, the only other gun that they have left.

It is near dawn, and the wedge of sky between the ridges is pale enough to dim the stars, but with the moon gone, it is still too dark to see much beyond the fire's glow.

Again, his father shouts the kanaka's name. Then tells the boy to light a torch, hand it over. "You stay back," he says. "Out of the light. I get shot, take the pistol, leave the torch." It hits the boy then—if the kanaka *had* the rifle, who might now?—but before he can get out a word, the man snaps, "Shut up and listen."

He tries, but as he follows the torch toward the mules, then farther up the bank, his ears fill with the river and he can only hear his own breath, his own bare feet stumbling on stones, his father's footsteps ahead. Until they stop.

He sees the shovel first. The one his father had driven into the ground to stake their claim. Its handle is a bright line of flamelight leading to the blade reburied now in the gravel beside a splayed-out body. The boy looks away, but the image stays: the blood spread out beneath the kanaka's smashed-in skull, dammed by his dark mustache, the man's sockets shallow pools drowning his stare.

Then the firelight is whipped away. His father letting loose the torch, the flames flapping madly as it turns over above the river and drops and, in an instant, disappears.

They wait out the last of the near blackness crouched beside the body, trying to stay silent despite their shivering, and when the night begins to lift, they creep into the scrub to hide, moving only to keep among the drifting mules, till it is light enough they can make out each other's shapes, then faces, then eyes. His father's pull away.

When the first sunlight hits the tips of the pines at the top of the ridge, they stir. Giving the boy his pistol back, the father sends him searching for the other gun. Then gets to work. From his wandering, the boy catches glimpses of his father down by the bank dipping a bucket, sloshing water over the body, hauling it by the ankles across the stones. The boy's own legs are stiff with cold, his stumbling too loud. He stays shy of the woods, the trees alive with the rustling of birds. A buck bursts out—sudden, crashing—and the boy stands watching, heart thudding.

He never finds the rifle. Back at camp, his father is covering the kanaka's body with the man's bedroll. "Keep the birds off him," he says. It is hard to tell if the stain seeping into the wool over the bulge of head is blood or just wetness left from washing. His father snaps a stick of kindling, starts building back the fire, and the boy is glad to get moving, bringing the water pot down to the river, trying not to spill too much carrying it back. He gathers up the can of coffee, the metal mugs—just two: a hollowness swoops through him—grateful for the few more minutes that he won't have to say what he wants to do. Go or stay, they both make his gut ache.

But in the end his father never asks. Sipping coffee, they watch the sunlight's steady advance down the far ridge, the mesmerizing flow of water over rocks. On the bank, the rocker cradle waits. "Here's what we'll do," his father says, and, when he's laid it out, looks at the boy as if there'd been a question.

"Okay," the boy says. Then says it again, steadying his voice.

His mother said he was too young, but his father had insisted that he come, and the boy had walked beside the man more than two thousand miles, worked like a man himself all the past year. Though never near this high, so far upriver. *Bring it back*, his mother said when she'd gifted him the gun. Some sixteen months ago, before he'd even turned thirteen. "Okay," he says a third time now, and stands first.

All day they work. The river gifts them gold as if it has longed all its life to hear men's whoops of glee. But despite their growing pile—more than the two of them had ever struck before—neither can seem to muster much to break the day's stunned silence. Maybe it's just they know he's watching. Or that *it* is. Sometimes the boy hears it in his mind again—the screaming, the stones—and wonders if even his father has no real sense of what they're up against.

That night, when it is almost fully dark, the boy stands blocking as much as he can from sight while his father props the kanaka against a rock, wraps a blanket around the dead man's shoulders, even wedges the empty whiskey flask into a hand. Almost gently, the man settles his own hat on the kanaka's bashed-in head, then, unbuttoning his pants, pisses on the fire, the light dying out around his legs, leaving only a scattering of still-glowing coals.

They bed down beside a boulder big enough it should keep them in shadow once the moon is up, close enough his father can keep an eye on the abandoned camp, the mules beyond, the hidden shore that, in an hour, will be blasted with moonlight. Sitting back against the boulder, bedroll bunched in his lap, pistol in his grip, his father tells him to get some sleep.

"What about you?" the boy says.

"Tomorrow."

And in the simple answer the boy hears again his father's words that morning: *Either we get him tonight or we get out of here first fucking light.* Or other options left unsaid. The boy climbs under his blanket, no chance he'll close his eyes. Turns his head on his crushed hat so that the river's roar recedes just enough to let through his father's breathing. He can feel the coming moon, sense its presence slipping into the canyon, its brightness on the far ridge, the water, the stones of their own bank, and when the glow sweeps over them, the boy sits up. His father was right: they are still hidden in the boulder's shadow. But out there, the kanaka is lit. Maybe it is just the hour the boy has spent waiting, maybe it put his head in a strange place, but he has the feeling that the kanaka is on watch, that any moment now the dead man will shake himself awake at some sound, stand up, and walk off to investigate.

"Sleep." His father's whisper is a command. But the boy is sure he won't, can't.

The second his eyes snap open, he knows he shouldn't have. In his ear: the boom of a gunblast. On his chest: a weight like a rock. His father. His father's face. Fallen a few inches away. The big beard is mashed against his cheek, warm and wet, and in the moonlight the boy can see gunk glistening in his father's hair, his father's too-close stare, eyes open wide and shaking in his father's shaking head, and before they go still, the boy knows, knows it but will not let it in, is squirming away, shoving to get free, get his dead father off him.

Soon as he's up, his eyes catch smoke; he drops back to the sand. No gunshot. Just the dissipating ghost of whatever killed his father.

Beside the body again, the boy can hear a moaning—not his father, not a sound like that—and then he sees the pistol in the still hand, and it strikes him quicker than thinking: the shrunken shadow of the boulder, the moon crossing the sky till it betrayed his father, the clear sight the shooter would have had in the same bright light that now shows the boy. And grabbing the gun, he launches himself into the remaining sliver of shadow, strains to see some moon-shown movement where he had spotted smoke.

His father's blasted-open face, his eyes rolled back and still. Wrenching his mind away to what is left—the smoke, the moon, the shooter—the boy is peering so hard, trying so hard to quiet his breath, that he does not realize what he's heard until it's almost disappeared: footsteps. The low clatter, below the river's roar, of someone crossing fast over the bank above. Sucking a breath, he scrambles around the boulder, steps out just enough to scan the rocks upriver, and it is there—a figure running, his back bare, his long hair shaking—and the boy fires. The spin of the six-barreled cylinder, its kick, the smoke. The air clears and he is still there, running. The boy watches him leap from rock to rock. Fires again. The runner veers toward the river, starts to cross, and the boy can see the rifle held out as if for balance, the litheness of the body, how steadily it gains the boulders, and these things come to him: that his father is dead, that this is who killed him, that he will never have a clearer shot, that he has had two good ones already and twice missed, that his father is dead—and he squeezes the trigger, misses again.

Then he is running toward the river. If he can just get to the water, narrow the distance, steady himself and still his breath and aim. But the man is nearly to the far bank, and the boy splashes in, sets his legs, watches the figure drop behind a rock and out of sight.

Standing there, the frigid river rushing around his ankles, feet slowly freezing inside his boots, he stares, trying to shove from his mind everything except the act of seeing. But if he lets the man escape, he will be back, won't he? In his own time, picking the place from which to pick the boy off too? Might he not be reloading now?

Already sighting? Or maybe something has gone wrong, a faulty round, a hammer jammed: Why else would the man have not yet shot back? For a second he wants to run, back to the mules, climb on and up the ridge, ride as fast as he can, away, but soon as he imagines it, he knows whoever killed his father knows this land much better, would cut him off, catch him long before he could get clear. *I'll go,* he thinks, a voice within him pleading to no one who can hear, *leave like you told us,* and knows too that whether white or Indian, the kind of man who'd do what this one had done would not care. And then he's there again, a movement leaping into the boy's sight, less shape than a shaking in the far bank's brush, and all the boy's thoughts flee, his body crashing ahead into the water, chasing.

It takes him longer to get across the river than he had hoped, but pistol held above his head, his other hand clinging to rocks, his legs shoving against the current, he keeps his eyes on the ridgeside, knows if he can just get free of the water's drag, onto dry rock, start running, he'll have a chance, his pistol with three loads remaining, the man's gun maybe stuck, the best—maybe the only—chance he's got.

But when at last he's out, up on the rock, he stops. There at his feet: a circle, white. Big as a boulder drawn flat on the ground. It seems to glow, bright as a twin to the moon above, but made of stone. He stoops, scoops up a handful of tiny shards. Quartz chips. Translucent as shaved ice. Gathered by the thousands, tens of thousands, by someone who then used them to make this impossibly perfect circle here. He drops the bits of stone. A tinkling. And, as if the sound is a feeling on his skin, whips his head around.

Another circle, black, six inches from his face. Behind the muzzle, so close that he can see the dark pupils cut in the whites of the man's eyes: a face blown bare by moonlight. There is the tattoo, a single line splitting the visage straight upward from nose-bridge to forehead, the netting stretched over the shock of long hair as if to hold it in place, but it is neither thing that is most strange. Beneath the net, his hair is brown and streaked with white, and beneath that, his beard is a massive shag the color of gold dulled by a coat of dust, and his cheekbones are hard as river stones, the skin stretched over them rippled and sunbaked. Though not so much that it can hide that he is white. And it is not even that that is most strange, nor the trembling of his cracked lips, nor the intensity of the stare, but the fact that he is crying.

The boy stares back, waiting for him to pull the trigger. A second. Another.

Against the boy's finger, his pistol's trigger presses too. He watches the wetness in the man's eyes, the streaks on the man's cheeks, watches his face shake, the beard shivering at the other end of the long barrel, and feels the pulse pumping in his own throat, the tiny shift that it would be to flick the barrel in his own hand up just enough to point at the man's belly. And does. And never even hears the blast.

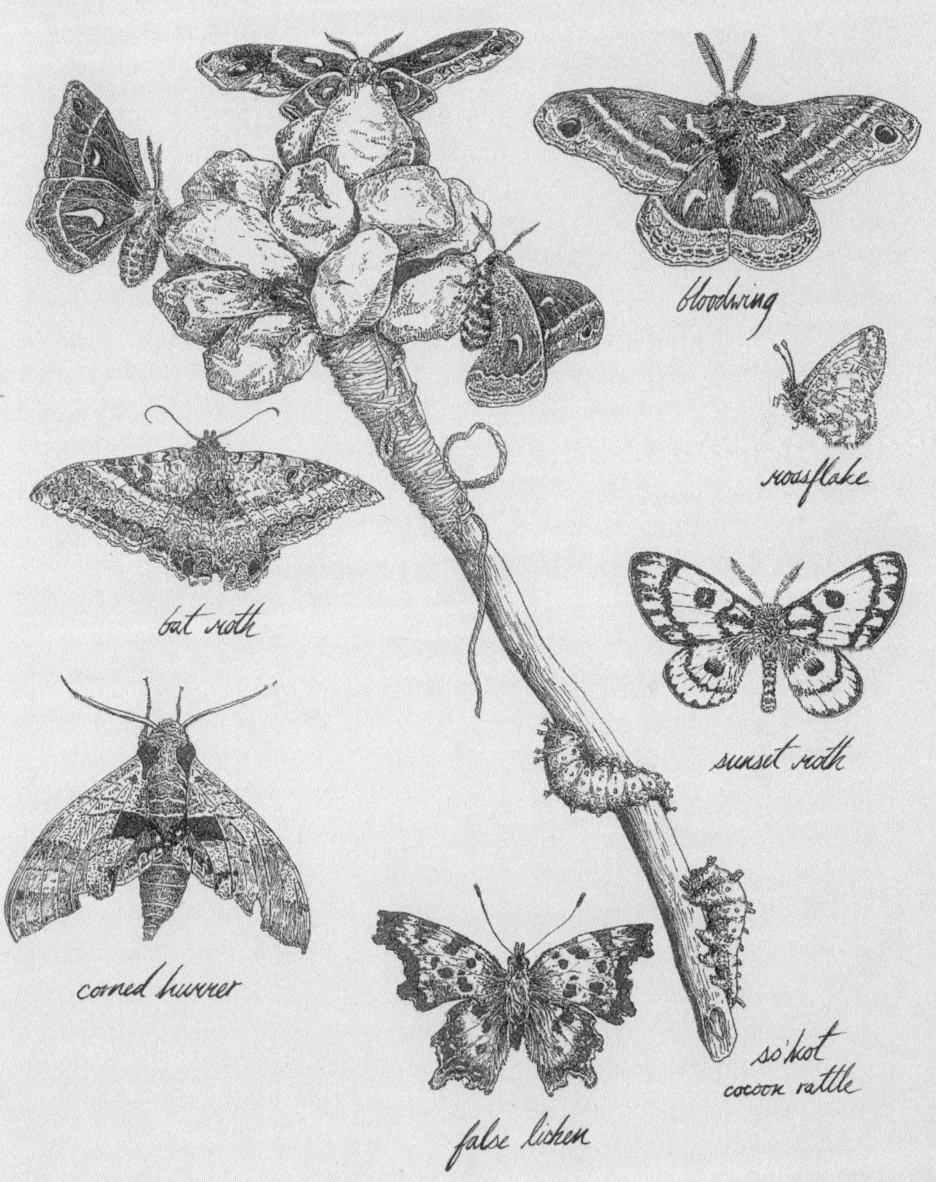
bloodwing
mossflake
bat moth
sunset moth
corned hummer
so'kot
cocoon rattle
false lichen

You will want to know why. Even if you do not think so. Even if you have tried to cut loose. From me. And done it. Still one day you will want to. I know cause I have tried to cut loose too. From you. Your mother. She used to call you Shash. We used to. Yes cut loose & done it & still I am here 12 yrs later in these last hrs I will have in this place that has bcome my reason why for everything for all of it has bcome me. Your father. And still here I am now writing to you.

It is temsampauto. Season of small trees freezing. Octbr 49 maybe novbr. Cold outside enough to snow. But in here warm with the fire. Fire & smoke & so they will find me. Outside I have set the traps. 20some springloaded spiked steel jaws waiting in the woods round me. For whoever comes.

The nisenan say when you die your heart stays. A few days longer. Goes round to all the spots you knew in life. Now as your ghost. To do again all of the things you did bfore you died. I have been thinking on it. Is it for the spirit? Or for the living who are left? The living do not know the ghost is there & if they did they cld not see it. The spirit knows the living are near but cannot allow itself to see them either. If it so much as looks at someone the one who it lays eyes on will die too. So it has got to redo its life all over in a kind of blindness. Of its own making. A kind of dance. Reenacting memories longside those who also lived them. But now alone.

Here is what I think. I think it is for both. To give time to the living & the dead to let them make them force them to feel. I think that is why they cannot see each other. So they will look into themselves instead. And grieve. Maybe then when the heart at last goes west to rise off of the earth it can leave bhind its regret. Its sorrow. Which wld make this that I am writing now really for myself. Except if somehow I can get it to you. Then I will have got round the rules. Let you see me.

Your father. Back when I was a boy of three or four. Bent low and moving slowly through shadows of branches and leaves. My earliest memory. An afternoon in must have been 08 or 9. My mother brother sister. The four of us gathering walnuts in the grove just outside town. When from somewhere beyond the trees there came a murmur. Low. Like a breeze in the canopy. But rising too suddenly building too steadily already become too loud.

I was crouched down filling my sack. Lost in the rhythm of reaching for each windfall nut each hard green shell nearly too big for my small hands. When I looked up. Around me leaf shadows stirred gently as before. Above the branches seemed undisturbed. But beside me Hinton had stood up strangely straight his half-filled sack swinging from his sudden rise and beside him Adnah reaching to still it. Both my siblings turning to find our mother.

She was a few trees away. Staring behind her across the field toward the closest windbreak. The farther glints of roofs marking the start of town. The two steeples spiked white against the sky's low edge gone strangely dark. Less like some stormcloud coming than a strip of night that had simply refused to leave. Now bent on returning.

We watched it widen. The darkness climbing off the horizon over the steeples' tips. The quickness with which it filled the sky catching my breath. Its sound by then had swelled past anything like wind. Become something more akin to thunder. A ceaseless rolling clap that kept on coming. Loud enough to clear all else out of my ears by the time I realized it was birds.

Passenger pigeons. A flock so huge it blackened the sky, blocked the sun, cast the land below into a sudden dusk sweeping fast across the field toward us.

Around me I could feel the others fleeing, my brother and sister running for the cover of the thicker canopy, my mother turning as if to follow, then seeing me and pausing. By then she had learned to keep me separate from my siblings, to place herself between me and their playing, had come to know the way that sudden shifts in my surroundings could set me off, and in the sweeping shadow of the onrushing birds, her face betrayed her worry. But I was calm. Beneath the bird storm I stood completely still—my two fists gripping two walnut husks, my face turned up—the roiling blast blowing away all other movement, blotting out all other sounds, encasing me.

The beauty of those flashing feathers. Slate-blue and copper, snippets of greens, streaks of tarnished silver. The movement of the flock surging, swooping, swerving, so that the sky itself appeared to lift and dip.

I do not know how long it lasted. Only recall the overwhelming peace. The blur of birds above. The sense their passing would never end. And then the falter, a snag in the flow, and out of the flock the first one falling. Another. Some were still flapping, some plummeting, some careening wildly out of the rest, the sound even louder. Nearly enough to smother the shots.

They had come running by the scores. Townsfolk clambering over fences, leaping off carts, women with dressfronts wet from washing, men calling back at wives to bring their guns. Already nearly a hundred were following the flock, firing upward with pistols in both hands, reloading muskets on the run, flinging nets into the air or climbing roofs to hack with scythes and rakes, the rest just grabbing whatever was at hand and hurling it into the birds.

My own siblings were throwing walnuts, flinging the rock-hard husks and stooping and throwing the heavy shells again, breaking the slate-blue wings, snapping the copper-colored necks, bringing down body after flailing body to lie whapping at the ground. Then I was throwing, too. Whipping the stone-heavy nuts hard as I could at my sister and brother. They were a few years older—Hinton seven or eight, Adnah nearer ten—and on their faces there was a second of stunned shock. Quickly replaced by fear. Their frantic screams, the quaking of our mother's voice—*Sy!*—shouting my name—*Sy!*—as she came running.

To me? To them? I have no memory. Nothing between then and when—a few breaths later, or half an hour, or half a day?—I must at last have come back to the world. A flock that vast might have taken all afternoon to pass over the trees, out of hearing and sight, to finally leave me a boy of maybe four sitting in the fallen leaves amid the bodies of fallen birds beneath a canopy turned white. Branches pale as the grass beneath. As if it all had been dusted in ash. I took in my own white legs, felt the coating on my arms, in my caked hair, smeared face, and knew that it was scat. And it was comforting. To my eyes, my mind. As if the frenzy of everything always around me had been subdued.

Until a whimpering. A movement catching my eye: a body rocking, rocking. No: three. Huddled away from me. My mother, sister, brother. She was holding them. Shushing, rocking. Only then did I realize that I was rocking too. And stopped. And, in the sudden stillness, saw my father's cart coming across the field, the horses driven at a trot. Before it had quit clattering, he had leapt off. I remember his trousers growing gray with smears, his suit jacket streaked, hat tumbling to its ruin in the guanoed grass. I remember Hinton, stripped to his waist, covered in bruises, an eye swelled shut. Adnah's hair stuck to her cheek, her bloodied ear. I remember not understanding why, inside my mind no hint of what had happened between my first few throws and this. An emptiness that slowly filled with the terror of knowing that whatever violence had come upon my brother, sister, mother, had come from inside of me.

Would again and again. It could be something simple as a scent: bread rising on an afternoon of baking with my mother, and my father barging in reeking of his veterinary work, lighting a pipe, smothering the small back kitchen. Or I might be waxing boots, lost in the whisk of cloth on leather, only to hear my mother's humming break through my peace and feel it coming. Already by four or five I'd grown to recognize the flare at its first flicker, and seized by a terror that those around me would see it too, I'd grasp for any way to make it abate, keep it inside. Might force myself to join my mother in her humming, my brow bunching under the strain, struggling to keep the small vibrations from becoming tremors in my face. Taking the rising dough into the farthest corner, I'd lift the cloth over my head, bend my face so low inside the bowl's buffer I'd feel the yeast's warmth on my eyes, my desperation increasing with its heat, till, rearing up, I'd find myself hurling the bowl toward my startled father, the ceramic smashing, my mother's humming ceasing beneath a screaming I would not even remember making.

Tantrums, my parents called them. Fits. Words that, as I turned five and six and the episodes only increased, fell away in their inadequacy. Replaced simply by *it* or *one—he had another one; it happened again*—my father pleading with the pastor for his guidance, my mother whispering to friends who brought their children over while the women worked together: Had they experienced anything similar? Seen it in another? The other woman speaking then of Susquehannock mothers she'd witnessed swaddle children as old as three, or how a high-strung daughter benefited from hot baths, a son from bee balm tinctures, teas made from catmint leaves. None of which seemed to my mother to touch on what was wrong with me, what she might do to help her six-year-old sitting in the corner, knotting bits of discarded wool into an ever-longer strand, hidden behind the spinning wheel, its spokes like bars between him and the other kids. Beside my mother, the other woman saying something about some cousin, the way he'd flap his hands or set to moaning or rock when he was riled *like your son*. How he'd become so overrun with what was wrong inside they'd had to keep him on a rope, ready to restrain him, till at last they'd found relief in dosing him with laudanum. And all the while my mother trying to keep the conversation from my ears—muffled beneath the whirring wheel or clacks of chopping—her glances flicking to the other woman's daughter or son drawing ever closer to me. Long as she could, my mother would resist intervening, give me a chance to change, before, seeing me break, she would rush over. Sometimes, distracted by her visitor, she arrived too late. Sometimes the other mother got to me first. Though by the time that I was five most of her friends had learned to leave their children home when visiting. By the time that I turned six, most found it best simply to stay away.

And who could blame her, then, if there were times she came

undone herself? If her shouts would overpower mine, her prayers to God for help give way to curses against the devil in me. If, slamming out of the house, she'd simply flee me the way that I fled everyone else. If, one day, as another mother carried her own child—hand bitten hard enough my teeth had hit bone—out of our home, my own had hauled me before our parlor mirror, held me in place. Despite what she knew it would do to me to clamp my bucking back against her chest, trap my flailing arms inside her clasp, restrain my struggling body with her own. I can still feel her bruising grip as she snapped, *Silas! Look at yourself!* Words she would repeat till they would be subsumed by her own sobs.

My father by then had come to accept that he would never hold me, never wrestle me the way he did my brother or seat me before him in the saddle the way he'd taught my sister to ride. At first he tried to fix me. In his work he'd seen animals altered by things they ate—poisons that traumatized the mind, sullied the spirit—knew cattle to get soft-brained from hollow horn, had himself sawed off the tips to pour in vinegar and salt, and he would pry his instruments into my ears, put me on his examination table, probe my belly, underarms, spine. But as the years passed, he set all that aside. Instead, he simply observed me, the same sharp eye and alert senses that had brought him renown as an animal doctor now brought to bear on his son.

The way my rocking would increase with each new person entering a room, abate as they withdrew. Seeing the way I'd stiffen at a still-distant sound—my sister chatting to a friend as they ascended porch steps, my brother playing with other boys out in a field—he'd set down his work, observe me tightening my body against the coming burst, till, breaking, I'd slam out the kitchen door. And crossing to the window, he'd watch me run for the woods, my limbs loosening with each step taking me farther from them. My family. Though with anyone else, it was worse. The mere clatter of an approaching cart enough to send me fleeing, a visit from my grandparents consigning me to a far room. From which I would refuse to emerge till they had left.

And if my grandmother was to speak to me through the shut

door, my father would know, soon as the thudding started, that I was trying to knock her voice out of my head, would whisper to her to leave it be. Though sometimes, in the rare moments of peace that could descend upon us—me crouched beside a rivulet of ants, handing them torn flower petals; or standing motionless, my arms outstretched, as butterflies alighted on my body—he would forget himself, let his hand rest on my head, feel me shrink away.

But I could sit for half an hour picking ticks out of our collie's coat, fingers roaming so gently they would send her to sleep. Might stay atop a horse all day, give it the reins, lie resting on its withers as it grazed, its shifting drift beneath my chest working on me much the same way. I could even set my hand down in the path of the ant colony, let them climb up my arm, trickle across my skin, the feeling unhinging nothing in me but the smile spreading over my face. Till, feeling my father's stare, I might turn in time to see him look away.

Sometimes as I watched him fight the urge to meet my eyes, it seemed he must have been looking less *at* me than *into* me, through to whatever inside me kept me away from my own kind. But then he would give in, glance back, and I would see in his eyes the weight of his failure to find it. The barrier in me that I could not escape, found simply by looking back into his face. Or at my mother's. Or anytime I tried to feel in me what I saw on my sister's, brother's.

Oh, I could catch the glow in Adnah's face as she returned from riding with my father, the pleasure in his as he helped her off her horse. Could know it was borne of their experience together. Could hear my brother's laughter as he rounded the house, chasing a friend, recognize the peace inside my mother came from the happiness she saw in him. Could even feel it in myself, for them. In them, for me.

But in between us always, the barrier of me combined with anybody.

In the schoolhouse, there was a score of children packed in the single room. At seven, I was among the youngest. Not that age mattered: the press of their small bodies hit me the same. I could feel it even before I entered, a density to the air in there that pushed out through the walls, so that, as I drew near, the morning's crispness would recede, the cheery call of a towhee disappear, my own slowing footsteps smothered by the voices coming from inside. Even the dawn's last chill burned away in their leaked heat.

There was their scent—the unwashed staleness of kids my age, the riper stench of older boys, the stink of slops and excrement from morning chores—and their noise: banter, laughter, boot-thumps. The way their breath got in my lungs. But none of it would have undone me if it hadn't been evidence of them. Their presence. I could feel it. Clear as if they'd somehow crammed the mass of all their bodies into my skull, crowding my mind, the pressure of it all too fast become too much for me to bear.

A thing that, before the schoolmaster was even aware of a new pupil in the room, drew the attention of the rest. So by the time he turned from marking his slate, they'd already begun to mimic me. Some jerking with exaggerated rocking, others clamping hands over their ears, grimaces turning to grins, laughter catching the entire room.

Except my brother and sister. They'd gone in before me—Hinton stomping stiffly ahead, whispering warnings over his shoulder; Adnah, too flustered to remember touch was worse, offering to hold my hand—and now sat still, refusing to look at me. As the teacher, shouting for order, stilled the others too. All but me, rocking and moaning amid the silent rest. Until I wheeled around to flee. Maybe if the teacher hadn't caught me, hadn't dragged me to a chair and forced me down, maybe I could have held myself together long enough to avoid the worst.

You can imagine. What it did to me to be tied to the chair. And then, when that failed to quell my fit, to have two older boys carry me, still bound, into the closet, shut the door, leave me there. No doubt the schoolmaster meant it a punishment, but it was what saved me. Let the tremors leave my body, the crying die in my throat, the pressure ease off my mind. Just enough wall and door and darkness between me and the rest to let me sit in quiet.

He left me there all day. And the next morning, when it happened again, he did the same, no doubt having decided mine was not a mind that could be taught. For five hours each day I sat there, bound in the chair, listening to his lessons, grateful for the way the closet muffled his voice, smothered my classmates' answers, grateful for the door that hid their stares. If I let my mind drift, I could almost forget they were there. At the end of each day, my siblings would be sent to retrieve me. Standing near enough for me to hear their breath behind the door, they'd wait till the room cleared. Then, in the silence we'd grown used to, enter the closet and untie me.

Though, on the third morning, I crossed straight to the closet on my own and shut the door behind me. So the schoolmaster left me untied. Only, later that day, to open the door himself, beckon me out. And speaking slow and overloud, gesturing as if even those few words might be beyond me, he directed me toward the board.

I was aware that it was covered with the signs of a language we were supposed to share, but beneath the weight of all the other students' stares, I could not shake the sense that the chalked lines were marks not meant for me. The teacher barked more words. My trembling hand went to the board. Held the chalk chattering against the slate. I tried to press it still. Failed. And lifting it away again, stood looking down at the white stick, my thumb and forefinger rubbing at it, twitching ever faster with each word the teacher shot at me, till the chalk snapped.

Maybe one of my siblings spoke to him, maybe my parents. Because from then on, he let me stand outside the school and watch. Through the open door I could see him at the board, could, if I cupped my hands behind my ears, hear just well enough, backed by just enough sound of the woods around me, to make it through.

On dry days I'd sit on the ground, cupping my ears, elbows propped on knees, trying to hear through the whispered mockery. When it was wet, I'd stand beneath an umbrella my mother gave me, rain drowning the teacher's voice, struggling to focus past the gestures of older boys—their fingers and thumbs mimicking the way I'd rubbed the chalk, the meaning of their stroking lost on me till my knuckle-bloodied brother was compelled to tell our father—my eyes finding the teacher's face each time he turned, learning to read lips as much as what he taught. Still, I came a second week, a third, working with stick instead of chalk, dirt for a board. Still, when those nearer my age would be released for midday break, I'd watch them play. Games of chase or hopscotch, hunt-the-slipper, rounders, shinny. The rhythms of their rope-jumping thudding through me standing far to the side. Sometimes I'd match it with my own, jumping an imagined rope held by imagined turners. Sometimes, if a ball rolled close, I'd brave throwing it back. Though if it was returned, I'd let it fall, retreat so that the thrower could retrieve it on their own.

Once a girl a little younger approached the hopscotch grid I'd scratched into some dirt, asked to use it when I was done. Though I'd already stopped mid-hop, begun to flee. Something in my reaction catching inside her too, so that she turned and fled from me. A thing I felt so bad about that the next day I made myself approach her. Stood a rod away, looking at the ground, mumbling there was something I wished to show her. To my surprise she understood me, to my consternation agreed to come. Turning, I led her toward the maple tree I'd found at a far corner of the field, her following too near behind so that I kept quickening my pace to keep her from getting closer, both of us running by the time we reached the tree. Where, standing beneath the spreading branches, I stopped, tilted my head back, told her, through the too-hard hammering of my heart, the too-tight clench of my chest, *Look up.* The canopy was completely covered in seed clusters, each pair of winged samaras that all late summer had been pale green now turned brown, dried perfectly. The previous few days I'd kept an eye on them, willing away ruinous rain or too-wild wind, neither knocking them loose, so that I knew they now were ready, waiting too. We stood there watching, the air around us still but for her breathing, mine. And then a gust, and they were falling—a thousand whirls of spinning sunlight spiraling down around us, a whole summer of butterflies alighting all at once—and I was whooping, running round and round the tree, arms out as if the wind was blowing me, the samaras landing in my hair, fluttering against my face, filling my sight, so that I didn't even see that she was not looking at them, but me.

It was only when I rounded the tree again and, passing by her, sensed her stillness, that I stopped. She was as covered with seedpods, her hair as filled, their wings glowing as bright with the sunlight, but on her face, there was a startled, stunned confusion that I watched darken to fear. She turned, started to run. From back where we had come: another fluttering, a movement that for a second, I thought was another tree's loosed seeds. Then realized was the crowd to which she'd fled, the others gathered in the distance, a whole classful of fluttering fingers and flapping arms that, for a moment, filled me with a surge of glee, a thrill—that they had seen it, felt it; that I'd shared with them what surged through me—until I heard the hooting, their imitations already breaking into laughter, and looking down at my own hands, realizing what I'd been doing, clasped my arms around myself and clamped them still.

But for a second, before I'd begun circling the tree, before my hands had started flapping, hadn't she seen it, felt it, same as me? I could still hear her inhale, still see her smile start to emerge, could still sense the curtain of swirling seeds the tree had sent down between us, the way it had allowed me, even so near somebody else, to feel such glee. The way that simply knowing the thousand winged samaras had been there, waiting for someone to see, had given me the strength to approach her.

It was a morning, not long after, that the season gave me another gift: a box turtle, passing over the wagon tracks not far from school. Its shell was mottled mud-gray and gold, head raised, legs shuttling slowly across the path. It had grown cold enough I knew this one would be among the last we'd see till spring, and I would have called ahead, but Adnah and Hinton were already out of sight. Instead, I carefully slid my hands beneath her belly—the bottom plate lacking the dip that marked a male—her head and legs drawing into her shell with a panic that made me pick up my pace, whisper to her it would be okay, that soon as I'd shown her to my siblings I'd carry her back exactly where I'd found her, even if it made me late to school.

Maybe one of the others overheard, maybe they'd gathered to wait for someone else, because as I caught sight of the schoolhouse I saw the cluster of boys. My brother must have gone in already, otherwise they wouldn't have dared halloo. Usually he kept an eye out for anything he knew might throw me, took it on himself to stop it.

Usually I'd sense the danger first, remove myself. But I was holding the last turtle I'd touch till May and the wistful thrill was coursing through me.

What's its name? one said.

A box turtle, I managed, bolstered by the small weight in my hands. Turned her to better show the pattern of her shell. You can see her—

The nearest boy grabbed her from me. Look at that, he said.

The other: You ain't give her a name?

I shook my head.

C'mon, the oldest among them said.

And from the one who held her: He's all clammed up. Or maybe he'd said: She's all clamped up. Because he started poking at her, jabbing at the crack between her shells. I jerked as if he'd jabbed me, and springing a grin, he jabbed her again.

C'mon, the oldest said, we gotta go in.

You could give it *your* name, the other said.

The one holding her jabbed, jabbed, turning the shell, making his way toward her withdrawn head.

C'mon, the oldest said again, and, reaching for the turtle, took her from its torturer. As if, wishing to get to class, he'd give her back to me. But instead he grasped her in both hands—C'mon, he said, I want to see the duncehead flap—and lifted her above his head.

I fought with every muscle in me to stay still. Felt the panic spread through my body, cramp my chest, start to make me shake. Closed my fingers into fists. Please, I said. But I should have just let it come over me, given him what he wanted to see. Because, instead of giving the turtle back, he only shrugged and, with all the strength he might have put into swinging a sledge, slammed the turtle onto the ground.

The crack went through me as if it had been my own back. But it was hers. And, before I could more than shout, they were upon her, stamping their boots, hooting with such glee I couldn't tell if they were mocking me or too excited to restrain themselves. One kicked the turtle out of their scrum, flipping her over, and, for a second, I could see her legs emerge, her head. Then they were on her again, moving as a cluster. Two of them had found tools to swing—a shovel with its iron head, another just a handle—the others standing back as they took turns, and I could hear the thudding, feel the slamming in my feet, the shaking coming over me as I saw, between their legs, the turtle struggling. Watched, above their heads, a pair of hands raising a heavy stone.

I do not know if I hit him before he hurled it, if by the time I reached the turtle she was already dead. I only know that when I spread myself over the shell I could feel, beneath my chest, bits sharp as broken bone, a wetness slick as my own blood.

That morning I walked home alone, the sounds of the schoolhouse—children's chatter snuffed out beneath the start of a lesson I'd never hear—slowly receding behind me. By the time I limped into our yard, the tree shadows had shrunk back to the woods, the day grown bright enough to let my mother see what they'd done to me before I reached the porch. She was down the steps and halfway to me before she forced herself to slow. When she was half a rod away, she stopped. For a second I watched her eyes search mine before she pulled her gaze. Though I could feel it find the blood in my hair, tears in my clothes, the bruised swelling of my face, before it settled on the smaller smashed body I carried.

When she asked what happened I could hear her ironing her voice, the strain it took, knew if I answered I would not be able to do the same.

Sy, she said again, what did they do?

But no matter how she tried to get it from me, I could only shake my head, keep my gaze from meeting hers, tilt my face toward the sky. Up there, a buzzard sawed, its circling marking the silence that my mother let settle then. Though she must have been watching the sky as well. Because, after as long as she seemed able to stand, she said, her own voice pressed steady as the buzzard's glide, That bird follow you back?

Not looking down, I managed a nod.

All the way?

A nod.

Was it there? Her quiet question seemed less inquiry than simply wondering. The whole time?

And when I did not shake my head or jerk my shoulders or do anything to indicate that she should stop, she asked me gently, What did it see?

It was a question not quite like any I'd been asked before, but after that day it would become a way we could communicate, a way of placing just enough space between us to let me speak, of letting another set of eyes or ears bear witness—a barn cat that had been nearby, a songbird I'd heard beneath whatever happened, or just our dog, so often by my side—so that I could recall what had disturbed me without having to stir it in me again. So that, that morning, after I'd told her, I could still follow her into the house, sit in the chair she drew out for me, remain in the same room.

Our kitchen often contained creatures in cages, victims of wagon wheels or cats or orphaned offspring that, bringing them back, I might implore my father to save. That day there was a wood thrush, its wing wrapped in a bandage, that my mother carefully carried to me. So she might exchange it for the turtle I still clutched. Easing the crushed body out of my arms, she slipped the bird's softer one into its place, waited to see me feel its heartbeat, my hand to start a slow stroking. Then, dipping a cloth in water warmed over the hearth, she began—touching me ever so lightly—to clean away my blood.

That was the last day my parents sent me to school, the end of their attempts to set me in society, the start of a life spent all but alone within the confines of my family, a family that over the next months—then years—would grow around me, the way a tree comes to encase a nail.

Till then I'd slept in a small closet in the upstairs hall that my mother furnished with tick and blankets to spare me sharing my siblings' room. But I was seven, soon to be eight, and so my father offered up his study. He'd taken a lease on an office in town, less for his practice than to relieve the house around me of one presence. By then my siblings had learned to leave me be as well. Waking for school, they'd wait to emerge till I had left the house for the barn's safety. Washed and ate while I watered the horses, harnessed the team. Climbing on our father's cart, they would refrain from wishing me good morning unless I—staying behind, whispering into the team's twitching ears—might break our silence first. After school, Hinton invariably went to another family, visiting the homes of friends he couldn't bring to his own, returning alone in time to do pre-supper chores. Adnah no longer tried to teach me knitting or grasped my hands to practice dance steps, instead avoiding me even more sedulously than the rest, scurrying out of sight soon as she heard me coming, often leaving behind a gift—a stone I might find pretty, a piece of embroidery—small surprises I discovered scattered around the house, each accompanied by a note that I would read, knowing her eyes were on me. Though mostly she was waiting for me to leave. Then, for however long I might be gone, she'd let herself loose—play dress-up with our mother, practice her flute, maybe just relish the chance to chatter away unhushed. Which, returning an hour or two later, I might see. Watching through the lit windows, listening amid the silence of my stopped steps. Sometimes I'd stay in the study all the way till night. Then lie flat on the floorboards, listening to them gather in the parlor, their voices rising through the cracks beneath my back. Father, Mother, Adnah, Hinton. Their laughter and easy company. Their relief it didn't include me.

Only my mother seemed to know how to do more than avoid me. Shut in the study, just the two of us at home, I'd hear her creaking room to room—the scrape of sweeping, thump of her ironing—and might come out, stand beside her. She'd smile at me, maybe touch my cheek before turning back to her task. When I was still small, I'd find her sewing and climb onto her lap and she would hold me, saying nothing, moving nothing but her foot to keep the rocker going. For hours we might stay like that, till my awareness of her and hers of me became as soothing as the dog's breathing beneath its fur, the stroking of a thrush's feathers, the noses of the horses on my palms. Though I can see now it was not easy for her, that for every minute of our time together she had to work. The way she'd resweep the rooms over and over so long as I still stood there listening, or might rock with me while the time for starting supper passed and the fire went out. The pain in her voice when she would have to wake me.

Mornings, my mother left me breakfast outside the study. Along with the day's lesson she'd prepared. And an apple that I would leave untouched till I felt ready to withstand instruction. I'd place it then outside the door: our sign that it was safe for her to enter. Some days I never set the apple out, just stayed alone till dark, filling pages with careful letters, sounding out words in books my father left me: an encyclopedia of horse anatomy, experiments in military surgery, an illustrated guide to birds that I loved best. Sometimes I read aloud so long that when I stopped, my voice kept on inside my head. Sometimes I never made it past a single picture. A print I'd hold against the window and trace. And trace again. Those days the apple was all I ate for lunch, and when the smell of supper would invade the study, I'd venture out into the house. Feel the air change. A pause in activity as my family became aware the footsteps on the stairs were mine, their silence not a sign of regret or worry, just a consciousness that I was there. And I would wonder then if they might glimpse what it was like to live as me. Except my consciousness of others never ceased.

Only when I withdrew enough would it recede. Following the split-rail fence toward the hill to our west, I'd feel the pressure lift around me, the house sounds slowly drowned out beneath the crickets' chirring, the rasp of my walking, till, cresting the rise, I'd start down the other side, the earth a wall behind me blocking the rest. Picking raspberries along the stream beside our house, I'd lose all sense of time, as if the hours ticking by beyond the brambles were swept away under the current's babble. And a peace would sweep over me that I never felt back in the world of others. People, I mean. For there were the crickets, the cows, the streaking swallows, the sparrow kip-kip-kipping, picking at the same berries a few feet away. Why did its singing not disturb me the way my sister's would? Why did the water striders' breaking the smooth surface of a pool not break my calm? I cannot say. Beyond the fact that to me other animals always seemed simpler. I do not mean in their abilities, but in my ability to understand them. The signs sent by a horse's angled ears or the tone of a dog's whine easier for me to read than hints contained in people's posture, hidden signals flitting across a human face.

No wonder, then, my mother came to depend on creatures as our intermediaries, to rely on them to reach past my reticence to tell her what was in my mind, draw from me feelings I never otherwise would have revealed.

What would she have done, then, with the trees? The grasses? The stones? The stream? If I had told her. If I had told her what even then I knew that I could not. No more than I should now tell you. Except it is the truth.

Elisha, do you remember when you were young? Young enough that you were still my son, and I your father, us together. How I'd sit you on my shoulders and take you to the great Monongahela's bank and we'd talk to the water. Call it Old River. Ask it what it had seen upstream. Old River, you'd say, what did you see today? And I'd answer in its voice, tell you a tale of high adventure, catastrophes averted, disasters overcome, till you would interrupt to ask why I'd let such and such happen, had not done this or that, as if the river could make a choice, act, might be as alive as us. The way children young enough can still imagine rivers and rocks and trees to be. When did you stop?

Sometimes I'd listen to the rustling of leaves and imagine I could hear them speak. Not words, not to me, but just communicating with each other. Sometimes I'd imagine they could see me, would picture how I might seem to the cow-cropped maple in the center of a field, or to the branches passing above my father's cart, or to the giant old elm that sheltered our house. And it would calm me. To see myself from such a height, so placidly. As if my pulse had slowed to match the movement of their sap.

Or the flowing of a wheat field in wind. Or the rippling of the stream over my toes. Or the solidity of soil beneath my feet. Sometimes I'd remove my shoes and simply stand. Sometimes I'd rush from the house and throw myself into the grass, lie back feeling each blade resettle into stillness around me, and that would be all I would need. Sometimes I'd talk to it. Hullo, Grass. Hullo, Lone Maple. Big Rock. Old River.

Our Elm. It had been there since long before the house—centuries, my father said—its branches overspreading the roof, its crown reaching a hundred feet, the trunk so wide it would take eight of me, my arms stretched out, to circle it. I knew because I'd done it.

Though mostly I would just hold it. Pushed by the others' presence from the house, I'd press my cheek against its deep-fissured bark, listen through my rushing mind to its rising sap, my breathing easing till I could not tell them apart. Back when I'd been too small to stop him, my father had nailed planks to its sides, and now, when the pressure was worst, I'd climb the massive ash-gray limbs until the highest branches would begin to bend beneath my weight. Then sit, feeling their shaking subsiding into swaying, stilling.

In summer, I'd climb to the tree's center just to be within such density of green. In autumn, when the yellowed leaves would thin, I'd sit inside their trembling, feeling the rising wind, the entire canopy shivering in anticipation of a gust. Then it would come, shaking the branch, sending the leaves into a fluttering so great I could hardly keep from letting go. Though by then I'd learned to mostly constrict the flapping of my hands. And when the snows stenciled the branches white, I'd race to stand beneath the distilled shape of the tree, staring up, giving little hops whenever birds shook off some flakes, shouts at each flurry that squirrels released. Each spring I watched it from my window, waking each day to see if any branch tips had begun to bud, any buds to redden, blossoms to burst, till one morning I would open my eyes to such a surprise of pink I could not breathe.

And through it all I'd feel the elm watch me. It was the only tree that could see into the house, hear through the roof, and when the presence of people—the Susquehannock women my mother hired to help clean, the few relatives she'd rarely risk inviting over—would grow too great, I'd listen for the scrape of branches on the slate, retreat to a room nearby the tree, stand staring out a window, seeing my own reflection as the elm might, smoothing my brow, loosening my jaw, slowing my breathing, growing still beneath the stillness of its gaze.

In exchange, I picked caterpillars off its leaves, combed its bark for beetles, saved my urine in a jar and, diluting it the way I'd seen my father do for fruit trees, sloshed it over the ground around its roots.

Still, by the time I'd grown big enough to circle the trunk in seven embraces instead of eight, the old elm had begun to show its aging too, its bark seeming to crack a little deeper, its canopy to thin, one spring a limb simply failing to bud. Centuries, my father had said, but not how much longer it might have left. Though when I went to him, he tried to assuage my worry, assured me that, in all likelihood, it would long outlive him.

But me? The thought of it dying filled me with such anxiety I could not eat. At night, I'd lie listening to winds, waiting to hear the crack of a limb, would grow so afraid in storms I'd wake the whole house with my pacing, my muttering become a moaning I wouldn't realize had risen above the drumming rain till my father pounded at the study door to ask was I okay. More than anything I had grown terrified of lightning, could not stop picturing the splintering tree, erupting flame. Incoming thunder brought me to tears, whipping me into such frenzies my father finally hired men to wire a Franklin rod onto the tree. Pointed out the gleam above the crown, the heavy ropes with which he'd had the tree-men secure the limbs, hoped it would be enough.

But by the time I was ten even he had to admit the elm was dying. Two roped limbs had begun to lose their bark, and one that had been left unsecured already had rived off, missing the house by inches. The winter I turned eleven my father stood outside my door explaining into the silence I sent back why he had to act: that my room would be the first to go, that the failing tree would crush me and anybody else below. And if I did not scream at him, did not hurl myself against the door, did not say a single word, it is because I could feel the tree watching through the window, could hear how the one word that would not leave my mind would sound: *good*—that it should kill me—*good*—crush them. *Good.*

The only reason I let my mother in was that she asked me what I thought the tree would want.

But once inside she tried to convince me. She'd brought a sack like a small pillowcase stuffed with feathers. Though when she opened it for me, I found it full of elm seeds. The dry, brown, paper-thin disks of the samaras fallen last autumn. There must have been a thousand that she had gathered, saved, said we'd plant that spring, all around the house, as if that might make it all right. As if it didn't just show me that for months she'd known, discussed it with my father, planned for exactly this.

You know what it would want, I told her. And did not have to say the rest. Because what could it want but the same thing as everything that lives? What life itself will always want? What else but to exist a little longer?

Still, I do not think it was my words that swayed her. Not even what she saw on my face. But what she'd seen in me all the past thirteen years, all of my life, what she knew was waiting in there should I break.

I swore I'd sleep in the barn in case the tree crashed down at night, promised if an overhanging limb should die, I wouldn't fight it being taken off. And in return, my father promised he'd leave the tree alive till spring, see what shape it was in then.

All winter I lived in dread of the same snows that once brought me delight, but by March I knew the worst was past, that the tree would see at least another season, that soon I'd look out my window and find the branches blushed with buds. So I was wholly unprepared for what one evening I saw instead.

A flock of birds, not millions or even thousands, no more than a few hundred, but catching the late light in bright flashes of green, streaks of scarlet, glitters of gold: a cloud of Carolina parakeets descending all at once upon the tree. I'd seen them before, of course, but in far fewer numbers, nowhere near as close. Now they were outside my window, big as crows, landing in such a mass they sent the branches bowing, swaying, clattering beneath the screams and squawks. So loud they drowned out the noises of our house. Or the whole house had seen them and been struck dumb.

Though when I rushed outside I found the sound so all-encompassing it silenced the tree frogs and chickadees, left only the sight of the huge old elm abloom in a canopy conjured from some tree-dream—the birds' emerald feathers, their ruby faces, golden hoods, beaks a hundred sparks of sunlight—the tree covered in so much color, movement, sound, I could not even feel its gaze. As if for once it was saying instead, *Look. Look at me.*

Not one week later I woke to the voices of men. It was still dark, and on the ceiling, I could see the shape of the window faintly flickering. A lamp. Outside, below. The realization struck me at the same time I realized they were talking about the tree, and I was scrambling out of bed, over to the window. Three men, down there, standing beside the elm. The same who years ago installed the rod, the ropes. But this time holding axes.

To this day I do not know why my father did not block the study door. Maybe he was worried that, trapped in there, I would not hesitate to break the window, leap upon the tree or the men or to my death. Maybe he thought it would be better if he could talk to me. Because when I tore out of my room and down the stairs, I found him standing by the front door. Wheeling, I rushed for the kitchen, only to see my brother planted before the exit at the back, his stance wide as if expecting me to ram him with all my force. He was sixteen, near a foot taller, and all the years of defending me had turned him into a seasoned brawler, but in the thin lamplight I could see that he was scared.

I could see also the other way through to the foyer, my father stationed there, holding up his hands as if he thought that that could stop me, or as if to show me they were empty, as if that would make him any less guilty than if he'd been holding an axe.

They're locked, he said.

Through my breathing I could hear somebody crying. My mother? Sister? Both? The sound coming from some other room, behind some other door. From outside, the dog began to bark. Between the barks: the men's wall-muffled talking. A metal clank. A long, loud scrape like something being dragged from a cart. Or like a branch scratching at the roof with all its weight. I could feel it up there, could see it out there. Dawn must have just been breaking because through the squares of windowpanes, beyond the reflections of flickerings inside the house, I could make out the huge dark limbs, the smaller branches, the black lines of the tree sketched against a barely brighter sky. And then: the long, ragged rasp of a saw.

In the seconds before I smashed into the window, there was this: my sudden lunge, somebody's shout, the sawing, the crying ceasing, my footsteps slamming, footsteps behind, the sawing, a screaming, my name, my name, my name, the saw blade biting, its teeth tearing, the ragged, raging, dragging cut carving my flesh, the shape of the elm lit by their lanterns, its branches drawn in firelight, shaking, shaking, and, growing over it, the sudden sight in the window glass of my onrushing face.

Why did I not wake earlier? Why did I not hear them coming up the drive? Why did I let myself fall asleep the night before, or any night, knowing what my father thought needed to be done? Why did I not climb the tree when I still could and, high in its crown, tie myself to its still-standing trunk? Why did I fail it?

Questions I have not stopped hearing since.

No more than I will stop seeing that face.

Not the reflection in the pane before it shattered, before I clambered through the shards and cracking muntins over a sill already slippery with my own blood, but the face that afterward would come to me instead of what came next. Whatever happened then—between me and my father, me and the men—would be wiped from my memory, replaced with the same image that always comes instead of any recollection of what I've done. As if my mind would hide what it is capable of from itself.

Silas, my mother had said, look at yourself.

And I did. Do. Ever since that time when I was six and in a fit bit through another's hand and my mother had dragged me to her, clamped me tight, forced me to look into that parlor mirror. Ever since then, every time, after I've snapped, that I hunt through my memory for hints of what I've done, I can see only this: a small boy's face, teeth red, mouth smeared with blood, spit-flecked from screaming, head snapping back and forth, whipping the rest into a blur. Except his eyes. They stay. Stare back. Though in the mirror they might be squeezed shut or rolled into their sockets or just a streak in the convulsing, though I know that they no longer see, that the mind behind them has gone somewhere even its own knowing can no longer reach, still I see them look back and recognize me.

AUTUMN, 1849

The boy is dead, dropped twisted at the edge of the white stone circle, blood spread out black beneath his skull. It is dawn. The fleeting blue-glow. The sky and river and boulders and chips of quartz and the boy's skin seeming to emit a phosphorescence. And Silas: the pale pelt tied over his shoulders, the big cat's head hung down his back, the netting holding his nape-long hair, the silver streaking his beard, breath-steam and dried tracks of tears and the glistening coming again into his eyes. Crouching, he touches the boy's, brushes a beetle off a cold closed lid. Within the hour the crows will dig the eyeballs out. Already there are ants on the lashes, the corners of the mouth, crawling into the hole blown through the forehead.

Something moves. Somewhere across the river. He stands. In the growing light the mules are newly visible, hobbled in the trees. Or at least two are: the dark brown one, the dun. The gray is missing. He scans the bank: packsaddles, panniers, the woodbox mining machine, the fire circle and propped-up body and boulder where the other two had lain in wait last night. Beneath its ledge the lingering blackness is barely thinned enough to make out the lumps of blankets, the body or not the body. He stands a long time looking, the patch of night slowly becoming morning, till he can be sure the bearded man that he had shot, thought surely dead, is instead gone. Then his eyes move quick, skipping boulder to bank to river—impossible to tell till it grows lighter if the spots on the stones are blood—and from behind he feels another's gaze, as if he is the darkness and his eyes are watching him, and whips around. But it is only a raven. Perched near enough to see its glinting eye. It cocks its head, ruffles its feathers.

He flings a piece of quartz. The bird's wingbeats: hollows of sound filled by the roaring river. Loud as it had been all night. Loud enough to cover the sounds that must have come from the other bank: the bearded man somehow wrenching himself out of his dying, dragging his body onto a mule, riding away. Or had he stayed? Hiding, hoping to make it through the night, till there might be enough light to shoot.

Slowly Silas scans the whole ravine, a smooth steady swiveling of his head—each gleam, each shadow—the world sharp as if he'd just broken through the river's surface, been submerged for the past hours. He has not slept, has stayed by the boy's cooling body, keeping coyotes and minks away, staring at the moonlit open eyes until, at last, he had lain down and shut his own. But with them closed he could hear better—that whooping when they found gold, that bull-calf bellow by the fire, the word shot from the boy's mouth the second after the bullet hit the father: *Pa!*—and Silas had squeezed his lids—*Pa!*—the squeezing spreading into his cheeks, brow, mouth, chin, till his whole face lay crushed with it, the boy's word coming back to him like the gunblast's echo: *Pa!* He'd opened his eyes, lay staring at the moon. Watched it cross the gorge till it was gone. The sky filling with more and more stars, much as it would have the night before, or the night before that, or the week, month, year. As if it all had not been forever altered. Could be forever lost. Would be, if the one he had thought dead managed to make it back downriver. Where surely there would be more men. Who would come back up. In search of him.

And here is the raven again. Creeping, stiff-legged, out of the shadow of a rock. A couple crows landing farther away.

"Get," he says. "Go on." And to himself, his fingers already untying the hide-cloak from around his shoulders: "Go on, go on."

Rolling the corpse onto its side, he moves as if with muscle memory, the blood-gunked back of the head, its bits of bone and brain, little different from the carcass of a bobcat or bear, even the thick-curled hair. But the ear stops him. Pale, perfect. Slowly his finger traces the whorl till, coming to the hole, his face begins to crunch upon itself again and he pulls away, wipes his shaking fingers on the boy's shirt. In the opening he's left, the raven lunges, stabbing at what's stuck to the stones beneath the boy's head, and Silas smacks at it, the bird flapping back, its caw close, loud.

He spreads his hide-cloak out, rolls the boy's body onto the cougar skin. Around the boy's waist: a small cinched sack strung from straps tied in a bow. Double knotted. The way a kid learns to do shoes. His fingers stay steady enough to work it loose. The pouch is soft and heavy as an organ taken from the boy's belly; he tosses it toward the pistol lying nearby. The boy's belt he unbuckles, draws free. Then, slipping one arm beneath the boy's knees, he bends them upward against the chest, with his other hand grasps both thin wrists to meet the shins and, binding the limbs elbows to knees, cinches the belt.

As if sensing their chance slipping away, the crows come closer. He hacks a hand, barely sends them back, their racket rising as, crouching, he takes the cougar skin's four legs and draws them tight, shrugging the boy's small shoulders together, bending the head, curling the body back into its first-known fetal shape it held before emerging into the world, knotting it all into a package balled up like any other human buried by the tribes high in these mountains. But for the boots. He yanks them off. The soles of the feet softly arched, shockingly white.

A black ruffling, beak stabbing. He swings, boot slashing where the bird had been, wings beating away, the flapping-cawing all he can hear, and he is flinging the boot at the rising birds, reaching down, hurling the first rock he finds. Another. Above, the raven hits the ridge-blocked sun. Even higher, a vulture glides, circling, circling, as if trying to make sense of the sight below: the lone figure stooping and throwing, stooping and throwing, surrounded by a rain of stones.

Slowly, he goes still. A last clattering falling around him. Then only the far-off cawing. Then just the river. He stands there, letting it fill his ears, skull, brain, blood. In his hand: a last stone, smoothed by the water, his fingers turning it over and over. He watches the sheeting current, his breathing easing, heartbeat slowing, fingers growing still.

Sometime later he stirs. The line of sun is still high up the ridgeside but slipping down. The birds are gone. When he sets the first big rock on the boy's body there is a faint cracking from inside, the weight pressing out air almost like a sigh. But instead of an intake after there is just the next rock. The next.

When he is done, the mound looks like something constructed to complement the circle of quartz beside it, blood spattered over the one, body buried beneath the other. And between: the boy's money pouch, boots, gun. He picks the pistol up, takes in the strange flat hammer, sightless barrel, heavy rotating drum, the three still-loaded bores, slips it into his belt. The pouch he uncinches, turns over the water, pours the gold out, the heavier pieces sinking straightaway, the dust sparkling in pools, a few flakes flashing downstream like bits of stolen sunlight. And there, where the canyon curves and the sun touches it first, another color: red spots bright on a newlit rock.

By the time he reaches them, the sunlight has lit others, a bloodtrail dripped and smeared on stones and leaves. The barrel of his musket is still empty; he draws the boy's pistol out. A few half-moon hoofprints sunk into gravel: the man must have clung to the mule as it stumbled, swum. His eyes hunt the banks below: Shake of a willow? A barrel's glint? With each step Silas takes, he half expects to hear a blast. But rounding the bend, there is no flash, no crack, no wandering mule, no waterlogged lump lying face down. Just blood. Slicking rocks and smeared on branches. So much the wounded man can't have gone far. But somehow has.

Back upriver, the birds have regrouped. Gathered on the opposite bank around the brown-skinned once-propped corpse now toppled beside the fire, cackling and flapping at each other, their movement making all the rest more still. Making him more aware of his own breaking it as, leaping boulder to boulder, he returns on the same route he'd used last night. That side is still in shadow, and passing back into the cooler air, he wades through the complaining crows and buzzards, lifts the blanket off the corpse, throws it around his shoulders. So wrapped, he drifts among the cookthings, picking crust off an iron rim, upending the coffeepot over his open mouth, chewing the grounds as he stuffs each skillet and spoon and cup into a nearby pannier. Beside the boulder where the boy and father tried to hide, he finds a pistol case containing powder flask and ammunition pouch, and a small sack that he shakes out: a tobacco pipe, its bowl still smelling sweet, stem pitted with the marks of teeth. Made by the boy? He shuts his eyes, hears *Pa!* Or by the father—he opens his eyes again—maybe alive, maybe even now making his way downriver.

Standing, then, he turns to the mules. They are so spooked that, soon as he nears, they shy away, stumbling in their hobbles. He waits, his hands held out. The dun molly calms first, ears easing, the darker john still blowing, and Silas talks to them—"It's okay, it's okay"—offering some ripped-up bunchgrass just close enough for them to reach, necks stretching, huge eyes watching him back. "It'll be okay," he whispers, their breath warm on his fingers, the brush of their muzzles.

The john was left readied for escape, sawbuck empty, reins looped over its neck, and making soothing sounds, he checks its rigging, loosens the girth—the front elbows show sores from rubbing—shifts the saddle back, raises the britchen so it won't hit the hip.

When he has rigged the molly too, he loads up everything, strapping on the old cracked musket, hatchet, all the mining tools except the heavy rocker box, which he drags to the fire, burns. While it's crackling, he sweeps the camp for anything he might have missed—bits of paper, cloth—and burns them too. A pile of dogshit: he hides it under a rock. A whittled stick: he tosses it on the flames, scatters the shavings. The blood on the stones he washes away—filling the kettle again and again, pouring it where he'd shot the father, brained the other, finally over the word he'd painted on the rock, splashing the *GO* till it is gone—each time taking the bank back a little more toward the way it was before they came. Only the body remains. The birds and others will finish that. But for the clothes. So he wades into the crows again, stripping the corpse, throwing cloth or leather on the already fading fire. When it has devoured all it can, he kicks it out. Smothers what remains with stones. Each turned blackened-side-down till even that last trace has disappeared.

Packing up his own camp goes more quickly. He leads the mules across the river, up the slope, wending between chinquapin and tanbark and madrones, oaks leaning out over the canyon's drop, to a spot beneath a stand of fir where the needle-duff is flat from months of his sleeping wrapped in the cougar pelt now buried with the boy. The rest of what he'd brought up that spring lies within steps or is already on him: buckskins, moccasins, otter-hide slicker, hat of woven reeds. His belt axe and big knife, horn handle at his hip. The two smaller blades—folding French clasp and swell-end jack, its stone spud sharp for fleshing—carried beside firesteel and flint, needles and awl, a bit of jirk and his tin cup, all inside his possibles bag. A few sacks: pine nuts, ground mountain sage, dried snakeroot. His small frypan. A four-holed flute. A fishing spear and a skein of netting, and a bentwood bow strengthened with sinew, its quiver made from a whole fox skin pulled inside out. And a small square tin, dented and scratched, stacked on a flat wood case. Each leaning against a canvas-wrapped packet, big as an open Bible, waterproofed with wax, cracks sealed with salmon-skin glue so that it gleams as if shellacked. Smells of the river. Takes up the entire bottom of his rucksack.

A backpack fashioned from a saddlebag that he now fills with all the rest: axe and spear tied to the sides, rolled slicker secured beneath the top flap, hat hung off the back. Lashes the whole thing to the brown mule's load. The bow and quiver onto the dun's. Then stands a moment longer looking around. In the past six months he'd found two dozen snakeskins—red little bloodbellies, fools' heads with their bulgy tails, rattlers, garters—strung each from an alder, and in the breeze they'd blow like streamers, sun shining through, so when a gust rose up they seemed to make the wind itself seen, when hanging still, the calmness visible. Behind them: the mountain ash and steeplebush gone gold and red and rust. He'd hoped to stay till the first snows, see the skins set within a world of white.

But the men had come instead. And now he spends his last few minutes going through their guns and ammunition. The boy's revolving pistol takes the smallest balls. The rifle's bigger shot prepacked in paper sacks. Peeling one apart, he measures the powder, studies the strange way it loads: a bar below the stock levers the breech, eliminates the need to stand and jam a ramrod down the muzzle. Brass caps in place of flint and frizzen. Faster surely than his musket. Though it is only feeling the spiral grooves inside the barrel that he guesses its accuracy, lifts the lockplate to his cheek, squints at the sight: the bead and notch offset oddly to the left. Lastly, the musketoon: flintlocked and smoothbored, it is a shorter version of his own, down to the patching. Though where his musket is repaired with rawhide shrunken tight, the musketoon's fore-end is wrapped in rags, its barrel cracked, clear why nobody bothered to load it. Still, two bullets fit—big .69 caliber balls, same as his takes—and he drops them into his ammunition pouch, reloads his musket, the rifle, the revolver. Then, loosening his belt to fit its six-bore drum, he jams the handgun in against his waist. The rifle he wedges beneath the molly's pack straps where he can grab it fast, ties the broken musketoon to the john's load, and, with his own musket in one hand, the lead rope in the other, stands for a moment in his camp.

A breeze. Above, the snakeskins flap. Turning, he leads the mules away. Behind, the alder shakes—branches flailing, molting snapping—for a few last seconds framing his shape.

Switchbacking against the steepness, shoulders resisting the molly's pushing, slowing their descent, he drops until they reach a game trail beside the river. Without the mules, he'd be down in it, scrambling rock to rock, scanning everything, missing nothing, but it is impossible terrain for a hoofed creature. Unless it swims. What the one carrying the shot man must have done. The blood-sign comes—red flags bright in the sun—and when there's none, he secures the mules, dirt-slides down to the bank, clambers over boulders till he spots a smear or satisfies himself he has not missed the body. Though in the end it is neither that stops him, simply a trail: the far embankment busted by a great weight, its shore scarred with the half-moons of hooves.

Leading the mules across, he crouches to touch a ball of dung. Hard to tell in the warm sun, but when he breaks it open, it's colder inside—left some time last night—and he looks up the steep canyon-side to where he knows a ridgetop path runs wide enough to let three riders pass. Though it would have only needed to carry one.

By the time he's scrambled up, his breath is gusting, the mules wheezing. The trail is recently burned, running blackly along the ridgetop like the inverse of the river below. Behind him, the mules blow at the ash, and from a flask he pours a little water into his palm. While they drink, he scans the singed trunks and brush. But there is no sign of a body crawled in to hide. None, either, of the border guards who, hearing his ascent, might have been waiting with arrows notched, kawim witak'pes wanting to know his business in their territory. No sign of anyone but for the footprints of all the hundreds who had passed. For a second, staring at the evidence of so many others, the litheness that had been in him down on the river leaches out, his face graying as if from kicked-up ash. He brings the waterskin to his own mouth, closes his eyes, throat bulging beneath his beard with his big swallows. And when he opens his eyes again, the hoofprints are there. Stark and clear. A long line disappearing down the ridgespine, westward toward the lower hills, the wider canyon, his home.

When he moves, the river is in him again, the flask slung back over one shoulder, musket re-scabbarded across the other, his hands wrenching the straps loose from the molly's pack. He works around her in a rising circle of gray dust, letting everything drop—his worn-down hatchet, rusted-out frypan, cooking basket frayed at the rim—a slow rainfall of all he will replace with something newer from the intruders, until he has unburdened the molly of almost all her load. The few things he doesn't drop he shifts instead to the john's back, last unshouldering his own rucksack to lash on top. Then, when the molly's packsaddle is bare, bends down, half disappearing in the ash-cloud, eyes squinted, breath held, till he lifts the bedroll out—the one the boy had slept in—and sees them: Two men, each with a magpie feather in his hair, bows drawn, their arrowtips two sharp, still stones.

He holds the dead boy's blanket just as motionless. Both his hands on it, the pistol at his waist hidden behind it. "Homaa kani," he says. The words come out too quiet, and he tries again, loud as he'd spoken to the raven, the crows.

"Homaa kani," one of the guards says back. The other saying something too low for him to hear. Other than the word *honpetayim*, the word *woole.* Madman. White man.

"Haan," he says. Yes. The single small word sticking in his throat, his lips slow to make the shapes of language when he adds, still speaking Nisenan: "You know me."

"Haan." The one who'd whispered, his bowstring easing.

And the other, slackening his too: "What are you doing up here?"

"Going home." Eight words now made by his mouth for others. Eight more than it has made in years. The weight of the last—*hupu*—still heavy on his tongue.

They look from him to the mules to him.

He can feel the mules starting to drift, the ash-cloud settling, and beyond the men the air is clear where the other's mule had disappeared, its ash kicked up how many hours ago? In his hands the blanket's stillness suddenly seems heavy. He asks, "Did you see him?" Then, in their silence: "What did he look like?"

"Like you," the one who'd recognized him says.

"Except," the other says, "missing his face." And, placing the blade of his hand below his nose, swipes down as if wiping everything from lips to chin away.

"But alive?" Silas asks. The man shrugs. Why wouldn't they have slit such a gravely injured intruder's throat? Ended his pain same as they would some wounded game's? Then he knows: they wouldn't. It not their charge but his. Same as if he gut-shot a doe, his right to follow it across their border, his responsibility to finish it. "How long ago?" he says, and, at the other guard's shrug, turns as if the motion looses his body too, throws the blanket over the sawbuck, secures it with rope while the kawim witak'pes watch. Silent till he's done.

Then one tilts his head at all he's left scattered in the ash. "These are his things?"

"Yours," Silas says, reaching across the mule's withers to heave his body up. "I'm giving them to the people of Yamako." He threads the lead rope through in his fingers. "My thanks," he tells them, "for letting me pass."

Beyond the guards the sun is already low in the west, its light slicing between the trees, the moss on the black oaks glowing, the leaves on the live oaks lit like sparks, while behind him the clouds are rolling down from the east, off unseen peaks, coming like an avalanche of sky. Leaning over the molly's neck, he nudges her flank, leads her past the guards already passing by the other way to see what he left, urging her into a trot, a canter, the tether between her and the john flapping to their galloping, the clouds filling the sky fast as if trying to run down something too, until they are above him, billowing like the mules' dust magnified a thousand times. Below, he rides with moccasins gripping the molly's sides, body rocking, beard blowing, hair flapping at the musket across his back. He passes a deer skull and hooves hung from a branch, a little later fresher antlers shedding their molting, later still a set of twirling jaws abuzz with flies, the sky grown dark as the dust churning behind him, night drawing close, the path before him nearly black.

He can no longer see the hoofprints he is tracking, but he can hear them in his mind. When he stops, it is only to hear them better. He has not ridden in nearly ten years and his back is tight, his thighs rubbed raw, his body as bruised as it is tired. He knows the hoofbeats do not come from the mule ahead, no more than does the molly's huffing breath, knows he should get off, give her some water, but can't. Behind, the brown john stamps, too sapped to even search for grass. The dun hangs her neck low, blowing at ash. A cloud of it he can feel in his eyes, nose, beard, his body coated gray as a ghost. For a second, his eyes close. As if they would drag him into the sleep he has not had now for two nights. But how could he lie down with his heart hammering so? That other mule's hooves beating upon his chest. They'd break it. Through the sound, he tries to listen to the river's murmur far below, let it slow his pulse. But in the distant clap of cataracts he can only hear hooves disappearing ever farther ahead, in the roar of rapids only the cover that last night let the other man escape, in his own heartthuds only the other's beating, beating. It shakes him, shakes his body like the earth-rattling stampedes of buffalo from long ago back in the world outside his own, and he can feel the quaking, as if beneath a hundred thousand hooves. But this time in his mind. Coming from the footsteps of men.

Now you will see it. That face in the mirror. That shaking head & blur of bloody teeth & red smeared chin & eyes of that small boy staring back & no no you see a man's. Your father's. As you last saw me. Must see me still. Even aftr all these yrs. Even here where I have lived now near a decade. Even in the hush of snow & rush of the river & the scent of alumroot & mint & the ringtail drying her fur nearby the fire like a cat & the coonfat burning in the slush lamp. Even though the only shaking is its flame. The only blurring my own writing. Smeared by the age of my own eyes.

Even so you will see my bandaged hand. Note the way I step with caution through the woods close by my home. Mark the traps that I have set. Strength of their jaws sharpness of teeth my urgency to finish this bfore the others come. And be afraid. Of me.

And if I bid you calm yourself the way you wld when you were 3? Reach for my face & feel my beard & scratch my stubble till you were soothed. I know that you wld be too scared. Wld think your fingers sure to come back smeared with blood.

But it is just a beard Elisha. Grown thick & soft & streaked with gray.

And though you may imagine what I have done. Think me a violent man. Grown from a violent child. I am not. Was not. No if there was ever a violence it was not in me but btwn me & the world. My skin a wick. My blood oil. And everything that tried to touch me sparks.

Even my father. My mother.

The night aftr they felled our elm I lay on the flr of my rm listening to their voices coming from the bedrm below. Their whispers lifting & tamped back down. So that I cld only make out the worst. Adnah & Hinton were long since gone to bed & I had lain unmoving on the boards so many hrs they must have assumed I too was sleeping. Instead of simply unable to rise.

Most of the day they had been forced to bind me. First to keep me steady enough my father could pick out the bits of glass. Stitch up my cuts. Then to keep me from doing it again as all day the hired men murdered my tree. They had carried me bound out to the barn. My brother holding my arms. My father my legs. Set me in the stall hoping the horses might soothe me. But there was my mother's presence too. For she refused to go. Then when at last my sister convinced her I would do better left alone there was the horses' shuffling. The rustling of swallows in the rafters. The distant rasping of the saw.

They must have brought the huge-toothed blade round the houseward side to cut. I had caught a glimpse of it as I was carried across the field. The steel flashing sunlight where it leaned upright against their wagon. The tool was taller than either of the men who would use the handles at its ends. And still it must have barely spanned the trunk. The distant rasping going on and on. Till finally the cry went up. The crack. The crashing. The boom. The silence. My pounding heart. And then the sounds slowly returning. The voices of the men. The thwacks of bucking. Thrash of limbs dragged clear.

Now it was night. My siblings asleep. The workmen due back the next day to haul the sawed logs away. And though my father and brother had fetched me from the barn and carried me to my room and unbound me, now that it was done, I could not move. The moonlight too bright. Its window-cast shape too clear of shadows. To rise would mean seeing what I knew was out there. The sprays of sawdust beneath each limb. The cut rounds pale as bone. The stump's inside exposed.

From below, their voices again: Getting too big, and Wrong with him, and Bethany, my father said, do you remember when my mother died? How he hardly seemed to care? His own grandmother. Yet this, this tree . . .

My mother said something that drew their voices down again.

Till he burst out with Nearly twelve! and Strong enough, and Hurt you, Adnah, Hinton, maybe worse.

He told her then he had been talking to other fathers, ones who in their own boyhood he'd known as brawlers, some known instead for the troubled reputations of their own sons. Had come away with little more than admonitions against leniency, assurances that what was wrong would, through time or whippings, correct itself. Only a seaman, long-since-turned tanner, a man rumored to have once sailed with shipmates who wound up hung, seemed to grasp my father's seriousness, answered with his own: Send him away. Where? my father had asked. Wherever he won't be near nobody he can hurt. And when my father reminded him I was merely eleven, alone might not survive till twelve, the seaman, my father said, had merely shrugged.

A movement that, lying there listening to my father repeat the words, I felt in my own shoulders, twitch my own spine.

There were some souls, the old seaman had said, so skewed by misanthropy they would do near anything to their own kind.

But you don't believe—my mother's voice now rose above my father's—*I* don't believe . . .

No, my father said. He's just . . .

And the silence that stretched between them then seemed worse than anything they might have said.

If I could have, I would have told them. If I had understood it any better. If I had been able to get up and go downstairs and knock on their door and stand there in the room with them and feel their presence so near and still stay long enough to try. I would have told them there was nothing I wanted more than to be able to climb in bed between them, to sit at supper with my family, ride my brother's shoulders, listen to my sister read me stories, accompany my father on his cart, hug my mother back. Would have told them all that and more if I had not been an eleven-year-old boy lying on the floor above my parents, unable to stop feeling them beneath me, trying not to cry.

Elisha, have you encountered men afflicted by a fear of too close quarters? Who cannot stand a coach or closet? Who, if shut in a cell, will start to sweat, shake, shout till they break? Do you think they hate the cell itself? Or simply what it does to them? Did to me. My cell the world, its slamming door the sound and scent and touch of others, their unrelenting presence the key turning the lock again and again.

When I woke the next morning, it was to hoof clops and wagon clatter. The tree-cutters returned, I knew, to haul away my elm's remains, bring it bit by bit to the mill on the Sewickley. But when the clatter stopped beneath my window, it was my father's voice that shouted my name.

Always I rode in the springless back, shaking among his juddered tools—trocars and drenches, bone saws and twitches, blankets stained with the blood of creatures he treated, the musket for when he failed—but that morning he slid over on the driver's bench, bade me climb up.

I know it's hard, he said, a firmness in his voice that left no need to say the rest. Instead, in silence, he handed me the reins, waited while I threaded them through my fingers and clicked the team into a trot, guiding me solely with gestures as he let the horses' steady rhythm try to shake the stiffness from my face.

When finally he spoke again, he asked me what I thought they would make from the boards. A boat? A floor? Perhaps, he said, great tables for some banquet room in Philadelphia. Or the new capital. Or beams for a house like *that*. He gestured at a new-built place we passed. A house—he looked at me, his voice broken by the ruts—much like our own.

I let the ruts shake his sound away.

But he began again: And if I had let it die of age? Or some disease? Some years hence? If it had chanced not to collapse upon our home but fall the other way and lain there then? For what? A decade? Two? Rotting away? For *what*?

Beneath our weight the steel spring squeaked, squeaked.

Silas, he said, I know you used to climb it. Long ago, I used to. My father built the house beside it so we could. So it would give us shade. The sight of it. Even whatever it must have come to mean to you. To *you*. To *us*. Which is another way of saying its *use*.

I gave the horses a quiet Hup!, sent a ripple through the reins over their backs.

When your grandparents came here, he continued, *that*—his gesture swept the pastures dotted with sheep, stone walls and split-rail fences, patchworks of maize and wheat—*that* was all woods. Forests so filled with elk this time of year their bugling would wake my parents every morning. In winter the hungry herds would leave cover in search of grazing, so many they filled the square in town, churned up yards, trampled the snow brown outside my parents' windows in the time it took to load a musket. A winter's worth of meat without leaving your porch. One buck even tried to eat a wreath off the door. My father simply stepped out and cut its throat. One swipe of a corn knife. Can you imagine? A beast twice the size of the deer that we have now. At least that's what I was told. By the time I was your age, the herds had been so thinned I never saw more than a handful in the distance. By the time you were born, they were gone. Not just from here but anywhere that I have heard of since. Why? To make way. For *this*. For *us*. The mutton we eat. The bread your mother bakes. The plenty God has provided us. Such variety! Such bounty! The bounty that we have been able to raise and sow and harvest in their place.

In all the shaking of the cart beneath us, I could feel the steadiness of his gaze.

You doubt, he said, it could be so reasoned. That one thing could give way to another not simply due to fate but through some greater plan.

Ahead a track branched off, and when he directed me to take it, I hoped his talking might be done, that wherever we were going might be close enough we could ride on in silence beneath the louder clatter over the rougher tracks. But he only gripped the bench a little tighter, raised his voice.

Do you know, he said, what all the best pastureland in Westmoreland County was not long ago? Swamp. Bogs from ponds dammed up by beavers. And do you think the men who hunted them ever imagined how their riddance would affect this land? How, without dams, the bogs would drain? How rich the ground beneath would be? Do you think they ever dreamed they could create this landscape? No. Because they didn't create it. But we—those who stayed, those like my father who came after—we watched it change and knew what to do, how to make use of it. So it would not go to waste. Yes, it is true, God gave us the beasts of the earth and the winged things of the sky and the fish in the sea, gave us dominion over all of it. So we might subdue it. Yes, the Bible tells us everything that lives is to provide food for you and me. But *how* is up to us. Is *incumbent* upon us. To use what God has given us as best our reason will allow. Our minds—so unlike those of any other creature He created—to use our minds to make the most of it. Whether land left behind by beavers who had unthinkingly enriched the ground or carved from woods once so overrun with elk they would have eaten anything we grew. Or an old elm. That had to be cut down.

The wagon track had passed into an older forest, daylight dimming beneath the denser canopy. Old maples mixed with silver-barked beeches, tall ashes breaking up the green with their white blooms: the kind of woods to which I'd flee when overcome by those around me. But my father sat there beside me. *For this,* he'd said. *For us.* And passing through the sunbeams slicing down, the hoof clops sounding closer beneath the trees, I could not help thinking, instead, *For him. For them.* For if there was some greater plan of God's, it had begun to seem one from which I only wished to escape.

I felt the horses hear it before I did: a nicker. Distant, distressed, growing nearer. I looked at my father—his muttonchops bulging his already big jaw, his brow a sharp slant flat as if smacked by a board, his nose-tip sharper than my own, so that his head seemed almost wedge-shaped, his mouth pressed hard against the shaking of the cart, his gaze unchanging even as the whinnying became more frantic, was answered by another sound somehow worse, the sudden banging of hooves striking wood—and when I looked ahead again, I saw the clearing.

It was wide enough to have contained a small-town-worth of homes, but on all the trampled ground between the grown-up scrub, there was only one cabin, long and low, rough-hewn with wax-papered window holes. Around it: the remains of maybe a dozen wickiups. Most now mere mounds—piles of rotted skins and collapsed poles smothered under soil spiked with saplings—with a couple high-domed skeletons still standing, beams arced like ribs over the leaning lodgepoles. All but one, still half-covered in skins, that as we neared, I realized had become a barn, the mud-churned yard astir with hogs and chickens. The cattle, I knew, would be off in the woods, fending for themselves—the way the Susquehannock and Haudenosaunee were wont to let them—but the horse was there. Just one. A mare pacing the fence, trotting toward us, wheeling away, her worried whinny filling the air.

My father whoaed us slow, his gaze on the mare. I told them, he said, to keep her separate too. Then he was off, jumping down before I'd stopped the cart. Though instead of heading for her, he walked away, calling for me to secure our unnerved team.

By the time I caught up, he'd stopped outside a small log shed, a storeroom hardly big enough to have held me. Let alone a foal.

Inside, it was tied by a rope around its neck, the shed less to keep it in than others out: the hogs and chickens, dogs barking from the house, the mare. She was still whinnying. While we watched, the foal called back, lips blowing, and for a moment I could see the black gaps and bloody gums, the froth of pinkish spit. It had been chewing the walls, the splintered logs slick with saliva, and it lunged at us, baring its remaining teeth, before the rope yanked taut, wrenching its neck, its rear hoofs lashing out to crack against the wall. Hooves still too small to do much damage. Except to themselves. Landing, one seemed to buckle, the foal collapsing to the ground as, craning its neck around, it clamped its teeth down on its own offending fetlock.

Worse, my father said, than a week ago when the family had called him out. Then he had not been so sure as he was now. Sure enough that when I asked what he could do, he only shook his head.

Returning to the wagon, we saw the family—Lenape Indians, my father said—coming out of their cabin, starting toward us. He raised a hand in greeting, called back and forth with one, but I was no longer listening, was watching more and more spill out of the door till at least a dozen filled the path, men and women, children running ahead, watching me back. My father was saying something about a village, the pox, these people the remnants of half a dozen families, the last of hundreds who'd once lived there, and as they neared, I felt the clearing crowding—the stares of the kids, the adults' bigger bodies, the memories of all those dead—the presence of the entire village suddenly pressing upon me. The dogs got to me first. I let them sniff my fingers, tried to focus on the feeling of their breath, the easing of their hackles, the low and steady voice my father used with animals.

I did not realize I had been talking too until he stopped. His hand was on my shoulder—the kind of touch he rarely risked—and in the firmness of his grip I understood he'd stilled my rocking. Then he was lifting me—hands beneath my arms—the way he had not done since I was young.

He sat me on the wagon bed, our faces level, barely a foot apart. It's okay, he said. It'll be okay. In his voice there was still some of the slow, soothing simplicity he'd used with the dogs, and I wished he'd keep speaking like that. But the tone was already slipping. You can stay here, he told me, if you want. Or come with me while I do it. Whatever will be better for you, okay? Your choice.

He told one of the Lenape he would meet them at the shed, and when he turned back to me, his gaze was even steadier than his hand had been and all the animal-talking softness had left his voice. Your choice, he said. In this and everything. You get to choose. Your mind is good. Listen to me, he said, seeing my confusion. You have a good mind. That is God's greatest gift and he gave you a fine one. Your only job is to figure how best to use it. Mine, to help you. You understand? And when I began to shake my head, he reached out, stilled it in his big hands. There is no poison in you, he said. No disease. No sickness soon to kill you. You are not *that*. His own head jerked toward the shack. You can get well. Then: Look at me! But I was afraid to; he seemed about to cry. You can get well, he said. Silas, you can.

Then his hands were gone, reaching farther into the cart, drawing out the gun.

I could not then comprehend why he seemed so near to tears—no more than why he'd brought me there—remember thinking his distress must be from what he'd have to do. Though you, a few years older now than I was then, will see it was instead all he'd already done, all that he'd tried. Not with the foal, but me. All those years observing his son, all the friends and strangers from whom he'd sought advice, the pride he'd set aside to consult even the tribes on herbs and tinctures that somehow might help: he simply no longer knew what to do. For all his faith in God's great gift, for all his belief in learning, in the mind's ability to find its own answers in the world, his own had failed.

And so, as I'd discover later, he turned to others, began writing long letters to doctors, detailed descriptions of what seemed wrong with his son, received even longer ones in return: suggestions for compresses and purges, emetics and blister rubs, requests he bring me in for ice baths, rotations on contraptions meant to draw blood off the brain, that he let them drill into my skull in order to relieve the pressure or simply deliver me to them for confinement and study.

I do not know why he refused them. Rejected even the use of laudanum. Maybe it was just that he had witnessed what it could do, experimented on high-strung dogs, mean-tempered cattle, observed the way a hound would lose all interest in the hunt, a heifer in her own calf. Maybe it was what my mother had seen in her own niece, a girl once deemed overexcitable who now rarely worked up the energy to speak, seemed to have forgotten how to smile. Or maybe it was just the change that they observed in me. For I'd come back from the homestead scared. Less by the musket crack or the short-lived thrashing or even the mare's screams than by the memory of tears in my father's eyes, his anger when he'd returned. Driving home, he'd told me how he warned the Lenape not to touch the dead foal for a full day, even then to do so only with gloves. And still the colt's owner had entered the shed as soon as my father was done, crouched by the body and with bare hands brushed its eyes shut, stroked its neck, leaned close to its lifeless ears to whisper. I know now how much that meant—to the bereaved man, to the foal's kukini—sensed it even then. Though my father could only rail against what he decried as the old ways. *That*, my father said, his voice rut-rattled driving away, the fact they can't get past that kind of thinking. You'll hear a hundred reasons why they've wound up how they have. The pox, the game killed off, too little land. But none of it matters more than *that.* The last word he would say the whole ride back. And in his silence I could not stop hearing the Lenape's singing that had drifted over from the foal's shed, the slap of beaver tails echoing off ponds no longer there, the bugling of elk, the old elm's leaf-filled branches brushing the roof above my room.

In the days and weeks and months that followed I tried in ways I never had before to find my place among my family, fit into the space life left me, create a way that we—the world and I—could work. Shooting, I discovered, could allow me to spend hours beside my brother, the two of us honing our marksmanship, the eggshells we used for targets holding my attention such that if I let the rhythm of loading, packing, priming, cocking take me shot to shot, I could nearly forget all else. The way that, tapping a beat on a side table, I could not only stay in the room while my sister practiced her fiddling, but help her keep time. The same was true helping my mother: if I had burs to pick from wool, cherries to pit, sheets to iron, I could—so long as I stayed focused—remain in her company nearly at peace. And when someone would bring an ailing animal to our door, instead of fleeing the visitor's presence I'd force myself toward it, find refuge in the creature's need, my ability to calm it. And soon as I felt it start to fail—the eyes of whoever held the animal watching me, my mother's voice breaking my count, my sister's laughter growing too loud, my brother calling a ceasefire to set new shells—I would silently excuse myself and slip away. Usually to somewhere where I could draw.

For I had found that if I could locate a scrap of paper, a little chalk, I'd be all right. Hunched over the page, lost in remaking whatever was before me—a ladle, a leaf—I just might keep the rest at bay. For this is drawing: Clearing something in the crowded world of everything around till there is only the thing itself. Taking that into yourself, your mind, where you can free it of all else—a line, a point, a shade of gray—till you put it back in the world with your own fingers. The same line or point or shade now on a sheet of white. Then the next scratch of lead, stipple of ink. And there on the paper is the thing that, till then, only existed in the welter of the world. But you have freed it, same as if you cupped it in your hand and lifted it out of the mire, saved it from life's clutter or the confusion of your mind. Either way less a construction than a clearing out. Of everything that would obscure the thing itself. And then you set it down, back in the crowded world, only now protected by the edges of the page.

Without drawing, I don't know what I'd have done. If my mother had not made sure to keep my study always supplied, first with black chalk and Conté, later graphite wrapped in string. If my father had not found a way to make it more than an escape. If, one day when I was the age that you, Elisha, must be now, he hadn't instead made it my work.

The task my father gave me was more serious than any asked of me before: I was to illustrate his book. Or at least try. He could not have imagined that what his son of fifteen years would draw could truly wind up in it, must have just meant the job to occupy my mind with something other than what plagued me. But it saved me.

At first he brought me specimens—carcasses deformed by cancers, born missing parts—and, secluded in the study, I drew for hours, the house dropping away, the others forgotten in my determination to transfer world to page. Sometimes, while studying a bird's big-knuckled foot, I'd catch sight of my fingers and find them strange—that they were mine—or, sketching a creature's heart, would be struck by the similarity to my own and feel a surprising peace. Which more and more I managed to sustain. Even leaving my room I'd bring a pencil with me, the smoothness of the cedar-encased lead beneath the ceaseless rubbing of my thumb enough to soothe me.

Now, coming down to supper, I'd reach into my pocket, feel the whittled tip, run my thumb along the length, the rubbing soothing enough to let me sit with my family. All through the meal I'd take my hand out of my pocket only to tear or cut, return it while I ate. Might this way manage to make it through, maybe even join my father and brother in the parlor after, the pencil out of my pocket now, my thumb on it the only rapid movement in the room, the two of them talking around me as we'd become accustomed to. Though increasingly their conversation contained a pleased awareness I was there. For a minute. Two. Each night I tried to hold out long enough my father, watching out of the corner of his eye, might see my hand become more frantic, sense my growing struggle, and reaching over, give me his pipe, let me take a draw. So I could plead, through the smoke, to be excused.

Ever since the elm, I'd been unable to sleep in my room—the empty view, the silent roof—had taken instead to sleeping out in the stable. Now, sometimes, waking, I'd wander outside to make my water and see him in my study: the lamplit window, my father's stooped still shape. And in the morning, I'd find his notes beside my drawings—*the lateral cartilage is too inflamed; this line of ligament obscures the ring-bone*—as if he'd spent long minutes poring over my work, as if he'd begun to think of it as something that mattered. To his. He never spoke of this—the change from child's project to part of his life's work—no more than we ever spoke of what it meant when he began taking me with him on calls. In silence we'd ride beside each other, and when we reached the farm, he'd leave me without a word. Sometime later, I'd hear my name called from house or barn, take up pencils and paper. Though when I'd arrive the family would invariably be quiet. Children staring, parents giving me space. As if my father had given them warning. My son, he'd say. And those two words would get me through to drawing.

Sketches that, at home, I would convert to ink. That, when the book at last was done, near half a decade after I'd begun drawing, my father brought to Pittsburgh with the manuscript, insisted all 220 illustrations be etched in copper. Which the printer refused. Did my father know how much an etcher made per hour? How many hours it would take? The price they quoted him was near all he was owed as author. Later, I overheard him tell my mother he'd agreed to leave the drawings out, was already on the street holding the folder of my work when he found himself going back in. Dropping the folder on the printer's desk. Telling them to take it out of his fee.

A thing he only told my mother many years later, after *Hall's Anthology of Animal Ailments and their Treatments* had sold more copies than even the printer had dared hope. The day that I turned twenty-seven he revealed to me that half of what we made from what he called our book was mine. By then my brother was at sea, my sister married, our home made up of just my mother, father, me. As had come to seem likely for the rest of their lives, the bulk of mine. Over the years we'd managed to find ways to pass our days around each other, intersecting only at set times, both of them long since having learned strategies to avoid sparking against me. While I—much as I'd managed to turn hand flaps into the finer motion of thumb on pencil, transpose the moaning of my childhood into a kind of hum—had learned to navigate our home nearly as if I lived alone. So by the time my father offered me my earnings, it seemed to me we'd come to live together almost easily. What, I protested, did I need with my own money? The question seemed to pain my father. My mother was past fifty, my father sixty. If I didn't need the money, at least I could alleviate a little of what I'd wrought on their last decades. A maid, I told them. Would my share be enough to pay a maid?

My parents chose your mother because she was a mute. Hoped that, without a voice, she might be half the presence of another. Less, if she avoided me. A task she took to heart. Inside, she worked in stocking feet, listened for signs of my approach, vanished from rooms just as I entered. Even setting pots on the hearth or hauling water, she hushed her movements as if I was a sleeping baby. Which I was not. How could she know that the more carefully she made her sounds, the more they drew me; the less threatening her presence, the more I might feel it without recoiling? She could not. Though she had to know sooner or later we'd find ourselves in the same room.

My study. One morning. She had gone in to dust. Or at least there was a duster in her hand. Though when, still in bare legs and smock from having worked late and overslept, I opened the door and so surprised her, she was holding one of my drawings in the other. She dropped it. We watched it flutter. A sound too loud for paper. She bent down quickly, darted her hand out. Then, careful as if the ink was wet, she lifted a corner, rose. So smooth and steady the paper barely whispered as she replaced it on the desk. Perfectly. I mean exactly as before, at the same angle. I mean that she remembered. Then turned to leave. Which meant toward me. I stepped back from the door. She stepped across the room, and halfway through the opening, and stopped.

I'd only ever seen her through the doorway to another room, or passing below the stairs, or behind a pane of glass. You can imagine. Her mouth was twitching. The way it would when she was trying to restrain a smile. Though that first time I saw it, I thought it was her wanting to speak, maybe apologize. Which pained me. Because, of course, she couldn't. Instead, she reached into her apron, drew out a slate, some chalk. I watched her write. Words made of letters I was not reading. Was instead listening to the quiet around the clacking, seeing the smooth gray space she left between the lines, feeling the strangeness of her way of speaking without sound.

When she was done, she handed me the slate.

You draw beautifully, it read.

In some reflexive need to keep the quiet free of speech, I reached to her—her hand—took the chalk out of her fingers.

An act that even writing of it now pauses my pen. Maybe it was the years I'd practiced being near my family. Maybe the fact that, with Hinton and Adnah gone, she had become the nearest thing. Sometimes I'd find a bit of chalk around the house, and for a day or two, it would replace the pencil stub I rubbed, slowly turning to powder under the stroking of my thumb. Or maybe it was merely the reality that I had passed the last near decade alone with just my mother and father. And now was in my twenties' latter half. And this my opportunity.

Though only once I was holding her chalk did I realize the gap between my wish to reply and knowing what to write. Which surely should not have been, *You write beautifully*. But was.

The twitching of her lips again. And already I had learned it hid a smile.

Thank you, she wrote. Then: *You do too*. Wiped the slate clear with her sleeve and wrote again: *But you don't have to*. Her smile breaking out of hiding. *You know I can hear don't you?*

And when she looked up from the slate and saw my face, she laughed. Soundlessly. A moment of happiness on her face free of a single distracting thing. Till she turned to the slate again, wrote the word *laughter.* Then put it inside parentheses.

She had a sense of humor, Delia—Phidelia Field, your mother—an easily offered kindness, a quietude that could seem almost cunning but was just her reading a room or mood or someone's need with an ability I'd only seen in animals—the way a dog might lift its head, a mouse might twitch its ears—and eyes so bright they fooled you into forgetting they were small, and hair red as fox fur, and a face that tapered to a tiny chin as fine-tipped as her nose, and freckles, and a faint scent of sweat always about her, unmissable as musk, and none of that was what drew me to her. When I say it was her muteness, you'll think I mean her inability to speak—and it is true, that did alleviate the pressure of her presence—but I mean what being mute had done to her, how having to fit into speaking society had shaped her, the way she'd been forced to find her place in a world made for others unlike her, that *that* was what brought us together.

At first simply in the same rooms, at the same times, the way we'd found ourselves that morning in my study, but now on purpose: where once she'd moved through the house ahead of me and out of sight, now she'd linger so I'd find her; where once I'd paused, waiting for her to clear my path, now I quickened my pace, hoping to catch her. Often only for a few moments—Delia raising a broom toward a ceiling already free of webs, her dress stretched tight across her back—at most a minute—me stopping in the parlor to prepare a fire I'd not till then intended to make—but all of it such a break with the expected pattern that each second carried the charge of transgression. It was not hard to keep it secret from my parents. They and I had our own patterns that kept us separate for long stretches, often left the house to me, and even if they happened to be home, my and Delia's meetings seldom lasted long enough for them to find us. Before the same sound or movement or simply sense of her presence that had drawn me into the room would begin to press again, the part of me that so desperately wanted to be near her undone by all the rest.

Outside, it was easier. I might beckon her to see a chrysalis starting to hatch, or an owl pellet we'd break apart for clues to what it ate. And she would show me mushrooms she found along the road from town, milk caps and hen of the woods and yellow fairy cups, her face lighting up less at the morels and penny buns my mother would gather for supper than at the colors and shapes of others even I knew not to touch, but that she'd be so drawn to she couldn't help but reach for with her fingers. One evening I took her to hear the peepers in a pond I'd gone to at dusk each spring as long as I could remember. And we had stayed—me sitting just beyond her reach, her seeming not to mind—until the swallows had begun to sweep across the sky. Then both of us had lain back, looked up, surrounded by the tree frogs' fluting, secluded in our own enclosures of high grass, somehow strangely, separately, together.

Another time I told her about the elm. My parents gone for the day and us eating berries I'd picked in anticipation, sitting on the stump in the full sun, its sawn surface so wide we could be side by side and still three feet apart. It was her idea to count the rings. I'd tried, of course, but never gotten far before losing my place. Now she took out her slate, sat quietly making a mark each time that I reached ten, a stripe through the lines to indicate one hundred, two, three. By the time I reached four hundred I was crying too hard to continue. I'm sorry, I said. At first to her, out of embarrassment. Then as an apology for losing count. Finally to the tree, over and over. Her chalk gone silent, her gaze unwilling to pull away, her bright eyes even brighter wet.

What did she see in me? Someone even less well equipped for life? Something strange that, despite herself, she knew she shouldn't touch? I do not think, for all her generosity, it was just that she wished to help, to fix me up the way each day she did the house. No, I suspect it was the same for both of us, born into shapes that did not fit the spaces others left, the hope that somehow together we might make our own.

I was out by the creek the day that I first drew her. An early morning in midsummer. I'd come to sketch the ducks, was so intent on capturing the way they moved I failed to sense her till she was there, a couple rods downstream, staring at me. No, merely my way. Her gaze moved on past. Gave no sign she'd seen. As if she knew that was the only way that I would stay, that safe in the invisibility she granted me I could begin sketching again. The hinge of her hips as she removed her shoes. The angle of her wrists as she loosed the day cap's straps beneath her chin. The way her elbows winged when she reached back to undo her dress. She was so thin the nubbins of her spine cast shadows in the low-angled light. When she was in, her shoulders, above the surface, were smooth as stones. But so much brighter.

By the time she turned to wade back out—my gaze averted and pencil down in a pretense of privacy—I'd filled four sheets. And in the days that followed, I would fill more, sometimes taking my drawing board into the room where she was working, sometimes sitting alone working from memory. She never once mentioned the creek, never acknowledged what it had started. No more than I would have brought her my sketches. Though at night I left them out, scattered around my room, knowing one day she would come in and find them.

But not that she'd wait there for me. Opening the study door that evening, I walked into her already-leveled gaze. No drawing in her hands. Only her board, her chalk. Both of which I could see shaking. Though, when she wrote, the words were clear: *now draw me closer.*

The wisps of hair curled at her nape, the neck-skin beneath sun-rough as someone's twice her age. Her earlobes were free, unpierced. Her eyelashes barely there. But red as her hair. She'd chewed her lips, and drawing the raw flesh, I could almost feel its roughness beneath my fingers. In my mind, I touched the chapped surface, brushed the wisps of hair, smoothed her eyebrows. Imagined being somebody who actually could. And felt the pencil stutter, my breath grow tighter, my teeth begin to clamp. Stepping back, looking away, I tried to keep the trembling from my voice. Asked did she want to see what I had done. Sensed, more than saw, her shake her head. And when I looked at her again, she spoke. Not with sound, but just the movement of her lips. *I want,* she mouthed. *I want to* something. *I want*—I watched her add the gesture—*to draw you.*

I do not know how long I sat feeling her eyes on me—my own shut tight, my mouth set hard—only that it was long enough that for a breath or two or more, I found myself forgetting she was there. Gradually my jaw ceased shaking, the muscles of my neck released. Beneath my still-slowing pulse, all I could hear was the pencil's scratching, all I could feel its tip. Drawing me. Clearing away all else. My shape become a line, a point, a bit of shading. And sitting there, my eyes still shut, I could feel the welter receding, the page approaching, the cup of her hand. Her hand: What would it be to feel that truly—her fingertips, her lips—back in my body?

From far away, hoof thuds and rattling: my parents returning from town.

The pencil's scratching stopped.

When I opened my eyes, Delia was looking away. As if she knew where I had been, was trying to ease my transition back. Or maybe it was just from embarrassment. Because when I asked to see what she had done, she shook her head. Then clutched the paper to her, starting to flush. Her other hand flew up as if to hide her face, and seeing her begin to shake, I found myself somehow crossing the room, reaching to her, lifting her hand away. But she was laughing. A silent kind of chagrined hiccup. And when I pulled the paper from her grip I realized why. It was perhaps the worst drawing I'd ever seen, a childish stick-figure that she had managed to spend half an hour darkening to a stick-smudge.

Still, I tried to say something. Got as far as *It's* . . . before one of the cart horses, pulling up beneath the window, let out a groan.

And we were grinning. She tried to retrieve the paper then, and tugged me with it, and suddenly she was too close.

Outside: the creaks and thump of my father climbing off the cart. In a few seconds, I knew, there'd be the sounds of his helping my mother down. Knew it as surely as I knew that if I lowered my gaze, it would meet Delia's looking up. I stood there, careful to keep staring straight ahead. Slowly coming to know that I was wrong. Her breath on my shirt: she was as carefully staring straight past my chest. Outside, my father climbed back on the cart, started to bring it to the barn. Between Delia and me: the hoof thumps in the air.

Downstairs, the front door slammed. And I could feel the shudder ripple through the house, the faint shake of the floor, an even fainter flutter passing briefly through the inch of air between our bodies.

After that night I found I could not draw her. Did not want to. Anything other than actual touch just seeming to mark retreat. Instead, I tried to teach my body, prepare my mind. Petting our dog, I'd bury my fingers in her fur till I could feel her heartbeat. Feeding the horses, I'd stand letting them nuzzle my neck, lip my hair, cover my face with their warm breath. Holding a ladder while Delia fetched something down from the attic, I'd feel her footsteps through the rungs, shaking the wood, grip tighter. Now when she'd climb into our wagon, I made a practice of offering my hand, would stand in our brief grip, steadying myself as much as her. And she, in her delicate way, would try to help: might chalk a request for me to hold half of a sheet that she was folding, let our knuckles brush together; or if her hands were stuck with dough, might beckon me with a gesture of her head, with another ask me to roll up her sleeves, so for a few seconds we'd be beside each other, almost as close again.

Later that summer the Carolina parakeets returned, the first flock I'd seen since the felling of the elm. Sometimes, though less and less frequently, passenger pigeons still filled the sky, and occasionally a handful of parakeets had passed by in the far distance, but it had been a decade and a half since the horizon had released such a burst of gold and green and ruby. I raced outside to be beneath them, the big birds flapping by not fifty feet above, their caws and cackles raining down so loud I couldn't help but call out too, my squawks and whoops breaking into laughing as, swept up beneath the rush, I forgot myself, slipped back into the boy I'd been when last I'd seen them, ran through the field, circling, swooping, my arms held out like wings, my hands fluttering as I'd not let them do for years.

And what more can I say of Delia than that, instead of turning away that day, she came onto the porch and down the steps and, rushing into the field to join me, ran her own path through the grass, swooped her own loops, her head thrown back, dress fluttering, arms wide, lifting and dropping with her leaping, her smooth graceful flapping less an aping of mine than something she'd made her own, so for the first time in my life I could give into the ecstasy of the release, feeling no shame.

I think I simply did not want to lose that feeling—the parakeets already nearly gone, the last of the flock straggling by, their calls already thinned—think I simply did not want to feel what she had given me leave to. And so when she swooped by I caught her. Or she caught me. Either way, we tumbled together into the grass.

It did not last long. All the past weeks of preparation I'd hoped might let me hold to what had grown between us tight enough to keep the rest at bay. But it was nothing like anything I had imagined, her touch a hundred times more pressing than anything I'd felt before. Her breath, her body, her presence. If it had been even a little less, I like to think I would have been less desperate. If she had sensed a little less fear surging through me maybe she would have been less desperate too. Instead, there was just my rising anxiety, her trying to help, both of us unsure of how to keep from coming apart except to keep pushing ahead until we'd be too entwined to separate, as if, enmeshed together, the rest could not help but be overcome. But it was worse.

To be inside another's body. A part of me more sensitive than any other, that no part of anybody else had ever touched. For *that* to be inside of her, surrounded by her, not simply by her presence but by her pressing, pulsing, engulfing self.

She tried all that she could: I felt her hands let go, saw her hold them away, fists clenched as if forcing herself to keep from touching.

But to be inside.

She shut her eyes.

Inside another.

Seemed to stop breathing.

For me to be inside of someone else.

I would not think it could have lasted long enough if it had not been over even as we started, if by the time that I was fully in her it was not already done, my blood drained from me with my seed, my shrinking part already slipping out.

We lay beside each other, our breathing quieting, all around us the stalks stilling, the sky above empty of birds. By the time their calls had vanished too, our breathing had become a silence filling the air around us. As we lay there untouching, with each passing second growing slightly more chilled, more separate, more awfully apart.

The way we would stay in the days after, and then the weeks, again returning to our old pattern of passing through the house around each other. Moving separately among the rooms. Except now the sounds of me shut away in mine set her to crying. A kind of toneless breathing shaking out just loud enough to reach through the walls. And send me shaking. Even my drawing failing against the constant presence of her despair. So that I took to leaving most mornings before she would arrive, staying away out in the barn or woods till evening when she'd be gone again. But when I'd return too early or need to retrieve something from my study and we'd find ourselves alone together in the house, what could she do but stand outside the locked door to my room, her quiet knocking met by my silence. My shame.

Elisha, if she is still alive, I wish that you would speak to her for me, tell your mother that my regression was never anything to do with her. That I know how hard she tried. That I could never blame her for our failure any more than I could the world I was born into. Oil and wick, I told you. Said, Everyone else the spark. But no. No, son. No, the truth is that I was always the flint and tinder too. What fault of others was it, then, if when I struck against them, I lit? And in the conflagration burned up what I and those around me had tried so carefully to build.

AUTUMN, 1849

He wakes to a fluttering of wings. A sound or a feeling, his dream or the morning: for a moment he is not sure. Night, he knows, has given way—the doves already singing, the rising warble of a vireo—but above, the sky is unchanged, black as the branches, and though he knows it is just clouds, the brightness building beyond soon to win out, lying inside the bedroll of the man he's hoping to find dead that day or kill, it seems a reprieve. Not only from what's coming but from what already has. The world held still. Time passing by above the clouds but down around him paused. Again: the fluttering. Somewhere above. And from below the whisper of the river. Quieter and distant, but the same sound he has awakened to each day for near ten years. Same as it was before he'd been here, will be after he's not. As he listens to it, the rest seems small. Above, the branches have begun to show a little sharper, the cloud cover a little grayer, and lying there beneath the barely brightening sky he sees the birds. Black shapes frozen midflight. Not roosted or perched, but in the open air between the treetops, wings spread, yet still. Staying eerily in the same place. There is something strangely peaceful in the sight. Until one tries to move and stirs another, their struggle rippling the air all the way across the swale in which he lies. Doves—he sees their shape now—snared in their flight path over the ridge. A net stretched by someone who soon will be back to wring their necks. He rises.

Leading the mules to the spring, he throws the blanket in which he'd slept over the brown john's back. A second—the one the boy last slept in—he throws over the dun. Then goes still. In each dark corner there is a single star embroidered. By the boy's mother? Sister? Peering closer, he can just make out stitched letters: *IS? 18?*

All day he descends along the ridge, following the river's incessant falling far below, inside Silas the ever-stronger pull of home. Usually, it is the faintest tug, but moving at such speed, it is a wrenching. No slow following the autumn out of the higher country, dropping so gradually the season would suspend itself beside him: leaves golden at six thousand feet, and turning golden as he goes lower, still the same color when, a month later, three thousand feet farther down, he'd reach his winter home. Now his dust-churned descent plunges him backward through the fall, the ninebark reversing its red, the yellow leaching from willows, ash leaves regreening. Only the clouds, traveling fast as he, seem to carry the coming winter. He watches them begin to shred, rain riddling the path, rushing at him—a cold hard drumming—and retrieving his slicker from his pack, he draws the otter skin over his head, the hood narrowing the world to just the trail, the hoofprints he's following disappearing beneath the spattering, blending into the ash, gone.

Still he rides on, watching the brush for broken branches, the muddied ash for dung, passes a peeling madrone, its smooth pale trunk carved with a crossed diamond on its east, on its west three lines beneath three dots: the end of 'Ustoma, start of Kushna. And, despite the new grass growing on the less recently burned path, the molly seems to sense his spike in urgency, her breath blowing a little louder beneath her beating hooves, the mud flying a little faster, till suddenly—somehow already come to know his body's portents before his voice—she slows so sharply he's nearly thrown onto her neck. Stands stopped. As if her attention has been caught by the same sight as his.

A path. Not far past the faint foot-trail that for years has fallen away toward his home. But this one new since he had left last spring. And too wide merely for feet. Its strip ripped slantwise down the canyonside, its mess of mud churned by not just one set of hooves, but many.

Now he takes it slowly, the mules slipping in the muck, musket unslung and gripped beneath his slicker, the sound of the river swelling with his descent till it's so loud the scream barely comes through. He tugs the reins. In hoof-silence, hears it again: a distant burst of pain immediately drowned beneath the rain and river. Beneath him, the mare breathes, barrel swelling and easing, and it comes a third time, breaking through the roar, and he is off, splashing into the mud, hitching the mules, hurrying away toward the sound.

They are there, beneath the trees where the heron likes to nest, beside a pool where scaups and goldeneyes alight this time of year, a stretch of river, not a mile downstream from his, where the canyon widens enough to let a gravel flat spread out, a spot where he's seen Kushna hunters, women weavers, but never more than a few figures. Now thirty, forty, white men like him. Bearded, booted, hunched beneath rain-heavy hats, running over the open ground—gutted gravel strewn with shovels and picks—toward the town.

A settlement of canvas tents staked along the bar like deer hides hung after a village hunt, their old-bone paleness cut by the darker lean-tos, the cut stumps' axe wounds raw and bright.

He is lying on a rock, propped on his elbows, rain drumming his back, musket aimed at the men. Notched by his sight: the bald spot of a sleeping man inside an open lean-to, skull waiting to explode; outside, another's exposed throat, face to the sky; farther away, the chimney of an unbuilt cabin still missing walls, its roof a flapping tarp, revealing with each gust the figures gathered around the hearth. Sometimes a breeze blows strong enough Silas can smell their sweat and shit and piss. But if the screaming comes again, if on the bar some have resumed using their picks, he does not hear it. There is just the tarp, and a man's chest, and the tarp, and another's belly, and the tarp, and Silas's breath slowing, stilling. He is thinking of bullets. The thirty-seven paper cartridges he'd counted. The packetful of pistol balls. How far the pepperbox's shot might reach. How many men he might bring down before they found him.

A dog slips from a tent, picks across the bar. Mules shift in a makeshift corral. And the men are emerging from under the tarp, slapping hats, stomping into boots, breaking the stillness of the camp. Only then does he realize the river's roar has reclaimed the air, that he's lain there long enough the downpour has stopped. And through the last pattering, he hears a sound that makes him lift his eye from the gun's sight: the tight, clenched moan of someone wordless with pain. He knows it then, knows clearly as he knows it is no moan but a scream torn loose from what a scream should be, stripped of the shape a mouth would make. Listening, he feels it in his own jaw: an ache in the bone, tightening of cheeks, pressure on his teeth that makes him open his own mouth.

Again: the scream. Louder, as if brought on a change of wind, so clear the mules behind him cease ripping leaves, lift their heads, ears twitching. And Silas sees it then: the other mule down there doing the same, its gray coat washed by rain, but the puddle beneath it stained a muddy red.

From somewhere to his other side: a crack. Loud as a wind-snapped limb. But the trees are still. And there it is again, upriver to his right, so close it must be just around the bend. The chopping of an axe. Another. And then they're coming fast and stuttered as rocks knocked clattering into the canyon. But it is the trees that quiver: the tops of a few tall cedars just within sight, shaking as if from some gust unfelt by all the rest around them. And flapping out of one: a red-shouldered hawk, climbing away, shrieking its shrill *kee-yeeeir.* The bird rises into a slice of late sunlight, struck like a lucifer burst into flame and flicked across the sky. He shuts his eyes. Imagines a torch tumbling onto the camp. The canvas catching. The wind rolling the conflagration tent to tent. The panic of the men. There is the father's scream again. The boy's *Pa!*

But when Silas opens his eyes, the bird is gone, the only movement in the sky the high circling of buzzards. Below, men have begun to work again, and on the bank the tents are peaceful and pale as tombstones in the shadow of the ravine, the ridges already stripping the canyon of the day's last sun, the only sign of fire the smoke still rising from the unfinished cabin's chimney. He thinks of the last fire he made—two days ago, three thousand feet higher upriver—the big mining contraption that he'd burned, the scattered trash fed to the flames, how clear he'd left the bank of any sign of them. How much too late he'd been.

A shout rings out upriver, followed by a roll of thunder, a crack that stretches through the long crashing fall into the boom. He feels it in his heart, the rock shaking beneath him, the mules wrenching at their tethers.

He leaves them to their frenzy, lying silent on his rock. And only when they have calmed, the air returned to the broken quiet of axes' chopping, does he realize the screaming has stopped. Looking again at the tent that holds the man he shot, he sees another standing outside it, shirt sprayed with blood, sleeves soaked so red that, for a moment, Silas thinks at least the upper reaches of the canyon might still be safe. What the three miners found up there might yet remain unknown down here. At least for the remainder of the year. Maybe till spring.

In place of the screaming, there are the clangs and scrapes of metal on stone, and he thinks of his winter home, so near upriver, the thuds of the toolheads hitting his breastbone, the tent spitting out another man, another, half a score gathered in the cloud-shadow, speaking with an urgency he sees in their flung hands, strained faces. One makes his way to a still-standing tree and, swinging a stick, sends a clanging across the bar. All along it the men come then, back toward the one banging the pan, and from above the bend, there is the quiet of the choppers stopped as they begin returning too, and he can feel the air between squeezed by the presence of them all converging, feel it fully as the slicker's weight wet on his back. Above him, a fine last mist drops through the sunlight like embers reversed, and he can feel that too, burning his skin, lighting his hair, finding the beads of water on his cheeks, beard, lashes, breath, the flung lucifer finally landing, igniting, inside him.

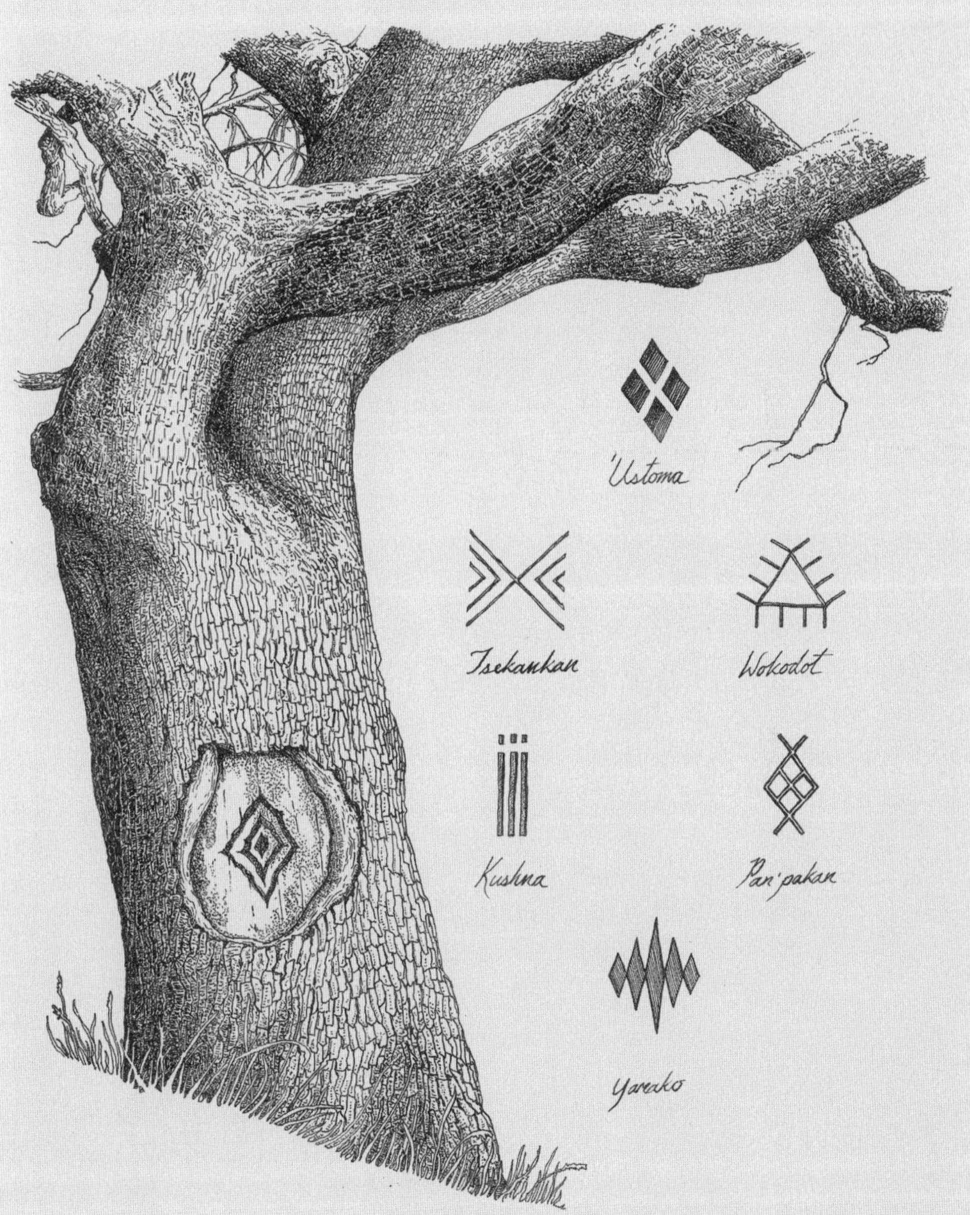
'Ustoma
Tsekankan
Wokodot
Kushna
Pan'pakan
Yarako

Last ko'no maybe wi'nuti what you wld know as march or april I went down to my river aftr a sudden rain & in a shallow puddle atop a boulder saw a flash of yellow green. A caterpillar. Drowned bneath water barely a finger deep. How hard the deluge must have fallen to fill the dip so fast it cld not crawl out. A tiny tragedy. Though huge to it. No less for all the 1000 others I might have found on that same stretch of river. The century old cloudpine struck down by lightning. The swallow knocked by a hawk out of the sky. This man in his 44th yr sitting in his small hut bneath the drumming rain lit by a single slush lamp writing writing writing. Waiting for the sound of riders or snap of traps or horses' screams gunshots whatever comes. To start my end. Set my heart on its last journey. One no greater than the caterpillar's or swallow's or pine's. Except to me. And I wld fill these pages with their stories instead. If not for you. For you are not son to a pine or swallow. Your story not begun by theirs but mine. Your own tragedy one wrought by me. Your hawk your deluge your lightningstrike your father.

It was from my own parents that I first learned I was to be one. Your mother on the day she quit working for them told them through tears she was with child. Mine.

Maybe, my mother said when later she informed me, it is a blessing. My father & she had grown too used to the idea of my never taking a wife. Selfishly so, my father said. And I was not sure if he meant my selfishness or theirs. But it was 1833. That fall

I wld be 28. And I knew they were right. That your mother's quitting cld not be an end. Must instead be a beginning. That I wld have to find a way to live with her the way I had with them.

The money I had intended for your mother's salary we used instead to rent a 1 rm flat. Pittsburgh was a 1/2 day's stage away & as her parents had alrdy passed I tried to argue that once the baby came we wld regret a move so far from mine. But my own mother insisted a marriage needed space & my father had alrdy found me an apprenticeship to an engraver & Delia believed it wld be easier for her to find work as a wet nurse. Maybe even hoped she might find help for me.

I had been seven the last time I saw the city. My father bringing our whole family to witness Pittsburgh's first steamboat lift anchor. And even then when the city was still a bridgeless town of a few thousand it nearly destroyed me. The crowds amassed along the towpath. Their cheering at the smoke-belch from the stack. And the horn blast and splash of the enormous wheel and roar rising along the bank colliding with the clamor of foundries forges mills till I was forced to flee. Leapt off our cart. Fought through the throngs toward the nearest trees. Even back then it took nearly a quarter hour to reach where the logging ceased.

Two decades later now it would have taken a full hour at least. Even in my parents' wagon piled with provisions for our new home we were still miles outside the city when the woods lining the road gave way to stumps and slash. The landscape become a mountain range of logs. Our clopping passing submerged beneath the sawmills' roars. Under each bridge creeks foamed with sawdust and grease spilling into the Monongahela. The river growing murkier as we neared the city. Sloughed soil from the bankside fields that we had left behind giving way to such a slurry of sewage and factory slag and leavings of mills that the polemen punting the boats knotted kerchiefs over their noses against a stench that even on the road watered our eyes. As if the smoke that hung over the city's sky had dropped around us.

For we were there, encased in the clangor of the crowd crossing the covered bridge, wagons and walkers and riders pouring out into the street, instantly subsumed by countless more. In the twenty years since last I'd been there, Pittsburgh had ballooned into a city of some fifteen thousand crammed on the wedge of land between the Monongahela and Allegheny. Workers at salt plants and rope walks, smithies and weavers, boatbuilders, coopers, tanners, chandlers: I could feel them all, their presence thick as if the smoke hovering above was made of breath, filling my throat, the foundries' pounding thudding my chest, the hooves on street-stone hammering my heart, the cart shaking my face, the grinding of its iron rims starting to scrape inside my skull.

That night, after we'd unloaded the wagon, carried all we owned upstairs to our new home, my parents gone on their long lantern-lit journey back, we found the flat we'd rented turned out to be above a bar. No shingle hung or way to know except that evening it was as if the street broke in beneath our floor: fiddle strains and roars of laughter, dance-thuds shaking the room. While from above, the sounds of two men arguing blew through the ceiling, and from our neighbors' side of a shared chimney, some family thundered through dinner, and how many others were around me? In that one building? The air containing breath from how many lungs? Already my skin was clammy. I shoved open the room's two windows only to let in a worse cacophony. Still, it was not the sounds that undid me, not the smells—chamber pots emptied, beer spilled on cobblestones—not the swinging lights and sweeping shadows, but the way each brought into the room the presence of all those massed so near, their pressing on my lungs till I could barely breathe, my heart till it beat like a bird's, my mind till it went blank.

I do not remember heaving the table over, shoving its top against the hearth. No more than I recall dragging the ticking off our bed, smothering the windows, stuffing the door-crack with our quilt, hauling our furniture against the walls, padding it all with pillows, blankets. I only remember standing in the cleared room, breathing hard, slowly growing aware my wife was there, silently watching. Surely scared. Though even more surely brave. Because she did not flee or come apart herself, but all that night did all she could to help.

Despite how weary she must have been, how late it had become,

Delia insisted we set up my drawing desk, lay out paper and pens. Though even as she worked undoing what I'd done to the room, I could do nothing but sit, forehead to tabletop, palms over ears, my body rocking, my humming growing into a moaning, filling the room.

It must have been a sound she'd never heard me make because, for the first time since we'd lain beneath the parakeets, she tried to touch me. At times, over the months, I'd caught her watching me as if she wished to, as if she thought she might feel the affliction in me, pinpoint where it resided, learn to relieve it. As if she could have lifted my skull-squeezing hands, or cupped my forehead to take the weight, or simply let her fingers break the space between us, without me wrenching away.

The way I did that night. Looked up into eyes filled with such hurt it seemed she'd found the pain inside herself instead.

Where did she find the strength to remain? To turn, open the door, disappear down the outside stairs, and not keep going? To instead return with a bucket of water. Demand I fetch another. In the fireplace she heated pot after pot, filling the wash tin till I could climb in, hide inside the steam, sink deep enough—curling my spine, bending my chin—to get my ears under the water, let it smother all but the thumping of my heart.

Thank you, I said.

And though my eyes stayed shut, my hearing muffled, I knew at the slight shift of water—a ripple stirring over my chest, brushing my throat—that she had dipped her fingers in, let them drift for a second a few inches from my skin. Then they were gone, her presence receding, the surface stilling. And I could hear, distant and distorted but undeniably there, the toneless gasping that was the sound of Delia crying.

Crunching my body further, caving my chest, I slid deeper, till my entire face was underwater. Down there I could hear a shushing—her brushing something? smoothing a sheet?—like shifting reeds, the cattail and sedge that once had grown all through the wetland now buried beneath the city. I could hear the water draining, the soil drying, the scrape of shovels raking salt from the mines. Her sweeping? There was the rasp of grass knives cutting fields of sisal, the footsteps of ropewalkers shifting the runner, thudding closer till they were loud as falling lumber, the forests collapsing in tremors I could feel in my chest, could hear the whine of saw blades starting to rip, and I heaved up, came crashing back into our room, the city, its paving stones and bricks and boards and iron and us, the swarm that had descended over all that had been here, as if we had fed on the grass and leaves, devoured beaver and deer, consumed even the dirt and trees, and for the first time I understood how the presence of others could contain such weight it would press from me even the ability to breathe.

Sometime that night I woke. The water cold. The crying stopped. In its place: the clogged and heavy breathing I'd come to know as Delia asleep. I'd soaked so long my own breath shivered and yet lay there on my sore spine, cricked neck, heart quick with terror at the thought that I might climb out and wake her. It was the deadest hour of the night, the presence of others thinned. In the clopping of hooves along a distant street I could almost hear the horses in my parents' barn; in the coo of pigeons on the roof, the hoot of owls; in the hollow draw of air inside the chimney, the wind, the woods.

That dawn I fled for the first time, wending down endless-seeming streets till I reached the city's edge, then turned upriver along the wrecked bank into the wasteland of brick-walled factories and cluttered boatyards, clambering across refuse and sludge till at last I came to trees: a copse of sumac and crack willows that, as I neared, began to stir—I stopped, breath gusting—as if motioning to me.

Inside I found a crushed and matted patch of weeds still warm, the copse closing behind me, the scent of deer still in the air. All morning I breathed it, screened by the leaves, listening to the calls of polemen blown off the river, steamboats chuffing by, their waterwheels like passing cataracts, while on the banks the boatyards boomed away, making new barges, broadhorns, brigs. The gristmill churned through bushels of wheat, the linen factory bales of cotton. Smithies banged out another nail, a hundred, a thousand. And, back in our flat, my wife woke to her morning heaves and no sign of her husband, slowly emptied the bath by half-full buckets, so in her state, she would not risk too great a weight. And the church bells all across the city rang nine, ten, and I could hear my father again—*winged things of the sky* and *fish in the sea*—and knew if God had given humans dominion over them, over this, I wished he hadn't. The church bells rang eleven. Knew it as surely as if my father—*so we might subdue it*—had instead of them meant me. The bells rang noon, and one, and the first day of my apprenticeship passed by, and all around me the next foundry shift arrived, making tinplate and iron and brass. And Delia maybe went out in search of me or work or something to eat, but, either way, returned to a room still empty. As it would be till evening, dusk, dark.

At last she opened the door to find me. Behind her, the single room was lit by a single candle and I could not see her face. But felt her watching mine. She turned away, went to the fireplace, filled a plate, placed it on a table set for supper. Our first in our own home. Though something in her stance or how she gripped her hands or just the fact that now her face was lit gave me to understand she'd already eaten alone.

I asked if she had been inside all day. She shook her head, gestured that she'd gone out as well. To look for me? Again she shook her head, picked up her chalk, wrote on her board's black surface: *to get you help.*

What from then on she called it. And it did. Was. An eight-ounce bottle of thick brown glass I would uncork each morning. A quarter ounce on waking, a second in the evening. The taste bitter as raw parsnip, but the feeling pure peace: a sip of softness sliding through me, a kindness in my veins, miraculous, as if my body could contain the shadows of the barn, my blood the woods beyond, my chest the warmth left by a resting deer, my eyes the sky through shifting sumac, my ears the whispered breeze.

That first day it let me make my way to the etcher's flat, face him with my apology, shake the Negro's strong-fingered hand, begin my study: painting wax and pitch asphaltum on copper plates, each stroke laid down without a sign of bristles; smoking the finished grounds with candle flames, the wick held a hair's width away. Careful work in which I found a focus that, for hours, could keep my need at bay. Though as the day wore on, I'd become aware of the etcher's movements, his needle's scratching, the commotion of the street, find myself biting back the urge to snap at the older man or bellow for quiet or hurl the copper plate at the offending windows. Till the day would end and, fighting five blocks of crowds, I'd climb the stairs to where your mother would be waiting with my quarter ounce. Or half. Once she'd found maid work, I would return to our home empty, measure my own. Mix it with whiskey. Fortify myself for the apartment to again be filled by her.

It took three weeks before the etcher trusted me to copy his drawings onto the grounds. By then I was hiding the tincture in my satchel, sneaking sips when he'd leave the room. Though by the time he'd taught me how to run the rolling press, transfer the lead, finish the acid bath, I'd quit caring if he caught me. One afternoon, as I rose, he stopped me. Told me to sit. Swiveled on his stool to face me. He had been offered a commission: ten etchings to be finished in half as many weeks. So much, on such a schedule, he'd need an assistant able to take each pen-and-ink to finished plate. I assured him I was ready, started to stand. This time he restrained me with a touch. The first we'd shared since the day we met. My transfer tracings had become shaky, my smoking showed the scraping of the wick. He'd had to turn the commission down. Because, he said, he could not count on me. And, standing, held out his hand.

For the last months till you were born we lived on what your mother made, paid rent with what remained of my share from my father's book—all I could contribute in my state. I could, of course, still manage simple tasks—hauling coal up from the street, making myself a cup of tea—if only I could have made any of it seem to matter. At least enough to lift me off my stool, make me leave my drawing table. After work, Delia would walk the city in search of commissions—flyers, broadsides—jobs I'd fail to finish, drawing instead the things inside my mind: strange creatures, impossible scenes, snippets of dreams that had begun to stretch beyond my sleep.

In the corner, I'd built a warren walled off by blankets, pillows, clothes I rarely wore. Could hardly find it in myself to shuck my smock, reach for a sweater. Ate only when Delia made me, washed only when she cajoled me. Though, working into her last weeks carrying you, she grew too weary to do more than leave me alone, started eating supper at her employer's with other staff, spending Sundays away at services I'd always shunned, the two of us living more alongside than together, the most we spoke her chalked asking if my bottle needed filling, my *thanks* as I took the new tincture. And again the grass would grow, the weeds thicken, the leaves cast down their shade.

I don't believe I even knew she had begun her labor till her pains had grown so great she could no longer keep from breaking through my haze. A thing Delia did with the same care that she did everything: stood silently beside my warren, waiting for me to see the writing on her board: *fetch midwife please.* I'd like to believe it was the *please* that roused me, the fear in her eyes what got me to my feet, the pain wrenching her face what rushed me out so quickly that, in my fluster, I forgot my tincture. When I returned, she was already groaning—circling the room, holding her belly—and the midwife pushed past me, filling the flat with her commands, the hurry of her helper heating water, the moaning of your mother. I could not bear to step inside.

Shut the door, the midwife said. And did not mean behind me.

I was already down the steps, out in the roaring street, by the time my hands flew to my pockets. Before me wheel spokes spun—surely a coin—hooves spattered by—surely enough for a mere ounce—men shoving past. Not a quarter, not a dime. Somewhere above, a window smacked shut. Your mother? Already she'd begun to scream. But the apothecary would surely know her, surely trust me. I'm her husband, I'd tell them. Tell them, She's my wife.

But by the time I made it there, the shop was closed. I stood by the window, staring at the bottles on its sill, their glints an inch beyond the pane. Reaching toward them, I watched my hand's reflection reaching back. Till the two touched. Behind me, the street was darkening, a few first lanterns flickering in windows. The way one would be in ours, the helper holding it over your mother, the midwife crouched between her legs. Her screaming. In the glass, the eyes of passersby glanced at me, their voices shoving—*Excuse me! Out of the way!*—their crushing rush pushing me ever closer to the window, my fingers pressing against the pane. Then my hand was gone, drawn back by the jerk of my arm, an emptiness where its reflection had just been. Before the streak of my fist smashing in.

I was in jail when you were born, crammed close to a wall smelling of piss, trying to keep from touching the others trapped in the cell. A cluster of men staying clear as if they feared me worse: my shaking, sweating, my speaking to myself, not as I'd done since childhood but strange sounds unhinged from words. While, not far away, your mother suffered in silence. Through the night? Into morning? When you drew your first breath, was I breathing through my need to puke? Crying as you cried? Your father. Though if by minutes or hours I do not know. Was not there in body or mind. Because the truth is, by the time that you were born I was not thinking of you. By then the reek of puke and piss and worse were mine, my body unable to retain its waste. And you will think of your mother, of her wracked body surely slower to heal, my own skin already leaking laudanum, my muscles calming, but my mind, my mind. Elisha, how does a father say that on the day his son was born he wanted—I wanted—what I wished to do, would have, were I not confined

No. No, all that matters is you know this: had I by then laid eyes on you, I never would have been able to consider such a thing.

A son, my father said the afternoon he came to pay my bail. And in the two small words I heard all the hope he once had for me. All the worry he now had for you.

In the corner where I'd made my warren, my mother had piled the birth-stained sheets atop my own rank bedding, and taking one look at me, she told my father not to let me touch anything but that. Leading me to the pile, he left me sitting on the soiled laundry, opened the window. My mother was already warming water, swabbing the basin, the sound a shushing beneath your mother's breathing coming from the bed, loud as it did when she was sleeping.

But she was not. Was holding you. Her on her side, you on your back, her mouth inches from your ear, her breath less breathing than a strained and urgent blowing. Though she was crying. From joy? Pain? Because of me? For you?

I would have gone to her then, risen through my weakness and shaking, if my mother—one hand holding the kettle, the other spread before my chest, careful not to touch me—had not stopped me.

Bathe first, she said.

I said your mother's name. Called it loud enough to reach her.

And mine hushed me. Said, so quietly I had to read her lips, She's trying to sing.

While my mother carried the laundry down to the lines, I sat in the basin trying to wash, my hands too unsteady to hold the soap, my body scrubbed by my own father. He scrubbed me hard, harder than he had to, and I knew that I would have to take it, to show him that I could. Toweling off, I tried to hide my shaking, but lying on the bed I was still trembling. On the other side of you: your mother's eyes. On me. Shivering faintly from my shivering on the tick. Between us your tiny body trembled too. Till my shaking woke you and set you screaming.

When Delia scooped you up, I was so sure she'd lift you away that when, instead, she placed you on my chest, I froze. You lay face down. I could see your crown dark with water or sweat, the fur fuzzing your ears, your nose mashed against my breast, mouth and one eye lost in its hair, but the other open. Motionless as my hands that held you. Still as my chest. I seemed to have forgotten how to breathe. And when at last I did, you moved, started to root, your mouth finding my nipple. I think my laugh surprised you as much as me. Because you froze again. And it was only after I had returned to breathing that I realized the rest of me had ceased to shake.

A thing that I will never understand. Do not believe anyone can. It just is. Was. What happened when I held you, when you touched me. And for the first time in my life the flint refused to spark, the wick remained unlit. As if your presence was not separate, but a part of mine. As if I'd been the one to carry you inside. And now you were detached. And it felt good to have our presence back.

Your mother touched her fingers to her lips, spread them out from her mouth in the sign for speaking. But I knew that she meant sing.

Shash, when I would sing to you, the rest of the world would slip away, my sound stripped of all but the need to reach you. The way everything seemed after that. So long as I was with you, I could keep all that wasn't us at bay. Even your mother, chalking song titles for me to put to tune, remained outside us. And I'd reach out, bear her wish into our world, perform it. In those first weeks we were the closest thing to a true family we'd ever be. Me bound to you. Her bound to you. She and I bound together by that. Nothing else mattered. Even my drawing. My focus on the lines and shapes that had steadied my mind replaced now by a focus on you.

Your mother had a harder time, would flee your crying, take to the street to get away. And I would stay, you swaddled at my side, attached like a baby on a squaw's back. A sight to make any squaw laugh. While your mother walked the streets, I'd walk the room, round and round as if your weight on my one side drew me into an endless eddy. And if that didn't work, I'd joggle you in my arms, the way a jomin shakes a rattle to ward off kukinis. Shook you as if marking the room, making it safe. So you could sleep. Sometimes I would too. Inside a space made safe by you.

Till your mother would return, or wake, take you to nurse. While watching, I'd be wrung by an emptiness as if my blood was being drained instead. And when, after barely a fortnight, she found work as a wet nurse in a home she'd take you to during the day, I'd feel your absence like part of my own body severed. Alone in the flat, I'd wait listlessly as I once had between allotments of laudanum, as if even that had been preparing me for you. As if my entire life had been. My awareness of another's heartbeat, breath. My days holed up inside my father's study. Even my drawing.

I had begun to work again. The etcher, though declining to take me back, would, out of guilt or pity, pass along surplus requests—advertisements, flyers, small one-off jobs—even, on evenings after he'd left, rent me his office, chemicals, tools. Though mostly I worked at home with you. Because as you grew, it seemed to soothe you too. From my lap you'd watch me crosshatch and stipple, scrape scenes out of blank slates of wax. And maybe it was that—the magic of something not there, then there—or maybe just all the dots of black, that hypnotizing repetition. When you grew able to grip a pen, I'd let you till I'd need it, then slip it from your fist, replace it with an eraser. By two you'd scrawl, sitting on my lap. Later, kneel by my stool, shading in misprints I brought you from the etcher's, the scratching of our pencils keeping time.

Sometimes, watching me sketch, you'd tell me, Make it happy. Or sad. Or angry. And I would do my best, bend a bridge's arch into a frown, darken its shading till it glowered; might droop a bouquet of flowers in despondency, or lift it with gleeful lines till by your laugh or nod or word—*Good*, you'd say—I'd know I'd got it right. Sometimes, forced to leave our flat—a commission requiring I study some subject or scene—I'd survive by turning it into an excuse to bring back a gift for you: a picture of a bluff from which I'd cleared away all buildings, a boulder freed of surrounding streets, one of the last city trees not yet cut down. Your face would light up as you took the page, warm me like a lamp. And when I'd tell you what each was, you'd say it back—*pine, pine; cliff, cliff; the rock on Watson's Road*—as if trying to remember the name of someone you'd just met. Maybe because you knew that soon you would.

Some days I threw you on my shoulders, your small presence still enough armor to let me brave the city. We made a game of searching out subjects I'd drawn, betting who'd spot each first—the hemlocks standing sentry by a gate, the old oak cloaking a cemetery—me always letting you win, wanting just the feeling of your excited squeeze around my neck as you'd call out. I'd carry you where you had pointed, let you place your palms against a trunk or grab at leaves, smiling when you'd say, *Hello, Hemlock* or *Hello, Old Oak*, speaking as if you still believed they might say hello back. And I, feeling their gaze upon us both, couldn't help but close my hands a little tighter around your ankles, hold your legs a little closer.

At home, we'd talk of them—trees, cliffs, stones—as if they had told us their stories, your mother listening at first with pleasure and then, as you grew older, increasingly with worry. The same expression on her face that she would get when you'd erupt in fits of screaming or when she'd catch you happily clapping your hands, as if she feared they might start flapping. Though it would be her own that fluttered into words. Which you would translate for me.

You'd learned to speak with her using your fingers—a thing I'd never truly tried, our inability to talk partly how I'd survived living together—as well as you had learned, even at two, to read your father. My moods, needs, fragilities. So that, between us, you became an intermediary. By then what had once drawn Delia and me together had long since worn away, but with you as a buffer we could at least regain some normalcy: cutting your food, feeding you bites, I might make it through an entire supper; curled around your sleeping shape, might manage to remain in our shared bed.

Elisha, do you know you were the only one I could ever hold? That simply feeling the swell and easing of your breathing could ease mine? Maybe something in you remembers too. The way when you were still newborn your mother would bring you to me, set your swaddled body in my arms, let me hold you to my chest, my heart beating fast as your infant's own, but slowing. The way it would when, by the time that you were two, a simple look from her could send you to me. By three, you had no need of being told—knew it in yourself surely as if you felt the strain rising in me—and you would climb unbidden onto my lap or wrap your arms around my back and simply stay. Waiting for my breath to calm, my heart to slow. Watching me try to press my humming back to singing, my struggle to rid the room around us of what I'd brought into it. Holding you the only thing that seemed to help. Till that began failing as well.

I cannot claim to understand its end any more than its start. Though I can say it was a thing worse than I'd ever known or have known since: the desperation with which I tried to hold what was between us, the certainty it was leaking away. You had long since stopped speaking of trees or rocks as anything but objects. Now you began turning from me at night. *Your breath is too hot*, you'd say, and when I'd ask if you meant rank, you'd only answer, *Your breath is too hot.* Hold up your hand, send me away. You were just three, too young to remember how we'd been, but old enough to make memories of what would come. And I can't but wonder if that was part of it, if the weight that once had balanced me, now, as it became your own—as you began to take the shape of the self you would grow into—had grown too heavy, begun to break away.

In its place the world as it had been crept back, the presence of others increasingly crowding again. Early that spring of '37 the publisher of my father's book engaged me for another. A narrative by an adventurer, a Clearfield County man who'd lived in Pittsburgh before he'd hied off west, worked as a trapper, gone as far as California. All recalled in diaries printed in his town paper. Now to be a book. Illustrated by me. Landscapes of land I'd never seen, faces of men I'd never known: it was a kind of drawing that took more of me than any before. And more and more I found myself turning to it, away from you, staying at my desk longer and longer, staring at the page like I was wearing blinders, going all day without speaking a word, working late into the night, my pen-scratching replacing my singing, the room thick with the silence of your mother putting you to sleep. I'd sit, hunched at my desk, feeling your hands talking with hers behind me. Clear as if they brushed my back. To feel that prickling, that heat, the air catching, flames flaring across my skin, and know it was not caused by strangers or neighbors or my wife or my mother, father, anyone, anyone but my own son.

Who had begun to bang on the wall with someone from the family next door. They would tap out a rhythm you'd tap back. All hours of the day you tried it—*tap, tap*—and if they returned the signal, you'd bang louder, then they in turn, till I'd tear from the room and, slamming the door behind me, break for the street, fleeing your mother's clapping, your laughing, the joy you took in bringing others' noise into our home, as if it came from some wish to cause your father pain.

Which could be true.

For if you remember anything, it will be your asking for another sheet, some help drawing a star, your pulling at my sleeve, wrecking my work, my hand slapping back, its crack across your face. The crash of the chair as I stood. A sound that seemed to come from your small body on the floor. If you remember my face, it will be that one so full of fury. If you remember my eyes, it will be the madness in my stare. For you would have been too young to recognize the fear, the horror, to understand my terror at not knowing how to make what was happening inside me stop, not being able to keep from turning back into the man I'd been, the man everyone but you till then had known, the one I did not want you to, would have had you remember any other instead. Even the one lying beside you on the next night, the last time you would see your father, the last time we would be together.

Late. Our faces inches apart. Your mother slumbering on your other side. Your eyes heavy too. Those tiny pouches creased beneath. The soft hair furring your ears. Your breath already scented of sleep. Hold me, you said. Turned over so I could. Your small body fitting the hollow of my chest, your head my cheek, your back my breast, your feet my thighs. We breathed.

Sing, you asked me. Sing, Dada, you said. And did I? "Early One Morning"? "The Rolling of the Stones"? Do you remember those songs? Did anyone sing them to you after I'd gone? Do you remember my breath? Or beard? Or anything?

Maybe your father, earlier that night, hunched at his desk, hands over his ears, pressing the sides of his head so hard it had begun to shake. His body quaking. Making a sort of hum, tremulous and low, like some vibration he was struggling to keep from leaking out, and failing, the hum rising into a moaning loud enough to wake you. A sight frightening enough to make you call my name, need me to hold you.

All evening, through your eating supper and readying for bed, I'd walled myself inside my work, inking a drawing of snowcapped mountains, intent on binding my mind to the page, back to the room, ears blocked with wax, refusing to turn from my desk till you and Delia were safely asleep.

Then I had stopped. To stretch? Knead the tightness from my neck? Retrieve a glass of water? I couldn't remember, only knew it was a mistake, had let in the scents of stew and ale, the fiddle strains piercing my wax plugs, the distant booms thudding back from the wharf, the city thickening inside my throat. I tried to swallow, breathe, finish the line I had been making. The nib's ink shivering. Inside my head, a thrumming. Sometimes it seemed what the wax let through got trapped there, the strangled sounds unable to get back out, stuck swarming, massing, against my mind.

How long ago had I begun to hum?

From outside the window: a shout. And my hands were off the pen, clapped over my ears—palms pressing, pressing, my skull near caving. Then I was tearing them away, digging my fingers into the wax, gouging it out, the shouting coming louder, clearer—a linkboy in the street calling safe passage: Beware the dark! My torch to take you there! Beware!—while in my body my blood beat, *Quiet.* Beat, *Please.* Beat, *Be gone be gone be gone.*

I could feel the linkboy's torch-flame touch my skin, the air around me burning. Though his voice seemed farther. Or just drowned out beneath my breathing, growing louder and louder till I was sure it would soon wake your mother, you. But fighting to make my breath quieter only seemed to make yours clearer: your quick dream-gasps, your mother's longer gusts. In sleep, even her breathing seemed a struggle, each inhale strained, each exhale ragged, as if dragging a bit of something living from her lungs. I'd learned if I simply stole over, eased her onto her side, it might abate. But that night I was afraid to let myself too near, instead stayed at my desk, took my pen back up, tried to press its shaking still. And still the breathing pressed at my back, the ink began to pool, the nib to stab the paper, its point gouging the wood. Your mother breathed another ragged wheeze. My fingers seemed about the break, the tip to snap. And in that second I could feel how easily the steel would pierce her skin, how soft her throat, how quick it would be to let that something living out. Then I was wrenching the nib out of the wood, jerking back as if my body would rip free from the thought, and in the screeching of the stool it came to me: It could. I could. Through my own flesh. How much more easily the nib would pierce the thin drum of my ear. How quick then the relief.

At first it was a small cold feeling, almost feathery, almost tender: the tiny tip probing, finding the hairs, drifting a little farther. Till it touched. I sat there breathing through the pain, the nib so deep it seemed to break the border between my skull and mind. I held it still, my shaking stopped, the steel point's presence pushing out all else. For a few seconds. Before it all came leaking through again. And I shoved the pen in.

The pain ripped my head sideways, shot down my jaw into my teeth, set the room sliding. Catching the stool, I stood breathing through the taste of blood. A trickle on my cheek, in my mouth. A slick of something else that shut my lips. I pressed an ink rag to my ear. And heard no rasp, no muffling, nothing but ringing. All the city disappeared. All but in my other ear. Where, thinned of the rest, the breathing only seemed all the more there. The rag over my ruptured ear was sticky, warm. Gingerly, I peeled it away—the deafness still unbroken by anything but ringing—and, carefully cleaning the nib, gripped the pen in my left hand, raised it again.

The point was already pushing into my other ear when I heard the flutter—a whiffling whisper—watched a moth flit into the lamplight. Shut my eyes, willed it away. The point still hovering before my still-unbroken drum, all the sounds of all the others still amassing in its canal, but beneath them now the palpitation—subtle as it was inescapable—of wings. Quick patter on chimney glass. A ruffling passing. Opening my eyes again, I caught a flicker fading into the dimness over the bed. And in the lamplight's farthest reach, the gleam of two other eyes: you, sitting in silence, staring at me.

Dada? you said.

Before you could say more, I blew the lantern out.

It was different moving through the dark with one side deaf: my footsteps quieter, the board-creaks weaker, my balance off. But it was the same lying beside you. The same enfolding you in the bend of my body, the same feeling your heartbeat meeting my own. The same *hold me*. The same songs whispered into the same small ear. The same long wait for you to slip to sleep. The determination then to remain still—the same. To not pull away—the same. The desperation as I fought my body's need to separate, the struggle to restrain my own rebelling limbs, the sadness knowing I'd fail. Already your heartbeat had begun to fall behind my thudding own, the faint weight of your head growing unbearable atop my arm, my own son's breathing filling my good ear same as my wife's. The fear then: the fear was new.

A need shot through me—jerk my arm free, my body back, shove you safely away—but, shutting my eyes, trying to breathe, I held still till I was sure you were asleep. Then gently slipped from under your lolling head, eased across the tick, walked to the door. Unhooking my coat, I searched its pockets, set down on the floor what coins I found, stood a moment longer turning the ring on my finger. But I was looking at my desk: dark bulk below the windowpanes, pale hint of paper. What would I say? That I'd fled to keep you safe? To find a way to become well? After all the ways you'd witnessed me fail? I could write that I'd send for you both when I was able, but why would you wish it? Why would you come? Could claim I'd send back money, but what good was saying it? You'd know if you got it. How much I loved you? Despite what my mind made me do? Despite what I had showed you?

When I crossed to the desk it was instead to retrieve my pens, slip them into their case, set my wedding band down in its place. The case I put into the pocket of my coat. The only thing I took. No money or food or clothes or anything that could be sold to help feed you. Just recrossed the room, silent in my socks. Slid on my boots. And left.

Though once outside I did not seem able to go beyond the landing. Stayed standing, forehead leaned against the door, listening. My ruptured ear wouldn't stop ringing, and after a time, I turned my head, pressed its good side to the wood, tried to hear through my wife's muffled breathing. Once I thought I caught yours. But it broke apart, became a rippling along the inside of the door, so near it was more a feeling passed through the boards, a pattering almost too quiet to hear, before it too disappeared.

AUTUMN, 1849

A strange hu, this—sheets woven watertight as skin, stretched taut by ropes, propped up on sticks—holding inside it the stench of blood and smoke and all the tight-packed bodies of the strange men who in their strange sounds call it a *tent*. Sounds the man they had hauled in, laid down, gathered around, seemed nearly unable to make. Despite his tongue trying inside the wreckage of his mouth, the torn flesh and shattered bone and bloody mat that once had been a beard, a chin, his jaw. Now a mangled place from which he had managed a few garbled words—*gun? son?*—between his screams, the men holding him down leaning lower to try to make them out. Before another, in rolled-up sleeves, calling for needle, knife, saw, started his work.

Inside the scream, inside the struggling of the wracked body, inside the blackness that the pain draws like a sheet over the sideways-slipping mind, the way when the wounded man had been a child he'd pulled the quilt over his face against his father's lantern approaching in the predawn dark, inside that memory another, nearer: the man's own son sleeping in the shadow of a boulder, moonlight creeping onto a curl of hair, curve of ear, the boy's face lambent beside him on the gravel bank, the same face—he sees it clearly—as it was when still a baby's. *Shhhh*, his wife says, nudging the cradle from her side of their bed, *shhh*, *shhh*—the same face it will be in a few years, grown into a man's. His wife goes silent. And when he looks at her, her eyes are on him, wide, filled with some urgency. As if she needs to tell him something about their son. But when she speaks, it is about the moon instead. *Its light*, she says, *it shows you too.*

The blast, the pain, the brightness outside bleeding in, flaring around the straining men, blood-spattered faces, staring eyes. Behind them: the canvas ceiling riffling, quaking. Wind? Rain? The pain that in another wave caves it all in, tent and men and brightness collapsing back into the black of night.

A gunshot, somewhere nearby: the pinched snap of the pepperbox. Clatter of footsteps receding fast, already gone beneath the rapids' roar. And then another pistol-clap, farther away. Followed by nothing. Nothing but the too-bright moonlight—why is he lying here?—the too-near gravel—why can't he move?—the too-loud river—where is his son?—the pain that comes flooding his face as if the hurt had burst a dam, as if he had been thrown headfirst into a river of agony. Through it: a third blast. This time maybe across the river. But from a bigger gun. The sound the only thing that could have stopped the scream still in his throat. That and the silence after. The only pain that could be greater the one brought then by the distant voice—not his son's—a sound above the river's and drowned beneath it and rising again that, when he came to seconds or minutes or hours later, he realized was somebody speaking. A voice that, as he lay trying not to slip away beneath the waves of pain, became clear was not speaking to anyone else. No other sign of life in the still night. Until a splash, a rustle, a scamper across small stones: not right. The mules stirring in the brush: not his son. The heavy hoof falls of one coming closer, its hobbled gait, its moonlit shape against the sky, its breath too near his face. And his own breathing and his own heartbeat, and the horror, the horror of what he knew had happened, growing beside the grief. Till they were too great to let through anything but his own pain.

Now he has fainted again and it is quiet in the tent, the others having followed the hanging pan's clanging call, all drawn outside in anxious confusion—what had the shot man slurred through his mashed jaw?—and angry talk of retribution—the others murdered by another miner, or maybe he'd said digger?—and growing determination to get their mounts and guns, find out just what those diggers know. While, inside, the half-faced man lies in the blackness of his mind, bandages wrapping his head from under his nostrils to where his chin had been, the gauze already red, the blood that he'd already lost wetting the ground around the table, seeping into the earth.

To K'aw, it tastes much the same as any other's. But the water—Moum, pooled outside in the puddle stained by the blood washed off the big, hooved beast that brought the man—knows better, having come from clouds blown eastward off the lower plains, carried over the far larger town down in the marshlands there, having seen the streets carved out, the creep of structures, the ceaseless coming of white men. Two autumns ago, there'd been so few wooles, living so far below, there may as well have not been any. Except that winter one had found the flakes and glitter, bits of reflected sun dug from the river, and by spring they had begun to arrive, by autumn had filled the lower foothills with as many of their kind as all the other peoples in all the villages in all the Lokum Yaman. Now there were ten times that number, so many wooles strewn along the canyon's bars and flats they might be a herd of paler humans driven up from the valley, filling the ravine, making their way upstream in some inexorable migration. Though to the trees that have watched the gorge for centuries, the stones for their silent millennia, it seems more a stampede. More and more each passing month, faster and faster. Till at last the horde has reached here. The banks of this river, Chapakakum Sew. All along its flats and bars: a coruscation of strange sun-struck sparks sending up an equally strange clanking. Sounds unknown as the scents of these new men. Men unlike any the buzzard circling above—Ts'ew-wenno, waiting patiently—or the hawk banking on a breeze—Tektek shrieking a shrill *kee-yeeeir!*—or the catamount or deer or even the oldest oaks and stones—Otak clinging to the slope with ancient roots, O' rolled to a rest by glaciers long ago—have ever seen.

Unlike any animal here except for the two-legged one in his otter-skin slicker, climbing away from all those of his kind below, scrambling back up the canyonside, pushing the four-leggeds hard up the scarp. Reaching the ridgetop path, mounting again, Silas turns the mules west, toward the only other humans that, till now, the Lokum Yaman has allowed among its folds: the village that lies a hard hour's ride downriver, the Nisenan living there as they have done for as long as Ole has sung his coyote-songs, as long as the five great ropes have anchored the world, ever since the earth was formed from the mud K'ocoj carried on his hump-shelled back up from the bottom of the sea.

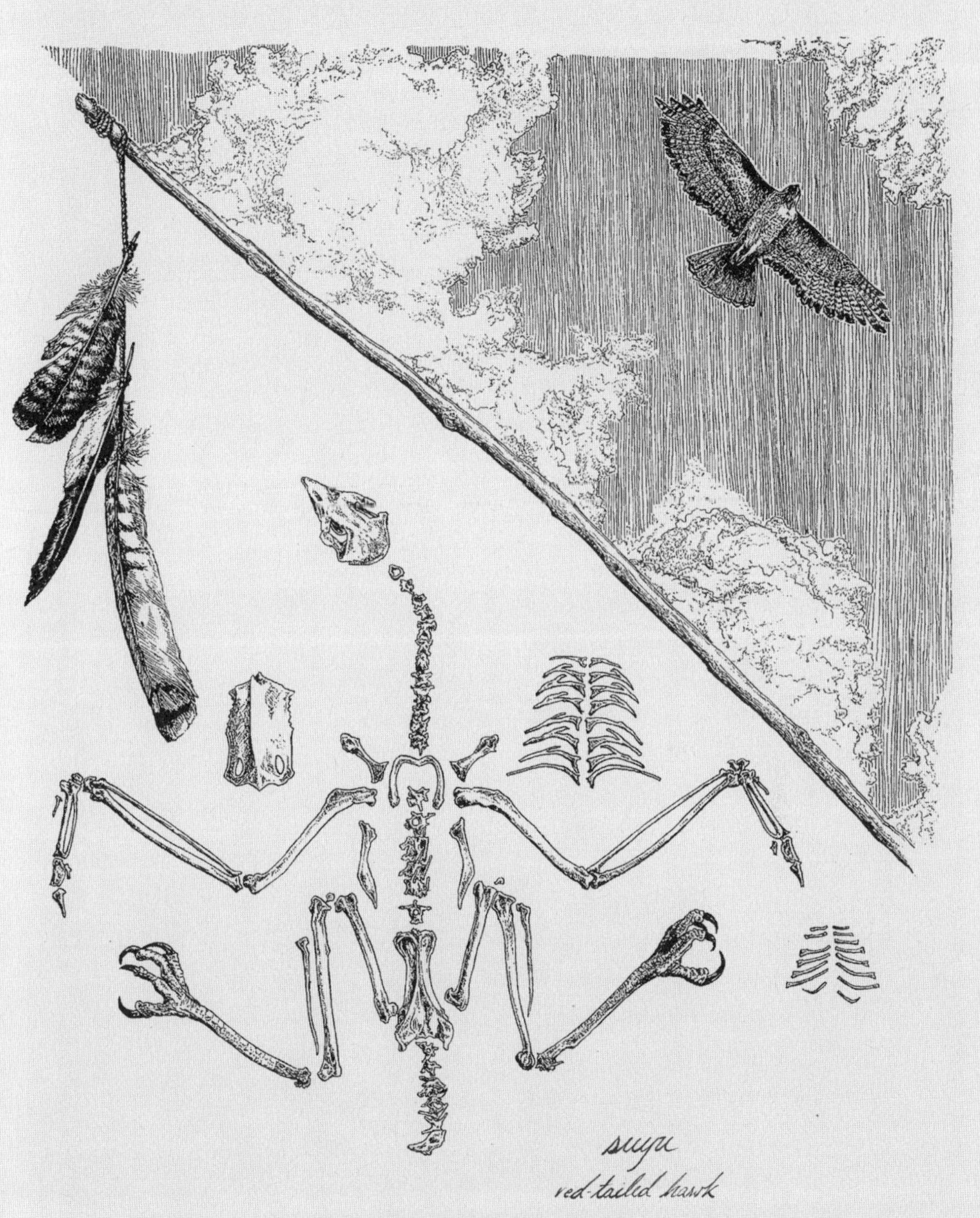

suyu
red-tailed hawk

And there we are. That door btwn us. The rest of our lives waiting on our different sides. And I sitting here 12 yrs later wld presume to tell you what you shld want to know. Wld make your words. Claim your questions. When I cannot even know your voice. Can only hear a 3 yr old's high Why? Why Dada? And you 15. Horrible horrible & worse to shut my eyes & try to find how you sound now & hear only myself. My own voice inside my head. Alone as it has been for yrs.

Still you ask me why in your terrible 3 yr old voice & now that we are here I do not know that I can tell you. That I want to. Why that night when you were 3 your father left you. Scared I said. Said the spark the wick my fear that I might hurt your mother or even you. Which is all true. But not the truth. The truth is I had alrdy lost you. Your presence becoming just anothr from which I had to flee. That to wait & see that happen was worse than anything I cld imagine. Except the other possibility. That you might return to me. Grow increasingly like me. Some day be unable to bear the breathing of your own mother. The presence of your own father. That I wld pass on to you the inability to endure a life alongside even your child. No the truth Elisha is that I left because of you. In order to leave you. Not seeing you again the purpose.

Now I have said it. And do not know that I was right to. For what good can it do a boy waking to an emptiness where once his father was? Maybe when you opened your eyes it was still dark. Maybe when you said Hold me your mother did. Maybe she assured you I wld be back. How long bfore she told you? Or did she ever? Or did the knowing just grow inside you over the days that wld come after? And then the weeks. And then the years.

If I had more time I wld start over. This letter. Wld simply say that I am sorry. Am sorry son. And I wld see how small that is. How meager. Wld pick up my pen once more. Redip the nib. And in the days or hrs or however long I might have left wld try again.

And if I told you how long it took to make myself turn from that door? How when I did it was because my breathing had become so strained I feared that it wld wake your mother. How each step down those stairs bound my chest tighter. That the only way I cld was the belief that I wld stay away no more than a few days a wk a mnth. Just long enough to find some way to make myself just enough better.

But outside it was so much easier to breathe. The linkboy gone. The dark street empty. In my right ear nothing but deafened ringing. In my left all the sounds of the whole city awake and sleeping. And then my flapping coat. My clacking boots. As I broke into a run. Strange stumbling limping. As if the sound from one side pushed me toward the other. Till there was just river. Whisper of water flowing below. My own footsteps echoing across the bridge.

That night I fled on the same road that four years prior had brought me in my father's cart. The coaches and drays now breaking the dark with drumming hooves and lantern flares that sent me scrambling into the slash and mud of mill yards. Pastures and fields. Eventually as I followed the Sewickley farther east a first bit of forest. Patches of woods that by dawn I had begun to recognize. Though in the decades since I had wandered them as a child they had much changed.

Most of the great oaks and hickories and chestnuts were gone. Their groves grown up instead in swaths of scrubby pine. So for long stretches, all the trees appeared the same. And where was the cloudburst of song and chatter? Instead of the thin mizzle falling around me. A wren's quick trill. Few pips of a thrush. So sparse I thought it just my damaged hearing. But as I crept toward the forest edge, the birdsong grew into a deluge of *twees* and *queedles*.

The pastures aflutter with bluebirds. Warblers. Only when I turned back to the woods did the sounds recede. Where were the titmice dropping acorns from the canopy? The flocks of chickadees popping branch to branch? Instead, as I resumed my rustling passing, the stillness only grew. The few creatures moving around me seeming quicker to flee. More skittish of me. A thing that, as I neared my onetime home, made me feel increasingly closer to them.

The house was the same. I do not mean the way it looked. I mean how it felt to see it: the sheet my father used for surgeries drying over a railing, my mother's bonnet dangling from a scythe, beyond the windowpanes the sense of someone passing. I mean to want to leave the trees and go inside and fall into my mother's embrace, watch my father's face lift at the sight of me, to need that more than I ever had, and yet to know as soon as I stepped through the door, there'd be the old anxiety, the same need to flee, the thing that had always been in me. I mean the fear that it would always be.

It had begun to rain, big slow drops hitting each leaf, the branches starting to bob around me, and watching the horses head for the barn—the roan rain-shy since he'd been born, the dappled gray following as always—I did the same.

Inside, the pounding on the roof was nearly loud enough to drown out the ringing in my ear, and I stood as I had through childhood, palms open toward the nearing horses, hoping, despite my lack of an offering, they might gift me with a soft nuzzling. When instead they turned away, I felt my own hunger curl through me. Almost strong as my need to sleep. Taking a blanket, I lay down in the same corner I'd spent so many nights in as a kid. They eyed me skeptically, as if to remind me it was midday, or that I was no child, or of the fact that they had known me when I had been.

Unlike the thinned-out creatures of the woods, they had remained. Same as the milk cow, the dog. And all the rest in all the other barns and homes. What had they known that the wolves and elk, titmice and parakeets, had not? How had they learned to live within the world of men, to fit themselves in the spaces we left—remake their natures, reshape their hearts, retrain their minds—and still seem so at peace?

The nearest I'd ever come had been the years living here with just my parents. Except for the years I'd had with you. Now you'd be at your mother's work, watching her nurse another child, helping her clean its diaper, trying to quiet its crying while she stayed in the privy overlong trying to quiet her own, failing to scrub from her face the redness you'd then see. And when the child's father, at day's end, leans down to kiss his daughter, or requests that you hand him his son, or just comes home?

Lying there, listening to the roar of the drumming rain, I tried to imagine how it might be to live here again. With you. My parents. Your mother? Already the drumming began to falter: Delia's sleep-breathing coming from my siblings' room. The leaves' rushing started to stutter: my parents moving through the house beneath my study. The roaring hushed: your voice calling for me. And turning over, I pressed my good ear to the ground, let the other's deafness drown out the rest.

I do not know how long I slept. Only that when I woke, it was to barking. An enthusiastic yipping I'd only ever known the dog to make when accompanying my father. I sat up in the empty stall—there was his whistle—and, before the dog could bark again, was slipping out the door.

Long as I could I kept to the woods, tried to survive off morels, cress, crawfish, crickets, but it was less than a week before hunger drove me to stealing: mulberries off a neighbor's tree, green wheat out of another's field, eggs from my parents' coop. Their horses' oats. Though by the time I grew bold enough to go back in the barn the team was gone, the wagon too, my parents somewhere far enough to keep them away for a whole day. And then another. A letter, I imagined. From your mother.

Knowing they were gone, it was impossible not to go further. The pole and tackle that I lifted from a corner of the barn had once been mine—but not the net, the basket, the hatchet I took for firewood. That evening I climbed into the loft, sat in the straw breathing the scent of mouse nests, bird feathers, the cats running their backs beneath my hands, while the high hay window showed the last of the sun. The dusk. Stars.

That night I slept as deeply as when I'd been a child. And in the morning, as if time had slipped back to then, there was my sister: Adnah, walking over from her nearby house, her young daughter beside her. They gathered what eggs I'd left, fed the chickens, filled a basket from the garden, and the whole time I watched them through a crack between the boards, fighting a tightening in my chest. My own sister, niece. Neither seen in over a year. And still: such relief when they were gone.

Climbing down, I went around retracing where they'd been, the sense of them still in the frenzy of seed-hunting hens, the head of lettuce missing from a row. It made me sad. That I could feel close to them only with them gone. That when I went into the house it felt so much better to be among signs of my parents' lives without them there. On the parlor mantel: my father's pipe. I drew a puff of stale air through, put it back. The kitchen counter was still spread with spilled flour. I finger-wrote my name. Then blew it clear. My father had reclaimed the study. The closet I'd once slept in had been filled. In my parents' room I could smell them on their pillows. The bed unmade. I lay down on it. Thought, If this was life, if only I could move through life like this.

A minute passed, a few, a quarter hour, before I felt the shaking. Faint in the bed beneath me. My punctured eardrum had healed enough to cease its ringing, let some sound through, but it was not till I freed my other ear that I heard the hooves. Leaping up, I left through the kitchen, fleeing for the woods like any wild creature. Except once I'd crashed into the brush I stopped, looked back: my mother standing there, staring at the spot where I had disappeared, her hand on the door, holding it open for a long moment more before she slowly let it shut.

It was the start of a pact between us. The missing tackle and hatchet, the dirt my feet left on their bed: they must have known that I was there. Even before I came again. That was my part. That I'd keep coming, keep taking eggs, sleeping in the barn, so long as they kept pretending I was not. Each evening, shutting the hens in their coop, my mother left behind half of their eggs. Each night, setting supper dishes out for the dog to lick, she placed a full portion on a shelf too high for him to reach. And after dark I might find a folding knife in the barn, a pair of boots, even a few blank papers, bottle of ink, pen. Its nib for writing. As if they hoped I'd leave a reply. Instead, each dusk before I snuck into the loft, I'd hide at the woods' edge and watch my parents sit rocking on the porch, the air between us filling with fireflies. My mother would sing, my father smoke his pipe. And in the dimness of coming night, I'd feel his searching gaze.

My mother never tried to see me, seemed not to need to so long as she knew I was there. Each dawn, I'd leave my empty dish on the stone steps outside the kitchen, watch her emerge and see the plate, her body lighten, as if each night she went to bed expecting in the morning to find an empty step. And when I would come near enough the dog might leave her side, dart to the woods, lean his panting weight against me, let me bury my fingers in his coat, I'd send him back, watch from the trees as she would call him over, hold him to her, stroke his fur.

One late afternoon, when my father was gone and she was taking laundry off the line, I surprised myself by stepping out into the open behind her. She turned her head—just long enough to glimpse me—then looked away again, back at the sheet hanging before her, her hands frozen on the line, her entire body still. I took another step closer. Around her the sheets stirred. A breeze. Settled and stirred again. I do not know how long we were like that. A while. Together the way we had discovered so long ago we could be. A feeling so strong I wanted to touch her, just put my hand on her arm or neck or shoulder, feel her breathing calm as mine. But I did not. Her breathing was not. Watching her back from a few feet away I felt its stiffness, the muscles tight as if to grip her lungs. I backed away. And it was only once I was in the woods again, hidden by the rustling leaves well enough to stop and let them quiet, that I heard her sobbing.

All the next day I stayed away. And when I returned that evening, everything had changed: two new horses in the pasture, a carriage by the barn, the house's windows bright as if each lamp inside was lit. Too far away for me to see more than the commotion, the passing figures. A woman: not my mother. I could hear the voices of men, children. Yours. My ear had fully healed by then, but even so my body knew it first. By the time the color had left the sky, the rest of me was sure. You were too small to show over the window-sills, so I stood waiting for someone to lift you up. Was still there staring when you came out. The dark porch suddenly split by lamp-light. The open door. You in it. Lit from behind, but still I knew. Would have even if your grandfather hadn't been beside you, hand on your head. With his other he reached behind and shut the door, and for a second I couldn't see you and, without thinking, stepped forward. But you were already coming down the steps into the dusk. I stopped, stepped back. Go on, your grandfather said. There was just enough light left for me to see that you were scared. Holding a basket to your chest. Okay, you said, but did not move. And I listened to him tell you about the latch and where to look and to remember to relatch it when you were done and you said you did not want to. Come with me, you pleaded. No, he told you. And then, What would your daddy think?

I think he knew that I was watching, knew it would be all I could do to keep from crossing the yard to you; that if I did, I'd tell you not to listen to him, would go with you, hold your hand. Just as he knew that I could not. Instead, you walked to the coop alone, struggled with the latch—from the porch he talked you through it—and then were in and, for the next minute, I got to watch you: the way you paused while the rooster beat his wings, said something I couldn't make out more than that it sounded spoken in fear, two words you repeated again and again, till I recognized them. *Go on,* you were saying, *go on.* Over and over. To the birds or to yourself. Each time that you reached down. *Go on.* For a while you were hidden in shadow and I could only see you in the movement of the birds and then you shouted to your grandfather and he reminded you to latch the door and maybe from where he stood, he couldn't see, but I watched you barely push it shut before you started running for the porch. The basket, the dark. Don't trip, I thought. And you did not. And when your grandfather brought you back in, shutting the door, I moved at last, crept to the coop, latched it for you.

Usually I was asleep by dark, but that night I lay awake late enough to catch a sliver of light shimmering crack to crack through the barn wall: a lantern coming across the yard, footsteps beneath the horses' shifting. I scrambled back far as I could into the darkness of the loft, and when I stopped, found the footsteps had as well. The light now inside the barn, flickering over the walls, the beams. I barely breathed.

Silas?

Not my father.

Sy?

I had not even known my brother was back. Had not seen him since before Delia.

He said my name again. There was the horses' blowing, their knocking against the boards. Then his footsteps leaving, drawing the lantern light out of the barn behind him. But not his voice. It stayed. My name in the air. Dawn seemed a long time away.

That night, after all the lamps had been blown out inside the house, I left the barn, took what things I'd gathered over the weeks, slept again back in the forest. And in the morning, when I returned to leave my emptied plate on the back step, it was not my mother who came to the door, but a woman I had never seen. That evening I did not check the coop for eggs, knew there'd be no plate of food, knew I'd been fooling myself to think it could go on week after week, that I could simply exist, alongside but separate. It hit me then how nearly happy I had been. Almost at peace. A thing I would have mourned if its end had not brought you. And you had been the nearly, you were the almost, the reason I was still there in the woods watching the house so full of others. My brother and his wife, my sister and her husband, their children, my parents, you. All but your mother. I don't know why, nor ever will. Maybe you do. Maybe you knew more than I believed. Maybe I was wrong about the last time you saw me. Maybe you glimpsed your father watching from behind thickets, between boards. I hate to think it. But I do not believe you saw me all that day and all the next. And I was watching closely enough whenever you came out of the house I would have known.

You seemed different. In just a few weeks. I think that was the hardest thing: to hear you speak a word I had not heard you speak before, to realize you'd learned to say *s* and *t* together—*stone* instead of *tone*, *star* instead of *tar*—to see you meticulously make each letter with a stick in mud, your grandmother at your side sounding out words. That night I read them in the moonlight. *Grandma. Grandpa. Mama.* Your footprints. A place you'd pressed your hands. I tried to trace the shape with my own fingers, stopped before I ruined it. Stop. Stay. In the coop I searched for eggs you might have missed. Found three. And a kerchief that must have fallen from your pocket. Tied the eggs in it for you to find. Did you? Did you wonder who left them? Did they seem a gift? Or just confusing? Once, I saw you sitting with the dog. Just sitting patting him. The way last time we'd visited my parents you'd been afraid to. And when you went off again, I whistled. Drew him close. And, burying my fingers in the fur where yours had been, held him to me.

Still, I should have known. The sending you to the coop. The way when my father played ball with you, he threw it always toward the woods. The strangeness of you wandering around the barn alone.

It was near noon. Earlier that morning I'd watched the carriage leave. Carrying my mother and the two younger women and, I'd assumed, you. Which was why I was so surprised to see you through the open barn door. No sign of anybody else. Silence from the house, the yard. All but you talking to yourself. About finding something, bringing it back. A muttering I knew you'd learned from me. Because you'd asked me not to. I think it scared you. And there you were doing it yourself. A thing I hadn't even known I had passed on. Wished suddenly that I had not. Because, watching you do it, it scared me too. Which is why I went in after you.

The second I was through the door, they moved: three men burst from a stall, one smothering you, covering your eyes, the other two on me, an arm around my neck wrenching me back, a hand grabbing my wrist, my father struggling to snag my other arm and, in his other hand, a musket—not pointed at me, but held away as if to keep me from reaching it—and then I realized he was lifting the butt above my head, and there is not much after that I remember.

He must have missed, or never brought it down, or let me get close enough to hit him with my free fist. Because he was suddenly gone, simply not there. I remember that. And the pressure on my neck, my brother's arm squeezing, squeezing, his chest against my back, and I have been in such a place enough times since to know what that would loose in me—that small boy's snapping head, those blood-smeared teeth, my spit-flecked face blurred in that mirror—a me I hope you did not see. And so will not show you now. You only need to know I managed to get loose, wrench free my hatchet, swing it.

I hit my brother. You will know where. How deep, how bad. I know only that he was bellowing, stumbling away, blood flooding the side that he was holding with the arm that had held me. My father's face was bleeding too. He shouted something, the gun now aimed. *Help* and *trying*. Words I heard through my own crying, breathing, gasping. Though none of it boomed like my heart. When it gets like that I can barely hear between its beats, but I heard enough of what my father said to know where they would take me, commit me. Then I was running—out of the barn, toward the woods—heard, beneath my thudding heart, my father shout for me to stop. Silas! he shouted. Son! Said he would shoot, shoot out my legs, would do it, do it for me.

Through my crashing into the trees I waited to hear the boom. Snapping branches and thrashing leaves and nothing. But your wailing. Which is the thing I'm most ashamed to tell you. That till I heard it, I had forgotten you were there. That when I did, I still kept running.

Though it would never take me far enough to stop hearing you.

Did you hear me? Your father screaming, bellowing, crashing away? Do you still? All these years later? Even these words heard in a voice exhumed from your memory. A snippet of sound. Even a song.

Early one morning, just as the sun was rising . . .

Wrong in your mind as your three-year-old's *why* is in mine. The voice of the father who sang those words to you no longer mine. Strange even in my own ears.

As it must be to the ringtail there in the corner clinging to logs, her eyes aglint with slush-lamp light, her stare on me as if she thinks another man might have taken my place. One that the mice she hunts would recognize no more than would the weasel at the creek, or the creek itself, or the boulders by the river, or the river. Which even now, through the drumming rain, calls back in its unceasing roar. Asking for me.

No, whatever voice you might remember is that of a man your father has not been for years, as much belonging to the past as that small boy's frenzied reflection in a mirror four decades old, a Silas so dead and gone I might have long ago blackened my face, pitched my hair, shorn my beard to mourn him. If all my life I had not been trying to kill him.

And there hangs the ringtail staring at me as if I'd said all that aloud, as if trying to decide if I've gone mad. Though just now when I assured her I have not, she did not even blink. As if my voice carried no sound at all. Nor my fingers when I snap them at her. Her wide curved ears not twitching, her long striped tail still dangling, her huge eyes motionless as if she had not even seen the movement of my hand, my head.

Maybe this is what it is to be a ghost. Maybe the Silas I became here is already as dead as the one I left. Maybe the dogs have already found me, the traps already cracked the horses' legs, the men blasted into my home, their bullets in my body. Maybe this is what it is to be a heart remaining, to linger in the days of memory after the ones of life are done. Maybe each heart revisits the living in its own way, mine returning here, to this table of stretched skin, this stump to sit on, this ink and pen and pile of papers, each sheet filled on one side with a piece of your father's world, blank on the other, waiting for another word, a word, a word.

Watch out, ringtail. Or I might return your gaze and take you with me.

But you, son, stay. For even if my sound is wrong inside your head, my thoughts are here. And so my voice. In the only way that truly matters. With you. Where I will remain. Through this night and the next day and however many more it takes to set myself down on the page, safe from whatever will become of the man still in this hut, beside this river, in this place that once was safe enough, this corner of the world that long ago, when it first took me in, saw me as I should have been. And so redrew me.

AUTUMN, 1849

Back on the ridgetop path, he haws the mules again into a run, sends them clattering down the canyon rim, the land around opening into an ever-wider expanse of rolling hills, long shadows, low slashes of sun, Silas—gun barrel glinting, beard a blast of gold—at last entering the high meadow where Kushna lies. Some fifty round-topped earth-mounded homes rising out of the foot-packed dirt less like built structures than features of the land.

Through the trees he can see the wisps of smoke, the dogs staked at each hu's east-facing entrance, the village farther than he'd remembered, the oak grove cleared larger in the three years since he was here last. Beneath the molly's hooves, the path is so packed with people's footprints he has to whoa her still, sit astride her heaving breathing trying to slow his own. His gaze searches between the trees. A gleam: the pond, where it should be. He clicks her forward.

Rising from drinking, face dripping, he stands in the mules' splashing and blowing, wondering why no women have called out to alert the village, no children seen him and fled. Hears, as if in answer, the drums. They thud against his chest like all the path's footsteps and, walking up the pond shore toward the pounding, forcing himself nearer, he sees the villagers at last: not standing on the ground, but on the roofs. Each hu holding a family gathered on its rounded peak, beside the house's marker pole bearing its pattern of hides and feathers: the women's hats like baskets overturned, long hair draping bare backs, bark tassels over their haunches, the naked children all turned away from him. All trying to glimpse the gathered men: the ma'ki, covered in his black feather cloak; the yo'hyoh with his black-painted skin, feathered horns and collar; the group of si'ling kukini painted black too, dancing with loaded bows, plumes shaking in their hair, faces hidden behind long veils of locks cut from their sisters, wives, mothers. The he'si. First dance of the season. He knows the men of the entire village will be packed in a new k'um built big enough to hold them all. Knows Pumk'uk'mi will be among them, won't come to see him till they are done.

So, wading back into the pond, he tugs the mules out, leads them to the trees to wait. At first he cannot find the place. The ancient canyon oak should be easy to see—stub-trunked and spread-crowned, its canopy thick green amid the sparser yellow of all the black oaks, tall and straight—but it is gone. No, he sees it: dead. The great splayed arms and huge humped roots still there, but the branches bare, brittle, gray. All but a halation of green moss clinging like memory.

The old stone circle is overgrown, but tethering the mules, he clears space for a fire—a twist of tinder, a flint-struck spark—crouches by the flickering flame, neck craned beneath the bare canopy, watching the last sunlight set all the surrounding trees' yellow leaves aglow.

By the time the distant drumming stops, the sun is down, the pond becomes a last bit of brightness reflecting the nearly cleared sky, the women and children silhouettes from which there rises a sudden whooping as the men come streaming between the hus—hundreds, nude and glistening—rushing the water, their splashing splintering the surface, skin-heat steaming in the dusk.

At the edge of his sight, another movement: two figures slipping away from the rest. The yo'hyoh, his black body paint half washed away by sweat, his running shaking his feathered horns like the entire black-feathered body of the ma'ki coming behind, the two breaking free of the village, disappearing into the woods.

When Silas turns back, No Rope is coming, his cougar-skin wrap pale as a piece of pond-sheen moving through the reeds. Around him, a few men that he sends back, then only children—he stops them too—then just the chief's lone shape, dimming as he enters the grove, all but disappearing in the canopy's shadow, before coming clear again, nearing the fire, there.

A man almost as tall as the one who stands to greet him, wet unnetted hair hanging over his shoulders, the skin around his eyes and in three lines over his chin pale as if it has been painted white, all but its ghost washed off, the rest of his face stained faintly red. A face built outward around its gaze the way wood grows in whirls around a burl. A long face a little bent—nose one way, chin the other—curving as if to cup the side of his mouth that is slightly caved in. Missing teeth when he speaks, smiles. Though the hu'k, stare taking in the mules, returning to the man, is not smiling now. He sighs—a breath through his nose: two tiny feathers piercing his septum shake—then reaches across the fire and, with two fingers, touches the other's shoulder.

"Silas," No Rope says.

And Silas, reaching to do the same, says, "Pumk'uk'mi."

Sitting then, they speak in Nisenan, Silas telling Pumk'uk'mi of the camp he'd seen, how many whites, how bad the wreckage, the hu'k just saying yes over and over—"haan, haan"—till Silas asks, "What are we going to do?" There is the fire's crackling. "No Rope," he says, "you have three times as many men. With Wokodot and 'Ustoma we would have ten times their number. With Tsekankan, Yamako—"

"Honpetayim Woole," No Rope says, and the words stop Silas's speaking. "I have seen what a woole with a *gun* . . ." The English word sounds stranger still and, in its lingering, the hu'k reaches across his body to touch his own shoulder where Silas touched it. "And"—his smile straightens his face—"I doubt they'll be as bad shots as you."

But Silas cannot smile back. Says instead, "We have guns also."

"*You* have—"

"You do too. How many were there? At least three muskets. With handguns—"

"Six," No Rope says. "And none that work."

"They work. You just . . ." In the hu'k's face: a hardening, as if something from the past is packing in behind his eyes. Silas shifts his glance to the mules instead. "On that dark one there are two more. And this"—the musket slung across his back—"this"—the revolver in his belt. "And all the powder and stones you need."

"Haan. And with Tsekankan and Yamako and Pan'pakan we would have a thousand men. And lose half of them."

"Not if we—"

"Where have you been?" There is the hardening, done, come out from behind the hu'k's eyes onto his face. "Where have you been?" he says again.

"Here."

"No," the hu'k says. And, pointing behind him: "There. And there." His finger jutting higher, as if touching a place farther upriver. "Among others. Even the Monaa."

"You know I do not see them," Silas says. "Nor them me. You know I have been on my own."

"Haan. And now you come here. After three years. And tell me *we*."

Behind him the mules shift, snort, and he can feel it too: someone else there in the grove. A sense so strong he nearly looks away from No Rope but will not. Holds the man's gaze. Searches for the word he wants. Finally says, "Friend." And strange as the word feels in his mouth, he knows it is as near to right as it will ever be for him. "Niki'upa," he says again, "I've been here almost ten years."

"I know," No Rope tells him. "I was here when you came. As suddenly upon us as they've come now."

From down by the pond: distant chatter drifting over, the women having joined with the men, all of them wandering back toward the village in the near dark.

When Silas speaks again, he calls No Rope *chief* instead, says, "If you do nothing, they'll stay longer than me. And bring more. And those will stay longer than you." He tells him then about the half-built cabin, the trees they'd felled as if to build another.

And the hu'k shakes his head, tells Silas no: "Wi," he says, "those trees are too large." The man's face is lit against the dark, and Silas knows beyond the fire it is still dusk, but to his eyes it seems like night. "They're for a new river," No Rope goes on. "A tunnel that will run through the air. This my men tell me. My men who work there."

Again a mule snorts, again Silas feels it: something out in the dark he cannot see.

And when No Rope goes on, his voice is softer. "Friend," he says, "you have been gone a long time."

"When did they come?"

"Spring. Surely not much after you went upriver."

"Your men are working for them?"

"Some. Some for the ones camped nearer to here."

"Where?"

"Down on the same spot where you first went. A bigger camp than the one upriver. One that already has many buildings made of wood."

The mule's footstep again. Then, no: a person's, coming toward them. Silas is already standing, reaching for the revolver, when he sees the faint sway of breasts, glint of earrings, and one of No Rope's wives steps into the firelight, a basket on her head. In one hand, she holds two smaller, stacked. In the other, a hunk of dark-charred meat. When she sets it all before them, both men thank her at the same time, Silas's and No Rope's *hestom ni min* coming as if part of a chant they have practiced together, and either that or the skewed way Silas speaks makes her break into a grin, a flash of teeth she must sense sits wrong because, smothering it, she turns to say something to the girl behind her. A daughter carrying a water basket, two tightly woven cups. Then they are gone, footsteps receding, the men alone again.

The smell of acorn mush and venison. The hollowness inside him: he cannot tell if it's hunger or sickness, brought by the food or what he's heard, as if whatever scoops his body out reaches into his mind as well. Then No Rope, pouring from the big basket into their bowls, says, "Eat," and Silas is thinking of nothing else, his fingers spooning the acorn meal into his mouth, tearing the meat, barely nodding when No Rope says, "You're hungry." Too hungry even to respond when No Rope says, through his own chewing, that he is sorry. "You bring me two guns and I bring you news of a hundred more wooles." Silas grunts. But he can feel it enter him—*a hundred more*—souring inside his body, so that, when No Rope speaks again, he stops.

"Where did you get them?" the hu'k asks.

Silas's fingers are sticky with gruel, the two he's used to scoop it glued together.

"The guns," the hu'k says.

He can feel it in his stomach too—too much, too fast, the grease—reaches for water. "Where I got the mules." In No Rope's silence, he hears them shift again, tells himself it is the woman or girl come back to clear the baskets or see if they need more. "Same," he says, "as everything else that I have brought you."

There is the fire's crackling, the splashing of No Rope washing his fingers in the water basket. "You know," the h'uk says, "we cannot take them."

From the dark there comes a grunt that both men know is not a mule and Silas is up, the pistol drawn, but not before No Rope has grabbed a branch out of the fire, whipped the torch toward the sound. Just a second of light spiking the dark, but enough for Silas to see the figure floating backward—the strange sight of a man who seems to have no arms below his elbows, no legs below his knees, no head—before the flame sputters and night sucks the image back into the blackness between the oaks.

No Rope is shouting too fast for Silas to understand, and from the dark, a shout comes back, a word too garbled or distant or simply one Silas doesn't know, though he can tell it's said in anger, meant to insult. A sound that makes the image he'd seen less eerie—clearly a man—and seeing it again, he sees the black paint on the limbs and face, says to No Rope, "The ma'ki. I saw him and the yo'hyoh go out into the woods."

"Haan," No Rope agrees, and between them there is the good feeling of having together come to an understanding. Then No Rope turns back to the fire and drops the stick back on it and the embers flare up enough for Silas to see his face better. For a second. Long enough to see there is no pleasure in it at all.

"Silas," No Rope says, "I heard about the man you shot."

How? Silas thinks.

"I heard there were more."

From the border guards up by Yamako?

"These are their animals, aren't they?"

From one of the Kushna men working on the bar?

"These are their guns?"

And he knows suddenly it does not matter, knows that before now No Rope should have heard it from him. "Haan," he says, the word little more than a whisper.

They are still standing, the firelight bright on No Rope's legs, dimmer on his body, his face lit from below, all flickering and shadow. "Last spring," the hu'k says, "in the season of black oak tassels, not long after the wooles came and made their camp, we heard from the people of Wokodot about a thing that happened farther south. Near Molma. On Yodokum Sew. A thing that happened to a village where I have never been. But where the wooles had been already. Wooles who took their women. Used them for wives. So their true husbands, brothers, did to the wooles what they would have done to any one of us. That day five wooles died. And the next day? The wooles returned. To kill twenty of them. Then rode to another village and killed more. And in between they used the women of those villages too. The girls. Since then, in that part of the world, that is the way that it has been. Do you understand what I am saying?"

While he had talked, the fire had begun to fade and, above it, the hu'k's face is now nearly all shadow, his features just flickered hints, and Silas knows his own face must be the same. "You are saying," he answers, "I should not have come."

"Wi." No Rope shakes his head. "I am saying you should not have shot those men."

He had forgotten the revolver was still in his hand; it feels stuck to his fingers, the acorn grit gluing them to its grip.

"I am saying," No Rope goes on, "you should not have brought their guns here. Or their animals. Or anything of theirs."

The hu'k's face is all but lost to darkness now, and on his own, Silas can feel the fire's warmth slipping away, a chill replacing it.

"Please," No Rope says, and something about the word said by the chief makes Silas glad he cannot see the man's features, "take them away."

His eyes are shut, head tilted back, beard lit by the last firelight, his face above it dark as the Nisenan's, but when he opens his eyes, he can see the tree. The whole underside of the old oak, flickering. Faint branches barely separated from the black, but there. The huge arms spreading above him, extending outward till they disappear.

"No Rope," Silas says, speaking up at the tree, "do you remember the floods last year? The end of autumn. Not much later than now. Do you remember how early they came, how fast? From nothing. Did you know that fall, when I came back from the high country, I found a log house just like the one they're building now. Built by wooles just like them too. But on the bank directly across from my own home. Did you see any of their logs come down past here? Carried on the floodwaters? Any of their bodies?" When he looks down again, the fire is no more than coals, No Rope a shape faint as the branches of the tree. But he can tell the hu'k is watching, listening. "Do you remember," he says, speaking across the redness, the hints of baskets, the food they'd shared, "how that first year, when I camped on the bar where you say the big village of whites is now, do you remember you warned me then? Warned me I would have to move?"

There is the flap of No Rope's cougar skin as he wraps it back around him, its breeze briefly brightening the coals. "It was not from nothing," he says. "The flooding last year. It was from the rain, the cold, the snow high up. The earth that it shook loose. Men said they saw a whole part of the bank fall into the water. It was the wall it made, blocking the river, filling the canyon like a lake. Until it broke." Crouching beside the fire's remains, the hu'k holds out his hands, dark fingers spread over red coals. "And you say this is from nothing."

Then Silas is crouching across from him. "No," he says. "What you say is what I'm trying to. All that, all that the kukinis of the snows, the mud, the rains, the cold, the high country, the lower bank, all that they did, the river did, to watch over us."

"Maybe," No Rope says, "but I do not think it will do it again."

"No. No, I don't either. But"—Silas reaches over the red glow too—"we can watch out for *it*. The river. If it needs a dam, we can give it one. Your men have axes now? Or can get them? Know how to use them?"

Across the coals, No Rope shakes his head. "Now," he says, "you sound like a woole." With one hand, he touches Silas's hand holding the gun. Gently, firmly, pushes it back out of the light. "Silas, the river is strong. Stronger than men. It's not the river that needs watching over." Reaching to his neck, he lifts a strip of leather over his head, the pendant—a small sphere wrapped in a knot of dry sinew—dangling against his chest, over his face, in his hand held out across the coals, hanging heavily, the glow drawing a glint from within the wrapping. "Take it," he says. And as Silas does: "Take it, and take the rest, and go." His emptied hand reaches a little farther then—two fingers touching Silas's shoulder, same as earlier—but, before Silas can return the touch, the hu'k has risen, turned, is gone from the glow, become just a movement in the dark grove, then just the sound of footsteps in fallen leaves, a quiet shrushing becoming nothing. Listening, Silas hears only the leaves around him, a light breeze blowing through the tall black oaks, their rustling like a living thing passing all through the canopy. Except for above him. The dead oak's branches leafless, its crown spreading a circle of silence around the man still crouched alone beside the last glow of coals.

The moon has been up for hours by the time he makes it home. The whole way back he'd walked beside the molly, the mules too spent to even match his pace, leading them along the ridge trail, cutting around the path down to the miners' camp, until they'd hit the turnoff to his own. Less path than just a place he knows, a patch of matted kitkitdizze that, as he leads the mules through, looses its heady pungency: a lemony resinous tang much like the smell of scraped green walnut shells that, for a decade now, has been for him the scent of home. And starting down the canyonside he knows he should go even slower, keep the mules from falling into a stumble-rush descent, but the kitkitdizze is in his head and his feet are following a pitch they recognize and, from below, the river's roar is growing louder, and despite the dark, he cannot keep from dropping faster, falling into a stumble-rush himself, his body knowing this terrain better than its own, till he is there, clattering onto the gravel bar, the mules crashing out of the brush behind.

Only then, standing again in the all-encompassing roar of his river, does he think to scan the bank for men. No fire-flicker, no shape he does not recognize. Across the water's glitter the boulders are huge in the half-moon's light, smooth and blank as ever, the far side's creek shimmering along its same steep slant, the tree-lined ledge that's held his hut these many months he's been away all dark and still.

Normally he'd cross a little lower, where the rocks are close enough together that, at least for another week or two, he could leap boulder to boulder, reach the other bank. But with the mules he goes upriver to where the cascades calm into a pool, a sweeping bend just wide and slow enough to let them swim.

He rides the molly in, urging her with whispers and nudges, his feet, knees, thighs stinging from cold, and she is kicking, splashing, the john crashing behind. Around their moonlit shapes, the air is so filled with river-sound they seem to swim in silence. Until they reach the other side, rise stumbling and slipping out, their clattering breaking through the roar, their shivering carrying the current onto the bank.

Up at his homeplace, he leads them across the creek onto the ledge of near-flat land where the steep slope levels out in a wide pad just high enough to be safe from floods, catch a bit more sun each day, the trees giving way to a small clearing, a scattering of stars: his cabin. The same, as far as he can see, as when he'd left it. He tugs the mules through the grass grown up and seeded and died since then, undoes their rigging, lifts off the sawbucks, uses the blankets to rub them down, working so hard to rid them of the river's chill that by the time he's done he's warm as well, and even more tired, and hobbling them beside the cabin, leaves them to graze or sleep as they might wish.

Around the walls he'd long ago packed soil so that the logs appear half-buried, as if he'd built the hut on a small hill and it had sunk. But the entrance is clear, just high enough he does not have to stoop as, pushing aside the door-skin, he steps in. Inside: a cave-like darkness that he moves through as if it's day, makes his way straight to the hearth and, feeling in his possibles for flint and steel, strikes a spark—his bearded face flashing for a split second into sight—then places the embered char onto a nest of grass he'd left for this, and picking the whole thing up, gently puffs a flame to life. In the hearth: a careful construction of kindling waiting since spring for him to ease the burning nest into its opening, blow it alight. When it is roaring, he sits back, takes in the room. Some small creature—pinyon mouse perhaps, perhaps a wood rat—scampers across the woven mats. At the sight, his beard seems to grow lighter. A smile. He looks around. The elk-skin door, its bottom eaten ragged. The window hole covered by a hide. Between the two, the wall is studded with some dozen antlers waiting like hooks. Above, brittled bouquets hang from the ceiling—wormwood, yarrow, mint—between strung lines of milkweed rope. The hearth is built from three big stones, the mantel a longer, thinner fourth, the chimney logs chinked tight with mud. To its right: a pallet of willow branches crushed nearly flat, topped by a mat of grass. Beside it: a mound hidden beneath a draped buckskin. More of the same amassed all down the wall. Along another, below the window: a collection of peltries so chewed they seem as much food as cover. Or nests. Behind them, and in the corners, and everywhere: the glints of eyes.

"Hello, the camp!" he says to them, the smile under his beard become a grin.

From the pile outside, he retrieves his rucksack, the rifle and musket and ammunition. Hauls in the blankets and hangs them from the milkweed lines to dry. Then steps out once more to take a piss. Walks a few feet away and lets it arc. His head craned back, face to the stars. Blurring and clearing in his breath. He feels the mules watching, hears them go back to eating. Beyond them, the screech of a fox. Rattle of something high in the oak. A great horned owl's *hoo hoo-hoo hoo hoo.* So far away it's nearly smothered by the river's roar. Still, he hoots back: *hoo hoo-hoo hoo hoo.* Waits for an answer.

And when none comes, he turns—the elk-skin door glows faintly from the firelight, as if it might already be warm to the touch; it isn't—and goes in. Inside, he adds a couple logs to the bright fire. Lies on the bed. Draws his otter-skin slicker over him. And listening to the river—there's the owl's hooting, closer now—at last sleeps.

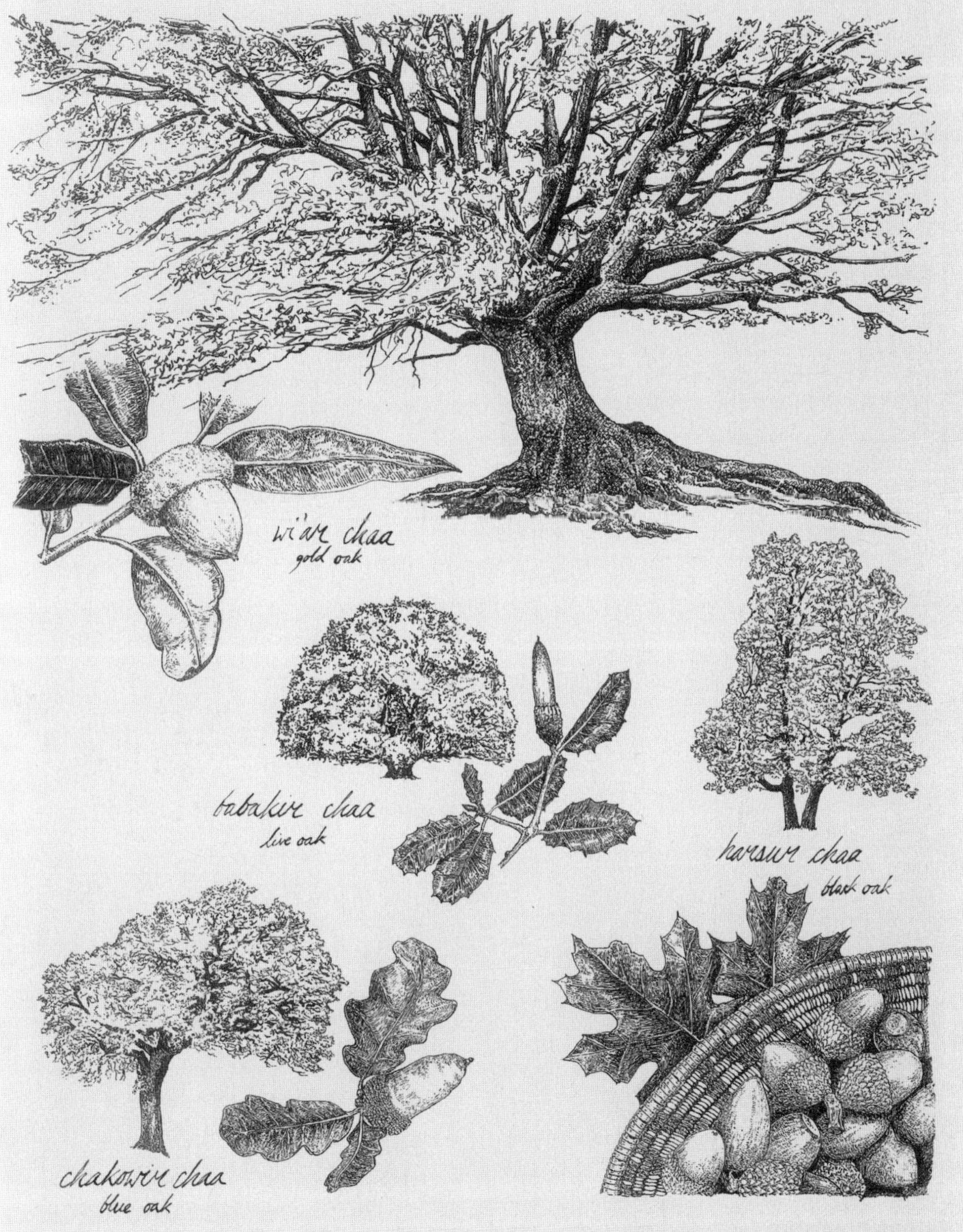
wi'ar chaa
gold oak
babakir chaa
live oak
harsur chaa
black oak
chakowir chaa
blue oak

More & more you visit me. Here in my hut. I hear the doorflap open & there is the darkness & patter of rain & maybe it is just the lack of sleep. How little food I eat. The little else that I have done but fill pg aftr pg writing to you all through the night now into my 2nd day. My only breaks my work upriver felling trees. Building the dam. Each time that I return the doorflap letting in a little daylight. The rm darkening again as I pass through. And yet though I have sat here all night & into dawn I swear just now there was a brightening bhind me. A louder patter. The flap hushing it again & the light redimmed & the hut back to my home of the past decade. But changed. The emptiness round me bcome somehow a little thicker. With the presence of anothr. Again. Each time it happens I cannot shake the certainty that it is you. I hold the spoon bfore my mouth or set down the pen or watch the inkspot spread. Feeling a shifting in the air. As if stirred by your coming in. Brushed off you. Agnst me. The closest we will ever be to touching.

You smell of soap. Or wheat bread. Or the waft of kerosene & axle oil & horse droppings that was the city. Or me. Sometimes you smell like me & then I know it is just in my mind. Which may seem troubling to you but soothes me. To know you are still in my head. Instead of here. Your soul not here. Your heart not here. Whatever part your ghost might choose.

Though there are times I cannot place the scent at all. A scent not of my world nor from my memory. And then I have to shut my eyes. Squeeze them hard. To keep from looking. At you. Squatted there across the hearth. Crouched close. Watching me shake. If you are dead how wld I know? How else? So I sit with my eyes squashed shut telling myself it is not your heart on its last journey. For what steps cld it retrace to bring you here? What history? How wld it find me?

And did I ever smell like my father? My mother? I cannot recall. Hard as I try. Cannot remember the scent of them at all. My parents whose hearts wld not be able to find me either. But that if they have passed away have surely tried. A thing I know cause I feel it in mine. The certainty that you are watching from across the fire matched only by the sureness you cannot be. An impossibility I know they must have felt as well. In the years aftr I left them forever.

No matter that they must have known that it was better. Why my father failed to pull the trigger. Holding the musket while my figure disappeared into the trees. His son become just stirring leaves. And you must wonder what would have been if instead of lowering the gun he had blown the running from my legs. Stopped me with a blast of buckshot. If my brother had limped into the woods and dragged me thrashing out.

Elisha I had seen the letters. Read them at near the age you must be reading this. The physicians responding to my father's pleas. Writing of madmen they had seen reduced to the state of the creatures my father treated. Contraptions built to correct corrupted blood too near the brain or cool a body till resistance drained away. One who recommended my father bleed me would routinely empty gallons from his patients' veins. Had once drained half a lunatic's blood in a few days. Reported profound docility. A state achieved by a different doctor through elongation of the body. A rack on which to stretch the spine. Separate the vertebrae. Free the skull of blockages pressing the brain. Some swore by vomiting. Some by blistering. One instructing my father to roughly shave my scalp, rub it with mustard powder till the nicked skin bubbled. Promised the infected pustules would bring pain great enough to drive the sickness out.

The machines I learned about because another doctor drew them. Sketches scratched across his letter. A cage for lowering patients into water. Instructions scrawled beside the drawing. Leave submerged till thrashing has subsided and bubbles ceased. Then raise with haste. Revive by slapping. Another page depicted a man strapped to a board spun rapidly around a pole. Feet out for maladies caused by too much blood on the brain. Head out for those caused by too little. Such bodily stress induced that thoughts could be clung to no more than bowels. And if such motion-treatment failed, there was its opposite: a chair in which the afflicted could be clamped still, ankles to skull, a bucket set beneath the seat for waste, the body forced into tranquility. For an hour, a day. However long till the mind followed. A result that, according to the doctor, such treatment rarely failed to reach. Though he allowed he had seen cases last for weeks before the patient could be released. Which, he warned, left lasting damage to a body. By which he meant me.

Before I was even as old as you.

And maybe he was right. Maybe it would have cured me. I do not know much in the way of science, have not studied the mind. But I have spent the last ten years in my own company and seen what a cure looks like and cannot believe it could be reached that way. Though it surely would have kept me. There in your life. Or close enough that you could visit—accompanied by my father, your grandmother, maybe your mother—once in a while. To sit and stare at me through bars. And wonder was that better.

And yet. And yet. Was there not something between the asylum and my absence? Between being locked away and fleeing forever?

That day, I ran till I could no longer hear your screaming, would slow just long enough to let the branches cease their thrashing, then, through my breathing, still hear your distant crying and begin again. Till at last your wailing failed to find me. And there I stopped. Just far enough to be out of your reach, but near enough I could one day return. A kind of border between there and gone. Where all that end-of-summer into fall, then winter, I would try to remain.

From New Cumberland to Colliers, between Wellsburg and Bethany, all down the wide Ohio's eastern bank. Not settlement to settlement so much as through spaces between. Fields such as I'd never seen, acres sewn wholly in barley, hillsides combed into rows of only maize, the beans and squash that, in my childhood, had always been mixed in now left to backyard plots, tallgrass replaced by timothy and clover, the land occupied by new iron implements—moldboards, grain cradle blades—forged in the same foundries I had fled. And I would flee again toward what woods remained between all that burned down for potash, vast tracts of stump-pulled earth pockmarked as if afflicted with the pox. Sometimes I'd come across an empty longhouse, its poles collapsed, bark walls caved in. Often in sight of a new cabin. As if one home had grown out of the other's ghost. Sometimes the bulges of burial mounds. A newer cemetery. Increasingly crossing the paths of those still living. So many people it seemed sometimes they'd done same as the homes, grown from the ghosts of deer, lynx, bear. For I saw little more than hogs let loose to forage, cattle snorting as I passed. Their owners rarely sensing me there. Even when I'd leave the woods, creep to an orchard, a garden gate, a cellar.

In exchange for what I stole I would pull weeds, leave wild grapes on porch steps, scoop caterpillar nests out of the crooks of apple trees. So, in the morning, a man bringing a burning branch to torch the silks might stiffen with surprise. A woman, scattering the past night's ashes, might stoop to retrieve my offering, peer searching into the swirl of breeze-blown gray.

And did I miss your fingers in my beard? Delia's stirring the surface of a bath? My parents' embrace? Sometimes I'd lie on my belly along the riverbank, hidden by reeds, dangling my fingers in, waiting for the minnows to investigate. Their nibbling so faint it was like touch itself detached from touching. Yes, yes, and yes. And yet I knew what I missed was them, her, you, as you could only be without me. Me without you.

Still I could not bring myself to cross. Would stand beside the towpath watching the Ohio's incessant flow, or climb a limb over the water and sit staring west at the distant bank, toward a place I knew only through someone else's memories written in a book whose illustrations I'd abandoned, a world where I imagined trees broader than any elm, forests wilder than any I'd known, filled with all the creatures who'd fled my kind. And in my chest a tightness would squeeze my breath till I'd have to retreat, retrace my steps back east. Not quite as far as where I'd last heard you, but close enough to feel the possibility—a few days' walk, maybe a week—close enough to stop me. The river and the idea I might one day return to you become, for those few months, the boundaries of my life.

For I had never meant to leave forever. Had hoped eventually to find a way to bring you with me, somewhere we might yet live together, the three of us alone. A place that would allow for such a shape. That, with enough time, I might manage to shape myself to fit it. Though as the weeks stretched to a month, another, and I began to know a life removed from others, I grew afraid. That, growing into my isolation day after day, I'd grow used to a life without you.

And so, with autumn's cold, I began what I would come to think of as my treatment. Would force myself each evening to knock on a new door, ask permission to bed in the barn. I chose homesteads so hidden—armed scofflaws, scorned Mormons, a Shawnee family—that some who answered lifted lanterns at me in disbelief, behind them their children staring in fear. Each time I'd stand well back, arms crossed over my punching heart, my body clenched against its rocking, waiting for the door answerer to speak. Though when they did, I couldn't, afraid the hum I'd been restraining might break into a moan, a shout, bark of anxiety—could manage only to raise a hand. A sign somewhere between hello and stop. My open palm pausing their talk, slowing the moment. From your mother, I'd learned to communicate without sound. Now I found myself feigning an inability to speak. Would cross my fingers over my lips, point to myself. Then, clasping a hand around my arm, would mime my shoveling or splitting wood. Answer their question by feeding my mouth with empty fingers, tilting my head onto the pillow of my hands.

We'd come to some agreement then that would leave them to go about their lives, me to work quietly, each existing in a strangely separate peace. As if the others, thinking I couldn't speak, made me blind and deaf too. Let me go about my washing or fixing or clearing or building as if encased in my own world. Sealed off from theirs. A feeling I found myself seeking with such an increasing need that, by the time winter was nearing, I knew it could only make me worse, take me farther from you, misshape me into a man who would never return.

Instead, as the breeze bore milkweed seeds and birdcalls sharpened, I began to refuse the refuge of feigned muteness, forced myself to call out the first hello, raise my eyes to meet another's gaze, break the quiet with my name. Silas, I'd say, extending a hand. Fighting to hold it steady long enough that we might shake.

Each time I made it through a new encounter, I grew determined to take my treatment further. One morning, waking in the early dark beneath a sawmill's roof, I rose, reached for the beams, leaped. Hung swaying till my shoulders began to shake, my elbows to pull apart, my vertebrae to separate, my mind stripped clear of all but pain. A thing I'd try again and again—from bridges, barn lofts—sometimes inverted, knees hooked over a branch, feet tingling, blood swamping my brain. Though in the end it worked no better than the bleeding. I began in the small places that, from my father's writings, I knew drew just enough—earlobe, nostril, back of my knee—and progressed to ever larger cuts till I spilled so much I'd be nearly too light-headed to tie the bandage, so much it could not fail to clear me out. Except what could replace it but what my own aberrant body made? Before long, the cuts became the first thing people saw. Scabs, scars, blood-crusted rags. A strange relief: to watch their worry, feel their doubt, know it came from something so easy to understand. Requiring from them only that they conjure a reason. Dogs? Thugs? They seldom asked. And, if they did, it was just a request that I supply the lie instead.

Though it was harder to explain away the burns. What could I say? That the night before, I'd sat by my fire lost in the flicker on my father's knife, thinking of a letter he'd received. A doctor who'd so believed in bleeding he'd cut his patients' jugulars. Just a small slice. Through which would gush such a blood geyser they were all but certain to be cured. Those were his words. I remembered them exactly. But could not recall how one might mend a cut like that. Could only see the letter crumpled in the kindling box, as my father left it. Where I'd found it, read it. Before he'd caught me and, ripping it from my hand, hurled it into the fire. An act that, only years later, holding his knife in the light of my own fire, did I realize was meant to show me what he thought of the letter's writer. A gift that let me fold the blade away. Though it was in my loss of hope for bleeding that I remembered the mustard powder, the patient's blistered head. I sat a long while, watching the fire dwindle to coals. Then knelt beside it, the burning growing on my knees till it seemed their skin would blister and, leaning over, shut my eyes against the glow, lowered my head, smelled singed hair and felt the flare of heat and shoved my crown down on the embers.

What was it? That let them see my burned-off hair and blistered scalp and still receive me? That made a camp of escaped slaves risk discovery to treat me? A couple ruffians uncock their guns and give me work they could have done themselves? What was it that had made those Shawnee offer me a berth inside their wickiup, those Mormons insist I sit with them for supper? A widow little more than half my age offer me her body if I would stay? Even as I shook my head or fled before first light or peeled her desperate grip away, I knew it was due less to anything inside of me than something inside them: the sight of me a warning of how it could be if they got worse, if whatever made them live their lonesome lives were to grow stronger. And I—who did not wish to share a meal, who preferred to sleep alone in barns, who could not stay even long enough to say goodbye, but who once had hoped to find in their lives a path for mine—I grew more desperate too.

The dawn that I left the widow-girl, I kept walking west till I came to the river. It was cold as winter. Hoarfrost spiking the bank like a white pelt grown overnight. I watched a barge creep into view, poled by men bundled in coats. A rowboat farther upriver, three fishing figures still but for their drifting. Yet even that enough to break the stillness of the rest.

From the towpath, I listened to them splash closer, the polemen's chanting. Across the river, the sky was already stained with chimney smoke. There came the clangs of bells, rumble of a mill. While on my side the chant grew louder, the fishermen's chatter shattering the peace. And when would it be otherwise? No matter how I removed myself, there seemed no place more than a mile from the next farm, nowhere I wouldn't stumble on a shack before long, another hermit holed up in his pocket pretending the world didn't exist an hour from his door. How I envied him. That he could do it.

When it came, it came like a reprieve: the sun breaking over the trees behind me, striking the westward ridge, releasing a line of mist I watched roll into that distant valley, smothering chimney-stains and hints of cows, returning the far bank's fields to stillness, curling down onto the river, crossing the water, till it was rising off the reeds before me.

What can I say except I wanted to be in it? Knew how soon it would burn off, allow the world back in. What can I tell you but what I told myself as I clambered out into the mist: that I would try just one more treatment—and stepped into the freezing water—would stay down just till I lost my breath—and searched for a heavy stone—no longer than the physicians' patients had remained submerged. Told myself I'd come up then. As, sloshing through the muck up to my chest, I hugged the rock, plunged in.

The cold. The current. I clamped my arms around the weight dragging me down, dropped through the murk till I hit bottom and everything stopped. The current tugged my coat, my hair, tried to roll me off the stone. Above, the sun kept burning off the frost, the mist kept thinning, the day kept coming, but its sounds stayed far away. Oar-splash and chant and chatter all going on as before. Though I was not. Was down where there was only the mud, the rock. My heartbeat. My lungs' release. So simple. I am not saying I did not wish to stay alive. Only that I wanted to stay down. Another minute, a little longer. Feeling my body trying to rise, I forced my lungs empty, with my last strength turned over onto my back, wrestled the rock onto my chest. Above me, the bubbles of my last breath floated toward the surface, broke it, disappeared.

This is what the doctors must have meant—this clearing of the mind, cleaving away of all distraction—the clarifying certainty they sought. It came like ice set on my brain, as if the freezing water had filled my skull, a thought past thinking shot through my body:

unclench your hands, shove free the rock. And when my body refused to listen, the command became even more simple: Move. Move. Which I could not.

And you will think I did this also because of you. Will think it and will be right. A thing I couldn't tell you if I didn't think it might make the rest easier to bear. Because when I was down there, I did not think of your mother or mine or my father or even you. Did not care for anything but living. That was the clarifying thought: My life was worth continuing for itself. Myself. Even without you. As hard a thing as I could say. Can only hope it might free you as it did me, that you too can see how anything else could not have worked, that there was only dying trying to live in the world that held you, or letting go of it, of you, forever. So I might live in a world that could hold me.

AUTUMN, 1849

Someone outside, west wall, the pile by the shack. The revolver is in Silas's hand. Beneath the ragged bottom of the elk-skin door: a slightly brighter strip of dark. Near dawn, then. The mules? Is it the mules? No. And he is up, across the room, slipping out, near silent but not near enough—the man out there swinging a gun—and throwing his motion back through the flapping door, Silas is inside again before he hears the voice.

"Honpetayim Woole." The words are hard low grunts. A voice he knows, though he is thinking of which gun he'd left outside. The ruined musket? Empty, even if it worked. If he is right.

"Honpetayim Woole." It is a call this time, a command. "Usip'putom." Come out. The words spoken with the roughness of an old man's throat. "Tooye'ewis 'ay ni musse."

Or he'll take what? The musket? The mules?

Out in the colder air it is already light enough for Silas to see he's right: the rag-wrapped musket pointed at him, one of the mules—the john—unhobbled, the rope run through its halter instead, caught under the tribesman's foot. Above the moccasin: the blackened shin. On the musket: the black fingers. The black-painted face. And now he knows it. That growled grunt back in the grove, that old man's voice: Too Much Water.

"It will shoot," Momhe'elimda tells him, using the Nisenan for loosing an arrow.

"Haan," Silas says. "You have learned to use it."

"Where is the powder?" the man demands. "The boo'let."

At first he does not understand, then does—and knows the man has learned some English too. “Inside,” Silas says, meaning the gun is loaded. But the man says, “Get it,” and Silas realizes he means the rest—powder and bullets—inside his hut.

“Too Much Water,” he says then, “you know No Rope is right. You cannot take the gun back to Kushna. Or the kawayu’.”

“The powder,” Too Much Water tells him. “The boo’let.”

“Inside the gun . . .” he starts, and the man tries to cut him off—“Wi!”—but he continues: “. . . the powder is wet. It will not shoot.”

The molly is drawing near, as if to join the john, and Too Much Water glances over, sees it’s only her, says, “Then get me the rest. The powder. The boo’let.” But the command has gone out of the words and left them questions.

“I will get it,” Silas tells him then, “if you give back the gun. Leave the kawayu’.”

At his voice the molly turns to Silas, closing the space between them, her big head lowering, her breath on his neck. The light has grown enough he can see Too Much Water looks even older, the shaman’s cheeks gaunter, his meager whiskers grayed, but his eyes—even in the dimness Silas can sense the roiling behind the calm that covers them like a glaze—are the same. Then the molly’s huge eye is there instead, blocking the shaman, and he says, “Hey, hey,” pushing her muzzle away, stepping aside, and when he sees the man again, it is his back, his long gray hair shaking with each step, Too Much Water leading the john away, still holding the gun.

“Hu’uku,” Silas calls, though he does not know if the man has regained the rank. “Hu’uku!” But the shaman does not slow or turn or even glance. “Too Much Water!” he tries once more. Then aims the pistol at the man’s back, says, “Hatip!” Stop. But the shaman cannot see the gun if he will not look. He could shoot into the air, break the quiet of his home, send the molly wheeling, the john lurching away, waste a round.

When the shaman is gone, the hoof steps subsumed by the river again, Silas reaches to the molly’s cheek, feels her lean into his hand, and, scratching, works his fingers across her jaw, her neck stretching to let him scratch a little harder as she blows low through her lips. “Well, caballo,” he says, giving her a pat, “I guess now it’s just us.”

Just him and the mule.

Just him and the mule and the river. And the scent of cedars. And the big madrone with its leathery leaves and rifts of peeling bark and clusters of red berries and the tanager moving through them. Its fluting call.

Just him and the mule and the river and the hammering of a distant woodpecker and the breeze fluttering the leaves of the cottonwood beside the bank and the clearing overgrown with grass and the three woven granaries crouched on their poles like companions around a fire and the bark-slat storage shack and his hut, its roof grown up in ferns and lichen, its hide-shade rolled over the window, its chimney waiting for the morning's first smoke.

Just him and his home. And the sudden croak of the heron. The great slate bird flapping slowly up the river's course, its long curved neck, bright slash of beak, legs swept back, wings rising and falling as it follows the canyon upriver out of sight.

Beside him the mule lets out a sound somewhere between a bray and neighing, so loud it draws his gaze: her huge eye watching him back as if to remind him she is there, or see if he has something to eat, or just to break his stillness, get him to work.

But wait, the colors are coming into the day, the dawn-blue letting through the cottonwood's green-gold, the yellow willows, crimson madrone berries and maroon manzanita and all the greens of moss and lichen, the low scrub's browns, the grass, the ground. He stands a little longer, knowing it might be the last time he sees it, knowing that, before anything else, he should prepare to leave again, repack his rucksack, resaddle the mule, fill his waterskin, wipe down the guns, decide where he'll take cover when they come for him—the miners camped on the nearby bar who by now will have gleaned from the one he'd shot enough to guess, the rest in the even-larger camp by Kushna—knows it and still he thinks, *To hell with them.*

Inside his hut, he ties back the door-flap, rolls up the window shade, moves through the brighter room lifting mouse-chewed skins off cooking baskets big as cauldrons, ewers leakproofed with pitch. One by one, he turns them right side up, flaps their coverings free of dust, drapes the antler hooks with nets, fishtraps, soaproot brushes, snares. Then, retrieving his summer hat, hangs it up too.

Last, he hauls a skin off something by the sole window: a tree stump and small log. The stump is overturned, its roots supporting a wide, flat basket covered in stretched skin shellacked with tallow. A table. Beside it, a log stool.

By the time he's done, sunlight is slipping down the canyonside, not yet in the trees but bright beyond their branches, and in the morning's remaining shadow he unsheathes his knife, crouches before the door, begins cutting the grass. Hands moving fast—fisting, slicing—the rest of him drifts slowly across the clearing, falling into an easy rhythm, the footpath forming in river-smothered silence from hut to storage shack, granaries to creek. Sometimes the mule lifts her head to watch. Sometimes a squirrel, paused in its gathering. Up in a ghost pine two crows pass their commentary back and forth. From there the paths appear clear as line drawings, as if he's adding to all the creations he'd made over the years: the sun-bleached tree propped up by stones, dead branches re-leafed in feathers; a mossy boulder, its green studded with small white bones; a mound of pinecones, startlingly blue, each seedscale covered in a flower petal glued on with sap. By the time the path is done, the sunlight is flashing in the feather-tree, lighting the blue cones bright as the sky. He lifts the cut grass up, carries it armful by armful to the cabin-side shelter, throws the sheaves in. Until, beneath the slanted roof, there is enough to make a bed.

Come look, he calls to the molly, see what he's made for her. Maybe it is the look she gives him back, as if trying to decide if he is crazy, maybe the fact that looking at the overhang he knows it is too low, maybe just that the sunlight has already reached him, but suddenly he knows the mule will not sleep there that night. Through the river's roar, he listens for the clacks of hooves, breaking of branches, but it could be any morning in November. Could even be the one that brought him here so long ago, all the years since still ahead, still waiting for him to live them. Could be, but isn't.

He had been about to go unearth his cache, uncover the cavern he'd camouflaged that spring, take out his cookpots, cups, bone gigs and buffalo robe, all he'd need for winter, but now he knows he will retrieve only his long-stored saddle, old flintlock pistol, re-cache the rest for whenever he might make it back. Though, before he ever reaches the covered cave, he stops, his gaze searching the air farther downcanyon. From where he smells the smoke—a gust swept from his cabin? the hu'uku camped nearby?—then sees it: a thin gray smudge over the western rim, wisps rising as if from the miners' camp caught fire. No. Farther than that, a fire far larger, a smoke cloud hanging over the same spot where each autumn Kushna's great clearing burns send billows up. Except he was just there. Knows the village's groves have already been burned clear.

Back at his hut, the cache untouched, still breathing hard from running, he repacks his rucksack—the last dried fish, pine nuts, belt axe—leaves the rest that he'd brought back all piled on his bed. Frypan and fishing net and spear. Stares for a second at the dented tin and wooden case and Bible-big canvas-wrapped packet, then leaves them too.

The guns he takes. The new rifle and his old flintlock and the boy's pistol. Rolling his slicker, he secures it under the rucksack's flap, ties a waterskin to its side, checks his possibles—pocketknives, bullet molds, needles, awl, firesteel and flint and tinder—slings the bag across his chest. Stops then, looking around the cabin, pausing on the ceiling-hung stalks. Stepping beneath them, he sorts through the crackling sheaves, takes down some yarrow, strips its leaves into a sack, is about to drop it in the slung bag when his eye catches the bottles. Small, thick-sided. He reaches for one, gives it a shake—brown liquid sloshing—takes it as well.

Again he stands still, taking time to think, look. Though this time at what he's left. The pile on his bed. The drying miners' blankets draped over ropes. Then, turning, he goes outside, around the cabin, to the midden of dead men's things he'd unloaded the night before. There is the shovel; he picks it up, takes it back in. And, lifting a mat, begins to dig. Through dirt packed hard by years of his own weight, down to looser earth, dumping each shovel-load onto the upturned mat, till there is a hole just bigger than the canvas-wrapped packet. Which he wraps in another skin. Same with the silver-rimmed case, the ornate tin. Then, setting all three inside the hole, he fills it back in. Packs down the dirt. What's left on the mat he drags to the woods and scatters. Then, bringing the mat inside again, begins walking atop it, ducking the hanging blankets, till, abruptly reaching up, he pulls one down—the boy's: pale stars embroidered in each dark corner—and spreads it out. Pulling down another, he lays it beside the first, stoops to the hearth, scoops out a spray of ash and, pacing back and forth, grinds it in: a path to the door. The last two blankets he sets outside atop the miners' piled rest. Then, for another minute, walks in and out, tracking dirt and ash over the mat until it looks like it's been there for years. And taking up his rucksack and guns, turning one last time, he pushes through the elk-skin flaps, calls for the molly.

A long, low whistle. A sound he has not made in nearly a decade. But still his sound. After it, a silence, as if everything else has paused to listen—the sapsucker, the crows, the mice and rats and mule with her head lifted—everything except the river. Eyes shut, brow bunched, breath stilled, he listens back, hard as if he might absorb its answer, take its roar into his blood, bring it with him. But soon he will give in, breathe, open his eyes, lead the mule to the hut and load her, the rifle and musket straps slung in an X across his back, the pistol pressing his hip as he climbs on, turns her toward the smoke, the miners' camp, the world of others.

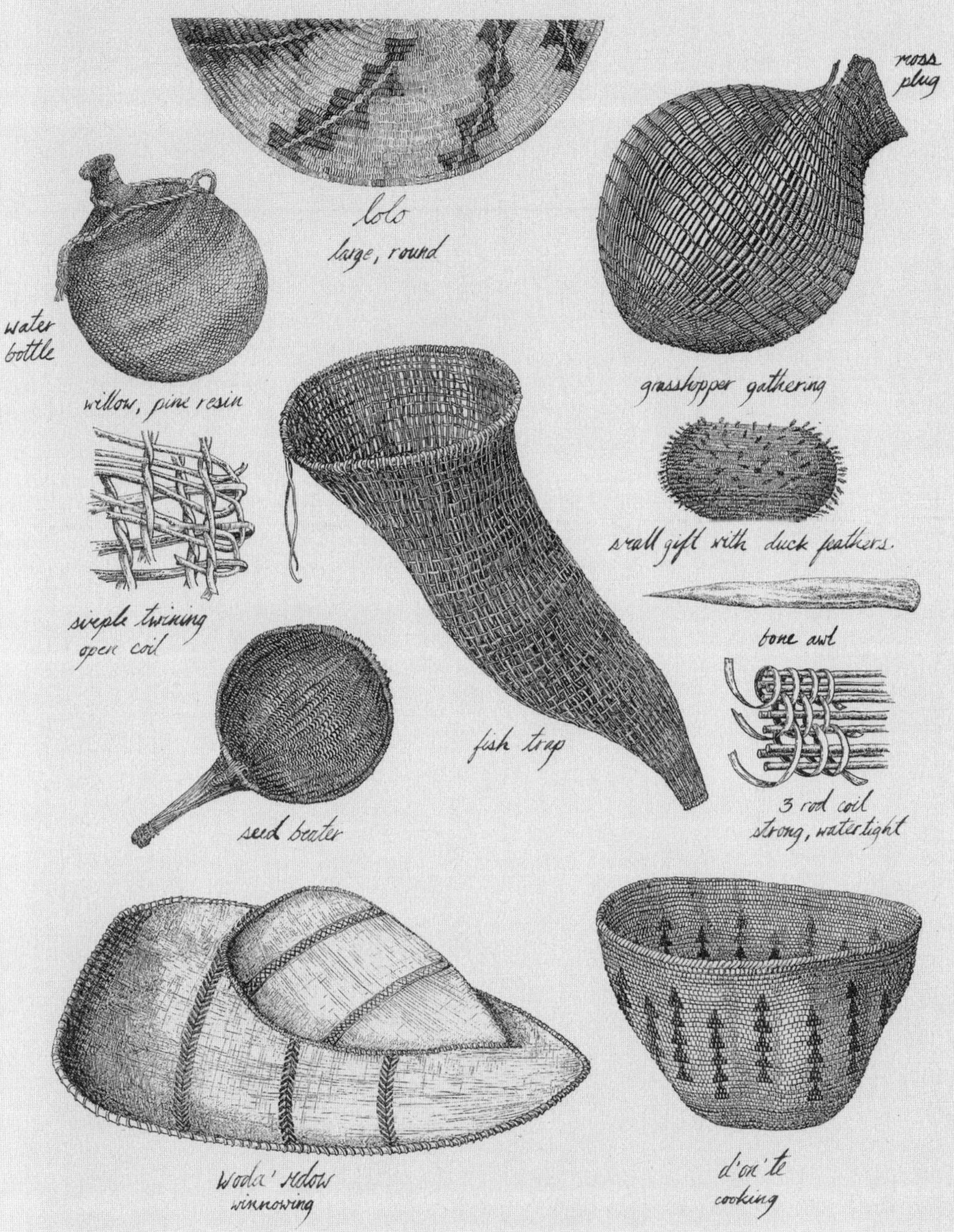
lolo
large, round
moss plug
water bottle
willow, pine resin
grasshopper gathering
simple twining
open coil
small gift with duck feathers.
bone awl
3 rod coil
strong, watertight
fish trap
seed beater
woda' sedow
winnowing
d'on'te
cooking

Dawn. A break in the rain & strangely cold. Where I left off logging last evening the trees I felled these past 3 days are ice sheathed trunks stretching across the river's boulders. Their shattered branches shaking in its rush. A dzn broken bodies piled atop each other. So far from enough to hold back the water it seems less a dam than a mass grave. A dzn hearts released. Though where wld they retrace their history to but here? Where they have stood since acorn or seedpod or pinion. A few score yrs maybe a century. Now reduced to drying trunks & dying leaves. Each bcome their own kukini. Watching over me.

Or merely watching. Choosing the next up the bank I cannot know if it has made its peace. Understands what I am doing. Wld want me to. Gripping my axe in one hand steadied with what is left of the other all I can do is listen to the river. And it is clear. Its cataracts alrdy rushing & above the dam the pool alrdy growing & the roar in my ears same as since I first came here. Since it first called me. To do this. So hacking a notch to drop the tree atop the rest I step upslope. Begin bringing it down. And though I know I am only doing what it needs. The river canyon boulders even the tree. Still I feel each whack inside my chest. Feel it even aftr the crack & groan & thundering into the water. Each heartbeat hurting.

The cold. The river. I remember lying on my father's sled. The shush of runners. Hoof thuds shaking my chest. Lungs aching as if stuffed with snow. The cold. The sky. My father framed agnst it dark in his hooded cloak. The clouds bhind him rocked. Pitched. Began to slide. I shut my eyes.

And when I opened them again he was still there. Though the sleigh had stopped. The rocking stilled. My breath still ached. My heart still hurt. But the face framed by the hood when he reached down to adjust the blanket round me was not his face. I jerked away. Will not stay awake. Was not sleeping. My eyes had simply not been seeing. Then were. Anothr's eyes taking me in. Brown irises. Dark skin. Lips blue as if tattooed. Or cold. For they were shaking. Shaking the long black hair framing his face. Hair wet and steaming. I lay there watching it rise off him. As turning away again he spread his hands before the fire.

Across it two other Shawnees crouched. Squatting between my steaming boots and soaked coat hung from a branch. Above me my blanket bent a bough with its wet weight. And what then was I wrapped in? A peltry. I sat up out of it. Saw the two across the fire start to stand. The other stayed. He clasped his own plew round his chest. But his arm was bare. Same as his legs. Same as I knew I must be beneath my fur. With his free hand he gestured. Scooping the air from me to him. As if urging me to speak. But what could I say that would not be too small? The awful paltriness of thanks.

Into my silence there came the others' speech. And the wet-haired one reached out again as if to help me up. Though when I went to clasp his hand he grasped my wrap instead. Tugged at the peltry. Pulled it free.

Then he was walking away from me. Toward the others already climbing into a boat. The fishermen from back on the eastern bank. Each took an oar, and as they pushed off from this western one to which they must have brought me, the man who must have plunged in to save me threw the peltry into the skiff. Leapt to its bow. Sunlight gleamed in his wet hair. Flared off the oars. They let the current take them and were gone.

On the far bank where I had waded in, the mist had burned away. The forest that all fall had been my boundary now a distant strip of gray. I squinted at it across the river. Trying to remember. The cold. Each heartbeat hurting. That same sun coming through that same hair underwater. His hands lifting the rock off of my chest. Breaking the surface.

Why had he done it? Why had they pulled me out? Why row across to the far shore instead of back to the one I left? For the sunlight on that western side? Their fire from the past night? Or had this bank just been a little emptier. Its towpath less busy. The three Shawnee less likely to be spotted with a half-dead white man in their boat.

Staring back at the last I'd see of Pennsylvania, the only place I'd ever known, I saw again my earliest memory of those like them: a field full of Lenape or Susquehannock or Haudenosaunee—I'd been too young to know the difference—slowly moving through high grass or bent over rustling leaves in the hours after that massive flock of passenger pigeons had flown by, after the massacre the rest of us had wrought, looking for the bits of the birds' bodies we had left. I'd only recently come back into myself, my father still treating the injuries inflicted by me on my sister and brother, and it was strangely soothing watching all the men and women dipping up and down. My siblings asked what they were doing and, when my father told us they were collecting the discarded carcasses—the ones too wrecked by rocks or rakes or shot to salvage—my mother said she thought it admirable, the way they made use of every part. Only for my father to shake his head. It's not that, he said. They do it out of respect. For the birds. As if—and his voice hardened—pigeons had souls, same as you and me. Or a rock. A tree. Which—the hardness sharpened—they also believe.

My brother laughed. More to release the tension in my father's face than out of any humor. And my mother, to do the same for us, pretended the whole ride back to speak in the voices of objects we passed. So that, by the time that we were home, Hinton and Adnah were crying out for her to do a hawk, a pail, a fencepost.

But I refused to join them, could not have if I'd tried. And when, six or so years later, my father had the elm cut down, after we'd returned from the Lenape homestead where he'd shot dead the foal, I'd gone to where the tree had stood, spent the rest of the day gathering what pieces of it were left. Raked leaves and twigs into a circle big as the shadow its canopy once cast. Pushed wheelbarrows full of woodchips into the meadow, tossed armfuls of sawdust into the wind. Piled the fallen branches in a great pyre that, once I'd lit it, I refused to leave all night.

When I was six, I'd seen a village burn. One of the last left in Westmoreland County. Just a handful of wickiups a small band of Susquehannock had resisted leaving a bit longer than the rest. But big enough that, when it caught, we could see the smoke from our home miles away. There'd been a rumor—a confederacy of displaced tribes gathered to the west, a war party strong enough to breech the wide Ohio—a threat my father thought real enough he'd fetched his pistols, handed me one, declared it time I learn to shoot. So when he saw the smoke, he knew. Just as he knew the Susquehannock he'd often traded with for roots and leaves he used in tinctures, whose children played with my brother and sister, had nothing to do with the Shawnee across the river.

We rushed there together—Hinton, me, our father, the three of us loading buckets into the wagon, whipping the horses to a canter—but by the time we got there, there was nothing we could do, the bark walls and sapling poles gone up in such an inferno we couldn't get the horses closer than a hundred feet. Close enough to hear the screams, smell the burning flesh and hair.

And though my father sent me home with Hinton, though only he stayed behind to use what medicine he knew, the stench remained with me for days. The sounds for years. And though by the time I turned seven, the Shawnee stronghold had been burned too, by nine their leader killed and coalition broken, the stillness on that following day, when we went back to bring supplies—the smoldering ashes, singed trees, utter absence of birds—never quite left me. It returned whenever I heard word of the war—the militiamen who'd killed the Shawnee chief had, my father whispered to my brother, made razor strops from his flayed skin—or when one of the surviving Susquehannock came by with a mauled dog or crippled cow. A stillness that, from then on, I sensed in them as well—Haudenosaunees peeling bark at the town tannery; Senecas bringing barges of lumber down from their mill; the Susquehannock women carrying brooms between houses they cleaned; Lenape girls gathered around mounds of dead parakeets brought down by the white hunters who paid them to pluck feathers, fill sacks, the air around them flecked green, gold, scarlet—a quiescence about their presence that never pushed on me quite like others', never lit against my skin as easily. Perhaps it was only the distance between our lives, the fact that when they went back to log homes, some still entered through doors of woven mats. That when their singing came from the woods, the sounds they made on flutes or fiddles were nothing like the songs I knew. That, though their world had been pressed into an ever-smaller space, it was still theirs, still separate, still somewhere outside of mine. Of yours. The one that, crouching bare-skinned that morning on the riverbank, I knew I could no longer share.

Staring into the fire, surrounded by my draped, steaming clothes, I could not quit seeing their boat drifting away, the way they'd saved me and then, at my first stirring, left. Without a word. Or wanting one from me. As if we had existed on different sides of some great pane. As if to show me how it could be.

What did my parents tell you? What did your mother? As the days turned into weeks and months and you turned four, then five.

What do I tell them? Words I would hear over and over in the months to come. In parlors packed with mourners or from single survivors sitting wake. All of them always needing to know the same. What do I tell his mother? Father? Brother? Sister? Wife? But more than any other, the children: his child, her daughter, son. *What do I tell them?*

Gone, they said most often. Sometimes to heaven, sometimes to God, sometimes to a better place. Sometimes to nowhere, saying nothing after. Only, *Gone.*

And I can hear them say it to you. And to each other. My father to my mother. Your mother's mute signing of the word. In which I hear you too. Your asking, Where? Why? Till when? And then your stopping. After a month? A year? Your silence. Your unceasing, unrelenting, unyielding silence in all the years that would come after.

Even here, even now, in each pause between the scratching of my pen, I still can hear it, clear as I did then, rising from that fire, and in the quiet between my footsteps as I started walking west, and in the birdless silence of a swale where, two days later, I stumbled on the half-burned shack that would become my home. Heard it in the charred starkness of the two standing walls, the rain-sogged ashes of the rest, the black stares of iron pots hanging from the remaining chimney. Heard it in the aching of my stomach in that week I tried to survive alone, the weakness of the sickness brought on by what few things I found to eat. Heard it the first time that I gave in, in the night silence of a road an hour's walk out of the woods, in the first sound to reach me: a distant wailing of someone weeping in a farmhouse farther down, its windows lit long past midnight. I had intended to find a smokehouse or cellar, take just enough to stay alive, but, instead, stood listening. The crying swelling and receding. Long minutes passing before, at last, I turned around, walked back to my shack, retrieved my pens.

And so began my life beside the dead. My nights seeking out doors hung with wreaths painted black. Sometimes merely pine branches dipped and nailed up dripping, a ribbon ripped off somebody's dress and knotted dangling from the knocker, a hat black as a hole. Once, just three words carved with a knife: *Dyde Last Nite.*

Farmhouses with dogs barking behind the door. Cabins betrayed by tree-splintered light. Mansions on backstreets, smoke pouring from their chimneys, crying through their walls. Sometimes things thrown and breaking. Sometimes taprooms filled with the raucousness of drink and loud piano-playing and someone calling to keep it down and the crowd roaring. A black belt hung from its buckle on a boardinghouse back door beside a tacked-up note: *Rm 4.* And me reaching for the handle, turning the knob, stepping in.

Even hotels, even taverns. I found I could go anywhere so long as it was late enough at night. Three, four. Even the alehouses quiet by then. Even the crying stopped. The street empty. The farm at rest. The lodge a morgue. My knock.

Hello? they'd say—the mother, grandfather, great-aunt, wife—taking in my tattered coat, mud-spattered pants, my unfamiliar face in the torch flicker. Yes? the manservant would say. The half-grown boy: What do you want?

And I'd hold up my case. At first, just the drawing tools; later, papers and board. Always I told them I would be gone by dawn, leave them a likeness of their loved one, allow them a few hours' sleep while I took their place watching the deceased.

All I asked for in return was a few coins—saved for the day I'd find a way to send them to your mother—and silence.

From me? some asked. As if they thought I was requesting it of the corpse.

Concentration, I'd tell them. Distraction. In fact, I'd say, if you wouldn't mind leaving the room . . .

Mostly, they complied. And alone in the parlor, surrounded by portraits turned to the wall, covered mirrors and stopped clocks and the stark stillness of the small death door waiting to be opened after the wake, I would unwrap my papers, take out pencils and pens, pull a chair close to the casket, turn up the lamp. As a rule it was kept cold against the smell. And still the air was dense with death, the scent heavy even on bodies newly cleaned and dressed. Sometimes the mourning family tried to disguise it with blocks of resin, lavender, bread baking in a hearth. But I welcomed the scent of the dead. Its essence replacing that of the living. Strange how such bodies could fill a room more than they would have breathing, yet be no threat to me. Perhaps it was their silence, perhaps the absence left behind by a departed soul. I know only that I could feel the lack of presence, the remains become merely another object in the room. Which allowed me to stay for hours alongside bodies that, when living, would have undone me.

So it was with some resignation that I altered their faces, re-created features. Nobody wanted the caved-in skull, the burned side of the head, the missing teeth. I was expected to undent the bone, unsear the skin. And peering at an eyelid's curve or nostril's crease, I found it impossible to forget I wasn't there only to preserve memory, but to sit wake, reprieve whichever mourner had entrusted me to take his place. Make sure the eyelid didn't twitch, the nostril didn't flare, no breath passed lips. Sometimes, while filling out the cheeks, smoothing a brow, I would confuse what I was doing with what I saw before me, and stop—pencil paused, pen mid-dip—have to resist the urge to call whoever I had relieved back in.

Sometimes they came anyway. Unable to resist checking my

progress, seeing if I could do as promised. Sometimes it seemed they confused the drawing and life too, reentered the room with such expectation on their face, as if somehow my presence might have shaken death's determination. Maybe that explained the disappointment I'd often see seep into their eyes, maybe it was just that no drawing can match the vividness of memory, maybe my skill wasn't what I thought. But sometimes it brought them peace. After so long staring at the dead face, I found I could perceive more on the living one: a loosened jaw, a softened mouth, a silent release of breath. They might place a hand on my shoulder, two on my cheeks, even rest their forehead against my own. And holding to what I'd seen in them, I could, for a second or two, abide.

Not so the ones who were displeased, who would return minutes after I'd begun only to stand over me, command me to correct a flaw not on the page but on the face. Please, I'd say. Ask them to step away. Once a man, gripping my hand, tried to direct my pencil. I ripped my fingers free, began to rise. And when he grabbed my other hand, slamming it back onto my drawing board, I slammed the pencil down as hard into the back of his. So deep I felt its point, pushed through his palm, prick mine. But what was I to do when they could not leave a dead wife or husband's side? When even the thought set them to weeping? When a mother who'd lost a child couldn't stop talking? Telling me what her baby liked to eat, the way he laughed, his favorite toy. Would say, Let me get it, let me show you, I'll be right back. I admit there were times I set the drawing down, left without payment, fled. And sometimes, while a tormented griever filled the room around me with anguished rage, I'd look to the small side door—used only by the dead and those who bear them—feel a sudden desperate compulsion.

A fallacy, the Quakeress called it—the idea the world we live in is not the true one, that there's another where our true selves exist—or maybe, *A fantasy*. She was pacing the room and the floorboards' creaks cracked through the word. A confused concept of heaven, she told me, as if a soul can rush its own ascension, as if it does not need body or mind. If it could only gain release of its shell and too-flawed heart and sicknesses inside its skull here on our earth, a better, truer one would be there all along. Just out of reach. Just an idea. But, she said, and staring past me at the corpse, tapped her own head, in a troubled mind, ideas can do much damage.

The gash in the deceased's neck was wrapped in wool, a knit scarf wound thick enough to hide all evidence but for the way the head hung back a bit too far. A man a little younger than me. Who, hours earlier, had slit his throat.

She had not been the one to find him, nor dress him, nor shave and clean him. Nor was she any relation. But the woman I would come to know as Sarah Lamont had been the one to greet me at the door. By then, I'd been living in the half-burned shack for a full year and autumn was again giving way to winter. That evening the sky had shed a first few flecks of snow and I'd set out earlier than was my wont, made my way to a house I'd often noticed on my returns from town. Though only that day had seen the black wreath on the door.

A big country manor set back from the road, surrounded by old cornfields, livestock loosed in the cut stalks. The hills around were brown with the bleakness that blankets the country that time of year, and the road was rutted with refrozen mud and still, somehow, the mansion seemed untouched by the dark months. The house was lit all night, every night, lamps lining the drive and the surrounding walls and beside the big front doors and in the windows candles always burning. Even past midnight when I walked beneath the iron archway of the always-open gate. In the moonlight I could see the scroll-worked words: *Let Them Make Me a Sanctuary*—then I was within the stone enclosure, passing a dormant orchard's rag-wrapped trunks, a stall breathing the scent of horses, a carriage house's yellow face. The house itself was yellow too. On cloudy days a square of saved-over sunlight, on bright ones all aglow. Even at night, standing there before I knocked, I could feel its color faint as buried coals. Maybe it came from all the lamps, maybe just the way the high enclosure blocked the gusts that cut through my own home. Maybe that was why when Mrs. Lamont met me at the door, I let her take my hand and lead me in.

Maybe why, even when she refused to leave the room, I stayed.

I'm sorry, she said, I have a certain responsibility. To the family.

For whom she told me my drawing would be a farewell gift. An expression, she said, of our condolences. Then shook her head. No no, she said, if I am being honest, I am hoping it will aid in our apology. You see, he was entrusted to us. To me. A trust that we, I—she gestured to the corpse—obviously failed to meet.

I asked her if she wouldn't mind moving to another chair.

Another chair?

A little farther, I said. Away from me.

She fell silent, watched me trying not to meet her eyes as I prepared my drawing board, then stood up from the chair she'd been in and, crossing to the room's far corner, chose another. One clearly too small for her substantial weight but that placed between us the greatest distance. And I could breathe. A little better. Enough to get out, Thank you. Before she began again to speak. Her broad bulk behind me, her big hands in her wide lap, the tightness coming again into my chest. Charges, she called them, though when she spoke of one, it was always Daughter This or Son That. Daughter Jeffries grew apprehensive, Son Kane refused. For aren't we all, she explained, children in the eyes of God? Brethren. No matter how troubled, how flawed. Charges and attendants and her. And you, she said, you too. I couldn't make myself look back, couldn't move my pen. Her words had peopled the house. It was three stories. How many rooms? Beds? In her pause I heard footsteps, rustling, high drumming of someone pissing in a basin. The sound petering off. A cough. I kept my eyes on the dead face, breathed in its smell.

It was not till she spoke again that I realized how long she had been silent. Surely staring at me intensely as I'd locked my eyes upon the corpse.

I meant Brother Mathieson, she said. When I said brethren, when I said troubled.

I tried to nod. Failed.

She said, I think you did not understand that you had come to an asylum.

If I had been able to move, I would have set my pencil down, closed up my case, taken my papers and board, and left. But I knew if I took my eyes off of the dead man's face, if I so much as shifted the lead, I'd be unable to stop from bursting into flight.

You see? she said. This, this is exactly why we do what we do here. Look at you, you're terrified. As at that word we all should be. But, Mr. Hall, I assure you, not here. This is a safe place, a happy place.

As if to prove her wrong, a moaning slipped through the ceiling. Soft at first, but growing. I could feel it fall upon us like dust sifting through the second-story floorboards, could hear the creak of her chair, imagine her looking up.

When she spoke again, there was a smile in her voice. Well, she said, not always. If we were always happy, we wouldn't need a safe place, would we? Bernice, she called through an open door. Bernice! There came the thump of footsteps climbing stairs. What she must have wanted to hear because she again addressed me, her voice rising with the rising moans, the footsteps quickening. Perhaps, she said, you have heard of the York Retreat? Or nearer here, the Friends Asylum?

Upstairs, the moaning seemed about to break into a shrieking. But instead it was enjoined by singing. A woman's voice softly spreading over the moans—a blanket settling—so, in the silence of our listening, the one sound slowly smothered the other.

Oh how lovely is the evening, is the evening when the bells . . .

Between the singing, Lamont continued speaking to me. Of troubled minds needing not binding, but inspiration. Of the necessity of reminding those gone mad they'd once been rational. Could be again. Moral treatment, she called it. A belief born of the faith she began then to describe for me. But I'd stopped listening, was thinking instead of the hospital she said was the model for hers—in the state I'd fled, not three days ride from my parents' home, where my father might have meant to take me—a Quaker hospital, founded in defiance of the very ideas I'd feared, that had instead embraced a faith in friendship and gentle guidance, the belief that a refined environment could lift man's temperament to meet it. And I could see it: My father taking me to a room reserved for my own use. My mother visiting monthly, accompanying me around the sculpted grounds or to lectures by professors from nearby universities. Perhaps joined by my wife. Who would have seen me tending gardens, herding sheep, working in the dairy. Might have even supped with me, dressed in her finery, same as I and all the others every evening. In the library, Sarah Lamont explained, the Friends Asylum had a thousand books. With which, I thought, I might have taught you to read. In the theater's lantern light might have sat you on my lap, the two of us taking in a shadow show. They had those also. Classes in painting, acting. Everything that might help right a mind, lead it back to a life that, after enough time, might rejoin the lives of others. A life my father and brother might have managed to help me find. Had I not fled.

I sat listening to Mrs. Lamont explain the ways she'd tried to re-create what she had witnessed. Adopted, she said, on our small scale, in our small way. No more than twenty-four daughters and sons. Each one attended by a caring companion. And hearing how the attendants would try each day to lead their charges gently into the next, imagining how it must be to feel that kind of help, I felt instead the foolishness of my attempts to heal myself. Knew I had been bound to fail. Would be.

Upstairs, the companion she'd called Bernice had switched to humming the same short tune over and over, a lullaby that seemed to thicken in the room around me till I realized Lamont was humming too. I turned to look. She lay back in the chair, face tilted up, eyes shut, still as the cadaver, but for her breath. Her restful presence. In which, I realized with blooming surprise, I felt strangely at peace.

By the time I finished drawing, she was asleep, softly snoring. Quietly I placed my pencils back in their case, rewrapped the board and papers, set the portrait beside the coffin and, turning, made my way to the front door. It was unlocked.

Outside, I shut it behind me so slowly it made no noise latching in place. And then I knew it had not latched, for it was opening again. In the foyer's flickering light Lamont stood looking at me, her eyes alert with sudden waking, her face perplexed.

I left the drawing, I told her.

She said she'd seen it, that it was good, worth more than I had asked. Here, she said, reaching into her skirts. But I held up my hand, shook my head. Surely you want something for it, she said.

The lanterns beside the door were nearly out. We stood in their guttering, her eyes slowly filling with understanding, on her face a patience as if she had decided that if she could not pay in money, she would in waiting.

Perhaps, I said, I could come back again.

Her wide cheeks spread wider with her smile. I hope not, she said. And the smile stayed amid the sadness that reclaimed her face. At least not for quite a while.

No, I assured her, not to draw them.

No? she said.

Not dead, I told her.

Alive then?

Maybe, I said, they'd like to learn.

To draw?

I could teach them, I told her. I could come back to teach.

My room was on the third floor, low-ceilinged and narrow as the dormer at its end but long enough to fit hooks, shelves, a feather bed. They gave me shoes too. And my first suit. Dove gray. Same as the bowler that I hung from one hook. From another: the long wool frock, too big but warm, that had belonged to a worker before me. During the day I was to dress in white: slacks and shirt and short coat, just like the charges' companions. I'd pointed out the problem of painting in such an outfit, so on the third hook, there hung my smock: an apron from the kitchen, brightly striped.

It was warm on the top floor, all the house's heat rising beneath me, the window facing south. A long clear view: the rose garden's pruned stalks, the smooth snow of the croquet pitch, a pond swept for skating. Beyond the wall: the silos, barn, cornfields stretching toward the hills that hid the hovel where I'd near starved. Now each day I woke in that soft bed and dressed amid the wafts of biscuits and bacon and eggs and stared out of the window of my new room and thought, What have I done?

It was all true—the performances and lectures and library—though on a lesser scale. The plays performed by schoolchildren, the musicians two town fiddlers accompanied by Lamont's piano playing sister, the lectures given by Lamont herself, the library mostly bare. But the affect still every bit what she described. The audience sitting mostly in silence or gathering on the dance floor to learn a step or clapping so enthusiastically the sister would consent to play an encore. For her talks Lamont drew from her late husband's books, lectures as likely to be on horticulture as on theology. Even one night on the fate of the Carolina parakeet. Birds she said that once flew overhead in flocks so thick that, alighting on the roof, they'd reshingle it in scarlet, green, gold. A thing last seen back in the twenties. Flocks dwindling each year till the past few brought none. Brave birds, she called them. The way, when one was shot, they'd all crowd round it as if attempting comfort; the fact that then the hunters could destroy scores more not a mark against their species' brains but a flaw in the character of ours. One we could mend by emulating them. Act with equal compassion for our brethren. Hope to warrant the same from Him. Yes, there were disruptions—a man who mimicked the parrots' squawks, another who whistled during concerts, a woman who cried, *Come back! Come back!* whenever a child thespian would exit through the makeshift curtain; even some who had to be restrained, carried out—but the only time that force was used was to protect them from themselves. And, mostly, the attempts to lift their spirits, focus their thoughts, trust them with their own minds seemed overwhelmingly to work.

I'd watch them, these souls wracked by such suffering. A woman I once witnessed nearly gnaw off her thumb become demure and delicate when dressed in jewels for supper. A man who'd daily been stricken by seizures now went weeks without one, so long as a hedge-clipper or a carving knife busied his hands. A girl who used to hurl teacups at walls was now trusted to gather eggs. I'd watch her cross the yard hugging the basket, watch him serve me a slice of ham, the self-biting woman laughing, a wineglass in her hand. Would watch any of them who seemed so clearly to get better. Watch their wounds begin to mend. And hate them for it.

At least when the perforated box was submerged, everyone succumbed, their lungs leaking air equally. At least when the mustard powder was rubbed onto one scalp, it blistered same as any other's.

God, Lamont would say in her sermon-like talks, gave each of us our reason. If we lose it, it is something we misplaced, not He. So is within our power to reclaim. If only we are willing to. And halfway through, I'd have to rise, hurry outside. At supper, I always secured a place at the table's end, ate too fast to speak, took less and less onto my plate. Before long, I was feigning sickness, bringing supper to my room, breakfast on walks. Lunch I skipped, claiming I wished to finish drawing. Became thin as I'd been back in the woods. Before long, Lamont observed one day, I'd simply disappear. Which, more and more, I did: learned the locations of the hall closets so, at the sound of footsteps, I could duck in; at evening entertainments I'd wait outside the closed door, listening, eventually retreating to my room. A place that I left less and less. Which did not go unnoticed. Not by the other minders. Not by Lamont. Who one day stopped me on my way from class, asked was there something she could do. Which nearly broke me, my whole face twisting with the attempt to hold back tears.

Did I not live the same life they did? Hear the same lectures? Eat the same food? Dress as finely? Stay as busy? Where was my wineglass? My warm gathered eggs? My clippers or carving knife?

Oh, it worked it worked it worked for most. But there was Mr. Garner too. There was his cadaver in the parlor with its self-slit throat.

The night after I nearly wept before Lamont, I lay in bed listening through my thin walls to all the others, their presence filling my room till I could barely breathe. Rose. The creak of my bed ropes causing a creak the next room over, a cough across the hall. I stepped to the window, opened it. It was cold, moonlit, quiet out there in a way only wide-open spaces can be, the sounds of all the animals and trees and wind and everything just what was woven to make the silence. I stood there shivering, stood till my chest was trembling and my face shaking, and would have stayed still longer if I had not heard the nicker.

The next morning when I came to my classroom, my hair was flecked with hay, my white suit stained, my skin smelling of horses. I'd been having trouble with my class. On the first day there'd been only two students, accompanied by two attendants till the charges grew comfortable enough to be left to my care. A thing that had seemed feasible. The third-floor room was low-ceilinged as my own, but wide and bright and sized to fit a dozen pupils, so with just the three of us, it had been a respite from all the other charges' touches and stares, their companions' gentle corrections and desire for camaraderie. That first day I prepared my two students each with a sheet of paper, pencil, eraser, a still life of onions from the cellar. Left them drawing at their small desks. Retreated across the room to where I had set up my own some twenty feet away. Them drawing the onions, me drawing them. My focus solely on transferring their two figures to the page. Where I could release them as mere shapes, break their bodies into lines and shading, fool my mind into nearly believing I was alone in that corner of the room. My own safe place. If not quite happy. Because, of course, one student would grow anxious, disrupt the other, fill the room with growing consternation till I'd be forced to set aside my board and, fortified by our minutes apart, come over, steer them back to their drawing, so I could retreat again to mine.

A pattern that had worked well enough in that first class to make me think it could continue. Till the next morning. When, instead of finding two pupils waiting for me, I encountered more than twenty.

By the night that I slept in the stables, three weeks had passed and I'd lost all ability to teach, would avoid the classroom long as I could, hunker in my nearby quarters till the charges' confusion and attendants' frustration would force me out. Would hurry then into the room packed full of pupils, assure their minders they were free to go, fight my urge to follow. And in the slight relief of their departed presence, manage to get my students started—speaking with my eyes glued to the still life I'd set up—before fleeing to my corner. Where I would stay, the page between me and the crowded room, for the long hour before, at last, their minders would return, lead them away. And I'd remain behind my drawing board, eyes on the paper, my intensity of focus an excuse for grunting in reply to attendants' greetings, students' goodbyes, till the room was empty.

But this, of course, was hardly teaching. As Lamont had pointed out the day before. She'd stopped me outside the dining room, taken me aside, talked of what I'd told her I wanted the night we met, what she'd expected, hoped. Why I was given my room and board.

And so I tried. That morning I stayed in the stable long as I could, then barreled across the yard and up the stairs and, bursting upon the class, began taking command. Sent the companions out, the students to their seats. My voice not quite a shout, my movements just shy of manic. I'd brought an armful of tack—bridles, harness—and, slapping it down on the still-life table, began making my rounds. Circling the students as they drew. Pointing out a mislaid shadow, a faulty shape. And if drawing is lifting something from the world outside yourself to place it within the private compass of a page, then how can someone else simply reach in and, with a mark, adjust it? A line to show where an edge should go, some quickly scrabbled shading. I tugged a pencil out of one's hand, an eraser from another's. And as I leaned over their backs, the room filled with confusion, their voices rising over mine, their gestures growing agitated as my own.

I should have known. Did. Had observed them close enough over a fortnight drawing their figures to know who would retreat from my critiques, who hunkered over her work to hide it or snapped at babbling neighbors to shut up, which ones attendants kept away from others, which threw themselves into their drawing with a focus that recalled my own.

I suppose I chose him because he was most like me. Though older, fifty or sixty, bald but for a ring of curls through which he'd rake his fingers. His drawing hand, once he began, never went still. His gaze, locked on harness and halter, never dropped to the paper. Not even to check what he was doing. Not even when I reached my rag down and blotted it out.

His skull slammed back into my chin, his shoulder sending me sprawling. I cannot say I was surprised, cannot say I did not expect his paper sent flying, his desk crashing to the floor. For I felt his bellowing in my own throat, lay crumpled where I'd fallen, not even wanting the attendants to come running, wishing, when they did, that he would throw them off as well, would keep on thrashing, screaming. But they knew him too. Enough to get him in a corner, use their bodies to shield him from the others' stares, the sight of me.

Still, even after he'd been subdued, the room remained unsettled, the commotion spread through the house, the air ringing with cries and lullabies and bouts of shouting like nothing I'd known since I'd arrived at the asylum. Which, shortly after lunch, Lamont asked me to leave. Just for a while, she said. An hour, two. Why don't you take one of your walks? Clear your head. Just long enough to let us clear the air in here.

When I returned it was, they had. I'd come back in time to dress for supper, procured from the cook a pail of warm water, was determined to wash off the horse stall, shave, change into the clothes that they'd provided, button my waistcoat, recommit to the treatment for which I had once held such hope. Still did. In that morning's lecture Lamont had spoken of self-control, composure, the importance of discipline in making oneself a welcome member of any society, any family. If only we are willing to do the work it takes. I would. I would redouble it.

The house was quiet. As if it knew, wanted to help. As it had so many others. It was dusk, the lamps inside all lit, the sense of someone having just been by to do it. But the foyer empty, the parlor empty, the center stairs undisturbed by any footsteps. I climbed them slowly, trying to quiet the clacking of my shoes, avoid creaking a board. A first small thing that I could do. As if to tell the house I'd do my part. Though when I reached the second floor I started to wonder where were the others. On the landing, I paused. The far-off clanks coming from the kitchen, small clinks of the dining room being set: almost enough to set me at ease, if, from the floor above, I had not heard a murmur. A quiet breathing that as I stood listening, I could feel amplified by a crowd. A weight as if every presence inside the house had been amassed in a single place. Somewhere above me. On the third floor.

They'd gathered in my classroom: every daughter and son, all their companions too. The door was open and I could see them crammed in there, could feel their close-packed heat. All but Lamont's. She stood outside the door, peering in, smiling. Turned as she sensed me. Come! she half whispered, and when she gestured, I made my feet obey. We thought, she said as I drew close, it might be a moment ripe for instruction. For them to see how good it is to receive correction. For us all to be reminded of the value of impermanence. The dangers of attachment. Come, she said. Come see.

In the room they'd pressed around my desk, the entire houseful craning to look. In their center one of the attendants held up a lamp, its flicker falling on the stack of drawings I'd done over the weeks. Drawings someone had spread out for all to see. Drawings on which the pupil I had upset that morning was now working.

Something, isn't it? Lamont whispered.

And I could feel her breath enter my ear.

To see them, she said, begin to comprehend.

Could feel it brush against the membrane there.

The importance of acceptance.

And push inside me.

Surely, a thing we all must learn.

Past my eardrum into the cavity between it and my skull.

Isn't it something, Mr. Hall?

Filling my skull.

To see them so soothed?

Pressing my brain.

Simply by knowledge. Isn't it something? she said again.

And I managed to answer, Yes.

Yes, she repeated. Yes, yes.

Each utterance a thrust at the surface of my mind, so that I knew before she said the word again I'd break—could see my hand slam over her mouth, hear my shout, feel the blankness waiting for me on the other side—and I was turning then, taking myself away, fleeing down the hall into my room, shutting the door, standing there shaking, my fists balled inside my pockets sending my pant legs quaking, my face doing the same, my chest pressed by the weight of all their presence just beyond the wall, my eyes still seeing them staring at my drawings on my desk—the shapes I'd set safe on each page—their pencil tips breaking the lines I'd made, raking the paper, and

I was out again, my foot thuds banging back along the hall, those faces nearest the classroom's entrance turning to gape, my own eyes barely seeing, my ears not hearing, my mind bent to the bodies bent over my desk—half a dozen others had joined the patient I'd upset, their jerking backs and jostling elbows wild with their work—and then my own elbows were hacking, my own hands shoving, my body slamming through—Silas! someone called—as, grabbing shirts, hauling at shoulders, I sent the lantern-holding attendant scrambling back and, reaching across the fleeing others, lunged, my slashing hand catching the lamp, knocking it crashing onto the desk, the glass shattering over the surface, the oil bursting into flame.

In my memory there is no screaming. No more repeating of my name. Not even the sight of all the patients panicking. Just flames. Crackling, flaring. The top of the desk wholly engulfed. And my reaching in, grasping for whatever was not yet ash, crushing papers in my fists and hurling them—at fleeing backs? at those trying to stop me?—hurling balls of fire with my burning hands.

It was brave of her to sit with me. Kind. The two of us alone in the parlor again. The air still stung with the acridity of smoke. A faint haze between us in the candlelight. From above, there drifted down the sounds of the rest of the house consumed with bedtime preparations, the evening's entertainment canceled, the attendants helping their charges into the peacefulness of sleep, one after the other starting to sing the same low lullaby. The ones who'd been in the room with me had managed to douse the fire before it spread. Though by then another had ridden for town. Would be returning any time now, Lamont said. With a fire wagon. Surely the sheriff too. Who, in the coming days, would likely come again accompanied by a doctor from the nearest university. An agricultural college with a new school of medicine.

It will be okay, she told me. They don't truly want to shut us down. Nobody does. Who wants these troubled minds let loose upon their streets? There was her jowly smile, its fading as she met my lifted gaze. The plea in it she must have seen. Son, she said, do you have any idea how much it costs?

I had already asked to stay; she had already told me no.

Any idea, she continued, how much their families pay?

I could—

What? She glanced at my hands. They were wrapped in bandages, fingertips to wrists, white and stiff as paws. Yet another kindness she had showed me.

Next, she said, you'll tell me you're a Quaker. Then stopped me before I spoke. Come, come, it's not a thing you simply . . . Her smile was sad, and then was gone, and there was just the sadness. It's not, she said more softly now, a thing you can just . . .

I watched my bandaged hands.

And when she spoke again her voice was quiet enough I had to look back at her to understand. I think, she said, of all the disappointments . . . She sighed. Of all the disappointing things . . .

In the silence of her trailing off there came the sounds of a carriage far away. Silas, she said, her voice stronger again, you know that even if I could, it would not work. Then, placing her hands upon her lap with a finality: Do you think that all this time I have not seen you? Have not been watching? Did not know till now? How could I not? It's what I do. And you, son—leaning forward, she brought her face nearer to me—you know it too. That what you need we don't have for you. Not here. Not in any institution. Or any home.

But to hear it. To hear it from her. If my hands had not been so bandaged I would have covered my face.

No, she said, it is not always soothing, is it? Leaning back, she straightened her skirt, clasped her hands before her. Not soothing, but still good to know.

Outside, the sound of hooves turned off the road, the carriage rattling as it passed through the gate. But she seemed too lost in thought to hear it, her gaze caught in space, her words, when she spoke, so low I almost lost them in the clattering coming up the drive. Good to know, she said again, one's limits. The limits of what one can do.

And through the clatter, there came the sound of another carriage farther behind.

She rose then, refocused on me. Out back, she said, you'll find a cart. A driver.

Out front, the other was already pulling up, and as I stood, she reached into her skirt, pulled out a piece of paper folded and sealed, slipped it into the chest pocket of my overcoat.

A promissory note, she told me. For the driver.

Why? I managed.

To take you as far away as he will go. In her eyes I thought then I would at last see anger, but there was only pain. For me. And I knew then she did not mean I should go far away from her or from the home. But from them both. From everything. From everyone.

Her fingers found the button at the bottom of my coat, the eye to slip it through. Go on, she said, and buttoned the next, another, all the way up to my throat. Told me, Go on now, son.

But when I turned toward the foyer, she grabbed my shoulder, turned me the other way. In the candlelight I could barely make out the two small death doors, their knobs pale hints of ivory.

From the entranceway: a knock.

And her hand was on me, pushing gently. Her voice a whisper: Through there.

Before I left, I looked back once. In the lamplight she was seated again, shoulders slumped, eyes shut, face slack with relief. As if all the weeks I had been there she had been sitting vigil over me, as if my leaving had at last discharged her from the duty.

And so left you alone to see me hunch beneath the transom, step through the two small doors, disappear into the night like some pallbearer bringing out a body. Though bearing only my own. Your father at thirty-three, face shaved, hair shorn to match the patches growing back around the burn scars on his scalp, his eyes mere glints of lamp-shine in the black shadow of his brow. See the shine go out, the lids slide closed, the cheek-skin begin to stiffen. Listen: a long, slow exhalation. Followed by the longer silence of his breath stopped. The Silas I had for so long tried to keep alive at last let go, left behind surely as buried. Watch close, Elisha. Because if there is any image you remember of your father, any description come from your mother, anything that you recall about his face, that was the last time it would be mine.

You will say no. Will say my lines and shapes remained the

same—the too-large ears you used to pull, the scruff that scratched your cheek—but it is never that, not for any of those who paid me to preserve the features of their departed, who hoped my marks might instead transfer the self that the lines and shapes had once contained.

If I could, I would do it for you. Draw myself as I was then, re-create for you the face of the only father you ever knew. Before I turned away from him. From you.

But I cannot. No more than I can re-create yours. For I have tried, mined my memory for the right lines and shapes, and failed. Elisha, I cannot remember what you looked like. Yes, your face in parts—your eyes already pouched, as if I'd given you not just their shape but all my years; the faint blue line along your forehead like a reflection of the vein down the center of mine—marks and shadows, but not the self. Why did I not stay a little longer? That night I left you. Carry some paper to where you slept? Make just a sketch? I would have had it all these years. Your face as it had been, the child you were then, forever with me. For was that not why they all paid? For the transference back again, this time from page to mind. Drawings meaning nothing but for what they stir in those still alive. Even the faces of the living useless except as guides to what lies inside. Which, maybe, you knew. Even at three.

Your breath is too hot, you said. And I thought you meant sour.

Dada, you said, your breath is too hot.

Elisha, after that night it would grow hotter. As if some flicker of the fire I lit inside the manor had stayed burning inside of me, feeding off the fuel of myself, waiting for a wind. And those two death doors opening up to let it in.

The way that life will do. Gust up and shift your course, blow you clear of who you were before, knock you into who you'll be after. And why am I telling you this? You who felt it before you'd even turned four. I who, while you slept, opened the door and ushered that gust in.

You know, you know. So pull your chair a little nearer, give the lamp a bit more wick, sharpen your pencil, smooth your paper, look hard at your father's face. Before he steps out of that door and it shifts into your once-was-father, begins to be the me I would become.

Do you draw? Did you get that from me too? Or maybe you would simply scrawl a few words on the page: *His breath was too hot.* Maybe that would suffice. For what else is this that I write? What but transference too? Of life to paper, world to mind, myself to you.

A picture: Through the back window of the stage, the mansion lit by lamps, and the driveway a ramp through the last two, and out the gate into the night, the asylum a dwindling light in the dark landscape, shaking in the shaking glass, smaller and smaller, till it disappears and leaves only the hint of hills and night-inked sky inside the window frame. The faint reflection of my face. My bandaged hands wrapped white as candle-spills. Nothing else but blackness inside the empty coach. Outside, the driver hunched on his seat, silent as he will be all night. The hooves of the horses, the swaying coach. The last night or nearly the last night or anyway it is almost the end of 1838.

When I wake it will be dawn, the back window a patch of growing light. Behind it: the brightening east. To the left: a wide and level strip of reflected sky. The grand Ohio, alongside again, having already made its wide bend so that the road along its bank now takes me west. While, through the side windows, all the river's crowded life begins to stir: the carriage factories and hog yards and abattoirs flashing by, the world outside the glass moving as fast as the flipbooks I used to make for you. Do you remember? How I would thumb through each packet of tiny pages before your eyes. A flower sprouting from nothing into bloom. A face changing maniacally from sad to happy. A man running, running, running, as if trying to escape page after page. Till, at the very end, he finally leapt forward and away.

AUTUMN, 1849

Ascending the ridgeside he watches the sky, the smoke seeming to spread as he climbs, its scent to thicken, the air grow grittier in his throat. Below, the river shimmers and twists, just near enough that, steering the mule onto a deer track, he can glimpse the cataracts and gravel bars, too soon the scars of troughs and reshaped banks, shovels stuck in the sand in place of men. For he sees none of them. Not panning or digging or chopping timber. Not even when he spots the fresh wreckage of new-logged cedars. Now that he's on the river's other side he can see the trees he'd heard falling the day before, the trunks already skinned, some split down their long center, a few half-hollowed out. But no one there to finish them. Nobody even when, rounding the bend, the camp comes into sight.

Slipping off the mule, he creeps closer to the cover's edge. As far as he can see downriver the claims are equally abandoned. The camp itself devoid of all but dogs drifting among the tents, the half-built cabin, emptied corral. For a second he wonders if all the miners are at that moment riding upriver upon his home, if somehow he'd missed them below, and then he catches the smoke-scent again, and—face hardening as if he smells the lodgepoles, the flesh and hair; eyes widening as if, even from there, he hears the screams—he knows, wheels, makes for the mule at a run.

It takes an hour—the climb out of the canyon longer on this side, the ridgepath so little traveled he rides bent to the molly's neck, ducking boughs and slowing through thick manzanita stands, spurring his mount to jump a fallen pine so huge she barely clears its trunk—and by the time the path swings back toward the canyon the sky is bluer, as if whatever had been burning is near burned out. But he can see, from just beyond the southward ridge, the ghosts of smoke still wisping, and, riding hard down the ravine toward the crossing where No Rope said the miners built their bigger camp, the unsheathed musket in his fist, rifle slapping his spine, a hope knocks at him with the mule's jolts: that, nearing, he'll hear amid gunshots the warriors' ululations, instead of women's screams the panicked bellows of wooles. He sets the musket at full cock.

But when the river comes into sight it's quiet. Across the water, built on a ledge just high enough to clear all but the biggest floods, the camp—the town—is twice the size of the one upstream, packed not just with tents and hovels but a dozen cabins, more being built, even a couple two-story structures made of milled lumber. And, running beside it all, a newbuilt flume: halved trunks hollowed to troughs and bound together into an overground canal, waiting to be filled with water stolen from upriver. Down by a bar, the river is wider, slower, and, where the Nisenan used to pole tule rafts across, the miners have rigged up a rope-ferry fit for a dozen men. Men who should be milling about the muddy street, thronging the tents. But across the river there's barely any sign of them: one leaning against a porch rail, another perched on a corral. A scant handful. But each one armed. As if left behind to guard the town. While the rest rode off into the hills, heading for Kushna.

Because of him. What he had done, had failed to. The boy, the father. The other miner. The mules and guns. The hu'uku.

The old Nisenan is down on the bar, sitting on gravel. Arms bent behind him, chest flecked with blood, wispy beard smeared wetly red. A bit away, two miners sit on driftwood in the sun. Behind them: the bright slant of a rifle leaned against the log. They seem to be eating. Flashes of knives cutting, lifting to mouths. One stands, brings a bit to the bound shaman, holds it out. The other laughs. A sound loud enough to reach across the river, rise the couple hundred feet to Silas. Though Too Much Water does not hear. Or does not show it. His face unchanged except to tilt a little higher, his eyes lifting out of the shadow, their gaze finding the mule, Silas astride it raising his musket.

A shout—one miner dropping what he'd brought, reaching to his side; the other standing, whipping a flash of sunglint to his shoulder—and Silas fires: the rifle flung, the man spun down onto the stones. Screening the remaining one: a cloud of pistol smoke. The crack claps from the bank—the bullet's whistle already past—and the molly is trying to turn, whipping her head against the reins that Silas grabs, voice in her ear—"Easy"—the miner who'd missed racing back toward the camp—"Easy"—and already Silas is shifting the musket to his rein hand, the mule calming just enough to let him draw the pistol, tell her, "Here it comes again."

His first shot hits in a spurt of bank-dirt above the runner—the pepperbox hugely front-heavy, the six-bore barrel not even outfitted with a sight—his second spatters stonedust a foot behind the miner's feet. And Silas breathes a stuttered breath—the man still running—aims—running—fires. Gone. Behind a tent. All but his shouting. Joined by the shouts of others. For a second, it seems as if the town itself is moving—tent flaps, cabin doors—and then the movement is beside him in the air, the buckbrush whipping behind his shoulder, bringing distant rifle-cracks, and wheeling the mule, snapping the reins, he sends her scrabbling up the ravine.

He pushes hard, heels hammering her flanks, till they are out of sight, then reins her to a stop, sits stroking her neck, over and over, as if not just trying to calm her but rub the shaking from his own hand, arm, shoulder, jaw, his head cocked, listening for sign from below. But there is just her breathing, the river, his shaking, the miner spinning onto the stones, the moonlit father's face exploding, the dead boy's *Pa!*, and Silas's hand abandons the molly's trembling neck for the pendant dangling from his own, his fingers working the heavy ball, tracing its sinew wrapping, till they are steady enough he can let go, reach for his powder horn, refill the barrel, wrap and pack the lead, turn to reloading the revolver. When he is done, he listens again. It's hard to tell if the thudding is his heart or hoofbeats. Then it isn't—the clatter coming up the slope he'd climbed, but faster—and he shoves the handgun back in his belt, wheels the mule into the steepness, tries to click her faster with his dry tongue. But she is already gasping, her breath more raspy than his own, her head hanging, hooves slipping in the mud.

He'd hoped to make the ridgetop in time to give her rein, open some distance between them, but when he glances back they are already there: a rider lurching with his mount's climbing, gun barrel jerking above its thrusting neck. Another muscling into sight. Three, four, more, fresh-legged and watered. He looks ahead—two switchbacks till they crest this steepest part—and when he glances down again the trail beneath the mule's hooves is passing slow as if he was on his own feet. Then he is. Lands with the reins in one hand, the reloaded musket in his other, the rifle across his back, and begins to run. Hunched forward against the grade, driven by an urgency the molly seems at last to grasp, he leads her straight up, crossing the switchbacks, a route too steep for saddlehorse, but her steps holding better than his slipping own, her close breath blowing at his neck, until, reaching the top of the false peak, he leads her on just far enough to hide her from the others' sight, and stops.

Together their gusting is too loud to hear whatever sounds come from below and, in the reprieve, he swings his water bag around, swallows, gasps, swallows again. Then the mule is there, nuzzling, and he squats, lifts his skin-shirt into a pouch, lets her drink out of his lap. A few loud draws before his tired legs begin to cramp. Rising, he leaves her blowing at the droplet-scattered ground. While, on elbows and knees, he crawls to the edge of the false peak.

There is the first one, climbing the final switchback, rider twisting in the saddle, spectacles catching the sun in the second before the musket thunders. Smoke and the flash of falling glasses. Silas flattens himself again—behind him: the crack of branches—lets go his emptied gun, whips the loaded rifle over his head instead, lifts his face just high enough to sight on the next rider, and, before he can make out more than bead-on-body—too quick to see anything of the man that might start him shaking again—he fires. Dropping his head, he listens to the screaming of the horse he'd hit instead. The strange rifle's oddly angled sights, too eager trigger. He knows he should reload the newfangled gun—it would be quicker, let him stay lower—but his hand is already reaching for his trusted musket. All the long seconds it takes to pack the barrel the horse keeps screaming, the molly nickering nervously behind him, and by the time he's filled the pan, her hoof-thuds are coming near. Even before he turns, he sees her as they will—ears appearing over the bluff, then head, neck, body—and he is scrambling back, snagging her reins, turning to run the other way, pounding by her side for a few steps before he swings on, swivels, aims the jolting musket barrel, sights on the drop—the unhorsed rider—fires. The man jerks but stays up. An arm? A shoulder? Silas doesn't wait to see, just swivels forward again, holding the musket's hot muzzle far from the mule's hide, slapping the reins across her neck, trying to spur her to a canter. Though a few strides later she slows once more, breathing hard as if still climbing, as if this stretch of near-level trail isn't the best—maybe the only—chance they'll get to put some space behind them. And, grunting an apology, Silas reaches the long musket barrel back over the mule's haunch, presses the hot metal to her flesh.

By the time they reach the fallen pine she's slowed again, her trembling legs so unsteady she refuses to jump the tree, balks even at wending between its limbs. He lets her stand, regaining her wind, though he knows she won't before the others thunder around the bend. Knows she's right: even if she could get over the trunk—mouth thick with froth, her cooling sweat making her shiver—what would it matter?

For the past minutes he has been searching for a way to disappear. A place he might lead her off trail, lose the others. Alone it would be easy—a low branch he could swing up on, a boulder that would hold no prints—and sitting astride her heaving back he thinks of leaving her, just slipping off, stepping onto the huge pine trunk, following it through the wreckage of its fall, the woods downslope crushed into mangled brush, the tree a line jutting a hundred feet above some drop. His heartbeat, the mule's breathing. Beneath them both, more feeling than sound: hoofbeats coming. For a second he can see how they will find her, the empty sawbuck on her back sign enough to send them crashing after him. And then he's off, leaping from mule-back to tree, reins in one hand, musket in the other, rifle smacking his spine as he lands on the trunk, and, with a jerk to yank her moving, starts down the pine. Running, he keeps her close—branches banging her legs, tripping her hooves, but the smashed boughs and scrub as good a cover for her prints as he could find—the canyon drawing their weight downslope till he is sprinting to stay beside her, scampering over snags—the nearing tree-tip shivering with his steps, shaking against the sky—trying to keep them going fast enough that when she sees the drop, the slope sucked away into a sudden slide of scree, she cannot stop; he feels her try, yanks the reins forward with all he's got, and leaps.

A second in the air—he lets go, releases her to land safe as she can—and then the slam of his own weight, the slide of stones and dirt trying to fling him from his feet, his speed sheeting steepness away till the brush rears up and, throwing himself onto his back, he shoves his musket before his face to catch the worst. Beside him, the mule crashes into the scrub as well, though she has kept her feet, or rather rear, sat back so far she's fairly sledding on her haunch. Seeing it, he can't help but smile. She shakes herself, struggles to stand. And when he sees she can the smile spreads to his whole face, lifting his beard, creasing his eyes, crinkling the line tattooed along his nose. "Want to go again?" he says. The mule shakes her head. He keeps his laugh inside his eyes, listens through the last clatter of dirt and stones. A fainter, heavier sound: hoofbeats high above.

He waits through their rising rataplan, the crash of the horses jumping the pine, thud of their landing, the drumming fading again as they ride on. How long before they realize he has not? Notice the hoofprints he had left that morning, lack of retreating ones? Turn back?

Not far upcanyon he knows a creek, makes for it, leading the molly through skunk bush and gooseberry, thickets of poison oak, tugging her away from attempts to stop and rip at anything green, till the ground dips, and he feels her scent the water, lets go the reins.

Upstream, crouched amid the moss and ferns, he drinks deep too. Then stands, listening. Wet beard cold on his chin. A burbling wren, rustling of squirrels. The mule splashing farther in. Some hundred feet above, where the trail cuts through the creek, they would sound much the same—the horses splashing back again, the men discussing where he might be—but down here the water's rush is loud enough it might just smother them. And, feeling himself trying to listen through it, straining to hear, he drops to his knees, plunges his head in. The water is freezing, but he stays kneeling, hands on the rocks, his face submerged, skin numbing, lungs starting to seize.

What had the hu'uku told them? What had No Rope refused to? What had they ridden on Kushna thinking must have happened to the three miners so far upriver?

There is the underwater clatter of the mule's hoof, the gurgle of her drinking.

Who, when they set fire to the village, had they been hoping to flush out?

He whips his head up, gasps. The mule has lifted her face too. Stands with her muzzle dripping, staring at him, silent in her sudden stillness. If she would stay that way, if he could stay with his ear this near the loudness of the creek. He can feel the molly watching him, as if thinking *What then?* and he does not want to look again. Instead, watches her legs. And that is worse: their shaking. As if the muscles will not hold much longer. Beyond her, he can hear the river, its deeper roar. If he were down there, on his own, leaping rock to rock . . . As if she hears his thought, the molly steps closer, snorts. But when he glances over she is looking away, upstream, toward the ridgetop. Yes, leaping rock to rock and leading them. After him. Up his river. To his home. He knows then he will not go again to either. Not so long as there are men left to follow him. Back the way he'd come from, there is their town. Up on the ridge, the trail full of riders. Between it and the water the canyonside keeps on upriver for another mile. Till it turns to cliffs. Bluffs of sheer granite, ledges jutting far enough out to fool you into thinking you might follow them, that the thin paths might take you all the way around. But they will not. The only way to get beyond the bluff: down at the river, over the boulders. Or on the trail high up. Between the two, no way to pass. Not for a horse. Or mule.

Soon as he thinks it, he looks away from her, down at the stream, its flow fast as before, its sound as constant, its current following the same twists and falls the land long ago set for its course, but the water itself changed: it has gone cloudy, turbid with churned mud, stirred by the passing, or the returning, of something up above.

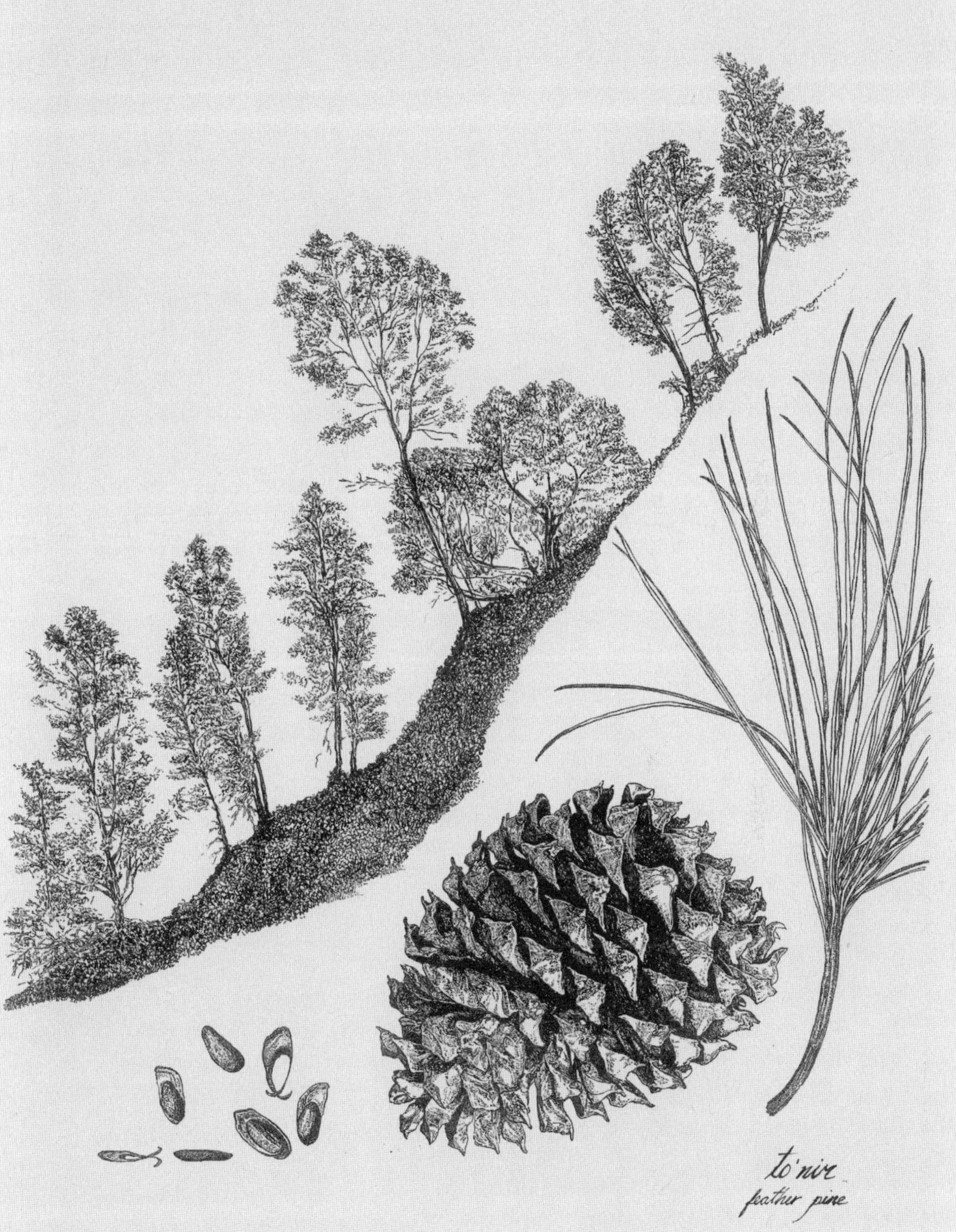
to'nir
feather pine

A picture: a giant floating pineboard box packed to its roof with 500 tns of salted pork. Your father standing on top. Bandages sagging loosening flapping away over the days till my hands cld grip an oar. Its handle 4 times long as my body. Me & 3 other rowers lifting & dipping our ft wide paddles in the ceaselessly flowing ohio. That whole first day out of cincinnati the river red with slaughterhouse blood. Surface slick with grease. A skim of fat clinging to our paddles as we plied our way west. Past banks of sewage-stained ice & cart-muddy snow. Wharfs & factories slowly giving way to farms & mills. The landscape near devoid of trees. But for the bucked logs choking the mouths of creeks. Backed up for miles. Waiting for the saw. Blast furnaces burning pig iron clean. Acres of forest to make 1 tn of ore. But each day that we rowed west the slash receding. Farmland dwindling. The woods returning a little more. Till it seemed we traveled less forwrd in distance than back in yrs. Decades. Twrd a time when we ourselves might disappear.

A picture: February. missouri. A mule cart. Me on the teamster's seat bundled in great coat & round-crowned hat. Wrapped in a blanket agnst the rain coursing off the mules' backs. Bside me on the bench an old potawatomi woman. Left bhind by her own tribe. Too weak to travel. Least according to the priest who hired me. Who rides ahead. His provisions filling the cart. The old squaw added to them in the hope that his returning her to her family will earn him a new flock. His faith that she will strengthen at the thought. Though each day she weakens. Slumping inside her robes. Till finally the Jesuit tells me to load her in back instead. Lay her atop the mound of supplies. So that she lies all day facing bhind. Twrd the place from which her tribe had been forced out. Marched west at gunpoint. The weak thrown on baggage wagons. Covered by tarps. Where they were baked. Unable to breathe. Smothered. Elderly. Babies. More than 40 the priest wld later tell me. On the day he found the old woman finally expired. In his fury throwing his own tarp over her body. Swearing she would gain him gratitude even delivered dead.

Another: Nearer the end of winter. Mid-March of '39. The town of Independence. A warehouse so huge it could have held all the remaining members of her tribe. But packed instead with furs. Plews stacked thirty feet high. Filling the building all the way back. Disappearing into its dark expanse. Through wall cracks streaks of sunlight. Stripes of russet and dun. Fox. Painter. The spotted pelts of cubs. Snow-white weasels and mink. Thin bands of skunk and broad ones of wolverine and the silvery gleam of otter. Black shag of bear. But mostly beaver. Mound after mound. Brown peltries piled to the roof.

And sitting before them dwarfed by the mass: a man. Behind a desk. Two handguns set on top. Their hammers cocked. Across from him: me standing in my suit and battered bowler. I had taken to keeping a pencil in my pocket again. For comfort as I had when I was young. My slacks pockmarked with holes poked by its tip. Held up by a cinched rope. My waist so thin it showed my hipbones. My voice still thinner as I tried to explain what experience I brought. To claim as evidence the fact of my survival. And then in growing desperation speaking of my part in the publication of a journal written by one of his company's own men. As if my drawings had been the reason I had left. Telling him I could not shake the scenes. Had traveled all this way hoping the American Fur Company might have some use for me.

Not unless, he said, you can draw me a ton of peltries.

But when I mentioned the author's name, the man's face changed. You say you know him?

The lie I answered with seemed as small as the single word it took. After all that I had read, I figured I knew the author better than the man before me. Found I recalled enough to make him think it too. Though in the end I don't believe that was what swayed him, but simply what so many others had already seen in me—the Ohio polemen keeping to themselves, sleeping with knives; the look in the priest's eyes, as if he thought the old woman died from something I'd done; Go on, Lamont had said, and meant away from her, from everything, everyone—what, flipping picture by picture, month by month, through my way west, you might see too: a darkening beneath my growing beard, a hardening deeper than hunger, the shape of your father freed from the need to fit into a space left by society. For I had tried. To fit a life alongside others. And failed. In childhood and fatherhood and my attempts at treatment. And plying northward up the Missouri, poling a keelboat loaded with supplies, making my way beside the crew on horse- and mule-back into such peaks as I had never seen, through valleys blanketed in buffaloe as wholly as pigeons once had smothered skies back east, our band of a few dozen men passing into a wilderness so vast it seemed to sweep aside all signs of us, I knew that I was done.

Do you remember when I was young, how my father reached to hold my face in his two hands? Told me there was no poison in me, no disease. You can get well, he'd said. Your mind is good. Insisted that was God's greatest gift. But I had long since ceased to believe in Him, His words holding no more meaning for me than for another beast or bird or fish. My mind increasingly aligned more with them than men. So that, as we made our way through such an endless expanse, I began to imagine how I might find within it a space for my own shape.

Though it was not till near a month had passed, our party at last crossing into the Green River Valley, that I caught sight of the life that I'd signed on for. The stockade where I was to start my post was like a patch of the crowded world I'd left behind set down amid the wide-open one to which I'd come. Though surrounded by such a vastness that the small square of spikes looked so out of place I couldn't help but hope.

In Independence, I'd mailed to your mother what little coin I'd saved over the past two years. Been outfitted at the fur trader's with pistol and musket, knife and hatchet and traps, promised a horse, mule, tack. Found them waiting at the fort. Worn rigging patched with buckskin and sinew, an apishamore reeking of another man, a cow-hocked mule and swaybacked gelding the stable hand said I should call Dutchman, smirking as if naming the roan after a crutch was comment either on its gait or how I rode. Though those first months I rarely did. My possibles stayed packed. My days confined to buildings clustered beneath a square of sky squeezed by walls so high they hid even the peaks. My life spent in the dark storehouse, revising my ledger, accounting for all the goods that the fort used, all the peltries brought in by freer men. Already they'd begun to come out of the mountains, a trickle of furs that spring would turn into a flood. By then I'd earned a reputation among the others at the fort: soldiers and officers, buyers and sellers, company men and free, some come up too late that season to go out till after the rendezvous, some recovering from illness, wounds, Pawnee guides grown more accustomed to whites than their own kind, Blackfeet wives left behind by beaver-hunting husbands, tending half-breed daughters and sons. All keeping clear of me.

I kept to the storehouse. Slept on floor-thrown skins behind my desk, took my portion of meat or porridge back to the stink of half-dried plews. Better than trying to eat at the long benches, men on either side. Better sleeping among the storeroom's nests and feces than in the bunkroom stifling with others' sweat and breath. Even outside, during the day, the open space seemed to contain an entire town crowded into an acre, so that by summer I barely ever left the storeroom, would keep the door shut till it grew so hot I'd be about to faint. Then fling it open, retreat again to the dark stench, sit sweating at my desk. While those who had business with me stood in the opening. Spoke from there. All but the newest knowing to leave me space.

A thing the new ones soon discovered. A wolfer who tried to trade his dog-stink furs for whiskey and, when I told him we had none, forced his way in, tore through the storeroom digging at piles of pelts and overturning sacks, kicking aside my own belongings, all the while holding his pistol on me. Till, as if he thought I'd hid a flask in my own clothes, he began pawing my body. One night a band of drink-corned soldiers thought to cut a shine by leaping on me while I slept, pinning me to cut my beard, a crowd holding me down while one hacked with his knife, some joker shouting how I'd lived in there so long I'd grown a pelt, belting out a price: Ten times a beaver! Another time it was a bug-tit sent upriver by the company to check on me, the waistcoated runny-nosed man insisting on reviewing the past months' books. Me seated at my desk, him standing so near I could feel his knuckles on the chair back, hear him sniff every few seconds in my ear. Long minutes into hours. Each sniff the scrape of steel on flint. Scraping, scraping.

Till I lit. Burst up out of the chair, my fist grabbing his hair, my other smashing into his face, over and over, before I must have turned, was slamming his head against the desk, spattering the ledger with his blood. Which is all I remember of the quiet after—seconds, minutes, longer?—my eyes held on the bright wet splatter, small spots that I began to notice shaking, only to realize it was my own grip on the desk, it slowly coming to my clearing mind that the red spatter had burst from him. And then, as if the knowledge cleared my ears: the sound of breathing coming from the floor.

The soldiers escaped with nothing worse than a gnawed hand, a palm torn by my teeth, a finger bitten near in half, a gash across the chest of the one whose knife I had wrenched loose.

But the wolfer would never see through two eyes again, one of them crushed by bits of cheekbone crashed into the socket with the butt of his own gun, the barrel still hot in my singed hand, the feeling coming back, as if my skin had forgotten how to sense pain. But not his. I can still hear him as he fled, his howling garbled through broken teeth, his hands holding the wreckage of his eye. And if I shut my own, I can see him too: his stumbling shape coming into my sight, my eyes clearing of the anger that had blinded me till then. And would again and again.

That elsewhere would have gotten me sent to the penitentiary. But there only set me free of the fort. I'd signed on to work as factor for a full year, wageless till my second one in exchange for all that the company provisioned me, but by that summer's rendezvous they'd sent word I was to leave my post, accompany a party heading up the Hoback. A band of bosslopers engaged with the AFC, a clutch of freemen tagging along for safety. Twenty-some trappers in all. Including one who'd never used the traps in his saddlebags or musket slung over his shoulder, who knew none of the other men and none of the country, but carried with him out of the Green River Valley into the passes of the Wyoming Range all of the hope that he'd held close to his heart all his way west.

How in all those days of picturing scenes I'd drawn out of that trapper's diary; how in all my nights imagining how it might be among those streams and swales; how, listening in my mind to quiet rippling after the slaps of beaver tails; how, in all of that, had I not heard the splashing of the others in the water, the way, returning downriver in the evening, I'd come around a bend and see a dozen men fleshing, drying, chopping, talking? How could I not have known that by the time I'd reach them there'd be nothing else that I could hear? Eating supper, I'd cross the river just to put its roar between us, forgo the fire's light and heat, find instead a boulder or tree behind which I could hide them from my sight. Though I'd have to remain near enough that they could hear my shout, bring my bedroll close enough in case they'd need to reach me.

Maybe five or ten years earlier it would have been more possible to go off on my own. Maybe I would have despite the dangers. But in that first year alone I'd see grizzlies destroy two men, maul a third so badly he had to be strapped to a mule like a load of peltries. Would watch someone lose half his hand in his own trap, another drown, more than I can count come down with sicknesses too bad to pull through without the ministrations of companions. Would learn the need for others to bring you food when you were weak, shoot a bruin when your gun jammed, help you work a rough press big enough to pack down a year's worth of peltries, man a mackinaw when it was time to boat them back. Still, there'd been years past when it was done: lone hiverannos making their way through the mountains on their own, meeting only at the rendezvous, all the year between hearing no other voices but those of Blackfeet or Pawnee. But that was decades earlier, before more than a score of trappers had ever worked the rivers or the first steamboat had plied its way up, bringing scores more, before Forts Bonneville or Vasquez or Saint Vrain had stood their walls around soldiers and traders, before the Blackfeet and Pawnee had begun to fight to stem the tide, before a party of two dozen whites had to expect to lose a few to raids, a smaller one risked being wiped out entire, a single man alone marked for lance or arrow sure as tattooed. A trapper heading off without another would have been reckoned dead before he'd left the rendezvous. Even a squaw man whose wife might once have meant protection from her tribe. Even one of the old voyageurs who, in decades past, might have trapped on his own.

By now there was no way to escape others. Or them me. Or either of us the fits that I grew famous for in camp, the fights that grew out of them, the thing that twisted my face into a sight they mocked to mask their fear. Though they could not have been as scared as I. As, day after day, making our way deeper into the mountains, I lost a little more of my last hope.

That summer we traveled down the Hoback, that fall made camp along the Snake, at each split into teams claiming sections of surrounding creeks. Despite my relief at being hired to keep the books, I'd lived with peltries long enough to believe that, when it came time to trap, I'd be able to do what I'd need to. But the first time I caught a beaver I set the snare too shallow, found its snout sticking up out of the water, nostrils breathing, eyes two spots of terror. I could not bring myself to slice its throat. Had to slosh in, drag the chain deeper, stand on the links to keep the creature under. Stood there with my eyes shut, hands over my ears, feeling its panic shiver through the chain up into me. A beaver can stay down near a quarter hour before its breath gives out. By the time the chain went still I was shaking so violently, breathing so hard, the bossloper tasked with training me came running, thinking I'd smashed my hand inside a trap.

After that I learned to stake them in water deep enough the heavy jaws around the beaver's leg would ensure it drowned. Found the lifeless bodies as free of presence as the cadavers I'd once drawn, their dead eyes no longer stares through which I'd witness myself standing there. And even if, after slitting a beaver's belly, ripping its hide free, I'd sometimes stare at the fleshed body, my muscles prickling; even if, each time I brought my day's catch back to camp, I'd feel the presence of my partners a little stronger, as if my skin had been stripped to the fascia as well; even still, I made it near a fortnight working alongside the two of them before I began needing to flee. Farther and farther, till I was trapping on my own. I'm sure they were glad to see me go. Each morning, riding past them sitting beside their fire or out checking their traps, I'd feel their watching, sense them wondering if they'd ever see me ride back.

I'd ride far enough I could no longer feel them, far enough the bellow building in me would subside. A thing that Dutchman seemed to sense, would stop and stand there, wholly still, ears swiveled back as if waiting to hear me breathe. Which I then could. And watching his ears turn forward again, I'd lie forward over his neck, let his heartbeat slow my own.

By the season's end I was staying gone three, four nights at a time. Long enough to feel how it might be: the rillet's babble covering their sounds downstream, the stars above unsmudged by any smoke save my own fire's. The space. Out there in those high mountains it was as if the press of others I'd felt all my life was simply lifted, their presence blown away by wind, so thinned sometimes I could imagine

And then a gunshot would break through. A distant whoop. A shard of laughter. Or simply, after a couple nights alone with just the creek and horse and mule and me, I'd be forced to pack, reset my traps, go back.

Much to the disappointment of the others. The entire party having placed bets on if I would return. Each time I did, someone cried out, Hall's back! Followed by groans. Unbroken by a single hallo. None asking after my hunting. Not even ribbing. Not a smile. Not that I blamed them. Or would have known how to take anything else. Let alone return a smile, call out a hallo of my own.

The most that I could manage was a brief thanks beside the cook fire. My cup filled with coffee, my bowl with broth, the others—kind enough to let me partake in what the party supped on together so long as, now and then, I brought in a doe, gutted some fish, took my turn peeling a batch of beaver tails—as glad to let me retreat beyond the firelight to eat as I was to disappear into the dark, their ribbing dwindling as I sought out the river's rush, slept near enough to make believe I was still a day away, up another creek. In the morning, I'd rise while the rest slumbered, be gone by the time they stirred. There were a few I could stand better than the others, who stood me better too, and we'd work together stretching parfleche, packing bundles of plews, digging out our winter cache. And perhaps if I'd not been given a glimpse of what it could be like without them, I might have even managed to make something like a friend. But coming from my days alone back into the others' presence only made it harder, softened the shell I built against it so that it hit me worse.

Though even that couldn't prepare me for what it would be like come winter. Those months after we'd cached our furs and built a lodge to shelter us till spring, rode out snowstorms so heavy we had to dig to reach the horses, their breath-clouds against the darkness of their lean-tos always a little shocking, as if in all that stillness it was surprising to find anything living. We kept ourselves alive by mostly staying shut up inside the lodge. The other trappers playing jaw harps or skin drums, singing songs, dealing cards around a circle. The score of us devouring whole bucks in a single sitting, the cold making us crave flesh and fat even as we grew fat ourselves, sick from eating solely muscle and grease. All of us packed close in that low building for those long months, the walls hung with carcass chunks, the floor smothered in furs, the air nearly as heavy with their scent as the stench of us. Sometimes it seemed the only way I was part of the group. I had again sunk into muteness, spent whole days hunkered in a corner drawing over and over on an already covered page. Till what little lead and ink and paper I had left was all used up. Turned then to coals, birch bark, anything to keep the rest at bay. There were days I'm sure that they forgot that I was there, days when, feeling them unaware of me, I could stop drawing long enough to let their speaking in.

At night the old hiverannos liked to talk. Afflicted by the sleeplessness of age, wistfulness too. Coon, they'd say to some younger trapper, you should've seen it then. Speak of the Shining Mountains before they were the Rockies, before there'd been more than a handful of men like them. Mostly French. Maybe fifty in all. On all the rivers, in all the holes. As little as two decades ago, when it was still possible to spend a season crossing pass to pass and never see another trapper, to call an entire range your own, belonging to you as much as to the Pawnee, Blackfeet, or Crow. Tribes that, back then, would befriend you or leave you alone. Herds of buffaloe so unbounded it was impossible to imagine them ever thinned, so much beaver a single bossloper would need an entire mule string to pack it out, prices so high you could buy a dozen more mules with one season's haul. Or get yourself a squaw and have enough still left to keep her happy. In a few more seasons, enough to retire, live the lazy life with a wife and little ones in a lodge up on a mountain all your own. They'd known men who'd done it, one or two who'd even gone it alone, would begin recalling who, till some younger trapper might interject about the world they lived in now, insist on how he thought they still had it pretty good. Only to be quieted by looks of pity. Coon, one of the hiverannos would say sadly, you should've got here twenty years ago.

And I would find I had to leave, would shove up from my corner in sudden clamor, the others' glances jerking to me, their stares following my mad rush out into the moonlit snow, my moccasins kicking a spray beneath my flapping robe till I was far enough away I couldn't hear their calls. Would stare up at the swaying pines, their branches sweeping futilely at stars.

I could have stood there for an hour, more, all night till I froze. Nobody would have followed, reached to my shoulder, said, Coon, you all right? Nobody would have been fool enough. By then the men who, all that fall, had bet on whether I'd make it back to camp had changed their wagers. Now, trapped inside with me during storms that blew for days, they placed great sums of beaver on which of them I would kill first. Who would kill me. None doubting that, before spring came, there would be murder.

And yet I made it to the thaw, and through that season's trapping, and all the way to the next rendezvous.

They were held midsummer—the close of June, cusp of July—the main marker of time for every trapper in that country as far back as the mid-twenties. Sometimes set as far to the east as the junction of the Wind and Popo Agie, sometimes as far west as Bear Lake, but mostly in the Green River Valley, along Ham's Fork or Blacks, or just below Horse Creek. Each year the mountains spilled half a thousand trappers out, the floodplain filling with bosslopers and mule skinners, free and engaged. Whole companies poled rafts piled with a ton or two of peltries, whooping as they rounded the river bend, so much gunsmoke from such thundered revelry the boats themselves appeared to have caught fire, men leaping into the water out of sheer eagerness to join the rest. Pack trains stretching half a mile, the muleteers shouting at beasts so laden they seemed huge mounds of plews moving atop their own hoofed feet, the whole range emptying out into a valley already loud with calls of traders hawking powder, lead, razors, buckles, haggling over the price of beaver—how many for a new knife, a rebored musket, half a flask of whiskey—liquored whoops ringing out at a first swig, or sight of someone unglimpsed since the last rendezvous, or simply from relief at having made it to another. All those humans talking in all that mash of English and French and Spanish and Arapahoe, Blackfoot, Coeur d'Alene, Pawnee. Whole villages set up along the banks, bringing the shouts of children, barks of dogs, the smoke of their fires mixing with the trappers' own in air already dense with the stench of horse sweat and mule shit and human scat and the rank remnant of death rising off packs of pressed peltries stacked high as hills. A reek so thick it seemed a thing that could be felt. The way all of it was by me, their presence pressing against my skin, each second building in me the need to flee.

The sole thing stopping me the liquor. Tanglefoot, some called it, some awerdenty. But to me it was simply the only way I could get through the rendezvous, could make myself come from the mountains into the melee, face the traders long enough to swap my furs for what I'd need to stay alive another year, my first trade made to keep me that way the next few days: an entire pack of beaver—seventy prime plews, a whole month's hunt—exchanged for a jug just big enough to last twenty-four hours, build up just enough buffer, seep through my pores, slick my skin, thicken like wax around a wick, till the crowd milling around me could no longer touch me.

Not that they would have tried. My reputation already spread enough by those I'd trapped with to stop the rest wishing to so much as speak to me. Almost as good as the awerdenty. Which I'd bring away from the worst churn, walk out beyond teepees and wickiups toward the herds. Take out my pens, new-purchased paper and ink, hope to make the whiskey last a little longer. Drawing corned worked even better. If I could stay just sober enough to scratch out lines, I could almost convince myself I was drawn too. As if I could be transferred to the page as well, walled off within the paper's edge. At least till the bottle I'd bought ran out.

I'd retained just enough beaver to buy another. But by the time I tried, the price had soared. And when I demanded why, the trader looked at me as if I must have been the last man in the valley to hear the news.

Hats, he said. Changing styles, silk. Spoke of how many greenhands like me the companies had shipped up the Missouri the past two years, the fewer pelts that came back even so, the beaver all but tapped out. Even that dwindling supply more than any company now could sell. Or would still try to. The word come down from the bushways that this July on the Green River would be the last of the great rendezvous.

I knew then why, as I had shoved toward the trader's tent, the throng had seemed to seethe around me with even greater urgency, their sound set to a higher thrum, every man among them corned. Other than me.

Otter, I told him, each plew worth two beaver. Offered him marten, black fox and red. All I had left. And when it still was not enough, I tried to pawn my pens, my paper and ink, would have traded in my guns if one of the others behind me in line had not revealed my name. The trader, soon as he heard it, refusing to trade.

By then I'd been dry of drink for long enough the awerdenty's buffer had melted off my skin, my skull begun to feel like it was shrinking, and when I finally got beyond the crowds back out beside my hobbled horse and mule, I sat down in the last light, took up my pad and pens, began with feverish fury to draw the herd around me. Ponies. The short and stocky paints and dapples belonging to a camp of Arapahoe. The children sent to guard them already grown bored of watching me. So that, as long as I kept my gaze on paper or herd, I could pretend I was alone among their grazing. An easing. The sound of their teeth ripping the grass, the feeling of their footsteps coming faintly through the ground. The nudge of Dutchman's muzzle at my back, his breath warm on my neck. The drawing almost letting me forget.

Till, just before dark, two men I didn't know came wending through the herd toward me. The horses' heads lifting to watch, dropping as they passed. The whole field seeming to ripple with the pair's approach. I looked back at the page, the dying light almost too low for me to see. The crickets had begun, their sound so thick my crosshatching started to match the rhythm of their sawing. Through it: the thinner rasp of pantlegs through grass. A nicker. I dipped my pen, started shading again. The crickets quit. And there was just the scratching of the nib. The brushing of the men's steps going against it. Then gone too. And my pen dry.

Nice horses, one said.

His voice in the crickets' absence was startlingly loud, and glancing up, I saw he was mere steps away. Peering over at my paper. He was the shorter of the two, his hair cropped close, shorn by the same blade that must have scraped his face, his welted skin still raw, the knife-burn on his neck somehow made worse by the red kerchief knotted around it.

The other man said, See? He was thinner, older. Said to the first, I told you he could draw. His face was freckled like a trout except where it was covered by a red beard, the hair gone gray over his cheeks, the color still deep around his chin and mouth. Above it, his eyes were baggy and bleary as my own felt.

Horses, the rashed man said. Like somehow they didn't count.

I set down my pen. I know you?

Holding out his hand, he told me, John Goss.

The freckled one said, Fancher.

John Goss and Fancher Hovey. They'd trapped together nearly three years—Fancher for a decade before that—all through the Tetons, the Wasatch, far west as Willow Valley. Unless, Fancher said, you count the coast of Calafornia. I sat there on the sawbuck looking up to meet their gazes, the page of sketches on my lap.

This your first rendezvous? Goss asked.

And Fancher answered for me: Second.

My forearms settled over the paper, as if to cover what I'd done.

Ain't you come up the spring before? Fancher continued.

I could feel the wet ink stick to my skin. What do you want?

A smile split Goss's raw face, the sore place below his nose wrinkling in a painful-looking way. What do *you*? he said. The smile slipped again behind closed lips, as if he thought he already knew.

Whiskey, I told him.

And from the bag slung over his shoulder he took out a small flask, unscrewed the top and swigged and, while I watched, handed it to Fancher.

And, I said, for the two of you to leave.

Through his throat-burn Fancher said, I heard you knew a man who'd been to Calafornia too. And handing the flask back to Goss, said, With Walker.

There was that smile again. Nip?

I took it, took a long slug. And when I was done, I did not give it back.

Leonard, Fancher suggested, as if he'd just remembered.

Heard, Goss said, you knew him so good he let you read his diaries.

They watched me knock back another swig. Big enough to make me cough.

And when I was done, the older one asked me, How much do you remember? Then, at my pause, motioned with his hand for me to drink again.

I could see Goss torn between watching the flask and me. Made it easy for him by lifting it back to my lips. Oh, I said, most everything.

Then tipped the flask to block them out. And when I brought it down again, I told them how I'd been hired to draw the illustrations for the book, required to read so closely I could see what old Zenas Leonard described in my own mind, how it had been inside there ever since, strong as my own memories. And, screwing the cap back on, I admitted that, to my knowledge, the book had never been sent to print. Which, I said, holding the flask out to them, must make me one of the only men ever to have read a word.

Hoss, Goss said, lifting his palm, patting the air between us as if to push the flask back to me, if you can write good as you draw . . .

Or, Fancher cut in, draw us a map.

. . . you can just keep it.

I did my best to give Goss his own smile back. Said, When you leaving?

Soon's you're done.

That right? I said to Fancher.

Is, he said.

You gonna read it first? I turned to Goss. Asked him, You?

We got a third, Goss said. He can read good.

Well. I tossed the flask back. Good luck to the three of you.

Goss caught it, shook it. Hell, he muttered. And, for a second, I thought he would be mad. But all he said was, There's a bottle back at our camp you can have too.

When I picked the pen up again, I could feel their eyes go to it, their weight shift as if they thought they might stand there however long it took me to write or draw. But instead of dipping the tip back in the ink, I brought it to my mouth, cleaned it, wiped it, set it back in its case, the stopper back down the ink bottle's throat, gave it a pound. And, standing, said, Tell you what. I will take that bottle if you take me.

It did not take long to agree to details: each for himself supplying mount and mule, arms and traps, all his own possibles; any other provisions to be paid for by the men already partnered; all guidance west of the Battle Lakes to be provided by me. That night I was to pasture my animals alongside theirs. Less to make sure our herd stayed safe than to ensure I stayed till morning, did not absquatulate with a hundred beavers worth of awerdenty. Already I knew I'd need the bottle to make it through supper. Though, when I told them I'd bed down with the horses at the edge of camp, they seemed to expect it. As if that was something Fancher had heard too.

All the while that I packed up, Fancher kept looking at the papers I'd set on the ground, glancing from them to the horses and back again, as if trying to pick out which was which. Or maybe just because he liked it. It made me like him better, made me think if I could mostly deal with him, I might just make it through. But when I'd rolled my papers back in their otter skin, placed my pens back with my possibles, saddled my horse, it was the one I'd already learned to call JG who mounted my mule as I swung up on Dutchman. Fancher, having already raised a hand, walked away to seek out the third man.

I watched him disappear. And riding beside JG toward the more crowded camps, I felt the presence of all those there come at me like a gust, thinning the already too-thin buffer of whiskey.

Don't worry, JG said beside me. Fanch'll find him. Fill him in.

I asked what was the third man's name again.

But JG only replied, It'll be fine.

From somewhere in the melee there floated a few fiddle strains, and reaching for the flask, I heard the drum thuds start, a jaw harp's distant twang, the music coming from a fire not far away. One of the hundreds burning all across the valley, the flames sucking the last light from the dusk so that the spaces between seemed black as night, the darkness, as we rode nearer, separating into silhouettes of men: trappers in the throes of dancing, whirling and stamping in time to the jangling same of squaws. Then JG was off the mule, and dismounting after, back on the ground, I could feel their thumping feet beneath my own, the drums shaking my chest, the fiddle bow on my skin. Unscrewing the flask again, I made myself continue. Took a slug, a step, a slug. And, by the time the whiskey was gone, I'd followed JG into the firelight's faint reach. Close enough to see his partner talking to another across the flames. To know, though I had never seen the man till then, that the fourth in our party would be Abail Ballou.

The Frenchman stood half a head higher than any other dancer, a voyageur whose name had run through the rendezvous as much as mine. With as much unease. Though, instead of cut with scorn, it was said with begrudging awe: his feats of curly wolfery, the glee he seemed to take in snapping bones and smashing teeth, simply his size.

Wait here, JG told me. And I would have turned and walked away if they hadn't already seen me. Fancher pointing me out, Ballou turning to peer over the flames.

The fiddler kept playing, the squaw beside him on the jaw harp too, the dancers stomping and swaying. But in those standing around, there passed a rippling that was both movement and stilling. The talking thinned. The Frenchman stepped away from Fancher, then through the dancers, his face forming as he passed by the fire—bright eyes above a long straight nose that seemed to cleave his visage more perfectly in half than most, his beard too thick to see his mouth, his knot of hair tied off his nape but for a few sweaty, loosed strands; he had been dancing and his skin-shirt was open at the neck, his shining chest covered in curls clumped wet and gleaming—and then the fire's brightness was behind him and he was just a dark shape coming.

The fiddler sawed, the drums went on. I flicked a glance at them, saw the squaw return my stare, the harp a blur of movement at her mouth, her fingers working it.

When I looked back again, Ballou was there.

I hear, he said, you've signed on to dance with me.

I made myself extend a hand. But instead of gripping it, he only raised his own huge paws into the space between us and sent them flapping, his thick wrists flipping back and forth, big fingers fluttering wildly. Behind them: his smile. I knew what he was doing; he'd known I would. His smile widened into a grin. Easy, bonich, he said, just showing you how glad I am to meet, the way I heard you like to—

My hand struck out, slapping to smack his flapping ones away, but they were gone, somehow already reaching round me, hauling me in. Even now I can still feel it: the press of his huge chest, the way he stooped to smother me, his beard mashing my face, his chinbone a stone on my skull. I pushed back, but his hug was like the chain and pole of a rough press squeezing plews into a pack, and jerking my face free of his reek, I told him to get off. Dragged in a ragged breath, shot out the words again.

Oh, I heard you, he said. And, squeezing harder: Hall, I have heard all about you.

My face was crammed so close against his neck that, craning back to breathe, I could make out the rawhide strip tying his hair, would have reached up and grabbed it, jerked that giant skull, but I could not wrench free.

He stood there pinning me, his heat crawling my body. I shut my eyes.

The drumming died, the fiddle quieted, the jaw harp went on alone. In its twanging I could hear the dancers' stamps dwindle away, feel their stares, and beyond the fire's edge, others watching from the dark, and farther still, the countless rest, and all their presence packed inside the Frenchman's grip, all of their breath contained in Ballou's own blowing hot across my hair, head, skull, his heartbeat thudding my cheek, my mashed mouth, my throat, the heat starting to rise inside me, the blackness to sweep over my mind, and pushing back, I heard somebody shout, Look out, he's 'bout to pop!

Ballou's voice came through his throat against my temple, less sound than feeling passed from his flesh to mine. That true? he said. You about to—

And I slammed upward into his chin, my crown pounding his jaw so hard I heard it crack, his bone or mine, did it again—his teeth, my head—was bellowing, Get off! or grunting it, or maybe not saying anything at all, but it was all that I could hear, the need so great I would have broken my own skull against his face if it would have freed me from his grip. But his chin was no longer there. My head snapped back into nothing but beard, and I was falling beneath his falling body into the slam of all his smashing weight, my head smacking the ground, lifting and smacking again, the back of my skull wildly seeking his face too far away to hit. Then gone. His grip gone. And in the second of relief, he flipped me, rolled me onto my chest, his bulk pinning me down, crushing my arm beneath me. My other was wrenched behind my back, cranked in his fist, lifting, lifting, and I could feel the weight of all the others pressing against the bone, about to break it, to snap the thing in me that always blew, that in all the brawls I'd been in had never failed to burst me free, that burst inside me then, and burst again, over and over, tearing through my own mind instead, trying to come out.

Scream, my father had said, and it will be the sound they hear forever. Every time you try to speak or they spy you, they will remember. Said it to me some two dozen years before, after he'd learned a neighbor's kids had taunted me, how I had lost control. Fight if you have to, he'd said, or simply run. So long as you don't let them hear your fear or fury or whatever is inside you. By which he meant whatever was wrong with me. But lying there, face in the mud, arm cranked behind me, I could not stop it, could only clamp down on the sound, try to keep it from exploding into a shout.

Through my moaning I heard somebody holler, I think he likes it! Then laughter. Then nothing but my groans, their swelling inside me swamping all else.

I only knew the sound had ceased when the Frenchman's voice came through the silence: You done? How long had he been saying it? Again, beside my ear: You done? Then just his breath nearby my face, his beard matted with blood, his bubbling lips when he said, Good. So close I felt the spray. Good, he said, I'm glad we got that out.

Rising, he released me, the night suddenly cool on the back of my head, my nape, my shoulders, lifting away everything except his moccasin jabbing my ribs. I let it push, my arm hurting too bad to move, till he had rolled me over with his foot. Stood above me, reaching down. His hand huge, his grin parting his beard. A smile wide enough to overcome even his bloody lips. Silas, was it? he said.

I said nothing, moved nothing.

Quiet, he said. Withdrew his hand. And, reaching behind his head, pulled his ponytail tight. Silas, he said, you stay quiet and calm as that and I believe we will make out all right.

I shut my eyes, listened to the sounds begin again—the fiddle striking up where it had stopped, the squaws' beads rattling, the thumping boots and moccasins—felt the berth they left around me in the scuffed dirt and busted grass.

But I could not stop seeing his bloody mouth, his spit-slicked beard. Feeling his fists in the bones of my wrists, his breath on my face. Could not stop hearing his name, pounding again and again, inside my head.

Abail Ballou. Abail Ballou.

You cannot know who the first man you will kill will be or even will you will you will you. But I will tell you, I will tell you this: he was the first I knew I wanted to.

AUTUMN, 1849

Here on the cliffside, where the sheer drop stops in a single ledge just wide enough to fit the mule, there is no cover, the roar of the river below unmuffled by anything but air. Through it, he speaks to the molly, stroking her neck, his torso twisted on the sawbuck so he can watch behind: a blast of crossbills exploding out of the trees, their specks spanning the canyon like a net cast out toward the other side, while on this one the canopy stirs as if with memory of the flock, instead of just the passing of the posse of miners riding beneath. For a moment longer, Silas holds the molly back, keeping her there until, hearing the shout, he's sure that he's been seen. Then, leaning a little nearer her ear, hitching the rein, he clicks her carefully forward again.

The cliff is granite, a bluff left by boulders tumbled off into the river, the water raging at their remains a hundred feet below, the rockface above him rising another hundred up. Riding between, he guides the mule along an ever-thinner ledge, broad enough for two to ride abreast back where it starts and, even here, before it curves out of sight, wide enough for one. Still, the molly balks, as if she knows. He pats her neck, says it'll be okay, and when she starts forward again tells her, "Good girl." Or tries: the words stick in his throat. Instead, he clicks his tongue, even that sound less certain than it should be. Around the bend, another, until she seems to have regained her trust in him—and the ledge ends. Broken off abruptly as if chiseled, the fallen rock shattered far below. She stands still, neck stiff, even her tail stopped flicking, only her sides swelling and easing. Him, on her back, as motionless. Her ears turn to him, twitch. Where is his sawing of the reins—*back, back*—his voice: Easy, easy. Gently he reaches to one of her ears, strokes it, its softness shocking. Though not as shocking as it must be to her to feel his shifting weight when, slowly, carefully, he swings over her cliffward side. The space is so tight he bangs his elbow, snags his possibles, before he steadies himself on the sliver of ledge between rockface and mule, his movements cramped as he sets down the musket, unlashes the rucksack, and, shushing at her scared stamping, lifts it off. Last, he tugs free the sawbuck pad, stuffs the blanket into the bag, cinches it tight. Her muzzle on his cheek, her eyes barely a foot from his, wide with confusion or fear or maybe merely understanding as, unslinging the rifle from his back, he shrugs on the rucksack.

From around the cliff-wall, ricocheting off the far ridge: a call that could be the high *keeeer* of a red-shouldered hawk, but isn't. Another, shouted back. Too far to make out words, but near enough to know they'll soon be here. Slipping the musket into its scabbard, he swings it over his shoulder, the old gun loaded with the last ball left that fits it. Except the one hung from his neck. For a second, he lifts the pendant No Rope had given him, feeling its weight, tracing the strips of sinew shrunken around the lead, his face hard at the thought. Then lets it drop, squats down, picks up the rifle.

This time when he holds out his hand, it is palm up, extended to the molly, as if he has something to give her. But there is just his bare skin, her warm breath, the softness of her nose. He shuts his eyes, keeps them shut until the breath is lifted, the softness gone. Then tells her, "Rest a while," and begins to climb.

Halfway up—the mule maybe fifty feet below, hidden behind the cliff-bulge now, out of sight around the last turn they made together—he finds what he is looking for: a rock-shelf jutting out just enough, another above casting just enough shade. Wedging himself prone, knees splayed, elbows propped on the stone, the rifle barrel safe from sunglint, he studies the canyonside back the way he'd come.

They are spread along the slope, a couple riders crashing above the trail he'd left, three others doing the same below, the bulk—five, he counts, then six, seven—riding in a line over the molly's prints. He sights on the lead one's chest, black nick beneath the collar, then shuts his eyes, learning the rifle's weight, balance, listening to the river below, its roar a whisper so near his ears its breath shivers his beard, his bunched brow smoothing—*easy*—jaw coming unclenched—*easy*—breath growing steady—*okay*—eyes opening just as the lead rider comes to the cliff and stops. The flick of reins, his horse's flinch. When they are fully on the ledge Silas shifts his aim to the next, trying to keep his breathing steady, discern the difference in the new gun's sights, anticipate its kick and barrel-rise, his only movement a faint fluttering of finger on trigger. The man follows the other out of view around the cliff. And Silas matches the bead up with the next. One after another, he sights, breathes, listens to the river, watches some stalks of poison oak for signs of breeze down on the rock, strokes the smooth metal with his finger, lets another rider pass, shifts to the next. Till half the men are on the ledge, the others funneling in to follow, just four more left on the slope, then three—any second now the one at the head will round a bend, find the molly empty-backed at the trail's end—and then the second to last is on and . . . There is the shout. An urgent holler that must roll back from man to man because the closest one Silas can still see reins at his horse, cranks his head to warn the others, the last still on the slope suddenly stopping, and Silas fires. Beneath the rider the horse whirls as if spun by the shot. But the man is spurring him, seeming unhit. The musket—Silas grabs it—the heavier boom: the last of the big caliber balls smashes into the rider's back.

In the time it takes Silas to reload the rifle—open the breech, half-cock the hammer, snap on the cap—the last rider manages to back his horse almost off the ledge, almost enough to turn. But the feel of the musket-shot is in Silas by then, atop the rifle-shot before, and pulling the trigger he does not even pause to see where the bullet hit—the man already falling, the horse starting to tumble—but lies flat to load another, pops up again. The third in line is gone, his horse's saddle empty. For a second, Silas scans the cliff. Climbing? Blocked from sight? Then there's a flash of shirt-color through the horse's legs—the rider dropped behind the animal for cover—and, aiming for the big rolling eye, Silas tries to squeeze the trigger, but the rifle is gone from his hands, replaced by the soft nuzzling of a muzzle, the eye become the deep brown of the molly's, and when he shoots he cannot keep the gun from jerking up off the horse. Maybe the bullet hits anyway—the rifle's sight skewing his aim again—maybe it's just fright from the ball blowing by, but the horse shies, slips, and, in a scrabbling panic, drops its thousand pounds down on the man. Raising the breech, Silas keeps his stare locked on his loading, tears the cartridge paper with his teeth. Even as, below, the crushed man's screams cut through the panic of his companions, the thrashing of something down in the brush: man or horse, neither meant to be here, die here, litter the canyon with its bones. Below the screams: the river's murmur. Silas pours powder with shaking hands. Placing the cap, his fingers slip. Above the rapids' sound: the crossbills' *kip-kip-kip*. He shuts his eyes, snaps the breech, cocks the hammer, and when he opens his eyes again he sees the two riders below, trapped between those ahead and the shot horse behind, frantically trying to back their own. The rearmost mount catches a hoof on the fallen body, slips, its rider desperately leaping free as, together, they tumble over the edge. And swinging his sight onto the other still on the ledge—the boom and kick—Silas sends him flailing after. Five men. Seven others safe around the corner, blocked from his sight by cliff-rock. But blocked from moving too.

Reloading the rifle, he crabs back out of the boulder's shadow and, leaving the empty musket behind, scrambles hold-to-hold with his free hand, fast as he can around the cliff-bulge that blocks his view, scanning below for a first glimpse of ledge trail. Then for the molly where he'd left her. Except she isn't there. Only the empty ledge. And then a glint—a man on foot, swinging his rifle—the crash and flare of Silas's own: the other seems to split in two, his body lunging toward the cliff, his forearm spinning away over the canyon, rifle still in its grip. And Silas is half falling himself in his sliding rush to reach the wounded man, alive or dead, but gunless. Unlike the one who is suddenly there, less than a dozen feet away, stepping out as if expecting Silas to be reloading instead of drawing a revolver, the pepperbox's first shot already sinking the man's shirt into his belly as the second booms—the fabric billowing behind his back—a third, fourth, fifth slamming into the man, the last blast from the spinning barrel finally sending his body off the ledge, cracking against the cliff-edge, caroming out. It's then that Silas sees the molly, her broken shape down on the rocks beside the rest—five dead men below, six still alive up here—and, turning, begins climbing again for cover.

Only when he's high enough to be blocked from sight does he stop, crouch with his shoulders against the granite, reload the rifle, eyes ticking between the two sections of ledge-path he can still see. But the men are equally hidden from him, the six of them gathered in safety till one decides to try a shot or make a run back off the cliff. Or climbs. Or all six do it at the same time. No—he can hear, over the river's roar, one whimpering—at most there will be five.

For some time then there is only the wounded man's moaning. The grunt and blow of horses. From somewhere farther down, a fevered nicker. Nearer, the thrashing of whatever is dying in the scrub beside the cliff. Nearer still, the voices of the others, all but smothered by the river. *Hey!* Silas jerks the rifle toward the sound. Held so close, it has a smell. *You okay?* Face-sweat, or fish-slime, or blood. *You need help?* From the brown-skinned one, his cheek bashed in? Grease of the father's beard? There is the boy, again: the hole blown through his brow. Down below: a movement. Silas looks, already seeing crows. But instead of caws: the far-off rattle of a kingfisher. He searches for its flicker over the water. Just the current, the rocks, the bodies on the bank.

From one: the bellowing again. It strangles out, seems done.

Still: the moaning man. Still: the thrashing in the bush.

Silas's stare stays on the cliff below, but the sky is filling up with clouds, a wind rising, and above him snakeskins flap, the alder's branches shake in the gust, and for a second he shuts his eyes, waits for the moltings to settle. When he opens them again his hand has drawn the necklace out, fingers turning the pendant over and over, as if the sinews wrap river-smoothed stone instead of lead.

The voices of the men, the horses' grunts. The vultures come. The clouds, the wind: it will soon rain. He straightens a knee, the other, bends into his crouch again.

Down there the river rages, waiting. Each time his eyes catch the bodies of the horses, he cannot help imagining them move. All five—counting the mule—fallen so oddly close together they seem less likely dead than cast under some spell.

The rainclouds drag the day an hour nearer dusk. Still an hour away? Two? And how long has it been since he last heard the wounded man moan? The other's bellowing seems a thing that belongs to the beginning.

In the growing dimness, the horses' bodies are blurred spots. Why can't they disappear the rest of the way? Rise and walk, or fade into the darkness, either one.

There comes a nighthawk's squeezed *pee-yah pee-yah*, but no sign of the bird. A buck, stuttering down the steepness, stops beside the ledge-trail and, sensing either the dead or living, bolts.

When the rain appears, it is still light enough to see it spot the rocks, then slowly darken the bodies and boulders far below. Letting go the pendant, he unties the slicker from his still-shouldered pack, struggles into it not fully standing, hunches again, guns out of the rain, only the rifle muzzle jutting from the otter skin. Far down, in the river's near dark: the flap of wings, slaty and slow. The heron. Strange: all these years he's never seen it so far from his own home. And then it is not strange at all and he watches its slow flapping flight till it has disappeared.

When it's too dark to see the horses, he knows it's time to go. Waits a while longer to see if the others will think so too, leave their mounts, try to sneak by on foot.

Between the drumming rain and rushing river, he can no longer hear them. Or they have gone quiet. And in the quiet he hears all the echoes of all the gunshots they have made, him and the men, hears the ones yet to come, the way they will break through rain and river, carry over the entire canyon, fill the air, become the last of him his river will ever hear. And he can see the heron, now long out of sight, break its smooth flight, its body flinch, its wingflaps stutter. The rain and the river and the darkness of night. *Go,* he thinks. *Go now.* Feels his heartbeat increase inside him. Says it once, out loud: "Go." And waits. Waits. And when they don't, he does.

some company

My mountains. My mountains. There were my mountains. There rising up out of 1000 miles of dry & bitter flatness. Of dust caking our skin. Stuck in our throats. Of rocks carved by winds so strong they blew our horses off course & us reining them back into the gusts. Hunching over their bent necks with rags wrapping our faces. Following creek bottoms lined with sand that when the winds died & the sun slammed down we wld dig up. Bury our bodies. Lie in the earthen chill imagining that it was wet. Water. For days we had seen near to none. Shallow lakes so salty their shores were crusted. Rivulets reeking of lye. And there breaking the line of sky bfore us: snow. A snow white peak. A single bright spike far to the west lit by the morning sun. My first sight of the mountains that I had tried so long ago to draw. That I had not known had ever since been drawing at me. Till with that first glimpse I felt it pull. As if my blood & breath & body knew bfore my mind that I had at last laid eyes on home.

Ahead one of the others whooped. JG & Fancher & Abail Ballou riding abreast. The frenchman's horse as usual a couple necks in front. All 3 separate from mine. The way it had been for wks. Each grown more wary of me in the mnths since we had left the rendezvous. Back then we had wound westwrd through the salt river range accompanied by a score of others. A remuda of some 50 horses & mules kicking up dust down to the bear. But ½ the men had balked then. Turned off twrd the desert route to taos. Anothr group split at lake bonneville when it came clear we wld need to spend the rest of augst fattening our horses & building up our stores of meat waiting for the heat to ease enough to let us traverse the flats. The cooler weather coming only ½ way through septbr. By then the others had decided to drop south instead. Doubtful of our ability to cross the calafornia peaks bfore the bigger snows. Hoping to cut round the range. Same as Fancher had some dzn years ago with Smith. The ones meaning to try it now wanting him to lead them. Which I believe he wld have were it not for JG. The clear affection the 2 had for each other.

Too clear for some. A few of those bound for the southern route refusing to follow Fancher if JG was coming too. The older man unwilling then to leave the younger. The two planning to homestead together along the coast. Raise cattle in the grassland Fancher had been dreaming of since seeing it over a decade ago. What Ballou wanted, I did not know. He had made it all the way to the Great Salt Lake in '33. Only to be left back with another party when Walker pushed farther west. And maybe it was just to erase that memory. Prove he could do as much as any trapper. Maybe he imagined opening another pass. Discovering a lake. Places on maps that would be named Ballou. The way the river we would follow west was named for Ogden. Salt flats for Bonneville. Or maybe he wished instead to find a place where no one knew his name and so had not yet learned to fear him. Though in the end I came to think all he wanted was what he had back in the Rockies. Before they were trapped out. A life that would let him live as he wished. Be who he was. Beyond the reach of anyone to right him.

No, you cannot know who the first man you will kill will be. Or even will you. But you can know you want to. And it is the wanting that makes it worse.

I hope at your age you have not yet known either. Neither the wanting nor the doing. Have not had the need to end a life beyond what you might eat. Perhaps then you will think it much the same. And in others it may be. For I have seen in some an eagerness to kill. A thrill at the ability. But I could barely bring myself to trap. Would have eschewed eating all flesh if I could have found another way to survive. If the others on that thousand-mile journey had not come to rely on me.

Not because I was a better hunter, but a better shot. JG could spot a sheep on snow a mile distant, Fancher cut sign as well as any white I ever knew. Ballou was always quicker, already aiming before his hands had raised his gun. But if I had some time—enough to stop and breathe, to let my sight adjust to slanting snow or glaring sun, the calm come over me—then I could hit most anything. A deer too distant to discern my scent, a jackrabbit juking a dozen rods away. So long as I had time to feel the world widen around me, my focus on a shape or shadow shaving all else away, a kind of peace overtaking me then not unlike the transference of image to page. As if, pulling the trigger, I might pin a fleeting thing in place, stop the world's spin. At least for the hare, the deer. Though, in the second after, the peace would shatter.

If I could have hunted without killing, I would have. Not just to spare the creature's life, but because of what the taking of it did to me. The hammer, the powder, the strike, the spark, my skin: a rush I recognized, too near what would come over me when I was pushed too far, what had led those with me in the fort or on the Snake to watch so warily, what they could see me holding, holding till it might be released. The sighting, the stilling, the blast. The relief of ceasing to protect that peace from me. And through the smoke, another being kicking or still. I could no longer tell through my own shaking, would have to set down the gun so the others wouldn't see.

Sometimes I fought it. When I would find myself alone, out of the others' sight. If we were well stocked with meat. Would stop my horse, lift my musket, draw a bead upon some creature, let it disappear. Then stay there—the barrel aimed where it had been—holding my breath, my heart hammering, hammering, as if trying over and over to ignite the spark, but the blast not coming, my mind remaining cleared of all but the stirring grass, the shaking leaves, everything outside my sight kept wide. For another breath. Another. Till the grass or leaves went motionless. And let the world close in again.

More than once I did it with him. Might ride back from scouting, crest a rise, spy the three of them: distant horsemen small as antelope drifting across the plain. Or, stepping away into the desert night to try to drip a bit of piss, might watch his shape cut from the campfire. Unsling my musket. Had let his silhouette swallow the small black bead. Held it on his distant horse-swaying body. And far out on the plain his hat would gleam, his voice drift back, just clear enough to make the antelopes men. And I would keep him in my sight, trapped by the muzzle tip, let the world around it slip away. And hold. Heart hammering, finger shaking, body prickling with sweat.

I can still feel it drying on my neck, the chill of a breeze, the time that Fancher caught me. Can still see the look in his eyes. Not shock or fear or even anger but a sort of sadness slowly growing hard. Something in the way he watched me after that more how he might a horse inclined to kicking, or a dog known to bite, than another man.

And Ballou? I believe he knew too. Just as he knew what it would do to me when he'd ride out after what I'd shot and bring it back still breathing—a jackrabbit with a blasted haunch, a deer bleeding across his horse's withers, flailing as he shoved it to the ground before me or tossed me the still-twitching hare—instead of simply slitting its throat where he had found it. A right he insisted was mine. Though he only wanted to watch me do it, to see me touch the thing that could undo me and have to hold it. Oh, he knew me. Knew me from the first. Spent the months we rode together learning me better. Probing, pushing. The way that, cutting across a basin a hundred miles wide, he'd trot up to ride so close beside me I could feel his horse shaking its mane, his stirrup knocking mine. Or when we came across a friendly tribe—fishermen floating on rafts of rushes; squaws scraping up flies the wind had blown onto a salty shore—he would, being the only one to speak a language remotely close, approach to ask for guidance, promise gewgaws in exchange. And, pointing, mark me as the one to dish them out. Knowing that while I untied the sacks of beads and blades, the natives in their eagerness would press tight around me. And he, seeing the strain come over me, would stop JG or Fancher from coming to my aid. Stand back and watch, grin widening, as if my struggle was a game.

One that, by the time we sighted that far-off peak, he'd been playing with me for months. It was October, the wind turned cold, five weeks since we'd split from the others, a fortnight since we'd finished our jirk. Since then, the only meat a single hare we'd split four ways. That night we agreed that if no game appeared on the next day, we would be forced to kill our weakest horse. Between us we were down to eight, two mules and two spare mounts lost on the way, JG's remaining horse already sticky-eyed and droop-necked, Fancher's mule stumbling. But I knew Ballou would still choose Dutchman. That night I served him sips of water in my palm, feeling his peeling lips, warm breath, his muzzle nuzzling my hair as if he wished it grass. Went to sleep listening to him huff at the dust. Told myself at least it would relieve him of his hunger.

Only to find, on waking the next dawn, one of Ballou's own horses gone. A sturdy star-faced grulla that he went after at first light. JG and Fancher with him. Me staying behind to guard the herd. Watching them ride away against the graying sky I could make out their shapes among the stars, bent low as they cut sign, before the near-black earth rose up and swallowed them. Around me the land was just as dark. I watched it, musket in one hand, reins in the other, standing close enough to Dutchman to feel his shifting weight, hoping to blend in with his shape. Listening to the others tearing salt-stunted grass. A long spattering piss. The distant clanks and creaking of the men riding away. Till I lost that sound too. Listened instead for anything approaching. My boots making their own scuffing as I turned in a circle. My gaze sifting the dark so slowly that, by the time it returned to where the men had disappeared, all but the last few stars had guttered out and bats were flits against the sky and, farther still, I made out smoke: a faint gray wisp rising from the direction the grulla's tracks had led.

The bark jerked me and Dutchman both. A dog bark, followed by another. From over by the smoke. A sound that woke the sounds of hooves, men's distant shouts. For what seemed a long time then I stood waiting—to hear a shot, a scream?—but there was only the barking, the hoof thuds muddying to a churned murmur, as if the men were milling around where I could just make out a hut, the dawn too new for me to see more than a sense of movement. And then a flash—its crack coming before my eyes had cleared—and in the space after: silence. Unbroken by a single bark.

Somehow the quiet made the waiting worse. No sounds of the men or their horses or anything but the herd around me. And then a shout. Cried out in pain or anger. And, after, nothing for a long time again.

By the time they returned, dawn had done away with night, the land separating into the shapes of shrubs and rocks, the riders coming at a canter. I glanced behind for a sign of chase, but there was just the stillness of the hut, the smoke all but disappeared. When they were near enough, I called out to ask what happened. Asked again as they pulled up. JG swung down. Fancher spit and followed. The two men leading their horses away to where we'd dug for water in the dry creek. Leaving Ballou to tell me.

He reached for his pommel as if he would dismount in silence too. Instead, threw something down. A dark mass I knew must be the dog. It lay in the dust, fur matted with blood, its stillness broken only by his second throw: a sack that crashed through sage to lie a few feet away, equally still. Till it moved. Lumps shifting like a large snake stuffed inside. I'd taken two steps back, snapped a look up at Ballou before I heard the whimper. What the hell, I said to him, my gaze snapping to the sack again. Where it stayed while he told me.

They'd seen the smoke too. Had pulled up to decide whether to follow the hoof tracks veering away, or circle the hut, or go straight in at a full gallop, when the dog had started up. Before it loosed a second bark, Ballou had known they wouldn't get the horse, the thief alerted along with anyone waiting in an ambuscade or working toward the herd and me. Where Fancher and JG wanted to go. But Ballou was already spurring toward the barking. At the hut, they'd found nobody but the dog. Which Ballou had wondered at—why it hadn't followed its fleeing owners—till he noticed the pups.

While he'd talked the wrap had fallen halfway open, and I watched, expecting six or eight to tumble out. But in the mass of furry lumps there was only one moving.

You seen her pups, I heard myself ask, *before* you shot her?

Then the wrap fell farther away and I could see the tiny bodies. Barely bigger than mice. Only begun to grow their hair. Some with heads smashed to a pulp. Some missing them all together. The mass stuck to each other by the congealing blood.

He had seen them and shot her and meant to eat her. Same as the others, he said. And I didn't know if he meant the other men had decided to eat the dog as well, or if he intended to sate his hunger on her and her pups. Till he told me the rest. How he'd climbed off his horse, stepped to the litter, slid out his knife. Pinned one with his moccasin. Sliced off its head. Same with the second. Then, turning to JG and Fancher, told them if they meant to share the meat they'd share the killing too.

I looked out after them—the two men standing by the dug seep letting their horses drink—watched them as if they might give me some sign of what they'd done. But when I looked back at Ballou I knew. He nodded toward the spilled-out litter, said, That one's for you.

I did not look, but I could feel it. Out of the corner of my eye. The tiny stirring.

Knife or rock or waste a bullet, he told me. Whatever you choose.

In the end he killed it anyway. And half an hour later they were eating. The three of them without me.

I can tell you I did not join them around that morning fire, but not that it was because I did not want to. No, it was because I could not stand the smell. Because it smelled so good. They sat in the sun's first rays holding the roasted puppies in both hands like spuds, their greased cheeks gleaming so I had to turn away, walk far enough I couldn't hear their crunching, chewing, the taunting Ballou tossed at me while the others kept their eyes on the next chunks that they cut free. No, I cannot tell you I didn't wish I'd killed that pup. Only that I couldn't. That, much as I'd wanted to, I knew that what it would have done to me would have been worse than hunger.

Which I know is not enough. Nor should it be. Not anything that I could tell you about Abail Ballou. Because I know this too: To want to kill a man is to want to kill him. No matter the cause. Unlike a deer or hare or even dog. Once the want is in you, there can be no other reason. Whether in anger or revenge or even to protect another, even to save yourself, it is the wanting to that makes it murder.

Sometimes in the days ahead, as we would struggle to cross the mountains, it would seem the cliffs and ravines and drifts harbored the same desire. Though at first the peaks appeared set on the earth to salve our misery, the whole range rising into sight white with snow. High by our reckoning as anything back in the Rockies. The whole day, watching them grow too slowly closer, we talked of the game we'd find on the slopes, JG hoping for buffaloe, Fancher for elk, Ballou running on about roast beaver tail till my mouth would have watered were it not pasted with dust.

Most of the way west we'd followed a route Ballou had heard about with Bonneville. Good enough, with what he'd gleaned from other trappers, to get us as far as Battle Lakes. But from then on, they'd relied on me. My memory. What I'd told JG and Fancher for a flask of whiskey. Though, in truth, I could only recall snippets of what I'd read, more details of scenery and deprivations than specifics of any route.

It was a dry, sloping, windswept country. Salt plains spreading east out of the foothills. The only grazing along a brackish creek we followed north. And even when we found a fresher stream to take us toward the mountains it seemed no game would come to drink. A week of nothing but a few foxes, the occasional lean hare, some sort of desert rat that scampered across our path, the four of us astride our horses loosing such a fusillade we lost the creature in our own smoke, broke into laughter, doubled over guffawing at ourselves. Even Ballou: his bellow and snort. Even me. In the quiet after we'd calmed down, the three of them taking me in as if they'd never imagined me capable of such a sound. Something about it seemed to please Fancher, relieve JG. Though Ballou had studied me as if he thought my laughter cause for suspicion. But what could he do other than trust me? What could any of them do but trust I knew the route, would recognize some sign, find a way into the mountains, show them the faith they'd placed in me had not been wrong?

Each day I tried. Would ride ahead till I was out of sight, leave them to search for game, and, alone again, would attempt creek after creek, follow each into the foothills till the folds closed in or crumbled to cliffs. Time after time, I'd be forced to retreat, ride slowly down toward the east, hoping to see some movement that would at least let me return with food. But spying nothing better than a gopher, which I slung over Dutchman's neck as if it was a deer; another time a five-foot rattler slung around my own, its heavy body banging against my chest to the gallop's beat, its meat enough to make the men nearly forgive me having failed again.

Sometimes I'd find them already eating—one having hunted more successfully—a skewered hare or fox all but picked clean. Once a couple buzzards spread steaming over the fire, their meat surely as bad as dog. Though better than the men's glances, the doubt that had begun to overtake them, the way Ballou, cracking bones between his teeth, said *time* and *draw* and *us* and *map*.

That night I did. In dirt and firelight. Put down each peak I'd glimpsed, each stream I'd tried, went farther into the mountains, across the ground, toward what I imagined. Knowing each scratch I made with the snapped branch made me a bit less necessary. Made it more likely I'd wake one day to find them gone.

And where in this, Ballou broke in, is Walker's route?

I took a step farther up the patch of dirt, pointed to a spot between two peaks, drew the winding line of a new river, told them I'd found it that very day. Though so far away, so late, I'd been forced to return before I could be sure.

I thought you said . . . JG began.

I am, I said. Told them that now, drawing it out, there was no question.

That night I dreamed of it. A river like the one I'd conjured, high cliffs streaked with silver falls, peaks white with unmarked snow, the beating of a single set of hooves beneath me as I rode off toward them alone.

And when I woke it was to the beat of hooves returning. Still night. Darkness surrounding a fire nearly burned down. Though, in the moonlight, I could see Ballou astride his pale horse, coming at a gallop, his body seeming to shake apart and remake itself in a strange flapping, the horse's sides doing the same, growing clearer as they came closer, till I could make out the things tied to his saddle and slung over his back: baskets and gourds and sacks bouncing with the gait, leaping around him as if trying to tear free. Though no more able than his own trembling beard. And in the moonglow, I could see the mud spattered up his mount's chest, scattered over the white like a dappled horse's specks. Except, as he pulled into the firelight, I knew that it was blood.

A basket of grubs, a gourd of dried flies, a sack of ground seed-meal, another filled with a season's worth of wizened fish, a mass of pemmican studded with berries and gleaming with fat stuffed into a basket with its lid lashed shut: enough, he said, to last us long enough to get us high enough we might yet find a goat or lynx or any of the larger game without which we'd starve here anyway.

How far? JG asked me.

To the river, Fancher clarified.

Beneath their stares I said we better start at break of day.

But Ballou just shook his head. Gave us the same beard-spreading grin that once had shown me bloodied teeth. Mes bonich, he said, I would suggest we go right now.

We rode all night and into morning, watching the moonlit ground rushing our horses' hooves—dips dropping sudden enough to fracture cannons, shadows hiding fetlock-snapping holes—lifting our eyes from the earth's sweep only to glance behind at the receding plain. Each time finding nothing. The only movement the scrub's shaking in our wake, the drift of shadows thrown by the moon's slow arc.

Each creek we came to, they looked to me. And I would shake my head. The four of us dismounting then, letting the horses drink, splashing our faces, stretching our legs, pissing and climbing on again. At dawn we eased our pace, sure by then we'd outrun whatever retribution Ballou had earned. Still, at each creek, we waded upstream or down before letting our horses cross, the day passing slowly that way till finally we reached the farthest place I had explored. And I began leading us a little farther up each stream, a little higher into the hills, hoping to find a canyon deep enough to let us wander far enough to fool the others for one more day.

Though in the end there was no need. As in my dream, as on my map: a river wider than any I'd yet seen, rushing down from the snow-clad range, its water sweet, grass on the banks. The one thing missing any sign of game.

The one thing that would stay the same as we went higher, the cottonwoods replaced by aspens on the bank, dense stands of bitterbrush and mats of shrub oak that snagged the mules' hooves, the ravine narrowing till we were forced to switchback up the steeper scarp, crossing scree so loose the horses balked. And all the time no sign of any sheep or goat or deer or even scat, even a print. Not even when, a few days later, we reached the snow. Thin at first, then soon too deep for horses, the four of us traipsing ahead on foot breaking it up. Slow work and draining and, at each day's end, nothing to eat but the last of Ballou's plunder. Then not even that. By the time we reached the lake from which the stream ensued we were chewing our peltries, boiling the plews till their skin was soft enough to scrape at with our teeth. Such meager sustenance our guts left nothing to excrete. At night we set whole fallen pines aflame to melt the snow, dry the ground enough for us to sleep. At least till the cold, seeping through even our buffaloe robes, shivered us awake to feed the fire. In the morning, we'd break camp hollow with hunger, repack the mules, saddle the horses, wrap our eyes with black silk strips against the glare, and, looking like some band of lost blind men, set off again.

Over what I assured the others must be the pass. Though even when we seemed to reach the crest it still stretched on for days without descending, an endless terrain of snow hills and windblown stone, bent and battered hemlocks and pines, the only movement their shaking in the gusts, swirl of a squall blown up, clouds when it cleared. Sometimes the distant sight of Ballou atop his horse, his figure dark against a cliff or breaking out of a copse, following beside me for a while, as if he had not split from the others in order to hunt, but to keep an eye on me.

Much as I could I rode ahead, stayed far enough in front to scout for signs we were on route, markers I assured the others I remembered. While, in truth, I sought snowed-over lakes or strange-shaped boulders simply so I could ride back and tell the others that according to my memory, we should soon be approaching such a feature.

Ballou I knew no longer believed me, but JG and Fancher seemed to. Or maybe simply wanted to and so supported each other's need. They rode always together, or walked together breaking snow for both their horses, talking constantly. Sometimes it seemed the subject didn't matter. I'd ride back and find JG, his red kerchief tied over his nose against the cold, merely describing what he observed—the gin-like scent of a crushed berry, the shape of a cloud—and, beside him, Fancher would offer sounds of affirmation. Till something the younger man said might spark the older's memory. And Fancher would say, Now that reminds me. JG going quiet then, absorbing his companion's words with equal attention.

At night they would bed down together, sharing their buffaloe robes for warmth. JG's hair grown into a tangle of curls matching the bison's color, Fancher's in the last months gone white. Their heads close in the firelight, their voices talking toward sleep. Invariably then they'd speak of the future. The seas of grass they'd ride through. The sound Fancher remembered of the ocean crashing against the shore. How he would take JG to hear it too, and see the seals, and watch the bullfights. The long-horned beasts pitted against grizzlies roped in the wild and dragged behind their mounted captors down to the arenas of the valley. Cattle herds so huge they rivaled buffaloe. The way the two men would one day own a thousand head themselves, ten thousand, a rancho with a real wood floor, a wheat field for making whiskey. A dog, JG would always say. A dog, Fancher always agreed. Asleep at the foot of a bed filled with so many feathers they both would have to leap up just to lie down.

On and on till Ballou would call across the fire, Enough! Either get to sleep or humping!

And I would lie there listening to them rustle and grunt or whisper off to snoring, wondering what it was like to want to be that close to someone. Their body, their heart. Surely what brought my parents together so long ago, what your mother must have wanted too when we'd had you.

My mountains, my mountains. If JG and Fancher had each other, if Ballou had his sheer strength of will, then I had them. Their wind and rock and snow and here I am trying to write them, show you with words, when all those pages of that journal I'd read might as well have been blank. My prints worth even less. For I could depict the lofty peaks, but not the way they would lift me. Could draw the snowcaps, but not know their glow beneath the moon. How, blown by wind, they'd breathe white breath beneath the stars. Lying awake, I'd watch my own blow the same way, listen to the soughing swell to a roar and ebb back to a whisper and start to rise again, and have to hold my hand over my chest to meet the pressing of my lungs. Would hear the echo of a loosed stone clack down a cliff, the burbling beneath creek ice, the distant thunder of an avalanche and, in the quiet after, the beating of my heart. And you will wonder why it would be so different from the mountains I'd already seen. And maybe it's as simple as the unmarked snow: its lack of a single track, trickle of smoke, anyone else. Though I knew there must be tribes wintering somewhere below, so maybe it was just that these mountains were unknown to me or any of my own tribe but the scant few who'd passed through before. Though, in truth, I do not think it was that either. Do not think it is a thing that I can tell you or even understand myself. No more than JG could what drew him to Fancher, or my parents what they grew into together, or you how you would lodge inside your father.

Elisha, I am trying simply to say they found a way inside me too. My mountains. That, even though my stomach ached and my bones showed and my skin stung with cold, even then it was them, my mountains, inside my mind and body, that in the end sustained me.

A statement that no doubt will seem the delusion of a man dying of hunger. So I will assure you I was in my right mind at least enough to recognize that the mere sight of mountains might not sufficiently sustain my horse. Already Dutchman was overburthened. Our remaining mules had been so loaded down we'd been forced to shift some to our mounts, though by then they were the weaker beasts, skin tenting their bones, so enfeebled that the four of us on foot would have to help them through the drifts. Some days we found no grass for them to eat, and when we did, it was sparse stuff yellowed under snow or pressed beneath the ice edging fast-flowing streams.

Then we'd break through, men and horses both, their hooves raking, their muzzles blowing great puffs.

A thing Dutchman was weirdly skittish of. He'd blow at the snow and the snow would swirl back in his face and he'd startle as if it had attacked him. An amusing thing to see had he not so desperately needed to eat. Instead, I'd shove great armfuls away till, brushing with a needled branch, I cleared enough he could rip up the grass. Once, out of sheer hunger, I even tried some myself. The way I'd eaten sorrel as a child or clover in the Rockies. But it was grass. And seeing Dutchman eyeing me, I held the rest out in my freezing hand, the warmth of his breath beneath the softness of his muzzle enough for me, for a few seconds, to forget my hunger.

Bonich, Ballou said, I think you like that horse more than me.

I was bent over, holding a fetlock in one hand, picking with my Green River knife at ice lodged in the hoof.

I think, Ballou said, you'd rather he make it through alive than us.

I could feel Dutchman shiver at his touch, refused to look.

That true?

The flash came so fast I was jerking my head back from the slashing blade, rearing up with my knife ready before I felt the spray across my face, saw the blood spatter the snow, heard the scream. Dutchman already wheeling into a run that buckled with its first steps, his great weight crashing into the drift, his struggling to rise again erupting in a burst of snow and mane and blood, stumbling away shaking his head, stopping at last to stand shivering, one foreleg lifted, back of the knee gashed so deep the rest dangled as if nearly severed, the cannon slathered in a red flood.

Too bad, Ballou said, he's come up lame.

Said it standing not half a rod from me. His Bowie bloody in his hand. No more than one quick lunge from my own blade.

The horse sucked in a ragged breath.

Fuck, I heard one of the others say.

And there was that smile, spreading that beard, blurred by his breath-steam, Ballou's voice coming through: I guess you best cut its throat instead. We need the meat. At least I do. If you ain't hungry, I'll be glad to do it for you.

I'll do it, Fancher said.

Fuck not, Ballou said back. And to me: Bonich, I am giving you an opportunity.

Even through my fury I knew it was true. Not what he'd done or wanted me to do, but what he could still keep me from if I did not. Through my fury I say, though it would be more right to say my hunger. A thing you cannot know the power of till you have seen it up close.

Still it took me long enough to force myself away, turn to the horse, that, by the time I did, Dutchman was so bled out he could barely stay on his feet, his body wavering, his wrenching neck dragged down by his head's weight, so tired by the time I reached him he could barely lift his face to mine. His wide giant eye wild with life.

I do not know how long I stood looking into that stare, holding my knife, my breath hiding his eye and clearing and hiding it again. I only know it was long enough for his breathing to thin, for mine to shallow and quicken till I seemed unable to get enough air into my chest, long enough for his eye to sink a little lower, a little closer to the blade I'd used to clean his hoof a minute or two before, long enough for Ballou to walk across to us, jam his pistol into Dutchman's forehead, and shoot him instead.

The blast blew through my stillness fast as the ball into his skull, and whipping around, I drove my knife with all my strength up at Ballou, thrusting for his gut, only to feel the hard bar of his forearm slam down, blocking my stab, his huge hand grabbing my wrist with such force I nearly dropped the blade. A second before my free fist smashed into his face. He must have bent to block me because his cheek or brow or whatever bone gave way was just within my reach, my blow too fast for his other hand to stop my second punch. And then I knew he was reaching for his knife instead and I smashed my fist into his face again, my other still in his grip, so tight around my wrist I knew that it would break, that the only chance I had was to keep hitting him too hard for him to think or move. But he already was, his face rising out of my reach, his fist working between our bodies, a second, I knew, till he'd find the handle of his knife, could feel it as if the blade was already carving into my gut and, trying to wrench away, I opened between us just enough space for his fist to slam up into my chin instead.

I came to tied, lying on my side, wrists bound behind my back, lips gummy with blood. When I opened them a spike of pain stabbed up my jaw, a shard of tooth sharp on my tongue. Across the snow-churned clearing I could see them cutting Dutchman apart: Fancher bent before the belly, scooping innards with his hands; JG gathering the huge intestine; Ballou hauling back on the flap of bloody hide, hacking at sinew, till he had the whole skin inside out—a raw sheet glowing red with sun, his dark shape showing through from behind—then dropped it and, with a hatchet, lopped off hoof after hoof.

They ate the liver raw, cooked hunks of rump flesh after, and then the tongue and, finally, the coiled entrails cut into foot-long logs and roasted over the fire, steaming the chyme inside. And all the while I watched them feast, their shapes near hidden by all the meat they'd set on spikes to smoke. But not enough to shield them from my stare. Fancher and JG unwilling to meet it. Ballou now and again shooting me a grin.

Though that night it was the older man who came to me. So quietly I didn't hear Fancher's footfall till he was already close, the snow-crunch coming between the snoring of another back by the fire. Out where I lay it was too dark to see much of his face, and he didn't speak, just threw down my robe, spread it quickly over me, took from his own a hunk of horseflesh. Crouched. Held it out toward my mouth.

I'd ripped away only a first few bites, chewing as best I could with my less painful side, when there came the sound of someone else crossing the snow. The meat lifted away with Fancher's standing. And Ballou was there, extending his hand, telling Fancher to go back before JG got jealous.

Crouching where the other man had been, he held the hunk of horseflesh out to me. Said, Here. And when I refused to open my mouth or crane my neck to reach it, he reached forward instead to mash the bloody mass against my lips. Kept it pressed there, smashing my nostrils too, while I struggled for breath. Till at last he withdrew the chunk and, throwing my head back, sucking air, I watched him take a bite and chew. Even in the dark I could tell it hurt him as well, the moon just bright enough to show enough with him crouched close: one of his eyes was swollen shut, his nose no longer straight, his beard heavy with blood. Though the rest of him was so slathered and gunked, it might have just been from the butchering.

When he was done gnawing the last gristle he wiped his hand on the robe Fancher had brought me. Said, Cozy.

I waited for him to stand and go.

Don't you look cozy, he said. All warm and cozy. He crouched there waiting, as if I could be the one to go instead. No? he said. Still cold? And standing at last, he wrapped his own robe tighter. Told me, Me too, me too. A few seconds passed. A few more. Him standing watching me for what I did not know. Till at last I shivered, and he said, Seems a shame, don't it? Fanch and JG all warm together. And us two—

For the first time since I'd woke I tried to rise, struggled to sit, my robe sliding half off before Ballou reached out and pushed me back. No, no, he said. No, no, no, no. His voice soft as his weight bearing down was heavy. Not buggering, he said. Nothing like that. I only mean for warmth. A little human warmth. What any man would want, wouldn't you say?

And when I didn't answer he shoved me onto my side again and got down on the ground behind me and, holding me in place with one hand, drew the two robes over us both, his other hand wrapping around my chest, hauling me close.

There, he said as I struggled against his strength, isn't that better?

I tried to smack my skull against his face. But he was faster, had my hair grabbed in a fist, my neck bent back, his breath blowing my beard, hot on my ear.

Any man, he said.

I could feel his breathing burrowing deep into my ear's canal, his beard in my hair, his buckskin-covered chest crushed to my back, his heartbeat knocking my spine, his arm over my shoulder, fingers on my scalp, nails digging through skin and bone into my brain.

Any human, he said.

And knowing then what he would do to prove that I was not, that he would wrap me in his body for as long as it might take to make me show myself as something less, I could feel the robes' weight great on me as if they still held the flesh and bones and guts of buffaloe. Or just of him, his heat. My sweat slicking my skin under my clothes, steaming, beading my face.

His voice, reaching inside my mind, saying, But.

And I could feel the scream inside me swelling.

But, he said.

Feel it about to burst my lungs.

But you aren't.

Feel it stretching my throat so that it seemed the skin would tear.

Are you? he said.

And lying there I held it in, would not give him even a groan or whimper. Lay there instead silently shaking, shaking.

Are you? he said again.

My body shaking as if in answer.

And I can hear your answer too. For what is there that makes us human except our minds? And where, then, is the line? Between the thoughts of man and other? Or if not, is it the body? Elisha, have you yet seen someone whose brain remains alive and heart beats on despite their mind having already died? The heart? Whose shape is much the same as any buck's or bird's. Or Dutchman's. The Quaker would have said our souls. Which the tribes here believe reside in every creature, even in trees, stones. Kukinis who know the thoughts of any man, who can step inside a woman's mind, speak to the spirit of a child, think and feel and wonder and fear. As well as you.

Are you? he said.

Were you? you wonder.

And when I tell you it was them that saved me—my mountains—you will think me mad again. But I have come to doubt the meaning of that word. For I was there—your father, the only one you have, the only one I could be—there on that mountain when the next morning we found the river.

I say *we*, but I was the one who heard it first. Though I was walking far behind, my tied hands hitched to my mule, its lead tied to another led by Ballou. Fancher and JG farther ahead, keeping clear ever since they'd agreed to let Ballou lead me on foot. To perish in the mountains or down into the valley, or till we found some Calafornio jail.

How they missed it I cannot say, the sound was so unmistakably clear: a roar like wind, but lower, steadier, thicker in my ears.

They were riding away and I followed with a swiveled head till I was sure, then stopped. Let the mule jerk me forward. Stopped again and jerked it back, the other balking up ahead, Ballou turning in his saddle.

Untying me from the sawbuck, holding the rope himself, he let me lead them back, me hurrying ahead, following the sound they still professed not to have heard. Then it was there, water sparkling and clear, winding away below a rocky declination, tumbling down a slope, marking at last the start of our descent. We scrambled after, sliding on shale, whooping and hollering, till we were near enough the river's thunder smothered our shouts.

And how could I not believe it had been calling to me? When all that day and all the next, for near a week, we followed it down, away from the windblown cliffs into a country thick with colossal pines, their cones long as our forearms, lake-blue showing beneath ever-thinner ice, till, sloughing off the snow, the ground grew soft with needles and leaves, lichen on rocks, moss on the trees, even a few oaks, and then a thousand, till the entire landscape seemed composed of their great twisting trunks, acorns crunching under my feet. Even the rain, when it came in torrents, seemed a thing of wonder, falling heavier than I'd ever known. Bringing at last the deer and bear, otter big as beaver, elk like buffaloe, their trails waiting for us to follow. Some wide enough it soon was clear others already had. Sometimes showing their footprints. Though it wasn't till we'd come into the foothills—grasslands rolling beneath the oaks, tall cottonwoods beside the creeks—that we first came upon some of the tribe that made them.

Two men. Coming up the same path we were heading down. Baskets on their backs, tump lines tight across their brows. Wholly unclothed but for a woven hair netting, bows in their hands, standing there for a split second before they ran. I was in front, watching them, when I felt the ball blow by, heard the blast, saw one stumble—flung basket spraying a rain of acorns—the other bolting for the trees. Behind me, all three men had drawn their guns, everyone shouting. But for Ballou, who, jabbing his heels into his horse, pounded past me and plunged into the brush.

Amid the sound of him crashing away we crowded around the fallen man. He'd been shot through the shoulder, the ball's exit blowing bits of flesh and blood over the scattered nuts. The other one had dropped his basket too, and there must have been a thousand acorns cracking and clattering as the shot man tried to stand up.

Behind me, Fancher said the Blackfoot word for *stop*, then *peace*, JG trying Snake or Gros Ventre or some other language I didn't know. And, turning to us with a stuttered flop, propping his weight on his good arm, the wounded man held up his hand before his widening eyes, the sight of our horses or guns or simply us striking him still. The three of us, for a second, gone still as him.

Before another musket blast cracked back out of the woods.

His body jerked as if he'd been the one who had been hit. But instead of blood, words poured from him: Kolom woototip mi nik. Kolom woototip mi nik. The same four, over and over. Kolom woototip mi nik. Between them the crashing of Ballou coming back. Kolom woototip. Till the trapper burst out of the woods. Mi nik. And put a bullet through the man's chest.

He was off his horse before it stopped, yanking the netting off the dead man's head, fisting his hair, unsheathing his knife, grunting at us as he began to cut, Who wants the other in the woods?

When he was done, he stood up with the dripping scalp, staring at the three of us still standing there. What? he said. I should've let him run? Back to his tribe? To tell them we shot this one? You all three lost your minds? Or ain't you seen what they do to men like us? Crow or Blackfeet or Pawnee. I know you seen it, Fanch. You too, JG. And you think this kind would do you different?

No, no they did not think so. And, though I'd been lucky enough to come through the Rockies with a party attacked just a few times—the last while I was out of camp, the others fleeting enough we had escaped with only wounds—I'd heard the worst: stories of captives cut up piece by piece, their bits fed to the village dogs, the dismembered parts of those already dead thrown at the faces of the doomed. Had seen, in the faces of the men who'd told it, enough to be scared now. Scared enough to start to think I sensed a presence gathering—in thickets of underbrush, behind rock pilings—a presence that as we traveled farther downriver seemed to grow. Even as we stayed off trails, stuck to the higher ground where the more level land would lend advantage to our horses. A presence that, as daylight dwindled, I began to feel against my skin. Increasingly seeming about flare. Like the hole inside a piece of wood rubbed by a whirring fire-drill, growing hotter and hotter. A feeling strong enough that, just before dusk, I called out to JG. He was farthest back, slowed down by me loping behind him, my rope tied to his saddle.

JG, I called, untie me.

Sorry, he said.

Untie me, I said again, and give me my gun.

At which he laughed. A sad, regretful breath puffed out. Just before the arrow struck his neck. They came with a whistling rush from either side, so thick they seemed bits of the forest itself blown at us in a sudden eruption: JG whole on his horse one moment, the next shot with a dozen shafts, his spined horse bucking his body into the scrub, the others ahead hit with the same. Though, in the second before the horse that I was tied to wrenched me away, I saw they had at least stayed mounted. Then Ballou was bursting through the braying mules, his eyes wild and cheek bloody and shafts jutting out of his body, but his hand snagging the horse's reins, hauling it behind him as he wheeled away. And I was flying—lifted off my feet, my arms jerked out, the rope ripping skin from my wrists—struggling to make my legs keep up, and failing, and then just trying to survive the bashing of the rushing earth, the horses crashing through the brush into a grassy opening, pounding up toward the higher ground, before another round of arrows hit them. The horses, the other men. I can only guess the reason they did not pierce me was that I was dragging so low, a body looking already dead, slamming along behind the mounted ones. Till they stopped. Ballou's horse buckling beneath him, Fancher's already down and struggling, JG's still trying to climb toward the others as if wanting to die beside its kind. A strange thing to see till I saw Ballou was dragging it, hauling it close enough he could reach out and slit its throat.

Before it quit gurgling I'd flung myself around its uphill side, the shaft-quilled body between me and our attackers, lay breathing hard against its back, feeling its own breathing stop. The others had done the same, lying behind their dying mounts—Ballou beside me, Fancher a little farther—reloading frantically, the Frenchman pausing between packing two handguns just long enough to snap the shafts jutting from his hip and shoulder. Fancher seemed to have fared worse: one leg studded with arrows, his shirtfront soaked with blood. Then Ballou was blocking my sight, rising to fire twice, emptying both pistols, slamming back down to grab his musket.

A hundred yards downhill the enemy began to break out of its cover: a dozen men, and then another dozen, darting rock to rock, tree to tree, climbing quickly enough they would be on us in a minute.

Again Ballou's gunblast—this time the musket—and in the thinning boom I heard him shout at Fancher, Fancher shout back. Something that made Ballou rear up and slap him hard across the face. I don't know if he was crying before the hit or only after, but it was then I realized the older man had not yet fired. For a second he caught my eye. A strange stillness between us as Ballou lay packing powder and ball. Strange because when Fancher raised his pistol it was at me, aimed at my face. You want me to? he shouted. And when I shook my head, he turned the muzzle on himself.

The blast blew pieces of his skull against Ballou so fast it snapped the Frenchman's face my way. And before I could ask, he was lunging toward me, reaching for my bound wrists, cutting them free. Then, whipping back to Fancher's body, he grabbed the pistol out of the dead man's hand and threw it to me. Reared up and fired off his own. And when he dropped back down, threw me that too.

Load, he said.

Fancher's was warm. I swung my powder horn around, poured

a charge, dug into my sack and found a patch and ball and packed them in. All the while watching the assault. There must have been a hundred now, so many moving up the hill it seemed the hill itself was rippling toward us. They wore a sort of armor, a shirt of sticks encircling their bodies down to their thighs, high as their eyes, so that when they would shoot, their faces would show for a second, then duck back out of sight behind their shrugged-up shell, the whole hillside seething with the movement, the sky whistling with shafts. The wet smack of arrows hitting horseflesh.

Ballou fired again, threw down his musket, held out his hand for Fancher's loaded gun, said, Give.

Instead, I stood straight up. An arrow sliced past. Another sliced through my possibles bag. A few scattered thumps hit the horse, a tree trunk somewhere behind me. Then for a moment, there were none. Below me the hillside seemed to go still. As if the stick-clad figures did not know what to make of this. And into the space made by their pause, I called out, Kolom woototip mi nik! Shouted the words loud as I could. Kolom woototip mi nik!

Bonich, I heard Ballou say close beside me, give me the gun.

And turning to him, I pointed the barrel at his face. Saw the fear come into it. And fired.

AUTUMN, 1849

That night he does not stop. The cliff is slick beneath the rain, handholds hidden by the dark, and climbing slowly, feeling his way, finally reaching the ridgetop trail, Silas does not even pause, just breaks into a splashing run, the night passing beneath his feet beating retreat upriver toward his home. Though an hour later when he reaches the turnoff south down the ridge, he will turn the other way instead, veer north into the woods and disappear. All but his prints left in the mud, a bit of fur snagged off his slicker. Signs that, in the coming dawn, will catch the eyes of those who will come after. Let them, the men from the cliff, the rest from camp. Let them, every miner in the canyon. Let them, so long as he is leading them away. From his river, his home.

Here. Where there will be nobody, then, to see the torchlight when it breaks through the trees. Only a barn owl up on a bough, a coon washing a root upstream. Nobody to see the posse spatter across his creek, ride through the clearing, shoot up the hut. But for a weasel watching from beneath some skins. Nobody but Wuut, unfurling his white-gold wings to glide away, Uhk dropping his root to disappear in darkness, Wibus darting out through the door never to enter again. So that, after the men have torn apart all that Silas left behind and, finding no sign of him, ridden away again, there is not even them to see the one who follows.

Not quite dawn, but the time between the night's retreat and morning's first stirring. In the ransacked camp: the quiet of no one, stillness of no one. Broken by a single movement through the trees.

A separating of dimness from dimness. Becoming a man. Atop a mule. Riding slowly. Sloshing across the creek, stepping through the wreckage the other horses made of the grass. The mule steered in silence, the rider mute. But for the moan he makes lowering himself off of the saddle, the final drop knocking a gurgle of pain out of his throat. No one left to hear it, nor see the fabric wound round his face, covering the entire lower half—mouth down to throat—the place where it should bulge over his chin strangely caved in instead. No one to see the wet-stained cloth and know it for blood. Or in its suck and flutter recognize the movement of breath. Each inhale a strained struggle. He breathes. Pushes the hut's door-flap aside with the barrel of his rifle. Breathes. Goes in.

Outside, the light grows bright enough to see the mule's color: gray. Somewhere a bluebird quavers. A sapsucker hammers. While, beneath the hut's fern-covered roof, the face-wrapped figure searches the wreckage left by the riders. Stops. Drops to his knees atop a blanket laid over the floor and, reaching to a corner—a pale gray star stitched in the dark gray rest—lifts it to his cheek, nose, breathes. Then he is crying. Or groaning. A bad sound—grief or pain or both—that, when he stands, yanking the dead boy's blanket up, suddenly stops. It is just light enough to see the woven mat beneath, the disturbed dirt when he rips it away, and by the time he's dug up the packet it will be bright enough to make out the gleam of tin, the silver case, the wax sheen on the canvas he unwraps. Inside: the stack of papers. Lifting one, he holds it so near his face it flutters from his breath, studies it for a long time. Then, leaning over the rest, peels off another, another, pushing pages aside, until, shoving the whole pile over, he stands again.

Emerging, he sends the clearing back to its earlier quiet—his lurch through the door-flap silencing the birds—but it is light enough now to see the stars stitched in the blanket wrapping his shoulders, the paper in his hands bright as a patch of morning, and walking to a place where the trees let through even more light, he peers down at the page. Marked like a map. That he stands studying. Even as the cloth wrapping his face begins to leak a darkness down his neck. Till folding the paper into a pocket, he wraps the rag a little tighter. Struggles back onto the mule. Turns her north toward the ridge. Begins to climb.

By then, Silas will have been heading north for hours, loping over the ridgeland between his river and the next, the levelness strange in legs accustomed to unrelenting steepness, as if the ground itself means to remind him he is leaving home. He passes the ashes of hunters' fires, sometimes a kapum hu alive with the presence of those sleeping inside, though he tries to keep to denser cover, coulees of reedy quags, moves through the hours—a night and a day and darkness again—reaching into his possibles mid-stride, chewing a bit of jirk, some piñon nuts, nearing another dawn by the time he stumbles down the steeper slope of another river, its murmur growing in the gorge, filling his ears, blood, heart, nearly like home. But not. And breaking out into the rockstrewn brim, he makes his way up not-his-river, letting not-his-water erase his prints, not-his-stones obscure his passage, until, crossing to the far bank, he begins climbing again up through the lifting night, the moonlight thinning, stars disappearing, as rising out of this other canyon, he reaches this other ridge, another path, and stops. Stands, chest heaving, before a sign carved in a sycamore: two short lines inside two circles. Clear in the dawn. And yet remaining as obscure to him as the name of whoever claims the land he's on. As if the land itself wishes to remind him that, close as it may seem to the corner of the world that years ago accepted him, this river, this ridge, this tree, have not.

The sun: its first rays breaking through the trees behind him, its small warmth cupping the back of his neck. He stands staring at his shadow suddenly there on the path—a long dark stain that, with its white man's beard and gun, must seem as strange to this still-unbreeched land as the river canyon had seemed to him last night—stands watching the grasses shake his shadow, the brush break it apart, the mist begin to lift his shape away. As if they would erase his presence if they could.

And yet, not long after he breaks into his lope again, less than a mile farther down the path, the same mist thins enough to show a sight that slows him: two tiny fencelines of woven reeds, each no higher than his shins, lining the trail to either side as far ahead as he can see. And all along their length: the brume-blurred shapes of birds, each a few feet apart, standing completely still. Quail. An entire covey. He takes a step. And sends them into a flurry of fence-shaking wingflaps, the whole flock tugging in panic at the lines noosed around their necks.

The gaps in the fences, the seeds scattered just out of reach: he scans the surrounding scrub for whoever set the trap. But there is no sign of any hunter and, crouching down, he reaches for the nearest quail. In his hands: the warm soft body frightened still but for its bobbing plume, its throbbing heart. It patters against his fingers, fast as if trying to pass him some message, no less than the marks on the territory tree, and he holds the bird a little longer, grips it a little tighter—the blood-warmth in his hands, the sun warming his face, the feathers ruffling in the same breeze brushing his hair, beard, the lashes of his shut eyes—tries to feel it a little better.

The second one's neck he wrings still in the snare, loosens the rope, slips the body free. From his possibles he pulls out the sack of pine nuts, sets a handful on the ground inside each emptied noose. Two small mounds left for the hunter, or some small creature, or a scattering wind, a soaking rain, or simply the earth of this place.

Though it is not until after he has plucked and gutted and blackened the birds; not until he's eaten each, one after the other, flinging the bones aside without pausing his walking; not until he's reached a third river, stumbled down another canyonside, that he recalls the darker rocks, mossier oaks, colder water; not until he's passed a tree cut with a boundary marker he remembers from years ago; not until he's standing again beneath the blackness of a cave high in a cliff above that his legs give way, as if his body all this time has known that it was coming here; is not until then, collapsed on his back, that he understands he has not been fleeing, but following; not till then that he knows where he will go.

This time there is no hint of lung-heat wisping out of the cave above. Down here no other's breath white with the river's cold. No one beside him as he rises off the rocks and starts to climb. Nobody inside when, clambering onto the slab before the cavern, he stands staring into its mouth. For a moment he waits, the canyon's chasm at his back, the cave before him a black hole wide as he is tall, high as his chest. Waits listening, scenting, still. Until, reaching to the scabbard at his shoulder, he draws the rifle out.

Inside, the ceiling is scooped high enough to stand. But he stays crouched, one hand in the dirt, fingers drifting through a fire's long-cold ashes. Farther in, he finds the bones: femurs big as rifle stocks, ribs like barrel staves, the massive skull and mandible picked clean. Even of teeth. Even the feet robbed of claws. As if whatever ate the flesh gnawed those off too.

A sudden flitting. He stares into the blackness, letting his eyes adjust—slivers of rodent bones, feathers, the stench of piss—listening to a crackling till he is sure it comes from nothing bigger than a coon. Reaching for a rib bone, he hurls it clattering into the dark, watches a marten dart to the bright opening and out of sight. Again he picks up a bone—a fibula—and tosses it into another part, listens for a bobcat's groan, the snuffling of a wolverine. Scoops up a handful of footbones and flings them scatter-clacking into the far reaches of the cave. No hiss or rattle or any sound but the river's echo, its roar rolling around the walls, surrounding him as he sets the rifle down, unshoulders the rucksack, tugs the blanket out. Though when he falls asleep it is to singing—*minki honi cheti* and *minki honi nik meti*, a boy's high shaking voice: *minki honi nik mei*—his eyes shutting against the flickering of flames, the sting of smoke.

hanpai

quail

I have seen men remade. Shed themselves. Molt. Make of themselves the them that they will be. Have bcome alrdy. Are. Are. Are.

Girls cheeks painted in stripes. Red black red black. The colors covered by skins thrown over all but their bare legs. Standing inside a ring of pine needles piled high & set on fire. Flames leaping all round them. And the girls running through throwing off their skins. Leaving their old selves bhind. Watching the flames crackle down to smoke. Then stepping back over the blackened circle into the crowd of singing mothers & sisters gathered to strip the new made women to their new skin & with warm water wash them.

Boys too dragged from their homes at night. Carried by arms & legs into the dance hall. Swung round the center fire. Ground meal sprinkled over their heads & kneaded into their hair & the hu'uku circling with his burning stick. The days & days of dancing. Calling out to south & east & north & west. Wadilna we'! Puna we'! Wailna we'! Nowina we'! All the once-were-boys spewing mouthfuls of water upon the one stripped nude & hunched & soaked with spray. Bfore he is wiped down. Dried. A new man climbing out of the k'um with his new name.

Have seen it in the same dance hall they took us to to die. Me & JG. Brought us through their village with all the rising hooting hollering of women & kids. Their yapping dogs. Stick armor clattering all round. Bneath it the drumming of what sounded like 1000 feet. Their dead & wounded carried bhind us & the wailing climbing & the pushing stabbing jabbing kicking. JG was long past walking or ever wld & so they hauled him up the packed dirt of a domed roof. To the smoke hole billowing. He had fainted from pain or blood or just the knowing what was coming but the smoke brought him back. I heard him coughing. Saw his head lift out of the crowd. His open eyes. Searching for mine. Then gone. A shriek. Then that gone too.

Even through the ruckus around me I heard him hit. Heard the din inside swell howling whooping. The warbling of some flute. The pounding stamping joined by a drumming I could feel through my own feet. As they drove me up. Beneath me the shaking roof. The drumming coming through the dirt. Drumming drumming. Then nothing but the shaking air. The hole. A ladder dropping down into a darkness cut by a single strip of sunlight. The fainter flicker of the fire. Faces brightening and fading and the crowd shifting and swaying and all their white eyes floating staring up.

Except from the still spot where JG lay. Fallen what looked like twenty feet. His body twisted. Arms bent behind. Leg at an angle bad as the shaft still jutting from his neck. Blood beneath his head bright red in the circle of sunlight. But for where my own head blocked it. My shadow shading his face way down there. And in it his eyes white as theirs. Open as theirs. On me. His mouth moving soundlessly. Though I knew what he was saying. Saying, Jump jump. Meaning: Your weight from way up there. Meaning: Aim for my head my throat my heart. Meaning: Please. And me wavering at the hole's edge. My wrists bound and arms held tight but my legs free. My weight enough. Were I just to rip lose. Take a step. Let myself drop. Jump jump, his mouth said. And I could feel his teeth on my feet his jaw smashed by my heel. Could hear the cracking of his skull. Please please. Then they were on him. Dragging him out of the sun. His eyes closing just before they disappeared. Just before the hands around me shoved.

I came up from the blackness sucking a breath of pain. A scream filling my ears. My sight filled by another's face so close my eyelids opening shocked him back. Her. A woman. Her own eyes flashing fear and then there between her eyes and mine suddenly a sharpened stick. Its spiked tip a glowing ember smoking so near my eye it raised the sting of tears. Its heat drying them right off my eyeball. The pain again. Come from my groin. And I knew the scream had been my own. The spike

But no, it was away, her face away, her lunge instead across the fire to thrust the smoking tip into JG. The screaming his. The spike driven between his ribs, hanging obscenely. A spout for what blood he still had left. Which could not have been much. He was quilled with the burning spits doused in his flesh, dangling from his chest, driven into his armpits, his gut, his groin. There came the stab of pain in mine again and I looked down, saw myself stripped bare as him. But nothing jutting from my body. The hurt come from my swollen knee, my shoulder—now I remembered: my shadow flying up at me, the fire streaking by, my feet slamming, body buckling, trying to roll—my left side radiating a pain so searing it swamped all feeling of the ropes that bound me to the pole against my back. Thongs tied tight enough to keep me sitting upright even blacked out.

But JG was standing—despite the jagged edge of a snapped shinbone shown in the firelight, the worse white of a wet knee flayed of its flesh—tied upright to his pole as if to better let them get at the rest. His body bristling with sticks and shafts. The broken arrow still jutting from his throat. While he miraculously, awfully, still breathed.

I barely could, the lashes digging into my chest each time I tried, my wrists so tightly bound behind the pole I couldn't feel my fingers. Only the pain flaming from my shoulder, pulsing from my knee, the drumming beating on my skin, inside my throat, against my heart. Its own beat stopping each time a hand reached out from the churn around me, or a face swung to me, or someone arced a sharpened stick out of the fire. Each time a crack cleared in the crowd of bodies long enough for me to see what they were doing to JG's. His ear. His screams. Hands cutting with the slow ripping of chipped stone, fingers inside his mouth, wrenching his cheek, its skin starting to tear, another pair slipping over his bloody face, seeking a grip, finding the socket of an eye—

Enough. I can see the word chalked on your mother's board. Can hear my mother telling my father. Him starting to talk at supper of something hard he'd had to do that day, her shhh, shake of her head. Your mother's tug at my shoulder, her frown, chalk clacking at her board. *Enough*, she'd write, hold up two fingers. Later three. Her eyes darting to you. But you are now fifteen. Older by five years than I was when my father brought me to see a hanging. Stood me in a crowd so packed I couldn't see the scaffold. And when I complained my view was blocked, he'd forced me by the shoulders to turn around, held me facing the faces of those watching, instructed me to watch them instead—their eager gawping—so I might burn that into my memory, bring it back before my eyes whenever I felt within myself the pull of our particular barbarity.

What would he have thought to see me shut my eyes now? What will you?

When I admit that, closing my lids, I felt only relief. That they were my lids over my eyes still in my head. That the sounds I heard—the drumming, shouting, even his groaning—were beautiful to hear. The fact that I still could. That when, opening my eyes again, I saw that he was dead, I felt not sadness or horror or even relief his suffering was over, not even fear that I was next, but just a rush of gratitude. His hanging neck bent with the weight of blood dripping off his mangled face and I was thankful, thankful I could still know I would be next, still feel the fear of it. I do not know how to describe it. Other than to say it was a kind of wonder. As overwhelming as what I'd felt for you when I first held you. But for myself. For my mind. My mind. Even for mine.

Across the fire a man who seemed burned black himself was cutting the flesh off JG's skull. Gripping the curls, ripping them free. He held the human peltry into the slice of sunlight, his eyes furious in his ash-smeared face, the clumps of his matted hair shaking as he shouted at me in anger or grief or warning. While, all around him, children flooded in, jerking the jutting sticks out of the body, the women calling encouragement over the ceaseless pounding of the drummers on their hollow half-buried logs, the churning crowd cramming together as men began dragging JG's body toward an opening cut in the building-wall, a faintly daylit exit barely wide enough to crawl through. But they were pushing the body in, toward what must have been others grabbing from outside, because it slowly disappeared—shoulders, chest, legs—till there was just the outside light again. For a second I could feel the air—the openness, the strange sense JG would finally be able to draw a breath, every fiber of my own body wanting to join him out there—before the light was snuffed again by all the bodies inside with me.

Why did the children not turn then, shove their fresh-blooded spits into my flesh? Why did the men not lift new ones out of the fire, burn stripes across my skin? I could not know, understood nothing. Not the shouting rising among the men gripping hatchets and knives. Not the blackened one lifting the scalp before them. Not another, older, covered in quaking feathers, his clamor loud, a rattle shaking in his fist. Not what seemed to increasingly rile the rest, their voices rising, the women retreating to the half of the roundhouse closer to me. No, I could not comprehend even as much as the smallest children standing amid their mothers' legs staring at me. Nothing but what my mind had always known, my body always felt, what—as my breath marked time, and time went on, and my mind remained alive—slowly began to replace my fear, as if till then terror had so thickly coated me that only now the presence of all the others started seeping in. Here is the strangest thing: it was almost a comfort, the sparks of them lighting the wick of me familiar in a way I almost wanted, almost welcomed. The reek of all those crowded bodies, their heat, their breath, their shouting, chanting, wailing, pressing around me. The harm they meant me mixed with the rest, saltpeter added to sulfur. The leather bindings cutting the blood off from my wrists, wrapping my chest so tight they pressed the bone against my heart, the thump thump thump of it: the rod tamping and tamping. And if the drummers' sticks struck my flint, what was not to understand? If the rattle-shaking old man when he spit into my face snapped my hammer, what was wrong in that? In me? All my life I'd tried to fix myself as if there could be something wrong with fire, when the only thing that made it so was others, others lighting it too near their skin or hair or things they owned. But alone? Without them? What could be wrong in letting it burn?

There was the blackened man, his face a foot from mine, eyes bright inside the ash, shout spewing spit. And into it I let out my own sound, all that had built in me all my years, that all my life I'd fought to control, that my still-living mind knew might be the last sound it would draw from my still-living body, a wordless bellow that roared up my throat and wrung my lungs and kept on coming, stunning the others silent, shoving back the soot-smeared man, clearing around me a moment of space.

I cannot say how long it lasted, cannot tell you how it stopped. Only that, long after I'd ceased to hear it, my body stayed shaking, my head hanging, my spit-wet beard mashed to my chest, my mouth agape as death. Belied by its own quaking, by my open eyes. Though I do not think that they were seeing.

Those physicians who'd written to my father, preached the benefits of restrained limbs, bodies wrapped tightly in wet sheets, maybe this was what they sought, what Ballou thought he could force: the calm that, as my shaking slowly stilled, came over me. Something that must have appeared like resignation or defeat, even tranquility. That was. The rage consumed, the fire burned out. A feeling I'd never known. That such near breaking could bring something so close to peace, come from being unable to do anything but breathe. Let my heart beat. Watch the world move on around me.

The drumming had stopped. Or maybe just moved outside. From somewhere beyond the k'um I could hear a distant thumping shaking against the log-lined walls of that round room dug down into the ground. In there, the crowd had thinned. Though around the center lodgepole it was still packed enough with men to hide from me what blood and remnants there might have been. Men squatting, standing, breaking away to climb the ladder to the roof-hole and disappear. More climbing down to listen to the rest speak. Their voices quieter or my ears returning to hearing. It didn't matter. I could tell they were discussing me. Though if one had turned and walked my way, I wouldn't have worried, wouldn't have flinched, wouldn't have believed that he could touch me.

A hard thing to explain. But even when children came close enough to brush my leg hairs; even when they grew braver, ran their hands over my curly chest; even when they buried fingers in my mess of beard, squealed at the wet, scurried away, it didn't seem they'd touched me. Not even when one of their mothers crouched close enough to prod my crotch with her hard fingers, lifted me and let me drop and, laughing, returned to the others. The feather-crowned man came back without rattle or spitting-pipe, gripped my fingers behind the pole as if to test if I could feel him, which I could not, and probed my displaced shoulder—there came the pain ripping into my back, through my neck—and watched my body jerk against its binding, and still I would have said he had not touched me. Crouching before me, staring into my eyes, he moved his fingers before my face as if I was someplace beyond his reach. And he was right.

I watched the slant of sunlight steepen, drift across the room, disappear and appear again, the smoke hole above me unchanging but for the clouds. The shape of someone climbing in or out, bringing a basket, hatchet, rope wriggling with fish. The scent of their steaming flesh, the baking loaves of acorn meal, drawing a rumble from my belly. The sight of the cooking women drinking from tipped gourds stroking a swallow down my throat. But I knew they would not reach through the space between us to give me water or food, just as I knew the men still talking, arguing, smoking, would not reach through to harm me. Knew it, though I could not know then the words that I know now I must have heard. *Hu'k. Te'. Woono. Nik'i.* Chief. Father. Dead. Mine. The blackened one trying to convince the others. Of what I could not guess, or in that state much cared. How can I explain it other than to say that I could feel and hear and see them all around me, packed near beneath that roof closed but for the dimming hole, the sunlight leaving, the stars starting to show behind the smoke, the firelight making the room all the more stifling, and still I sat there breathing calmly, my heartbeat slow, my skin unlit, my mind untouched by all of them. And if even their presence could not reach me, how could the rest? Even my injuries: the knee unmoved for long enough its throbbing had become part of my pulse, the muscles around my wrenched shoulder easing with each hour, freed of my body's weight by the tight binds. Sometime later, when they were gathered around the fire eating, I gave into the need to piss—let it flood the floor before me—and nobody noticed. I watched the dirt soak it in, watched the fire throw its shadows over walls and ceiling and, somehow, never me. Felt the throbbing of my knee, my burning shoulder, the numbness in my hands, the thongs still holding me still sitting against the pole. And, in the safety of my mind, slept.

That night I dreamed I was a bear. Hibernating deep in my cave. The only sound in there my breathing. Though, beyond the barrier of rock and earth between me and the world, it was all noise. The sounds of others. Even through my shut lids, through the cave walls, I could still see them: Ballou and Fancher and JG, Lamont and the rowboat of Shawnees who'd saved me, and my brother, father, mother, your mother, you. All of you living. Outside my cave. While the seasons changed to spring, summer, fall. And I stayed sleeping. All of us so happy that way.

I woke to them cutting me free—the pressure popping away from my chest, pain surging up from my shoulder—my body's drop stopped by my still-tied wrists. Then they cut those free too, and I fell—hands useless—slammed to my elbow, my side, my muscles seizing my slipped shoulder bone, must have cried out. In the echo of my voice, I could hear a murmur rise around the k'um: a crowd outside. The fire had burned down, the smoke a thin gray drift disappearing through the roof-hole into a dawn-gray sky. Or dusk. Or clouds heavy enough I could not tell.

Around me now there were only men. Most naked as myself. A few in skin-flaps, some with tattoos on chests or faces, noses pierced by feathers, hair pressed down by woven nets. All but the soot-faced one, his hair smeared with what, when he bent near, I smelled was sap. Pitch. His voice low and pitchy too. Though, close up, I could see he was no older than me. Still he seemed in charge, tasked with trying to communicate my fate, his hands pointing from me to him, him to me. He mimed shooting a bow, fingers stiffening to fly at me, stabbing like arrows—my leg, arm, neck, heart—till I thought I grasped what was to come. Till he turned his fingers on himself, stabbed his own body. He must have seen the understanding leave me then, because he grabbed my hands—dead blocks below my wrists unable even to feel his grip—and, lifting them, shifted my arms till the injured one was held out straight, the other bent. The shoulder pain threw my head back, severed my breath, but the others held me while he bent my good arm farther, angled its elbow till my numb hand brushed my beard: my own bow drawn.

Dragging me to the ladder, they tried to push me up. But my shoulder, my hands, my swollen knee. After a few attempts they pulled me limping to the wall-hole instead, pushed me onto all fours, made it clear I was to crawl.

A dirt ramp angled upward, barely big enough for me to fit. I could just see the surface, the feet of others flashing by, and lying on my uninjured side, I tried with my one arm scrabbling and one leg shoving to make my way up through the hole.

The light, the cold. Bright as the sun, but the chill sudden and sharp as plunging into snowmelt. I shut my eyes, hunched, felt hands haul me to my feet. The pain from my shoulder almost a welcome heat. And in its ebbing, the tingling flooding my wrists, forearms, a stinging that made me clench my fists—and find I could: my fingers struggling and the pain searing, but I could feel them. I stood in the November air, bare skin prickling over my body, my arms from fingertips to elbows tingling within, hands opening and closing over and over while, through my squinting, I took in the scene.

Huts and huts and huts and, in between, so many people packed so close they must have crowded in from all the villages around, come for the dancing, grieving, cutting, curing, eating of meat. It was the first thing that caught me: the sheer amount of it draped and hung and speared from every spike and rack near every fire. So much smoke that, even out in the open, it stung my eyes. And in its gray: the women working, arms gory, faces smeared, the glints of stones cutting at skins, the spray of others hacking at bones, breaking up carcasses. Beside each, a mound of innards steaming. Teams of girls and boys up to their waists in guts, sorting through the purple bulges, pulling out slippery parts to toss in piles. As if lifted from some buffaloe hunt back in the Rockies. But these were horses, their big bodies lying about in stages of dismemberment. And a bit farther on, tied in a stand of cedars: the living ones. Four mules, tugging at ties, knocking against each other in their fear. One must have felt me watching because it stopped, swung its gaze to me. And it was only when I tugged my own away that I saw the men. They were draped over a boulder: three bare bodies startlingly white, mottled with darker marks, stuck with so many arrows I could not tell through all the shafts which one was which.

Though, as I was hauled limping across the village, I passed close enough to see that it no longer mattered: enough left of JG's rashy throat to mark him, patches of Fancher's red tufts still on his cheeks, Ballou's huge body, but each man so hacked and flayed and missing so many scattered parts they may as well have been all mixed together.

The men who took me by them and out beyond the boulder were all armed. Bows and bludgeons and knives and spears. Some with our weapons too. Though, from the way they'd divvied up muskets and powder horns and pouches of shot, I could see they didn't know how to use them. My pouch was slung over one's shoulder; another held my horn in his fist. He saw me looking, shook it, grinned. But nearby him I spotted my big knife, my hatchet in another's grip, and I knew they knew how to use them. So I was surprised when the one with my Bowie crouched in front of where they stopped me and, with the tip, scratched a line in the ground. Then walked behind me and scratched another. While he did, the others tried with gestures and pantomimes to communicate what would be done to me. Or what I'd be expected to do.

Though I failed to understand till I saw the soot-smeared man step from the crowd. They had amassed as I'd been led out, hundreds gathered in the wake of my procession, women leaving their butchering, children coming running, men still weak from wounds, some naked, others seraped in skins, even a few smeared with the same pitch and soot. Though those were all women. And when the blackened man stepped forward out of the crush, there was no question.

He stood maybe six rods from me. One hand holding a bow, the other a single arrow. Over his shoulders, a cape of deerskin. In its shadow, something metal hung at his waist. Straight and short as the barrel of a pistol. Though it was the man with my big knife who walked across the empty ground between us and drew two lines again. This time in front and back of him.

It was cold enough I could see his breath blurring his face, his eyes behind it bright in the smear of black. Around me the men were talking louder, faster, moving in strange jerks and leaps, one snaking his limbs before me, till finally the one who'd drawn the lines stepped into the clearing and began dancing. A wild, spine-twisting swooping, so fast and fluid that when he stopped his breath was clouding his face too. But his finger pointed at my chest completely clear.

Clear as what it meant when the man six rods from me threw off his wrap. I felt the crowd behind me shift, glanced over my shoulder, saw a last few scatter. Nothing now at my back but woods, the air suddenly colder. I stood with my weight on my good leg, my shoulder dropped out of its socket, my body wracked by a shivering that would not seem to stop. All around me: the breathing of the hundreds waiting. From farther off: the blowing and hoof thumps of the remaining mules. The whining of a dog.

Run, my body said. The woods empty behind me, the mountains waiting. But my mind knew better, knew it would be an even surer death. Most likely in the seconds it would take to loose a shaft; if not, then in the few more to catch me. Though surely longer for them to kill me. And though I couldn't know then what I know now—what I was being asked to do was simply how the tribe had settled disputes for centuries, kept wars from killing more than a single man selected to represent the rest, to dodge the other chosen shooter's arrow, or be hit—though I could not know then how hard the man notching his arrow must have argued with the hu'uku to be allowed to avenge himself this way, how much must have aligned for the jomins to let him—that I had spared so many lives by siding with them against my own, that one of those we killed before I killed Ballou had been the village chief, that the man now sighting on me would succeed his father only if he proved worthy—though I could know none of that as I watched him draw his bowstring back, I knew enough to start to dance.

My eyes staring at his staring, my mind fighting to break my muscles' stiffness, the fletching reaching his cheek and my spine jerking, twisting, trying only to keep from stopping, my bad arm dangling, raging with pain, and the arrowhead a dark point floating before his gaze, and my hurt leg dragging, slowing me down, as I saw him release, and leaped.

It was my knee that saved me. Buckled at my jump and, instead, dropped me. The arrow a breath above my head, a slicing disappearing into the brush behind. I lay with my leg twisted beneath me, breathing, breathing. Till they were over me, talking loudly, reaching down and taking hold and lifting.

Across the clearing the chief's son stood watching. Then slowly set his bow aside.

Beside me one of the men held his bow out. I looked at him, at it. Remembered the one time when I was young, my father treating a Lenape family's hot-footed donkey, their son showing me how to notch a shaft, hold the string. I shook my head.

Through signs, I made them understand I could not hold it, not with my arm out of its socket. Made them understand, then wished I hadn't. A great debate rose up among them, seemed settled as quickly, their grips suddenly growing tighter, pinning my body still. All but the arm that needed fixing. It was only then I fully understood, tried too late to wrench away, saw one take hold of my loose elbow, another its useless wrist, met his eyes in the second before my own went blind with pain.

They held me up. Through the straining of muscle with muscle, the grinding of bone on shoulder-lip, the pop of it snapping back in, my nearly fainting, they held me up. And, when they thought that I could stand, released me. Held out the bow again.

Which was when I began to laugh. Stood there trying to keep from falling. Laughing, laughing, shaking my head.

A murmuring went through the crowd. One man reached out, lifted my arm as if to prove that I could move it, and broke my laughter, my cry making the crowd grow louder. By the time I'd sucked my sound back in, the whole village seemed thrown into confusion. Till the chief's son let out a shout. I turned to him along with everyone, and with everyone went quiet. He took a step toward me. Another. But what had silenced us was what was in his hand. Whether the pistol was mine I couldn't tell, but when, stepping forward again, he closed the distance between us enough to throw, I caught it.

He said something again to me, nodded, returned to his spot.

Slipping the ramrod down the barrel, I found it empty, searched the men around me for the ones I'd seen carrying the pouch, the horn, gestured to them, miming picking a ball, pouring the powder. Tried to hide the shaking in my fingers as I was given each.

I'd like to say I searched my heart then for what was right. As I measured the powder, packed the ball. Would like to say I weighed my chances wisely, compared what I'd done back in the fight to what I might do now. Would like to say I recognized the tribesmen had acted toward me as I'd been told they never would, that I reasoned I should do the same. Would like to say it was because, as he began his dancing, he was so lithe, nimble, even beautiful, his body so in its prime. Would like to say I read in his eyes the reason for his grief. Would like to tell you all of that, but the truth is this: I cocked the hammer, raised the gun, sighted against his chest and, finger on the trigger, let the barrel drift, follow his shifting shape, felt the world around us lifting away—just him and me: the quiet of it, the peace—and could not do it and lowered the gun, and, as his dancing slowed, pointed it at the ground between us and fired into the earth instead. The explosion froze him. Sent a shudder through the crowd that shook out in a burst of shouting, screaming, children and women running, men talking excitedly as if they'd forgotten what the blast was meant to bring about. All but the chief's son. Still frozen in his crouch, staring at me. Slowly he stood. Some of the men broke from the crowd, started for the crater the bullet had blown in the dirt, as if to see it better, but he stopped them with his shout. Gestured them angrily back. Stepped to the side. Retrieved his bow. Held out his hand for another arrow.

I looked at the men nearby me, half expecting them to show their disapproval. But they were only backing away.

This time I did not even try to dance, just stood, weight on my good leg, pistol in my good hand, and watched. His eyes. Made him watch mine. Heard the twang of the release and leaped. Meant to lean, to twist away, but there was just the arrow slamming into me, its power lifting me off my feet, my stumbling body crashing to the ground.

From the crowd: rejoicing. Beneath the shouting, footsteps of others running to me. I thought to help me up. Though they only stood looking down. And I could hear the disappointment in their voices, read it on their faces, only then began patting madly at my chest, lifting my head to see, my fingers hitting the shaft, pain shoving away relief, and then the relief: not my chest, not my chest, my shoulder; it had lodged in my injured shoulder. I didn't know how bad—bone or not or through or not—but knew I had to get up, grab my pistol, stand. The others made way reluctantly. As, anchoring the shot arm against my side, I loaded again. Across the clearing the chief's son stood, still holding his bow. I waited for him to set it down, begin to dance. But he did neither. I cocked the hammer, lifted the gun. If he moved, it was only to grip his bow tighter. The murmuring had risen again and now some in the crowd began speaking to him. But he seemed not to hear them. Did not move his eyes from me.

The barrel-tip marking his heart, I waited for him to start, to shift, so much as twitch. Go on! I heard myself shout over the crowd. Go on!

But he would not. Just shouted back something I could understand no better. Stood just as still. The two of us in all the crowd's commotion so frozen for so long I began to feel the pistol's weight, its tip starting to shake, and, stopping my breath, shifted the barrel a hair to the left, just enough to match the wound he'd given me.

It is a strange thing, shooting someone at close range. The kick coming back matched to the jerk of him falling away, the shot seeming made by you both: a kind of collaboration, body to bullet to body. A strange thing, if only for the one shooting.

For the other it is simple. I watched him fall, watched the crowd break from its shock, watched long enough to see his bare feet stir, his knee bend, the blood spread out behind his back. Tried to tell if

I had hit him where I'd meant. And could not. And then he was hidden by the rush around him and I looked at the few men still around me and took a step back. Watched them watch me do it. And took another, and turned, and ran.

Ran loping. Ran stumbling. Ran limping through the pain of my wrenched knee, wrecked shoulder, the shaking of the arrow shaft catching branches, ripping free. Ran naked, the earth cutting my feet, the brush raking my skin, the shot-pouch slung across my chest, one hand gripping the powder horn, the other the pistol. Ran scrambling downhill and clambering up, my breathing hard and loud and coming into it another sound, so like my crashing breath it seemed at first of my own making, and then it growing, overtaking my breathing and the clattering of stones beneath my feet and cracking of the branches I grabbed to keep from falling, the slope suddenly so steep I was more tumbling than running, the sound all around me now, echoing up the canyon, filling the air so that each breath I took carried the sound also inside me: the river. I ran to the river. And it found me.

I have been thinking about the ma'ki. Not the spirit who haunts the woods, sends unsuspecting hunters into deep sleeps, but the man who plays him in the he'si, black-feathered head to toe, who from inside his raven-skin cloak summons that bird's spirit into the dance hall, through his body, year after year. The same man in the same skins. Though another trains beneath him, a sort of disciple, who, when the ma'ki dies, climbs into the grave beside him, the feather cloak placed on a pole between their bodies. The disciple who, while the other kuksu members encircle the pit to hide it from the mourners' sight, secretly climbs out. Unknown to the grieving villagers who then fill in the grave, believing they have buried both. Only to find in the next he'si the ma'ki summoned again. In the same raven skins. But a new man dancing him.

And here I sit in your old father's skin, all these years since. And no one else to know it who knew me then, who knows me now. But you.

Surely you believe in resurrection. Raised by your mother and mine, my parents who tried to keep me beside them in the pews, and then to sit me alone in back, finally allowed me to listen to the sermon from outside, standing beside the Susquehannock beneath the open windows, their presence my excuse to slip away into the woods. If only for an hour, an afternoon. The world of others always waiting to reclaim me. The way the one to come would when I died. An idea that terrified me. Not the threat of what awaited if I failed to live a life of faith but the promise of what, if I succeeded, would be my eternity. Not all the ways that it would be unlike the world I knew, but the few that it would be the same. All those souls. All the souls.

You will say that, lifted from the world of men, mine would be different. Freed of my body, my soul would no longer suffer the same affliction. And sitting here in the home I've known these past nine years, hearing the rain come hard as it has each of those winters, the creek rushing by with the new life it receives every se'meni, the roar of the river now as much a part of me as my own heartbeat, I would say to you that you are right. Though it was not my body from which I needed freeing, but the bodies of others. Not my affliction that needed lifting, only the suffering.

And can you not then believe my soul is not the same? As it was when I still lived inside a world that would refuse me? Before I came to one that took me in?

AUTUMN, 1849

Then it is there, snuffling in, heavy head swinging, filling the opening, smothering the day, till there is just a glinting on its muscles—where is its fur?—slipping over its wet smooth side—where is its skin?—gleaming on its skull-bulge as it lumbers near, its face so close he can see the place its ears should be, the strip of cartilage along its muzzle, its toothless maw. Can smell the meat-stench on its breath. Its eyes, beneath the brow-ledge, are raw white spheres, its pupils black, still, staring. Till he tries to scramble back and it stands up, rears over him, the cave ceiling receding, the bear's peeled muscle pale beneath its fascia sheaths, its chest a massive version of his own, its arms elbowed the same, its paws, stripped of skin and claws, like hands with thumbs hacked off, fingers cut to stumps. And still somehow they grip, peel apart the muscles of its chest, reveal the breastbone, dig beneath, and, grasping its own heart, begin to rip. Its huge and toothless maw opening, opening.

A bark.

His own eyes open. The gasp of his own breath filling his ears. He lies there stilling it, his breathing stopped, letting its noise leak from the air. Outside: The dim light of dusk. Roar of the river. Almost loud enough to cover the barking of dogs.

And Silas is up, the blanket sloughed, rifle in his hands. Already the barking is closer, coming above the river's roar instead of through it, and stepping over the old yomkapa's skeleton in a half crouch, he steals toward the opening, slowing at the brightening, stopping just within the last concealing dark, the world outside still equally hidden from him. But not the sounds: at least three dogs, near enough now he can separate their barks, hear the shouts of men. Wheeling then, he is back at the bones, their scattering loud as he bends down, grabs his rucksack, begins jamming the blanket in.

A movement, the opening: dog-shape against the dusk. Snarling rolling into the darkness before a bark blows it apart, breaks the shape into a blur. He meets it standing, blanket spread in his hands, flung into the speed of the dog's leap, smothering its snapping, its body's lashing fury pressed squirming beneath his weight smashing to the ground, his hand releasing just long enough to reach his knife, the thing's face ripping free—a flash of teeth—before he can drive the blade in—the yelp—yank it free, drive it again, his other hand mashing the blanket over the struggling head, finding the jerking skull, as, stabbing the knife in just behind the bone, he jams it deeper, wrenching it back and forth against the squirming, the crack, the sudden ceasing. Stillness. His breath.

For a second he listens through it, his stare on the opening, the stirring of the dust kicked up, the stillness of dusk beyond: How long before another dog-shape breaks it? Before the men realize where the first disappeared? Or are they already gathered below, some covering the cave with guns while others climb—and then he breaks the stillness himself, rips free his knife, swings the rucksack over one shoulder, rifle over the other, turns to the cavern's back, its low receding blackness, hunches, crouches, disappears.

He moves with hands held out before him, the river's roar thickening around him as if the stone walls have soaked it in along with the scent of guano, the chill beneath his moccasins, knees, hands, elbows, wet in his beard, as on his belly he peers ahead into the dark and sees, at last, a rock-edge, a hint of quartz, barely a specter floating in black. But around him the walls have begun to change: soil. Its danker scent draws his face up. A blackness just as dark. But cracked by a thin line of sky.

From back in the cave, they come again—shouts and barks still too distant to be inside, but nearing—the cleft he's crawled in so tight he can't turn to check behind him anyway, can barely wrench the rucksack off, the rifle over his shoulder, lift it into the space above his head. Pressing his face into the dirt, free arm covering his skull, he probes with the stock—rain of soil, hail of rocks—hammering until the earth begins to crumble, becomes a deluge, and, slamming sideways, he raises his hands against an avalanche of stones, then is no longer holding it back but shoving through, past, grabbing a root, hauling himself up between two boulders, onto the slope above.

He kneels there, dirt-darkened in the deepening dusk, breathing the cleaner air, his only movement the slowing swinging of his slung possibles bag and powder horn, till they go still as him. Then he drops, reaches down into the hole, feels for his rucksack—slicker and piñon nuts, the last jirked fish—head disappearing back into the blackness, eyes trying to readjust: a blur of something coming fast, sound of its scrabbling, white of its teeth. He jerks up, yanks his hand out, is scrambling to stand as the dog's face breaks into view, maw snapping, bark blowing up the hole at him. He nearly draws the revolver—the barks bursting from the hole like a releasing of the earth's own rage—lurches to the side instead, rips up a rock and, lifting it over his head, slams it with all his strength straight down onto the snarling face. Before the bone-crunch has left his ears he's wrenched another loose, hurls it down too. Then, working fast, he fills the space with stones, covers them with dirt and duff till he's sure no light will make it down, at least not enough for anyone inside the cave to see.

From where he stands, he would not see them either—the other dogs bounding for the cave, the men climbing behind them—but by then he is already a faint figure slipping away between the dusk-dim cedars, dust shaking off his hair and beard, a pallid shimmer trailing him upriver as his shape sheds it, darkens, fades.

Though before he disappears, he stops—not yet around the canyon bend, still within earshot of shouting—unsheaths his knife, slices off the end of his dog-shredded sleeve. Then, reaching into his possibles, he pulls out the vial, pries off the plug—a reek of fish-juice and musk so strong his nostrils shoot out a gust of air—as, careful not to let the liquid touch his fingers, he drips some on the deerskin scrap, drops it at his feet. Moves on again. Straight downslope now toward the river, weight taking him at a thudding run, slowing only to shake a little more lure onto his path before he breaks out of the trees. Beneath the clouds the canyon is already nearing night and it takes him longer than he'd like to find a bit of driftwood flat enough to float with one side up. Onto which he drains the vial, lets the mixture soak in, then, crossing close to the middle as he can, lowers the reeking log into the current and lets go. In the near dark it disappears almost immediately. For a moment, he watches—a glimpse of it farther downriver bucking through a cataract—then, rearing back, hurls the empty bottle hard as he can. A glint arcing across to the far bank. The distant crepitation of its shatter.

Already, he is unlashing his moccasins, rolling his leggings up. Long as he can, he wades upstream through water so cold it seems to gnaw the flesh off of his shins, freeze his feet till he no longer feels the stones, before at last climbing back out, slipping into his moccasins, beginning to leap boulder by boulder up the river the Nisenan call Nem Sew—the North Fork—though to him it has only ever been Walloki's.

A strange sight, then—this lone figure leaping beneath stars and moon blotted by clouds, the canyon so black he would be lost to all but the nighthawks watching from the overhanging oaks, the owls silently gliding above, the catamount pausing to gauge his size and speed—a strange sight hour after hour to all who might see him pass by. Though not as strange as what he sees in the last hours of that night.

He hears it first: the thunk and clatter of weight shifting on rocks. Stops frozen on a boulder. Again: the clacks of smaller stones knocked loose. By something big. A buck? Bear? But when he peers across the roiling water—he'd long since crossed the river, the sound now coming from the bank he'd left—he can see it is too tall even for an elk, its mass breaking from the black rest only when it moves. The clack again. A horse. He crouches low, slowly swings his rifle around. But across the river there is no mirroring glint, no halloo to him or alert to others, and the longer he watches, the stranger it seems: the horse drifting at its own pace, picking its way through willows, ripping at leaves, as if riderless—but not. The more he watches the more he's sure: the way it shifts its weight, the mass humped on its back. A man? He stares, trying to tell himself it is only a pack, but something in him knows. Dead? A dead man slumped across the horse's neck? He waits for it to move again, the body to slide off. Hears a hoofstep. Thinks, Tied? A body tied? Stands to better see.

And the horse lifts its head. Silas goes still. But it must smell him. It brays—a mule, then—steps sharply away, lurching on the loose stones. And on its back, the movement is something Silas feels as much as sees: the dead body rising off the neck, sitting up. Then he can hear it: a noise somewhere between a word and groan, moaning loud enough to carry across the river. Before the splashing—the mule's hooves; the man urging it in—smothers the sound.

Something in Silas moves him then, though he knows he should stay still, sends his body leaping back to shore as if the rider's heels jab his sides instead. Though it is the sound—the moaning suddenly worsening into a wail—that stops him. Not just its eeriness, not the pain and rage that it contains, but the sense that he's heard it before—that scream torn loose from what a scream should be—and then the black mass of rider-mule is plunging in, water splashing around it, and Silas breaks bankward again, scrambles through his own too-loud sound up the steep slope. Till, reaching the deeper cover of the larger trees, he slows, stands listening through his breathing to the man's bellows. Which have not stopped. And don't. Not as the mule struggles ashore, clambers onto the bank only a couple rods downriver. Not as the rider, clinging to a rifle instead of reins, lurches so hard he should fall off, but doesn't. A sight that, like the bellowing, should make Silas go. He knows, he knows, but can't. Can only climb a little higher before he's stopped by the next screams, pauses to listen. Though the longer he does, the less they sound like something made by another human, the longer he stays the more they seem to come instead from the river itself. The canyon, the cliffs, even the dark. The longer he crouches there in the blackness before morning—three nights now since he'd last seen his home, four since he'd found the miners' camp downriver, seven since he'd shot the boy, the father—the more it seems a sound that could be coming from inside of him.

waksi
great blue heron

That day I found my river it was so cold the air over the water froze my sweat. The stones my feet. And still I leapt rock to rock despite the pain knifing my shoulder my knee. Till I was far enough out. Roar all round me. Crouched heaving. Body steaming. Somehow in all the exposed space bneath all that higher ground feeling completely safe. As if the river's roaring covering all other sounds cld hide me too. Hunched on that boulder. Still as the rock. Wishing only to remain inside that thunder. That canyon. Its walls keeping all but the clouds at bay. Let arrows whistle down. Lances clatter on the smooth stones. I wld stay till the current rose & smoothed me too.

And yet no lances came. No arrows but the one alrdy buried in my shoulder. The pain enough to stir me. Remind me if I did not move I wld bfore long be unable to. My feet felt frozen to the stone. I stared at them. The blood smeared on the boulder bneath. Knew it must be from their torn soles. Yet through the cold cld feel no pain.

Then I was splashing in. Up to my waist. Legs cramping so quick I did not know if I cld stand. Cld not feel my knee enough to know if it wld hold. Cld barely unseize my body enough to bend & plunge my shoulder under. My other hand clamped to the rock & my teeth clenched & my breathing stopped & I held it held it held it & came crashing out. Roaring onto shore. Then bfore I cld freeze up stumbled to the closest boulder. Dropped to my good knee. Gripped the rock. The arrow's fletching shaking inches from its surface. And with a bellow slammed myself agnst the stone. Again & again. Hammering the shaft deeper & deeper. Till the point popped past some blockage & I felt it break out bside my shoulder blade & by the time the notched end shattered against the rock the head was through. Snapping the shards clean off I gave the shaft a last shove farther. Far enough that when I collapsed into a willow thicket I cld turn my back to the bushes & jerking the barbed tip at the branches catch it in a crotch tight enough to hold. Then with one last roar I heaved my weight away. Felt the shaft rip through me. Was falling free.

That morning I did my best to stanch the bleeding. Scraped soggy willow leaves up from the sand. Pressed them into my congealing blood. Thick and sticky enough it might have held had I not been so badly shivering. My body shaking the leaves free. So that before I could weaken further I turned to hunting dry leaves instead. Buckeyes big and papery. Duff under pines. Twigs snapped off root balls. All of which I gathered in a pile on the beach. Poured powder down my pistol's barrel. And without adding patch or ball primed the pan. Cocked the hammer. Pushed the muzzle into the piled tinder. Fired.

All that day I barely moved from the warm flames. A few times to gather wood. First what I could find nearby. Then a little farther to drag back larger branches. Three hunks of driftwood big enough that spoking them round the fire I could feed it bit by bit for hours. By then my knee had swelled to twice its size and each time I tried to rise the poultice shook off my shoulder. So I stayed there repacking it. Crouched so near the fire my shin hair singed. My neck craned back in fear of rain. Trying not to feel my hunger. Sometimes I caught crows watching me. Thought about the few lead balls left in the pouch. How little powder. A few times tried throwing stones. Missed. Sat in the receding clacking letting the sharper pain caused by the motion drain back to just the steady hurt. And when the sky dimmed toward dusk I gathered up the blood-sopped leaves dropped from my wound and lay them on rocks beside the fire. Hoping they would scald and soften and I could get back inside my body some of what it continued to lose. Though even as I chewed, I knew it could not work. Even if the leaking stopped, the risk of mortification would be worse. Even without the fire's heat the blood-scent would draw bear or cougar. Unless the smoke drew men to me first.

There in the canyon it grew dark fast. The gorge losing last light even as the clouds above clung to their gray. Then that was gone as well and there was just the night. My fire. The roar of the river. The sounds inside my mind. Drumming and JG's screams and Fancher's crying and *Bonich*, Ballou says, *give me the gun*. The sight of the Frenchman's huge face. His eyes on me. Their glare steady even as his forehead caves. His hair blown out in a gust of blood and bone. That night I did not sleep. Though neither can I say I was awake. My mind in its rising fever become a haunting ground for memories I tried to shake only to find myself in others farther back. Till it began to seem that all my life till then had been a single relentless stretch of fleeing.

So that I was surprised to find myself still there that morning, surrounded by a mist so dense it hid all but my near-dead fire, the water's sound. That, in my ears, had already become the sound of here. I lay flat on my back watching the last thin smoke disappear into the thicker white, the sight of its drift making my own stillness all the more strange. I was so cold there seemed no difference between the stones I lay on and my skin. Yet I was still as them. As if, in my fever, my flesh had forgotten how to shiver. Unless this was simply how it would start, the still rocks and willows motionless beyond the mist, pines frozen against the sky, the world around me stilling in expectation of the final stilling of myself.

And then the stillness breaking: far downriver, a slow flapping, wings, appearing so suddenly they seemed ink-brushed into the mist. An enormous heron, slate-blue, its long neck snaked behind the bright spike of its beak, its legs two lines scratched in the metal sky. But moving, gliding effortlessly, almost to me. I watched it flap slowly by, slipping silently upriver, my head swiveling as slowly to see, and then I was rising onto my side, my weight on my good elbow, the great bird gliding toward the bend and gone, my own body beginning to shake.

Surely then it was my eyes: the flicker of red, a little higher up the bank, quivering as if brushed by a breeze. An autumn leaf? No, it hung too long and loose, then flapped again, and I knew it was a bit of cloth. Tied to a long black line too straight to be a stick. Then I was sitting up. Not twenty rods upriver, stood on its end, the swatch of red tied to its muzzle: a musket.

I made myself move, hauled my body over rocks and moss and through the pain and gained the slope and there beneath a stand of oaks found a mound so marvelous it made me doubt I'd woke. A pile of leather, metal, sisal, wool, topped by that rag-tied musket raised like a flag. For a long, bad moment I thought it was a trapper's cache. Then knew: the horn handle of Ballou's big knife stuck in a sawbuck I'd strapped a hundred times to my mule's back, the ripped fringe of Fancher's jacket, the red kerchief I'd last seen tied to JG's neck.

It was all there. Saddlebags stuffed with clothing, cookware, traps wrapped in their chains, apishamores smelling of horse sweat and buffaloe robes reeking of the men we'd been, and all our possibles, bullet molds, lead bars, fire steels, hatchets, two leather hats, a lone tin cup. Not all—the foodstuffs gone, some tools, most of the guns—not all we'd had. But all I'd need.

I am not ashamed to say I crawled up on a saddlebag, hauled a robe around me, sat there and cried. And I know that it was them—the same men who, a day before, had wished me dead—know they must have brought it all during the night, beneath the river's roar, my fire a beacon leading them—but I will tell you that from inside the blackness of that wrapped robe, it did not feel like an act of men. The mist had thinned. I could see the river's glint and I will tell you that, watching the cliffside oaks leaning protectively over the water, the smooth white boulders standing sentry beside the bank, I could no more make sense of the certainty growing in me than I could of what the tribe had done. But it was there. The gift they left. The sureness inside that I had not come here driven by years of fleeing, not even by my own seeking. But had been brought.

Above, the sun was in the oaks—their branches bare of all but moss, each soft-furred limb set so aglow with morning light the boughs seemed dipped in gold—and it was slipping through, down the broad trunks, onto me.

I shut my eyes, let the robe fall open bit by bit, until my face was warm with sun, the light bright on my lids. And do you remember spreading your fingers when you were young, the skin between lit red, the hint of bones within? Staring at the glimpse of what you were made of inside. Struck with wonder. Dada, you'd ask me, does your hand do it too? And I would tell you, Yes. Yes, Shash. Will tell you that day I held my hand out the same way, beyond my glowing fingers the air above the river alive with all the swirling specks of all the insects living off it, and beyond that the far ridge, and beyond that the rest of the world, hidden from sight.

Though I was not from them. One day not long after I finished my shelter—a lean-to of saplings small enough for me to fell one-handed—I found two men stretching six ropes between the banks, taut lines hovering above the surface: a floating fence. Which the two settled behind a boulder to watch. Though they seemed more interested in me. Till a pair of ducks landed downstream, paddled near, one of the men then flinging a stone to send them flapping into the trap, snapping their wings, their struggling shuddering the lines, the hunters splashing out to wring their necks. Afterward, descending the opposing bank, they'd watched me so intently their own necks twisted till they disappeared around the bend. The same where, on another day, a dozen women came slowly into view, digging with sticks, the babies strapped to their backs staring silently at me all afternoon, the mothers chatting happily, seemingly pleased, as if they'd planned on what the sight of me would do.

And once, after a weeklong rain, I went out at the first break, hobbled up the slope hoping to flush some game, nearly shot a man instead—beneath a doe's stiff ears and black-tipped muzzle his two eyes staring back, notched by my musket—before he leapt up wearing his headdress, waving his arms, behind him the deer that he'd been stalking erupting into flight. Grasping what I'd cost him, I swung the gun instead onto the juking shape, each leap stretching the space between us. But I could feel the straining in the buck's shoulders, the burning in his haunch, his fear. In my own shoulder, the burning of my wound; in my still-weak grip, the gun starting to shake. In my mind: Ballou's blown-open face, my fear that if I killed another man the act would surely snap me, the fact that it had not, the thought that if the deer had been the hunter instead—inside the decoy head, the man's—it might have been easier for me to pull the trigger. *Any human*, Ballou had said. *But you aren't, are you?*

In the quiet of the receding blast I tried, through gestures, to show the hunter I meant for us to split the buck. Watched the terror in his eyes recede as well. The two of us in silence making our way through the woods to the deer. Where he dropped to it, stroking its throat, speaking words as unknowable to me as to the buck, but the song he sang into its ear settling my breathing too. The hunter felt for a pulse, unsheathed his knife. Slitting the buck's belly, he reached into its innards, yanked out the liver, chewed the slippery slab in half. And, chewing still, handed half to me. I ate it hungrily. Then helped him carve the rest, the wordless time it took to butcher what was left the closest I would come to company. The voices drifting down from canyon paths the closest to conversation. The figures passing on the far bank as near, in those first weeks, as anyone would come to me. As near as we—the people of Kushna and I—would ever come to living together.

Though that first day that I'd awoke to what they'd left me, it had not seemed that way. Crying, limping, I'd hauled it all down to my gravel beach, only to find that all that time the men who'd saved me had still been there, watching silently from the trees, as if to see what they had wrought. Or maybe just hoping to learn to use the oddities I'd brought. Though when, that evening, over a dozen warriors emerged from the woods it seemed to me most likely they'd simply been waiting to see if I would die.

In my possibles I'd found my needle and thread, managed to stitch shut where the arrow had entered. But where I'd shoved it out, I could not reach, had barely been able to bunch JG's kerchief over the exit, cinch it with a saddle strap. It kept breaking open, seeping. Same as the wound I'd made in the other shooter's shoulder. I could see it as he came down the slope onto the bar, could tell his pain by the way he tightened with each jolt, his good hand grabbing roots and rocks, his wounded arm bound to his side by hide and cord, his blood soaking through too.

Against the cold he wore just moccasins, skin leggings tied off above his knees, around his waist a feather belt big enough to reach his sternum, a leather necklace swinging its small pendant against his chest, his septum pierced with a red feather bright in his still-blackened face, his hair still matted with pitch. But in his hand, instead of a bow, a pistol.

I had grabbed my own when I'd seen him start down, the forest full of others following. They carried bows, arrows already notched, and I watched them more than him, seen from the way he held the gun he wouldn't know how to shoot it. Though, as he closed, I watched his grip shift, his thumb come over the back, his finger find the trigger. Felt mine touching my own. And only then realized he was learning from me. Raising my pistol, I pointed it away from him. But instead of doing the same, he just switched hands, his gun held in the one bound to his side and, stepping near, lifted his good hand as if to touch me. Two stiff fingers, their tips held inches from my shoulder, pointing to the hole he'd made, his eyes on mine steady as if he were trying to speak through them to me. I tried to listen, watched. After what seemed a long time, I shifted my pistol to my bad hand too, raised my good one same as him, made the same sign, my two fingers nearly touching his wound. The necklace—I saw it now: the sinew strips binding a small black ball, hanging heavy as lead. To this day I do not know if it was the bullet I put in the ground or the one I put through him. Though maybe he told me then. Because he spoke. A few words. I shook my head. Said my words back: *Sorry*, and *Can't understand.* Though his grunt was clear enough to bring the same from me. No more than an acknowledgment of our impasse. And yet enough to break it.

He'd come to ask me to show him how to use the gun, made clear he'd watched me carefully, his hand miming loading the ball, pouring the powder, but then, instead of his fingers exploding outward from the muzzle, his palm turned up. His question clear as his confusion. Clear as it came to me that they had never seen one. A thing I'd never seen in men—even among the Shoshocos of the Salt Lakes enough tappers had passed by in recent years for them to know a gun—though I'd seen the way muskets had changed the Rocky Mountain tribes, tilted battles against their enemies, become the item they wanted above all else. And, standing there, it scared me.

I knew Spaniards lived farther down, between these mountains and the sea, Calafornios with horses, guns. Had heard Fancher's accounts, read descriptions in Leonard's diaries. But I knew too he'd seen no sign of them till he'd reached the valley, heard no Spanish in the hills, found on the ranchos no interest in grazing herds up among grizzlies, no wish to risk meeting tribes who might still think them evil spirits sprung from fevered dreams. Who might be right.

Already, I had brought them beads, blades, steel buckles, cotton clothes, coffee beans, a glass bottle smelling of awerdenty, the cork to stop it, the horses, mules, me.

I shook my head: No. Shook it again. Watched his brow bunch.

Strange how without words it is harder to lie. Passing ideas through your own face, gleaning them from another's eyes, the attention paid to each. Still, I tried to convince him I could not teach him, that what made the pistol work was not in it, but me, the fire come from my body, my hands tracing a line from trigger to finger, up my arm to my chest, back to the gun. Pointing to him, shaking my head. Trying to show him he did not have the ability, could not.

Mostly he'd ignored my hands, his face open to mine, his eyes on mine. Now I watched them darken. Just before he reached out and, with his own hand, stopped my motions, his finger pointing again to my shoulder. I was sure then I'd failed, that he thought I'd been claiming I was more powerful than he, his gesture a reminder that he'd shot me as well. But instead, he stepped to the pile he had left me, rifled through till he found the hat Fancher had worn, the moccasins stripped off Ballou and, reaching farther over my shoulder, tapped JG's kerchief bunched at my back. Then, gripping the pistol by its barrel, he pointed its butt at each article again—the hat, the moccasins, the blood-soaked bandage—and I understood: Why them? If the power was only in me, why could they make their guns work? I nodded, touched my beard, my arm hair, lifted my injured shoulder just enough to show the whiter skin of my pit. Then, with my good hand, began patting my chest, my neck, my cheeks. What did I see in his expression? A dawning understanding? A rising doubt? Reaching again beneath my wounded arm, I stretched toward the kerchief till my fingers came away red. Then, holding them above my pistol's muzzle, I opened my hand once more to mime an explosion. Wiped my fingers on my chest. Reached to his shoulder, found his blood, touched my fingertip stained with it to the pistol in his hand. Closed my fist. Shook my head.

Watching him, I wasn't sure that he believed me. Though I now know he did. Then there was only a brooding in his eyes, a deepening disappointment cut with something I feared was anger, but that I've seen enough times since to know was his way of finding in himself a difficult acceptance, shoving down the urge to fight a thing he didn't like. Slowly, he looked away, over the things he'd brought me, as if now wishing that he'd kept them. Then, with a sudden motion, he flung the gun onto the pile and, before it had thumped down, was striding back to me. Close again, hand raised again, again two fingers held an inch from my shot shoulder. Though, when I began to raise my own as before, he brushed them away. This time, he touched my skin where it was sewn. And, so lightly I could barely feel it, traced the stitches over the wound.

I showed him the needle, the sharpness of steel, bade him hold it while I demonstrated threading the eye. And, with our own eyes so close, his fingers holding the spike so steady, I knew what I would do. Took up the thread and tied one end. His hum of recognition at the way I made the knot, shorter one of surprise when I left him holding the needle on his own. His silence as he watched me unbuckle the strap around my shoulder, peel away the blood-soaked wad, nod and put my freshly bloodied hand over my heart. Then, nodding again, turn my back to him.

I sat on the apishamores, clenched fists shaking on my clenched thighs, while he sewed me up. Slow and careful, picking out bits of leaves or kerchief, his fingers sure, his face craning around to observe my stitching over the entrance wound, disappearing again before the stab of steel piercing my skin. Around us the others gathered, a tight circle of maybe twenty men trying to see. I shut my eyes against them, grateful for the pain bringing my mind back to each stitch, and when the stabbing stopped and the tugging began, I breathed into it, breathed harder at the congratulatory chatter that rose after his satisfied grunt, breathed my back into a stretch as much to deflect their presence with my pain as to test his sutures. Which held. He was already in front of me, my eyes opening to his.

Somehow completely changed. That thing in the eyes you look for when there is no other way of saying thanks. Or offering praise. Or indicating trust.

The best I could do then was offer the needle as a gift. Though he surprised me by shaking his head, handing it back. Before sitting beside me on the stack of blankets, starting to undo the binding over the bloodied leaves and sap that covered the hole shot through him too. Though it turned out to be a gouge—my bullet gone wide, ripping a finger-thick furrow out of his flesh—harder to suture but, I knew, quicker to heal.

Maybe it was the fact we sewed each other up, maybe my thread and needle left more movement in his arm than his own jomin's ministrations, maybe it was just that we'd faced each other, given each other the chance to live, each taken it, but from then on Pumk'uk'mi—No Rope, I'd learn it meant—from then on he what? Watched over me? Argued for me? The way he must have to bring me supplies that the entire village must have clamored to keep. The way, in the days and weeks that followed, he somehow convinced all of Kushna to leave me be. I do not know what arguments he made to those who surely would have rather killed me. I only know that they did not. That, forever after, whenever we saw each other, he'd greet me the same way: two fingers raised just shy of touching where he'd shot my shoulder. And I would raise my own, point to where I'd wounded him. Over the years the gesture becoming just what we did.

Though we would not see each other often. A couple ceremonies over the next few weeks. An invitation to a feast inside his home that I could not refuse. Once even of my own volition, me coming to him to ask he cut my stitches free, to cut free his. By then the rains had begun in earnest and we worked inside his hu, the earth-mound headman's hut bearing Kushna's tallest hide-and-feather marker, its lower entrance guarded by a staked coyote-dog, pine-needle floor carpeted with hides, the firelit inside, on my earlier visit, crowded with family—women singing as they ground meal on pounding stones, or chatting cutting each other's hair with glowing coals, children napping in hammocks slung from the walls, men rolling split-acorn dice, roaring and laughing. This time the only other one in there with us was the head jomin: the hu'uku, circling at a safe distance, shaking his antler rattle and feather wand, chanting words I could not understand. Though I gleaned enough from his hard gaze, the wariness with which the rest watched me, the way mothers called to their children. After all, had I not told them the explosions that had killed their fathers and sons were brought on by my own blood?

Or maybe they sensed something deeper, truer, about me. I know that No Rope did, know from the way, on my first visit to his home, I'd watched him take in my strain and sweating surrounded by his family, the way on that second time in his hu I'd started shaking. Not out of pain, not from his tugging. A thing he would have known since I tugged out his stitches first, since he had seen my shaking worsen as, outside, the chatter grew. Till I could hear them through the rain drumming the dirt-packed roof: all the villagers crowded out there, hundreds surrounding the hut, come close as they dared to the Honpetayim Woole.

What the next time I came I learned they called me. Though not yet what it meant. The words just sounds No Rope said now meant me. A thing I made no effort to correct. Was glad to leave behind the name my parents gave me wholly as I'd forsaken Son, forsaken Father. That day it was raining again, and cold, and yet I stood in my buckskin and buffaloe boots, hat dripping, waiting at the village edge for someone to tell him I was there. The granary guard dogs barking on their tethers. A group of boys out hitting pebbles with a scapula bat, scattering as they fled the worsening weather. And in the rain he came to meet me, raising his two fingers in greeting again.

There in the downpour I showed him the trap I'd brought, opened the jaws, set the springs with the steel dog. Then, with a stick, pressed at the pan, the steel circle snapping shut with such a crash No Rope leaped back a good three feet. Which I gave him to know was right, was what I'd come to show, why I set the trap again and let him press it with the stick. So he would feel the power, tell the others, warn them away. Gestured and drew in the mud till I was sure he understood I'd only set them near my camp, marked each with a red strip torn from the same kerchief he'd once tied to my musket.

And yet I think he understood more than I meant him to. More than I did myself. That day he never requested we go in from the weather, and, in the weeks that followed, sent fewer runners to my camp with invitations to ceremonies, seemed, when I would attend, not to expect I enter the k'um or hu. Appeared unsurprised when, near the year's turn, I told him I'd decided to move farther away. He waited while I tried to explain it was because of flooding—the river already risen enough to make me move my shelter higher—tried to let him know I'd go upcanyon far as I could without crossing into a rival's territory. And when I finished drawing and gesturing he only nodded, in his face no sign of wondering why I wouldn't just move upridge a hundred feet, in his eyes simply a knowing. As if he'd witnessed the women digging, the men clubbing ducks, the hunter with whom I'd shared the liver, all those whose voices too often broke through the river's roar, whose distant movements too often caught my eye. In his eyes: that faintly knowing smile that I'd grown used to. That, when he spoke—He'elkuuskuusin pokuu min, three words he'd taught me: *you need more traps*—broke out onto his face.

The first full smile I had seen. And in it, something more than mirth. Relief? His gait, when I glanced back after our parting, seeming somehow lighter. The rain had ceased and the sky was clear for the first time in weeks and he had come to me wearing nothing against the cold, but still, watching him as he walked home, it seemed he had thrown off a heavy cloak, as if what stiffness lingered in his shoulder had at last left.

It must have been the same for all of them. The relief of knowing I would go. The stranger who'd come into their lives spitting fire and smoke, killing their people and then my own, fleeing only to stay just near enough they could not quite forget. And so could not go back to the way they'd been before. For I was not one of them and never would be. Must have, in their minds, belonged more to the realm of spirits, the kukinis who keep to the edges of the world, who haunt mountain peaks and caves high up in cliffs, who make their homes behind roaring falls and in the depths of distant lakes, who appear nearly the same as any other man or woman, but are not. The kukinis who come into the dance house through the smoke hole, hang upside down, tongues unfurling to the ground. My tongue: my beard; my tongue: my skin. The blue in my eyes and the shaking in my body and the fire striking inside me at another's touch: How could they think otherwise? These people into whose world I'd come, who could no more be at peace with me among them than I'd been able to be among those of the world from which I'd fled. It must have been a relief for all of them. Though none as much as me.

All my life I'd lived on the outskirts of others. The woods beyond my parents' house, the forests full of hidden homesteads, the banks of streams just far enough from the presence of other trappers, in a deer bed beyond the reach of my own family. Now, at last, it was the woods and me. The deer and fox and squirrel and bear closer to my people than people would ever be.

AUTUMN, 1849

It comes out of the thinning dark, a susurration rushing through dawn-quiet woods, rising toward Silas like some upcanyon wind. Though the canopy is still, the understory still. And, for a second, he goes still as well, breath gusting from his climb. Till the rushing swamps his sound, breaks from the trees, and a buck leaps out—all heavy rack and hurtling weight—bounds crashing past. Before he can react, two more blur by—does—and then they are all there around him, the woods a cloudburst of stampeding deer.

For a moment, standing, chest heaving, he thinks it is the dogs that they are fleeing—last night, beneath the screaming: the first hints of distant howls, faint pulse of hooves—but the deer are running along the slope, not up from below, and in the torrent of them blowing by, he hears, coming out of the dimness far behind, a thin but rising chorus of ululating cries. A deer drive. In the same instant that he realizes it, he turns, deer flying by to either side, begins to run with them.

Through the crashing tumult of the panicked deer, he catches the first baying, a rider's shout, but does not once look back. His gaze stays searching the tangle of brush and vines ahead, while behind him, the baying nears, the riders' calls clear enough now to hear the words—*there*, *deer*, *him*—and where is it? How far ahead? How soon before the dogs are on his heels, the light bright enough for the riders to shoot? And then he sees the buck, the first that had leapt by, that should by now be out of sight, standing instead straight up on its hind legs, its forehooves flailing, rack lashing back and forth. Up the slope: another, stumbling. And they are leaping, catching their feet midair, falling in a bleating din of panicked crashing. Now he looks back, quick—three dogs racing up the slope, fast as the deer, the farthest veering off to chase a streaking doe, the next snapping at a passing other, but the third nearly on him—and he throws all he has left into his legs, lungs, burning chest, the barking closing, the deer's running a drumming beneath his feet becoming the deeper shaking of horses' hooves. Ahead: another deer caught in the net, and he can see the woven vines, the stakes shaking with impact, the tribesmen bursting from behind bushes, clubs in their fists.

He reaches to his side, draws out his knife, meets the fence already slashing, the big blade ripping netting, hacking a gash his body can smash through, on the other side by the time he hears the dog behind him hit—its yelp and thrashing—turns to see the second crash into the writhing first, a deer whirling away, veering instead into a hunter's club. The crack of skull, the falling thud, the man spinning to turn upon the dogs. Another hunter is already spearing the third, the entire fenceline suddenly achurn with men breaking from cover, such an eruption the ridgeside shakes—the slamming of clubs, thrusting of spears, flash of arrow shafts—the air filling with bleating and bone-cracks and, in the distance, another score of hunters coming, fast closing with the ones at the fence, the few surviving deer darting back and forth between the two groups in terror. And among the panicked animals, trying to control their mounts: The riders. Five white men wheeling, hauling at reins, drawing their guns.

The first shot breaks through the crashing of Silas's own running, his body dropping, launching for cover. Scrambling behind a fallen cedar, he peers through the scrim of its huge root ball: the fenceline, now a hundred feet back, separating the stillness of the woods he's in from the turmoil on its other side, the hunters scrambling, wheeling, tripping over the writhing of dying deer, fleeing the blast. Another boom. The whole ridgeside of hunters drops, rises almost instantly again to run. Except for one convulsing in some scrub. A second: crumpled nearer the horses. By the time Silas has unsheathed his rifle, brought a rider into his sights, a third tribesman is dead. He is about to pull the trigger when the miner he's aiming at jerks so hard the man nearly comes off his saddle, and then the second arrow hits and he does, and by the time his body lands, another rider is buckling, another arrow in his gut, the hunters, from their cover behind the bodies of the deer, loosing a dozen more. Then the gunfire is cracking fast, the tribesmen's shouts rising inside it as, wielding clubs and spears, they come hurtling over the carcasses at the remaining riders.

Through the gunsmoke, he sights again, touches the trigger, balks. All those warriors out there. Where are the boys? The ones too young to hunt but not to finish off the wounded deer? The girls who will accompany their mothers to butcher the bodies? Somewhere near enough to hear his gunblast, see his smoke, call to their husbands, fathers, brothers? Still, the only shouts come from the melee a hundred feet away, men being ripped apart by bullets, riddled with arrows. Another rider falls. But there must be half a dozen tribesmen dead, twice as many wounded, and how many more before his last pursuer dies? The white man has two guns out, one in each hand, some kind of rapid-shooting pistol Silas has never seen, letting loose shot after shot. Firing and firing into the tribesmen. This man that Silas brought.

The blast, when it comes, surprises even him. The handguns spinning away, the falling rider's face a burst of red in the dawn gray. Silas waits, breech at his cheek, for the shout—in Nisenan, or Notong k'oyom weye, or another language unknown to him—alerting them to where the shot had come from. The hunters turning to see. He'll stand, drop the gun, tell them he's not as he appears, is one of them—*Nisenaanim ni*—hope they understand. But no one shouts. Nobody turns. Nobody, he thinks, seems to have seen.

Then the rifle is gone, ripped from his hands, the fore-end shattered in a flash of shards blasting back into his face, snapping his head aside, the exploding gun and rifle-crack so close together he thinks *misfired*, remembers he hadn't reloaded, hears the echo again—it had come from the slope above—and then is hurling himself onto his belly, scrambling around the root ball's other side, just as its dirt blooms above his head. The boom. Soon as it comes, he's up again, squinting toward the sound, his eyes blurring with blood, one smothered shut just as he spots the shooter—the face wrapped in filthy cloth, the pale gray mule sidling—sees the ramrod streak and rising barrel and flings himself again behind the tree. Again, the root ball bursts. And it is only in the explosion of dirt and splinters striking his face that he begins to feel the pain. His left hand throbbing so hard he cannot tell where the hurt lies, he reaches up to wipe the blood out of his eye, his fingertips melding to the slick socket, some bit of hair pricking a part so raw it spikes a shard of pain straight up his forearm, jerks his hand away. And bringing it into the sight of his unsmothered eye he stares. The wreckage of his fingers. For a second he is not sure what he has left—the smallest is gone, a shredded stub, the rest mashed together into a mitt of blood—and then a wave of nausea and pain breaks over him and he has to look away.

In the clearing air: their shouting. With his good hand, he shoves himself up. Surely, the hunters have seen him now. But they are pointing higher, a few drawing bows, first arrows slicing by so near Silas can hear their whistling, the other hunters moving up the slope as if toward the shooter. But beneath his chest Silas can feel a thudding in the ground, a shaking so slight it could be from his own heart but isn't. Is hooves. Their drumming coming fainter, fainter, disappearing as it takes the other woole away.

Leaving only his heartbeat.

Only his heartbeat and the throbbing hand. And the pain. His little finger is lost. But his thumb—he leaks a breath—is there. The rest of his left hand is such a mash of blood and flesh he cannot see. Though when he tries to move his fingers, he watches the first two separate, his pointer unsticking from the gunk—whole—the middle following—whole—the fourth tugged with it in a ripping wave of pain. That one is mostly gone as well, what little's left held on by the coagulating blood binding bone to meat.

Only his heartbeat and the throbbing and the pain and the place where his pinkie should be, a joint of his near-severed fourth finger starting to dangle against the rawness of his missing fifth, and clenching his jaw, he wraps his right hand around what remains of his left, grips. The pain knocks his head back, rolls his eyes so far into their sockets the recti seem about to rip, the ache spiking down his face into his neck to meet the same spiked up his arm, the whole left side of his body wracked. And then he breathes and drops his chin, beard bunching against his chest, right fist wrapping his ruined left, the still-pumping blood leaking between his grip.

His heartbeat and the throbbing and the pain and blood and a lightness in his head he knows isn't good. Somewhere in the woods people are walking, their footsteps shrushing, voices just near enough for him to hear they're speaking of the face-wrapped man who'd fled, whether he'd been the one who shot the last intruder off his horse, or if there is another. And, farther away, there is the anguish of men wounded worse than he, their companions trying to care for them. Even more distant: the cries of women. Beyond them: the river. Its hushed roar. Not quite the sound of his, but similar as the language of these hunters is to that of Kushna. Not the same water, not yet, but will be eventually. When all three tributaries meet down in the valley. Something about that brings him a little peace, and he tries to listen through his heartbeat and the pain and the sounds of others to only the water. Listens until it is hard to tell the difference between it flowing down there and what flows from him, the soil beneath his ear seeming to carry the sound as much as the air. He lifts his head: the river's roar. Sets it down again: a different trickling, quieter, closer.

By the time he reaches the creek, the doves have stopped their three-note hooting, the warblers begun their later-morning cheeping. The women have come to tend the wounded, grieve the dead, their distant singing cut with keening. At first, he'd slid his body downslope, shimmying on his back, then turned over and crawled, an awkward three-limbed lurching, his wounded hand propped on his head in an attempt to slow the bleeding. Till, finally out of sight, he'd tried to rise, nearly blacked out. Then, wrestling his body up again, he'd made it another round of stumbling before sinking back down, his arm running its bloody flag back up over his head, his face bent near the ground, turned to better hear the creek.

Now it is loud. He'd followed the sound into a gully, letting his own weight slide him down beside the water, the warblers' *sweet sweet sweet* and women's distant grieving growing more distant still as he'd shoved his body across mossy rocks, his face over the surface, smothered all other sounds beneath the gurgle of the creek. His gulps. It is so cold he can't swallow much before his insides freeze, his lips go numb. Lying just above the rippling, he tries to see in his reflection what else the shattered stock had done—his stinging forehead, the blood crusting around his eye—but the current flows too fast. All he can catch is his silhouette, the lead-ball pendant swinging, the drops of red purling away, and flattening his body, he lets its weight rest on his chest, plunges his face all the way in.

The grieving gone, his heartbeat buried beneath the water's roar. For moment the cold is so great it even clears away the pain, the blood of his brow-wound staining the water less and less till it runs clear. Then he comes gasping up, rearing back dripping, and teeth chattering, beard leaking down his buckskinned chest, reaches for his possibles, digs inside with his good hand until he finds his needle, skein of chewed sinew. His arm, bent above his head, has cramped, his hair blood-glued to the wound, and tearing it loose, the pain clears the last of the cold, all but the tautness of the skin over his face, around his eyes, his mouth, as he forces his left hand's still-working finger and thumb to grip the needle. While, with his right, he threads the thin sinew through the shaking eye.

The wound is too smothered to tell where he might stitch. So, taking the needle in his right hand, he reaches his left over the water, plunges it in. At first the current's tug is so much worse he nearly yanks it out again, but then the cold begins to work, the skin to numb enough he can even open his fingers, what's left of them, let the water wash away the chunks of flesh and blood, the half-severed fourth one shaking as if trying to break free. Beneath, the red cloud billows, unthinning, and soon as he raises his hand, the wound is welling. Though not so fast he cannot see the smashed bone, mashed muscle, how little holds his dangling ring finger on. Quickly then, he plunges the hand back in, pins the needle in his sleeve, unsheathes his knife.

Three times he nearly faints. The first one feeling the blade slice through the skin and tendon, brought down with such force the steel sticks into the branch beneath, in the moment before he yanks it free, when he's unable to stop staring at the finger lying in the leaves. The second one when he has to lift his wrecked hand to his face, his right pinching the ragged skin over the nub of bone, his beard roughing the wound as, struggling to work his mouth around it, he grips the flaps of flesh between his teeth, begins to suture. The third one after he's made five stitches through the wound where his fourth finger used to be, fallen back onto the stones and, staring at the sky beyond the leaves, feeling the fresh pain of what he's done, knows that he still has to make himself sit up, pull together what he can of the wrecked flesh around what once was his little finger, do it all again. Each time it is the cold that saves him, the shock of plunging his blown hand into the creek snapping him back from blackness. His wound billowing blood, the water freezing the fainting away, the pain receding a little bit, a little more. He picks the severed finger up, spits out a bitten piece of flesh, finds another stick to set between his teeth, breathes in, clamps down, readies another stitch. Till—collapsed against the sloping earth, propped up against a trunk, his hand resting atop his throbbing head—he at last gives in.

It is the smell of smoke that wakes him. Or the pain. Or just his body knowing it must: the still-leaking blood, the threat of fouling, the feeling of the ants. At first the stinging is so intense he does not understand it and then, seeing them crawling over the wound, he throws himself toward the creek, plunges his hand back in.

When it's washed free of them, he draws it out again. The water has half cleared what blood had dried, the dark coagulations humped in fresh wet clods, and staring at the ragged suture before new blood wells up, he tries to tell if he'd covered the bone enough to prevent rot. The necklace No Rope gave him for protection keeps swinging out, blocking his sight, and snagging it in his good hand, he's filled with an urge to snap the string, rip it away. But already the stitches have begun to leak, brighter blood beading over the stubs, and dropping the pendant, he reaches to his parfleche, paws through his possibles, pulls out the sack of yarrow.

With his teeth, he undoes the knot, with his still-working fingers digs out a pinch of leaves, stuffs them in his mouth, sits with his eyes shut against the resurging pain, and chews. When it's wet enough, he drools a gob into his good hand and, steeling himself again, pushes the paste onto a knob of bloody flesh. Drools out another. Does the same. Scooping inside his cheeks, through the beard-dripped mess, he gathers the rest, mashes it over the wounds, pressing it on as best he can, face sheened with sweat. Then, taking the worn hide he keeps for patches to wrap his musket balls, he tears a few strips off with his teeth, uses them to bind the rest over his wound, leaving his thumb and two remaining fingers free. Above his eye, the cut has mostly quit leaking blood, but he presses the last of the paste onto the gash, waits for it stanch the rest. In the air, the smoke-smell is stronger. Many fires, but far away. And letting his eyes close, he listens for signs of anyone still near—the grieving women, the butchering of deer—but there is only the high burbling of the creek, the lower roar of the river, his breathing in between.

When he wakes, it will be night. Cold. Moonlight washing through the canopy, shifting with the breeze, so that the ground around him seems to ripple, drift, as if he is afloat on the surface of some gentle river, surrounded by water instead of earth. But when he stands his legs are steady, his breath even, his eyes, in a slice of moonlight, clear beneath his poultice-crusted brow, motionless above his beard matted with spit and yarrow. Until he steps into a strip of shadow and—slung bags swinging, empty gun-sheath flapping, his hair a tangle of moonlight and blackness and moonlight again—begins making his way back. That night he creeps up the slope till he can see the deer fence, the line of vines wound tree to tree all down the ridgeside, broken in places now, the moonlight bright on the crushed underbrush and branch-snagged bits of fur, dried blood shining blackly on leaves. All the rest has been hauled off or eaten, the deer butchered, the horses the same, their blankets and tack brought back to camp along with the meat. He can smell the smoke more strongly now, see the distant glow, firelit branches faintly flickering far up the ridge. Down here, only the dogs remain, their bodies skinned and bulbous, the thin layer of white over their muscles wet with moonlight. Something moves among them. More than one.

His good hand goes to his knife fast as if the movement below is human too, but by the time the blade is out, he knows it is too small. Martens or fishers, their slinking shapes slipping away at his approach. A hiss: something larger. He stops. Sees, farther downslope, a catamount crouched over one of the dogs. Its eyes two moonglints, steady on him. He stays as still, watching it back, his own eyes glinting the same, the two of them like that long enough the moonlight drifts on and leaves them dark, the big cat turning then, disappearing in a single leap. When it is gone, he goes to the carcass—a hound fleshed of all but the fur over its face, even the tailhide peeled away, only from the skull up resembling what it once was—and, crouching, makes a cut along the spine, slices away a strip of backstrap, lifts it dripping to his mouth, his beard shaking, jaw working ferociously, seeming driven less by hunger than some fury, his cutting tireless, eating ceaseless, minute after minute, as if he means not just to fill his belly but to make the entire body before him disappear, innards and bones, the fur of its face, its eyes glazed and globular and grown inside a beast that never should have seen the world in which it died, never should have loosed its sound beneath the trees, never should have been allowed to lead men like him here.

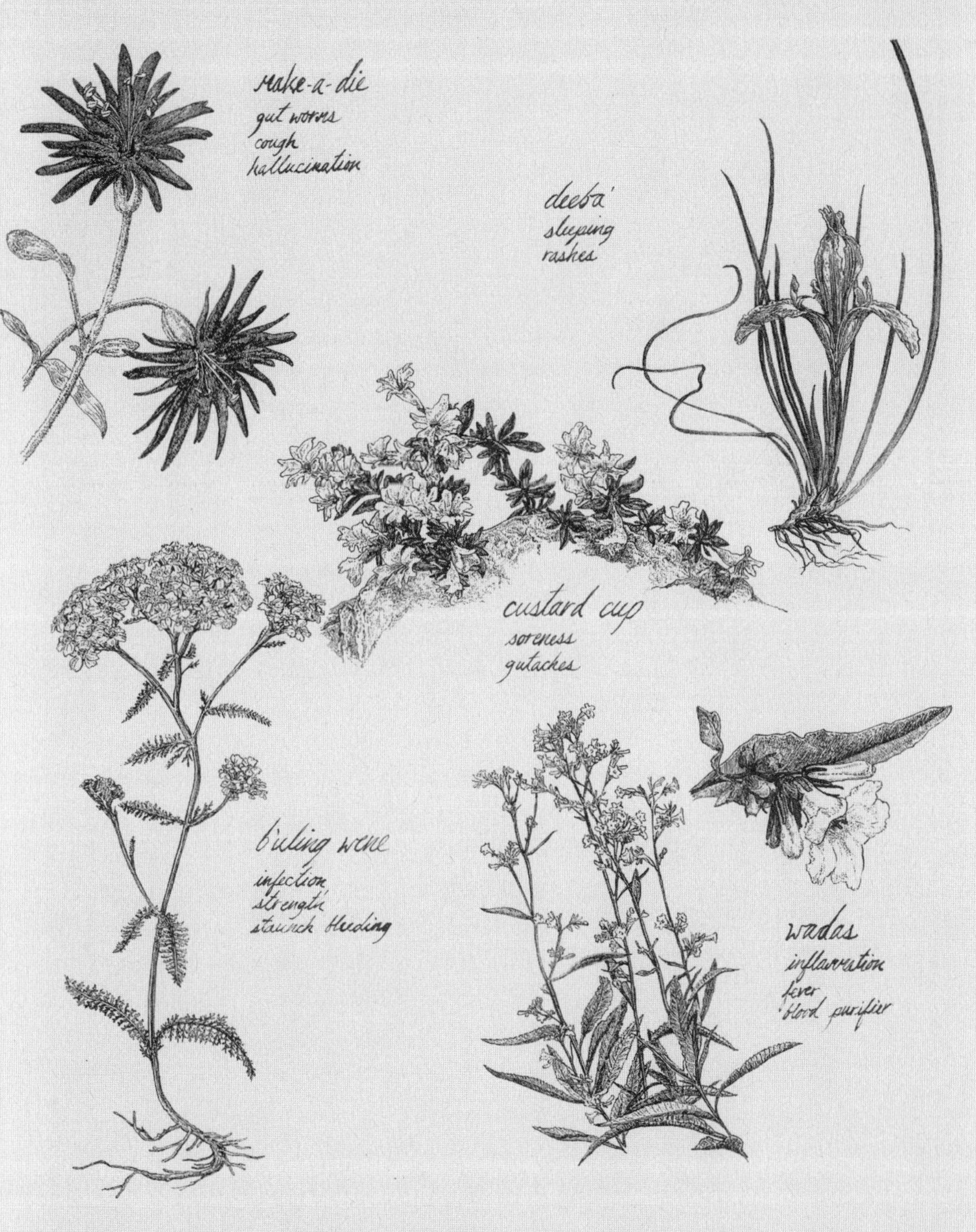
make-a-die
gut worms
cough
hallucination
deeba'
sleeping
rashes
custard cup
soreness
gutaches
biling wine
infection
strength
staunch bleeding
wadas
inflammation
fever
blood purifier

It was midwinter the day I went upriver in search of where to make my home. K'ummen. Willows losing last leaves & small birds puffed up agnst the cold & rain pouring down the way it is now as I write. Though that morning near 9 yrs ago the sun appeared for the first time in days & so I traveled in mere moccasins & buckskins my hat hung down my back to let the light in at my face. My shoulder still stiff & sore but my knee sturdy enough to let me leap boulder to boulder. Harder than taking game trails higher up. But they wld be out of the river's sight & above its roar & by then I had lived mid both long enough to know that though the sun came later & the air was colder & the nisenan all made their homes well up out of the gorge I wld make mine down in it. Nearby the water. Away from theirs. An hr's scramble upriver. And then anothr. Till ½ a day was past & the sun was streaming down & coming round anothr bend I stopped.

I can still see me standing there. My face lit by the sun. Beard not yet so streaked with white. Nose bearing no tattooed line. My body whole. Can see it even now through this small window cut through this wall. Myself near a decade ago struck still by the sight of here.

Across the river a sunlit rill spilled from a ledge above. The canyon's steepness leveling into a stand of larger trees. Their deeper green spreading over the outlet of some hidden creek.

And I was crossing. The river too high to wade too fast to swim. But seeming always to provide a boulder or fallen tree or log wedged just near enough to try the leap. Till flinging myself in splashing scrambles I reached a place I cld plunge to my waist plow through the rapids & with my wounded shoulder shaking from holding the musket over my head climb crashing out. Into the warming sun. Thin with the season. But bright & unbroken on that southfacing bank.

Above a wet sheened slant of cliff I found the creek. Followed its ferns & mossfurred stones onto a ledge of level land bneath the trees. A perch so hardby the riverbank some dzn ft below that the crown of a cottonwood growing down there seemed to spring trunkless from the ground. Its few last scattered leaves still shimmering gold. The land remaining level another hundred feet upriver till coming even with the bank again, it met the crash of cataracts into the sudden calm of a deep pool. A wide bend curving beneath a boulder bigger than any I had seen. Stacked with another. Stacked with a third. Three massive stones each the size of a small hill somehow balanced atop each other high on a bluff above. Like some hundred-foot effigy. Head and body and legs. Standing in silence over the river's bend. As I stayed there beneath its gaze, watching it back. Waiting. Listening. And in all that time catching no sound or sight or sign of anyone but me.

Me and the effigy. Its flat featureless face catching the sun's last light. Fading into the deepening dusk. Leaving only its stare. Silent as it had been when I had first rounded the bend. Too distracted by the scene back then to understand that I was being allowed to pass. The way the trees had laid themselves across the river. The water swept the logs against the rocks. The rocks held them for me to cross. Even the weather staving off rain for all the days after that it took me to carry all I had back. Hunched beneath a rucksack stitched of saddlebags and tack. Crossing the boulder-spanning snags with an adze or axe gripped in each hand. Till just hours after my final trip the sky above the canyon opened up. Loosed such a deluge it swept away my makeshift bridge. Removed all possibility of turning back.

Even the straightness of the pines standing where I would use their felled bodies to build my hut. Even the boulder resting where it would anchor my hearth. The cedar bark that peeled away in sheets for roofing. The soil that would bank the sides. Even the flag snake chasing off rattlers, keeping my cabin free of mice. The mink that watched me dress some game or gut a fish, darted in when I was done to clear the mess away. The crows that clattered down to clean up what bits it left. The heron that, as I'd sat beside the pool on that first evening, had glided by on its return downriver. Same as, each morning after, while I humped my supplies to my new home, it would pass me on its way up. Even in slanting rain it shaped itself out of the gray, barely discernible amid the downpour, but there, wings beating upcanyon each morning, down every dusk. Day after day. For years.

Here. Here, son, come in. Let me hold the door-skin for you, the elk hide shaking drops of rain. Inside it's dry, dim—the sole rawhide-covered window aglow with what faint light bleeds through—but I will roll my curtain up so you can better see. The hearth backed by that boulder, the bed of my old buffaloe robe, the rabbit-pelt pillow flattened by the weight of your father's head. Knock your knuckles on the hanging pot, see how the ringing lingers. Stoop beneath the strung-up sheaves of goldenrod and yarrow, the strips of smoked meat and strings of mushrooms hanging from near every inch of ceiling. The only space left for my head a narrow path from door to bed to hearth to desk. This root-ball table, its surface of stretched skin. Pull out the stool, its leather worn soft by me. Sit. Shut your eyes. Breathe in the drying fish and rain-wet moss and grease built up on iron pans over almost a decade. Baskets of alumroot, mint. The slightly sour scent of baking acorn meal. The slush lamp burning its wick. The paper, ink. And I would write you in. Despite the single stool, the only pillow, the sight of me standing there still, holding the elk skin open, the doorway empty.

As it would stay. Will. Has been since the first day.

The sound of the rain on my new-made roof a little sharper then, before the moss and ferns and lichen had grown over the bark. But the silence beneath it much the same.

That k'ummen the rains came hard and long, the moss on the oak trunks unfurling lush and green, between downpours beading with a million bright droplets of daylight caught. Frozen, in the coming weeks, to white sparks of frost. The juncos alighting on the bare willows: a hundred small birds popping from bush to bush, shaking the still lines of the rimed world. The sticklike stalks of poison oak, hoar-frosted river stones. The shocking red of flockholly berries, rustier clusters on manzanitas. Sunrise in the clouds above the canyon, crossed by the silhouettes of geese, their calls falling into the river's roaring. The sunlight slipping down the ridgeside to touch the frost-furred logs and in a second—two, three, four—the hoar-white disappears. Mist rising among the willows' new-sprung leaves, the oaks haloed with sunlit green. The alders' tassels blown by a spring breeze.

That wi'nuti I left for the first time—the season of fawns and subsiding floods, the water barely low enough to cross—waded in up to my chest, the plews I'd trapped held high above my head, climbed out on the far side into the shadow of the effigy that all winter had watched over me. Then turned downriver. And passing beneath its faceless gaze, made my way around the bend, out of its sight.

It was midday when I reached the place I'd lived my first weeks on the river, though the winter's floods had remade it so completely I nearly missed it. The beach where I'd hunched over the pistol-kindled fire was gone, as was the fallen trunk I'd sat on the dawn I'd learned I might survive. Even the bank had been carved back, stripped of trees carried downriver, my early shelter swept away along with the few belongings I'd left behind—sawbucks, spare horseshoes, Fancher's brain-and-blood-stained hat, Ballou's huge boots still reeking of his feet—as if the river meant to erase every last trace of who I'd been before I'd found it, the life I'd known beyond its canyon rim. For some time then I stood in its unceasing roar, afraid to leave it. Before at last, steeling myself, I began the steep climb out of the gorge.

Up the bright bloom-smothered slopes, through families of quail returned to their trails, the river quieting behind me, the roar dwindling away. By the time I crested the ridge it was a whisper; by the time I reached the village it was gone. Just my breathing and the crickets' sawing and a distant barking breaking out as I walked along the wide-burned path into the rising sounds of laughter, talking, a scent so strong it nearly stopped me. Not the waft of drying fish or stench of human scat, but the scent of them, their bodies. Same as I'd seen startle deer downwind of me, make foxes skirt my hut. The same as mine except increased a thousand times. The whole of the village milling around their earth-mound homes, the crowd thrumming with the thrill of the spring run, some pounding the new-smoked salmon to meal, others lining storage baskets with dried leaves, more stringing up the sharp-boned skeletons in long strands to hang inside their huts, later to be pulverized to powder, the children amassed around the piles of still-whole fish, tasked with keeping the crows and squirrels away. The scene so charged with excitement I could feel it fill the air around me, press my shape still. Still, I made myself take another step, another, my own body surely smelling as strange to them, as disquieting to see, my rucksack strapped with such a bulging mass of peltries my own buckskins and beard and hair might look to them part of the same. If they could see me. For a second, I was sure the self I had become in the past months would, in the presence of others, be an impossibility. But here came the dogs, running. There: the faces turning, staring. Shouts. Words I could not understand beyond the two, over and over: Honpetayim Woole! Honpetayim Woole!

No Rope was waiting for me in the great acorn grove, beneath a tree unlike every surrounding other. Amid the tall straight harvest oaks, the one I'd come to call a gold oak spread wide as all the rest were high, its gnarled trunk coated in moss, its overspreading canopy composed not of the buds studding the others' branches, but of leaves that had stayed dark and thick all winter. All but the undersides, aglow now with new green.

Beneath them, No Rope seemed younger, taller. The ash washed off his face, the pitch cut from his hair, the two feathers piercing his nose faintly whiffling with his breath. Which I could smell. Might have, from the mere shock of company, just turned around and left. If he hadn't reached out. My scarred shoulder twitching beneath the touch of his fingers, fighting an urge to jerk away. Till, lifting my own hand, I could bring myself to do the same.

And, as I tried to pass to him a sense of which supplies I wished to trade for, as he passed back to me the price in plews, as his children and wives brought baskets and tools, carried away my peltries, it seemed to me increasingly that I'd been wrong: he was not taller or younger but simply at peace. Because of what I'd brought to trade? Or because he knew, when we were done, I'd disappear again? Or just the way, over the past few months, life must have returned to what it had been, the thing I saw in him simply then who he had been before I came.

I still can't say. Though after I'd refilled my rucksack—acorn meal and dried chokecherries, glue scraped from salmon skins, skeins of milkweed string and nets of hemp and a stone pipe No Rope had given as a gift—after I'd left him at the grove's edge, returned at last to the deeper woods, regained the river's murmur, I could not shake the sense that what I'd seen was in fact not something in him at all, so much as a reflection of what he'd perceived in me.

I would come back again in fall, again in spring. Once each semem and each yoomen. Each year before I began my journey to the higher country that I would roam all summer, each autumn when I returned to the hearth-fire of my winter home. The two trading days a year marking the start and end of my migrations. As much part of the rhythm of my life as the month I'd spend slowly making my way upcanyon, a few miles each day, a few hundred feet in elevation, maybe a thousand in a week, moving at the speed of spring. Beside my climbing catkins unfurling on alder branches, dogwoods filling with blooms, cliffsides covered in the yellow-pricked purple of stars-at-dusk, clouds of cream-colored custard cups, ember poppies bright as molten gold. The warm air of the foothills following me ever higher, ever the same, even as each place I left behind increased in heat. As if I held the season inside my chest. Or it held me, carried my body up beside the flashing churn of salmon filling the river with the fervor of their spring run. And when, at the end of my months in the high country, bilberries would begin to bronze, the cold to drop down from the peaks, I'd do the same: follow the rusting mountainside, the swelling river, drifting down toward my bend, creek, cabin, effigy. The heron one morning coming upcanyon again to meet me, gliding back down in evening, its traversal steady as a heartbeat, each wingflap a pulse set to time's passing.

A rhythm that would wake me at first light, send me outside to make my water beneath a few last stars. Or, holding the door-flap over my head, I might piss out into a pounding downpour. Stoke the fire. Dip a scrap of buckskin into water warmed overnight and swab my face, neck, press the heat to my shut eyes. Stay still like that. Till, on the hearth, the water had grown hot enough to pour over the bark-curls in my cup and let them steep. Might make some cakes then, mashed christmasroot and manzanita berries baked in oak leaves, or swallow a handful of seeds, or gnaw enough off bones left from the night before to let me begin my day.

If I could, I'd bring you with me. Wading into shallows to stake a weir, or waiting with a raised spear, standing over a current quick as I am still, while the first spots of rain begin to dot the stones around me. Would show you how to skin cedar branches with a hatchet, whack their ends sharp, stake them around a basket, bind it with roots to hold the granary high off the ground. Some days you'd see me dump sacks of acorns in, others scoop out mast, grind it in a hollowed stone, my shoulders shifting with my hands' circling till the pestle is ground out, the hole worn deep, the season slipping into a year. Another. A third passing in the gathering of berries, drying of mushrooms, digging soaproot out of streams, fleshing creatures I'd caught, stretching their hides on willow hoops staked off the ground. And you would see me making my rounds, checking my traps, circling my home. Day after day. Year after year. Hear my moccasins brush through the leaves, the rock rasp round and round. The roar of the river under everything, always. Covering my humming, my heartbeat, my breath let out as I lie back on my plew-spread willow bed, rabbit-fur pillow, shut my eyes. Such stillness. As if my features had been drawn in ink, the blackness of the hut the blankness of a page, the log walls borders, the river's roar blowing me dry, the canyonsides two hands around me, holding.

Some mornings slants of sunlight came through the skins staked up around my camp, set a dozen hoop-stretched circles glowing red, the sight so striking I'd find myself leaving the peltries drying long after they had cured. In winter, I might pick through the remains of pinecones stripped by squirrels, layer a thousand seedscales over a boulder, one by one, till it was covered, then do another. In spring, might do the same with flower petals, leaving flashes of color all along my path up to the higher country. Might come upon the white trunk of a flood-drowned tree, prop it upright, spend days finding the feathers I'd tie to each bleached branch, leave it with a replenished canopy. That in a gust would burst into such wild fluttering it seemed as if the tree itself wished to take flight. And as I continued my own ascent, the canyon would grow narrower, the river dwindling, the gorge shallowing, ridges flattening to ever-wider expanses beneath an ever-wider sky. So much more blue. In my first days up there each year I'd be struck still just by the sight. Till mirroring the sky with a blanket of lupine blooms would be all I wanted to do. The way I'd paint rock-cracks with blood, taking such pleasure in watching the veins' color deepening day by day. Same as the peace I'd find at the first snow when, before starting back toward my winter home, I'd walk for hours, one foot placed carefully after the other, marking the white world with my own line, clean as a pen on paper.

A peace I pray you have known too. Though even as I write it, I hear your answer, your terrible child's voice come from a face already darkened by the start of a beard, a face I can see no more than I can you standing here in my hut calling me father. Your absence a hole leaking your silent breath. Blowing away the lupine blooms, the seedscales off the boulders, washing the blood out of rock veins, covering the line-in-snow back up.

At peace? you say. As if you've seen me stop mid-step, watched my brow bunch, when, at the sound of footsteps crunching the snow behind me, I'd know with sudden certainty that it was you, would spin, let out a shout, listen to it disappear into the emptiness between the trees. Till the air would fill back in with the yak of a magpie, a marmot's bark, the world I knew could not contain you too. Though, grinding larkspur blooms or custard cups or the twinberries I'd use to paint a bank of boulders blue, yellow, black, I would remember the bright colors you'd choose to draw your stars, hear your asking for a brush, a sheet, feel your tug on my sleeve, your mother's urgent signing, the speed with which I whipped around, the crack and sting. Would see your face suddenly far away, your welling eyes, their stare.

I have thrown snowballs by myself. Six thousand feet above the sea. Hurled them at rocks and trees, chipmunks and jays. Watched their cocked-headed curiosity, listened to their wingbeats flapping away. Disappearing into the snowy silence of that high country. The same that swallowed whatever sound the snowball, landing, might have made. So that I could still feel it falling, sinking, dropping through me.

At peace, I said, and still sometimes in spring I would find nests, the brown-spotted eggs of quail, the light green ones of goldeneyes laid in woodpecker holes. Once, a hummingbird's: bits of alder fluff and milkweed stuck with spiderwebs, delicate as the lichens on the branch that held it. Inside: two eggs, white, each barely bigger than my thumbnail, their shells so thin that, lifting one, my thumb sank in. And tipping it into my mouth I drained it. Stood holding the emptied shell in sticky fingers, the second unbroken in my other hand, feeling inside my throat the frantic thrumming of coming wings, hearing your small voice saying to itself, *Go on*, seeing the left-open coop door, you running for the porch. *Go on*. My stomach starting to flutter. The way, when I'd eaten a trout down to its bones and begun sucking its head, I would remember how much you liked to touch the eyeballs of fresh-bought fish, smooth beneath your fingertip, and, trying my own finger inside the trout's socket, would feel only the hole. As if my finger had instead reached inside me. Deep as when I'd dig through a gutted carcass, searching for the flattened lead. Would later melt it down, let it cool inside the mold. And lifting it out, find it remade into a marble of swirled glass. Held in a small boy's fingers.

At peace, I told you, when what I should have said is that I could have been. If not for you.

There is the sting again. Here on my palm. Its mark blooming beneath your stare. Your child's eyes asking why. Your grown ones asking only if it was worth it.

The sting returned, the burn on my own face.

What would be worse? If I said yes or no? Or find I can say neither, can only ask you the same. Your birth, your breath, your ability to hear and see and speak and think and feel and be. Your being. Your life. Was it worth it without me?

So now you know. How I would swallow the other egg, pick the flesh from the fish head, reload my musket with another ball. Leave you again. Though it sickens my stomach, though each gunshot cracks the world I've come to. A world that could not exist if you were in it.

A truth that needs me to admit this too: there was a pleasure in missing you. The missing itself the thing that I believe kept me from becoming a little less than what? Human? Living? Merely existing? Because the truth is, year after year, you were my sole relationship. My memories of you. The times when I would let myself reach back and touch them, or they would come for me, as close as I would come to touching anyone. Despite No Rope's two-fingered greetings, the children crowding around to brush my forearm hairs, the women cautiously cupping my beard. No, for a year, and then another, and then another one, you were the nearest thing I knew to friendship. The memory of you. That I could talk to and imagine hearing back.

Oh, the squirrels, the birds, the coon that, my first winter, joined me at the creek, washing his crawfish or snail while I, a rod upstream, scrubbed the scent of death off my traps. If he could smell it, he showed no fear, came ever nearer till, by spring, he'd take an onion bulb or a bit of root out of my hand, sit and inspect it, whiskers twitching. While I would ask if it was satisfactory, or should I take it back and try another. Though if I dared reach out, he'd shovel the morsel into his mouth. Some nights I'd lie on my pallet mimicking the calls of owls—the whistles of a saw-whet, a great horned's booms, the long-eared's mewling and shrieks—till I grew good enough to draw them into the branches above my roof, might drift asleep then beneath their sounds brought close. During the day crows kept me company. What can I say but that we spoke. Sometimes for hours, passing our thoughts or feelings or simply observations back and forth between forest floor and canopy, undaunted by a need for understanding. Mockingbirds mimicked me—my laugh, my muttering—as well as I did the owls, called to me much the same. Then a flock of jays would drive them off, take it upon themselves to clear my camp of all other birds, till, tiring of their bragging chatter, I'd chase them away as well. And I have played with minks and martens, games made up as much by them as me. Knew a fisher cat who'd fetch bits of innards I threw from gutted trout, dart after them and bring them back to eat beside me, wait for another. One winter I entertained a weasel with chunks of meat tied to a string I'd jerk to keep the morsel just out of reach. He'd leap and whirl and, when at last I let him catch the meat, would be filled with such glee. There is no other word for it. He would do flips, rolls, scampering dances of pure joy. Before settling down to eat. And watching him, I'd feel such a sweep of gladness for the little fellow I could hardly cease smiling long enough to eat my own meal.

Across the river, where willows lined the far side of the wide bend, deer would come down to drink, ears twitching while they watched me. As if they knew that, liking to watch them too, I would not shoot. Bucks and does and, one spring, a mother with her fawns. Two spotted siblings who each morning for a week I would watch wobble in the shallows, lose their footing, come scrambling out as if they thought the current an attack.

Till one dawn when, hearing a splash, I looked up to see their mother swimming out instead. It was after a late spring rain, the river risen in one last flooding, and back on the bank, her fawns were struck with terror, caught between the rapids and what I saw then: a catamount streaking from the brush, coming so fast it seemed strung to the current, nearly on its prey before at last they leaped into the churning water and were whipped away. For a time, the big cat followed, bounding boulder to boulder, till the fawns were too far out, their bodies bobbing in the rapids, legs like waterlogged sticks, heads wet stones waiting to sink.

By then the doe was almost across, neck craning after her offspring—one just a mass smacking at rocks, the other slipping through chutes still kicking—her eyes wild as they swept past. She clambered onto the gravel, started to run. But they were gone.

Maybe she knew, maybe she was just injured: her legs collapsed beneath her, her body crashed to the stones. On the far side, the cougar turned and slipped away. From where I stood, less than a rod upriver from the doe, I could hear her breathing—loud enough to reach over the water's roar—and giving her berth, I made my way around her, started down the bank.

I did not know which one I found, whether to leave the drowned fawn there or carry it back to camp and carve it up. In the end, I brought it to her, set the small body close enough that she could see it, reach it with her muzzle should she want. Though the whole time I crouched nearby she only looked at me.

Could she know I had not killed it? Understand I'd tried to find the other? That when I stood and left her, it was so she could do in privacy whatever she might need to. Grieve or die or just get up and leave. Gone by the time that I returned later that day. Though, in the days that followed, she stayed nearby. At first maybe because I left the body on my beach, but after the scavengers had carried its last bits away, she had remained. Came down each dawn to drink at the mouth of my creek, passing my hut in the half dark, so near I'd hear her in the brush. And if she was still there when I followed to the beach, she did not flee, just turned toward me before picking her way downriver, as if she'd been waiting for me to arrive before she'd leave.

Can that count as friendship? Even a bond? A trust? Does it matter that I moved my traps away from where I thought her route? Or that, leaving for the high country later that spring, I felt for the first time a hesitancy? That, when I returned that fall and she did not, I felt faintly abandoned. That when, early in the next year, I woke to the splash of hooves passing my hut, I knew. The way, in the absence of smaller splashing behind her, I knew she'd be alone. As she'd remain all that spring and the one after. That her return each winter became one of the ways I marked the turning of each year. That I believe she did the same.

And here I sit comparing the memory of you to deer. Fisher, weasel, coon. Can only hope you'll understand I mean their presence over the years. Not just their company, but its proof of my remove from others. A comfort your absence brought too. The fact that I could never reach you the other side of knowing nobody would find me. Can you see how, in an awful way, that was the greatest peace? How, so long as the world kept you away, I would be safe. Alone here with only my crows and owls, my ringtail watching me write, my memories of you, my fear.

Not of what I know will soon be here. Not the horses or guns or even men, the ones still downriver who, hearing I have returned, will gather again, ride up to do what others failed to. I will be ready for them. Above my home the river is already deeper, begun to dam, jammed at its narrowest with the trunks of all the trees I fell. A few each day. My axe cracking through cottonwood and ash, dropping their long bodies to mass between the boulders, bank to bank. Much like the driftwood that, my first fall here, I wedged into a footbridge. Which the first winter floods wrecked, smashing in seconds what had taken me days, shooting snags into the air, the raging water washing entire gravel bars away, sending its roar up through the ground into my body. Booms I still feel now. Each time I fell another tree, add it to the dam, imagine how it will sound when that stacked wall, so many times larger, at last bursts.

A thing I am not scared of either. Not the way I am of you. Who I can feel finally here, your presence filling the room behind me, the door-flap shutting at your back, shaking from the beating rain. Your face, were I to turn and look, surely shaking as well. As if you already know all I have failed to say. Your eyes watching my hand, my pen refusing to write, my fingers shaking too. Your father sitting here, beneath your stare. Alone with his creatures and memories and lies.

AUTUMN, 1849

He climbs up the night slope of the dark canyon, away from all that had befallen it the day before, leaving the roar of not-his-river ever farther behind. Above, beyond the treetops, the sky is lit with a glow that does not reach him, the woods around him black in the shadow of the far ridge, till, as he nears the crest, the first tip of the tallest tree dips into moonlight, and then another, the tops of the giant pines shining white above the cedars, and then the cedars finding the moonlight too, the oaks' limbs knitting its brightness overhead, before it's all around him, lifting the leaves and moss and lichen into a sudden luminescence. He rises into it too, the brightness lighting his shaking beard, painting the cross of straps pinning his bandaged hand against his chest, the pale strips of dogflesh hanging from his belt, his possibles bag swinging slightly with each step.

Breaking onto the ridgetop he stops, stands staring at his moon-thrown shadow, chest heaving, hand pulsing pain, seeing the mule-riding man again before he shakes it off: the idea it could be the dead boy's father unlikely as the chance the man had followed him here, lay somewhere nearby in wait. Still: another second of hesitation. His shadow staring blackly back.

Somewhere a coyote yips, yips. Somewhere a village dog barks out an answer. When he starts up the footpath it is away from them, away from his shadow's gaze, his gait taking him east toward the higher mountains, shifting again into the long lope that in the years since he'd come here has just become the way he moves. Beneath his skin-shirt the pendant knocks like a second smaller heart, and even as his hurt hand throbs, even as he fights the lightness in his head, grips his palm behind the bandaged stubs to squeeze against the pain, goes on with breath strained and mouth agape, he hears No Rope's *Take it, take it and go* and knows the talisman was never meant to protect him against wounds, but death. On his chestbone the lead ball taps, taps. He lets go his injured hand, presses the tapping still. Feels the pulse beneath his palm. Runs on.

Above, the stars are still, scattered faint and dim across the moon-thinned dark as hints of glimmer glimpsed through the surface of a frozen river. While beneath them his loping shape moves through a landscape just as still. And if he were to tilt back his head, fill his gaze wholly with sky, he'd seem to move no more than the path under his feet, the ridge, the trees. The world paused. At least the part that will still hold him for this night, perhaps another.

Somebody pin the moon, stop the constellations from their course. Push down the sun, hold off the dawn. For when it comes, the stars have drifted farther west, the moon is gone, the river thawed, the current rolling again on its unceasing flow.

But for another hour there is just him, alone. To either side, the forest coming alive with birds, the grass with crickets, the shadow that all night had loped ahead beneath the moonlight replaced with one behind thrown by the sun, a thin shaking line shortening with the growing day, following him along the ridgepath, climbing with his ascent, the pinemat slowly overcome by kitkitdizze, chipmunks flickering among the first aspen trunks, the fluttering of last gold leaves breaking the stillness of the woods to either side as he runs on between, so when he slows at last, it is not at some sudden movement, but its lack.

Four wedge-shaped posts, high as his knees. Stepping off into the grass, he crouches behind a serviceberry bush, peering through the rusty leaves for the women he knows must be nearby. But beyond the palings the rest of the meadow is hidden by a stand of alders. All but a distant swishing sound, barely a whisper, but there. Clear as the closer rasp of something stirred round and round. Cutting through both: a child's cry. Creeping closer, he sees the cradle-frames more clearly: each Y-shaped branch woven with rawhide caning, stem stuck into the ground, the swaddled babies all staked facing away from him so they might see their mothers.

Out in the meadow: seven women shuffling slowly though tall grass, each with a winnowing basket in one hand, a beater in the other, bodies bent over fall-brittle flowers, beaters brushing seed-heads onto the shallow baskets held beneath. Around them, in the early sun, the dew becomes bright arcs of spray. As, dipping, sweeping, they recede farther into the field. Their backs to him, same as their children's. But in between, an eighth woman—ancient, shriveled—staring straight his way.

She sits supporting a scoop-shaped basket so large it covers her entire lap, her hands inside it ceaselessly circling, her seat beneath the alders close enough to the cradle-stakes she can reach out and brush a fly off of a child's face. Close enough to Silas, crouched a couple rods away, she must see him. Will surely scream, bring others. But her creased face stays calm, unchanged. The only sound she makes a shushing. Which infant has started crying, he cannot tell—all their cradle-backs equally still—but he knows he should retreat beneath the sound, skirt round what older children or men might be nearby, is already backing away when she starts singing: Kassam, kassam. The words—lil hanpi—he knows them.

Bluejay, bluejay, gather the pine nuts . . .

Stopped there, still in his half crouch, he cannot keep from mouthing them—kassam, kassam—the words soundless on his lips. Lil hanpi. A trembling in his beard so slight it might be a breeze, or breath, but isn't. Unthinkingly, he reaches up—his injured hand: the sudden pressure, brush of beard hair—his thumb and remaining fingers squeezing his jaw until the pain abates. Then, with his good hand, he pushes aside the serviceberry, creeps closer.

By the time he's circled through the grove, the baby has ceased wailing—now he can see them: swaddled in furs, lashed to the cradle-frames, faces motionless as their bound bodies—and when he stops, he is so close behind the old woman he can make out the husks and seeds stirred in her basket, the lighter chaff her hands break free. Can feel it in the throbbing of his own. The circling of her palms and fingers: his pulse. The rasp of the distant beaters: his breath. Kassam, kassam, lil hanpi, the old woman sings, rocking slowly with her grinding, her moving making the babies seem even more still, almost unliving. All but their eyes, wide and watching, staring at him. He closes his own then, lids faintly trembling, the trembling only growing the longer they stay shut.

As if she feels even so small a motion, she stops. First her singing, then her hands. The shushing seeds go silent. And when he opens his eyes again, she's turned to him. Not fully, just a slight swivel of her head, so that he is no longer looking at the back of her neck, her thinned gray hair burned short, but the deep creases of her cheek, hint of a clouded eye, an ear, elongated by the circle of bone stretching its lobe, listening.

The swishing of the seed-beating far down the meadow. The whisper of the alder leaves. If he were to turn and go, would she suspect more than a deer? Hear anything in his retreat but another woman passing? And even if her ears discerned his weight and size, even if she cried out, what would she tell the others returned to find him gone? That she had sensed a man? A spirit? What would it matter, so long as she had never seen his skin, his beard, the color of his eyes. So long as she did not shout, *Woole!* Or, worse, not know the word. By which he'd know he was the first.

She sniffs, a long inhale through her old nose. The dogflesh draping his waist? His wound? Scent of himself? He nearly steps back, but she lets out a sigh and—ear still turned to him, gaze still away—her hands begin to stir again, her fingers sifting the seeds, as if feeling how far her winnowing has come. She lifts a hand, sucks a finger, raises it into the breeze.

"Nik'kotom," he says. Grandmother.

Her head whips to him and, before she can rise or overturn her basket, he's stepping near, saying, "No, no"—the word almost the same in Nisenan and Maidu: Wi, wiiye—and then, "The babies." And in her gasp, he hears the way she heard it: not what her scream might do to them, but what she must imagine he means to if she cries out. "No," he says again, crouching to steady her basket with his good hand. "No, nik'kotom, I am a friend." Nisenan, he tells her, watching her blind eyes twitch to his voice. "From the south,

Chapakakum Sew, Kushna." Tells her that is why his words sound strange. "Kushna," he tries again, shifting the stress, and another voice—*Kushna, 'Ustoma, Wokodot*—rises out of his memory. *You, me.* Beneath her silent stare his eyes begin to well. A sight that, could she see it, might have eased her fear. Sliding his hand along the basket's rim, he touches her trembling fingers, gently covers them with his own. But her shaking only spreads up his wrist, into his arm, reaches his face, nearly spills tears. He blinks them clear. Maybe she can feel even that, her body in its blindness attuned to movements others would miss, because into the silence he has left she speaks.

"Who?" she says. Or "Whose?" Her blind eyes gone still in her face, but the wrinkled skin around them lifting with the question. "Whose friend?"

The way she says *Homonik heskum maka?* The answer it asks for. Inside his beard, his mouth moves, but only breath gets past his lips.

"Whose friend?" she says again. Then: "What name." *Hesi yakupem,* she says, slow and drawn out, as if he is one of the infants, still new to words. Though when she repeats it, her voice is loud with fear or frustration or just the need to be understood: "What name!"

And so he tells her: "Walloki." Three syllables he has not made in as many years.

She grunts: Again.

Again, louder: "Walloki."

This time her grunt seems to herself. She shakes her head. "What village?" And when he tells her, her hand draws out from under his. "This," she tells him, "is not their land."

"Hew," he says, "but you know the village."

"No Walloki."

"A boy," he says, and thinks, *Three years,* and when she asks, "Yours?" tells her instead, "A man. A yomi." *A shaman.* "A panom yomi." *A grizzly shaman.* "Missing an eye," he says, and sees her blind ones blink.

The word she says then he does not know. Though when he says it back—"Kiunaddissi?"—it sounds more like a name. And then it is suddenly clear—of course: the name he knew would have been just for childhood—and he says, "Hew, hew." *Yes, yes.*

"Kiunaddissi?" the old woman says. "You want Kiunaddissi?"

"Hew," he says again.

And she must hear all that the small word holds, because her own words flow, nearly too fast for him to catch, something about a clan still in their summer camp, somewhere on a high lake around the mountain's eastern side, the old woman speaking through her work, describing distances and paths as, thrusting the basket up, she throws the seeds, catches them blindly, over and over, telling him how he'll rejoin the river, follow it higher, the suddenness with which the peaks appear, the signs—a lightning-struck tree, a rock shaped like Turtle with the world's first mud upon his back, a creek crossed by two rows of stones—before the trail will split. All the while the seeds rising between them, falling, the breeze blowing husks free, each time leaving the basket a bit clearer of chaff. Through it all the babies watch, their mothers in the distance reaching the meadow's end, turning to start their slow beating back. Though that is not what thins his breath, lifts his chest like the flung seeds, leaves him feeling the falling inside his body.

"You will find him," the old woman says when she is done. But when he thanks her and starts to stand, she stops him: "Son," she says, "do me a favor."

What she asks is so small—simply to tell her if she has missed some chaff among the seeds—that even glancing over at the returning mothers, knowing they will soon be able to make him out, he cannot leave, stays crouched across the basket as their brushing nears, the fingers of his good hand picking through seeds, finding a husk, flinging it away, returning to finish the task alongside the old woman's.

Until they touch. For a second more, his hand keeps stirring around hers gone suddenly still. Her face: as frozen. And her hand is on his wrist, her fingers reaching beneath his sleeve, feeling his forearm hair. Where, for a heartbeat, they drift. Then her other hand shoots to his face, and before he can jerk back, she's felt his beard. On her face he cannot tell if it is horror or fear or wonder or some mixture of it all and more. Can only stand, start for the woods before she might begin at last to scream.

Though, when they come, her last words are a whisper: "Panom," she says. "Kukini." *Panom kukini.* Meaning the spirit of a grizzly. Meaning a ghost. Meaning him.

"Hew," he tells her, as he slips back between the alders. "Hew, nik'kotom, hew." Yes, Grandmother, yes.

Once there was a boy. Near the same age as you. Maybe a little younger. At least back then when this that I am telling now was happening. To him. Same age as you & also lost a father. Though his had died. I do not know how or why. Only that it was winter. Sometime late in the season we call o'mi hintsuli. Squinting at rocks. But that he far up in his high home wld have known as bo'ekmen. A word I learned from him. It means the time of breaking open trails.

His name was Walloki. The boy in this story. No you wld have said. Wld have told me it shld be something else. The way you used to when you were 3 & I wld start a bedtime tale. No Dada, you wld say, call him

But Shash he was Walloki. His tribe the notong k'oyom. Much the same as the nisenan here lower down. But much different too. Their language barely close enough to understand. Their dead more apt to linger bfore taking their leave. The pains both tribes believe a priest can suck out of someone only the mountain people claim also speak. The offending sliver of bone or wood whispering into the ear of he who removed it the name of anothr who through his own dark art had sent it into the sufferer. The power passed down father to son among both mountain & foothill tribes but only the higher dwelling one making it a rite the boy cld not refuse. A responsibility he cld not turn from upon his father's death without bringing upon himself his own. Death I mean. Shld he reject his father's role. Decline to take a new name. Fail to bcome a locum for the spirit of the deer or coyote or goose or bear.

Panom kukini. Grizzly spirit. Or soul or priest or medicine man. Or something btwn. When his father died Walloki helped the other spirit-talkers wrap the man's body in the skin of the creature it had summoned when alive. A heavy panom pelt. Fur so thick it swallowed the boy's fingers. His hands still not full grown. His hair cropped & matted & face smeared black as No Rope's had been when I first saw him. But this boy's eyes inside the soot unable to meet those of the men. The yomis who had danced beside his father. The one who wore the condor wings and crown of feathers. Another who would peer through the eye-holes of a coyote skull. Grasshopper and duck and thunder. They had washed the body. Balled it up inside a net. The knees Walloki had ridden as a child bent to the chest. The hands that taught him to shoot and spear and roll oak galls into the holes of the he-laee game now bound to ankles. Around his father they had wrapped the massive panom pelt. The bear's huge heavy face flapped over the man's. And still through all that hide and hair he could feel his father's gaze. Feel it trying to make his own eyes look away. Up at the others. Meet theirs.

He would not. Not across the deepening pit he and the priests were digging. The snow cleared and ground blackened and the fire-thawed dirt dark beneath the nails of his cold fingers scooping it out. Would not meet their gazes as he helped them carry his father's body there. Or as they lay it down. Or as the mourning cry came from his mother and sisters. Their warbled wailing above the snapping of his father's bow. Crack of his snowshoes broken in half. They smashed his gambling bones and ripped his hair netting and broke his meal bowl and tore his moccasins and wrecking all he owned, threw it atop the bear-wrapped body in that shallow hole. All but his priestly things. His bird-bone whistle and antler rattle and shaker of dried cocoons. His headdress of black feathers. A necklace strung with three paws' worth of grizzly claws. The fourth was separate. Whole. Bones reinforced with rawhide. Five claws long as the boy's own fingers. Filed sharp. For what, he did not like to think about his father doing. Though after they had mounded the earth over the man, the others stuck the weapon into the ground above his body. The claw-rake planted beside the whistle and shakers and rattles jutting up. The feather crown a nest for the dead yomi's killing charms. Splintered bones and slivered quills and spines of fish. All piled beside the strings of oak galls. Small water baskets he had half filled to make the sloshing sounds. The nut-shell coat that had been his armor beneath the heavy panom skin. Not the fur cloak that he was buried in but the one the other priests now lay in a careful heap. Last but for the stares they lay on Walloki. The dead yomi's only son. Who still refused to lift his eyes to theirs.

And you, at three, would have asked me to begin again. Told me I was telling it wrong. Insisted I bring the boy's father to life. But by four would you have known the world won't work like that? By five have learned there is no use in wishing the dead back? One year more and I'd have been gone from your life long as I'd been beside you. Any memory of me surely become merely a missing. Why did he die? you would have asked by six. And I have said already I do not know. You are telling it badly, your forever-three-year-old voice tells me. And you are right.

And all I can tell you is all I do know. The way these yomis place pains inside their victims: waada summoned by a priest to invade a person's mind and bring him agony, the sharp pricks of sela spat or flicked into his body, slivers that lodge beneath the skin and bring on headaches, cramps, bowels blown empty, a thousand other ways a yomi can fill someone with misery. Lead him to death. Which will come too. Unless another yomi can pull the pain back out, suck it into his mouth and spit it into his hand so he can hold the waada to his ear and hear it name the priest who sent it. I've seen it done: the victim coughing amid pipe smoke, the yomi biting him about the neck, gnawing the face, till he finds the place and sucks, comes up cheeks spattered with blood, mouth frothing, hands cupping his chin as he drools the sela out. I've seen him hold it up and hear the name, have watched his face fill with fury, fear, the knowledge that now he must avenge the victim by afflicting his attacker with an even greater pain.

And I have seen these men alone beside a pool or stream,

summoning their charms to service, have seen one pin a rattler's head and lure it into striking a bit of liver over and over, seen Kushna's grizzly priest shuffling into the kuksu dance beneath his ursine coat and mask, have heard the water baskets beneath his cloak sloshing like guts, the oak galls' rumble, seen the claw-rake glint in firelight and been glad it did not come for me. As it does for some. The panom yomi one of the few who kills not only with spells but with the weapons of the spirit he embodies, gouging eyes, ripping throats, slicing open bellies, just like a grizzly.

A thing maybe Walloki simply wished never to do. Or maybe knew had been done to his father by another. Or maybe had too often witnessed his father return from doing it to someone else. Or maybe he was just scared. Of all of it. Of what his life from then on would be.

That night the spirits that had once spoken inside his father would enter him, kukinis who'd come to his dreams angry at having been abandoned by their yomi, doubtful of his son's ability to be a bridge to men. Kukinis that, in their ire, would sicken his sleeping body till he was too weak to rise. That, as he lay alone inside the hut nearby his father's grave, would haunt his mind with such sheer terror his body would try to retch it out, spray it in squats, wring it from his pores. Day after day. Five straight nights before the other yomis would at last come and, carrying him through the village to the central k'um, covering his face with breath-blown smoke, singing to summon their own kukinis, would strive to convince those once his father's to accept him as their new yomi—to come and test him, fill his fever-wracked body with their pains, cut him till he was bathed in blood—watching, waiting, for his bleeding to cease, fever to break, to see if the kukinis would agree to live inside him. Or find him wanting and let him die.

All that first night he did not sleep. Sat alone within his tent of leaned-together cedar bark. Feeding a fire, spooning two fingers into a basket of acorn mush his sister left outside, chewing each bite so slowly it liquefied. Outside: the scent of roasting meat, sound of the feast. His nephews playing with a ball, his nieces singing, the stomping of women dancing late into the night. Till a roar of flames silenced them all. Consuming, he knew, the home he'd lived in all his life. Then came the children's shouting, his mother's keening, his uncles' sad song, and shifting away from his own small fire, he'd lifted the door-flap just enough to see.

Out there, the hu's doorway was bright with flames, its earthen dome leaking wisps of smoke, and then the ceiling-bark must have caught, flickers licking through in bursts, till the whole thing caved, lodgepoles snapping, roof collapsing, flames leaping to light the faces of his family watching it burn. He looked for his mother's. Instead saw theirs: all the yomis of the kuksu staring back. As if they'd been watching his door-flap, waiting for it to stir, him to emerge.

Between them and him: his father's grave. The antler rattle and feather wand and claw-rake jutting up from the mound. Waiting for him to come and take them, bring them back into his kapum hu. Before another, seeking their power, could sneak over, steal them, claim the kukinis who'd resided in Walloki's father. If he'd been younger, his mother would have claimed the sacred symbols for him, hidden them till he'd grown. And how he wished to see her leave her mourning now, creep to the grave, take his father's rattles and wands away, make it okay for him sleep. But there was just her keening, their burning home, the yomis waiting for him to cross the snow, pick the pieces of his inheritance up from the grave. He shut the door-flap, drew back in.

How did he keep himself awake all night? Stoking the fire? Pricking his skin with his scratching stick? Another thing I do not know. Nor if, in the hours before dawn, he heard the yomis creep close. The clapping shakers, rustling skins, their lion coughs and crow caws as they encircled the small hut. I do not know if, had he been sleeping, their chanting might have sounded less like men, become sounds of spirits instead. And who's to say that they were not? That it was not kukinis outside the kapum hu growing ever angrier as the dark thinned, his fire flickered, waiting for him to slip into a dream that they could enter? I only know that they did not, that whether it was the kukinis who would have climbed inside his mind or the yomis who would have poisoned his mush, the sickness meant to consume him never did. Because he never slept, stayed up till the first sounds of dawn—a whine, whimper, bark—made him shut his eyes. Even through his sleepless haze he could tell which of his father's dogs was dying first. Second. Last. Old dogs whose sounds he'd known all of his life. And still, listening as their throats were slit, he could not help but hear a new thing too, something in them that was not them but a sound crossed over from the world they were about to enter—the thing he'd shut his eyes against—and giving into the darkness of his lids, he at last saw it: a face, not his father's and not a bear's and yet not neither, its eyes on him with such a stare they snapped his own open again.

Though it was what he did not see that scared him worse. When, later that second day, he at last succumbed to sleep. Woke before night came. And in between dreamed nothing, saw nothing, heard nothing, was visited by nothing. As if the kukinis had already deemed him lacking and, abandoning him before he could even begin, left him the same boy he'd been before his father's death. Except now it was after. And that boy could not exist.

Not even to his mother. He saw it on her face as she brought him supper: piñon nuts and acorn bread and the tender inner bark of tamarack scraped into curls, pale green and smelling so powerfully of sap they cut through the scents of smoke and cedar and his unwashed, scared self. She could have let him dig out the bark with his own fingers, but he knew she'd hoped he'd be too weak, the tamarack meant less to ease his hunger than the wrenching of his innards from the anger of the kukinis working upon him. Except they weren't. Which she saw soon as she entered.

Outside it had started to snow, in the hut's opening a few flakes drifting at a slant, as if the world had come untied from its great ropes, begun to tilt. Between him and it, his mother crouched, a dark still steadiness, her face hidden by the brightness behind. Then the flap closed and the firelight showed her eyes in her ash-smeared skin. On him.

I woke you, she said.

The first words spoken to him in days. In them a searching strong as her stare.

He told her.

They'll come, she said. Told him he had to help them. And when he said he didn't want to, she made the sound she made when frustrated with him: a quick clearing of her throat behind pressed lips, as if what vexed her had risen from her stomach.

You are too strong, she said.

And he said, Niknem—

I mean, she said, too stubborn.

Mother, he said again.

She shushed him. You think I don't feel too young? Too scared? You think I want to be your uncle's second wife? You think I could choose not to?

Niknem, he said, they did not come to me.

Then sleep again.

And if they don't? If they know I'm not—

My little boy, she said. And the words stopped him. Words same as all parents called all sons in their first years, but ones he hadn't heard spoken to him since his earliest memories. Niki p'ube, she said again, you are your father's only son. Lifting the bread, she brushed at the char left by the leaves it had been baked in. Said, Still, he was older than you when he was called to take his father's kukinis into him. Almost twice your age. Already himself a father. You already his son. Though too young to remember his going through it. But do you remember his first bear hunt? The first where he would be the one to speak with the grizzly? Do you remember him in his panom skin? Taking his bow and pipe? How he left our house already shaking his rattle. Shaking it and shaking it. Because if he had tried to hold it still, it would have betrayed his fear.

She held out the cleaned loaf.

But instead of taking it, he said, What if he hadn't gone?

She drew the bread back, broke off one edge, held the bit toward him. The last weeks that you were in my womb, she told him, I didn't want to let you out. She pushed the morsel nearer his mouth. Open, she said. And when he did, she smiled. He could remember when she'd added the fourth and fifth stripes to her chin, how he had liked to place his small hand over them, watch her smile spread his fingers till he could see the tattooed lines. He'd tell her to stop smiling so he could hide the lines again, but she never could, would wind up laughing, his fingers unable to hold her shaking chin.

Now, closing his mouth around the bite that she held out to him, he felt her fingers on his lips. Then gone. And through her smile, she said, Don't fool yourself. I wanted you out. I just didn't want to have to get you out. I had not borne a child yet, but I had seen the pain that others went through. Had seen two women die of it. Was terrified. This time she held the remaining loaf out for his hand. Aren't you glad, she said, I didn't refuse? Can't you see how glad I am I couldn't? How grateful that there are things in this life for which the world leaves us no choice?

While he ate, she sat with him, their silence settling back with a new weight, as if each snap of a stick she added to the fire or pop of burning pine or simply his chewing were all small betrayals of the quiet that should have contained him. But when the food was gone and the tamarack set aside, she stayed sitting, breaking another branch, feeding it to the fire. Before at last taking the empty basket and getting to her feet. Hunched beneath the low roof, her face near level with his own, she said his name: Walloki. And he had the strangest feeling. That she was saying it the way she'd earlier said *boy*, a word already consigned to memory, as if she had already begun turning herself toward whatever name he'd take after the ceremony. Walloki, she said, if they don't come, you have to make them. Do you understand me? Even if they refuse, if you can't feel them inside you, you have to claim them. Now. Before another can. Do you understand? You have to trust you'll feel them after, after the others have carried you into the k'um, after they've tested you. You have to trust they'll come. But right now, you have to help them. Do you understand, son? You have to. For your father. Your family. Me.

By the time she left, it was already dusk, barely light enough to show her figure, the faint depression of her trail, the village just sounds of children and dogs coming from the blurred gray. He watched her disappear into it. And after, stayed crouched in the open door, letting in the cold, watching the deepening dark cover the huts, the trees, till they were only a dim shifting beyond the cemetery, the clean snow there seeming to glow, smooth and clear but for the few black lines still jutting above the new-dug grave, somehow still sharp, refusing to disappear.

And still he would not dream them in, the kukinis who'd been his father's nightly companions, the spirits of rocks and waters, weather and beasts, that would have become his if he would only sleep. Which he managed not to till morning, waking that afternoon into the same regret and relief and shame. But worse. He missed his father. And in his grief, wished he could meet the beings who'd known his father better than any other, could speak with them as his father had done. Would have let them in then. If they had come.

But his only visitors were from the village: his younger sister bringing wizened roots, more acorn mash, the roasted larvae sprinkled on top the nearest he was allowed to meat; his uncle filling the kapum hu with his lion-skin wrap and long black hair and loud berating; even the chief, an old friend of his father's who sometimes shared a pipe inside their home and had a laugh that could set everyone at ease. Though, entering Walloki's cleansing hut, the old man looked as if the laughter had collapsed inside him, a weight within seemingly dragging at his eyes, sucking his wrinkled cheeks inward as he talked. Of how he understood the fear, how scared the boy must be of what might happen were he to fail. How, if he would not try, the might becomes a certainty, the other priests tied to the demands of the kukinis. Who, once denied, would harden irreparably against him. Talked of the inescapability of what till then had been only a chance. Told Walloki he'd done all he could to give him time, had come to tell him there was none left. Only his father's priestly things still waiting above his grave, unclaimed. And the night coming. And nothing he could do for him by dawn. Not even as chief.

Rising to a stoop before the door-hole then, he said, You must be a man. But halfway out, still crouching in the opening, he turned again, his voice full of the kindness Walloki remembered from when he'd still been a child. Do you want me to get them for you? the old man said. And bring them here?

No, Walloki assured him, trying to sound sure. No, Grandfather, I'll get them.

But by the time he at last went out it was long after dark, moonlight bright on the surface of the grave. The snow now bare. The wand and rattle and rake no longer there.

That night it was not hard to stay awake, listening through the pines in wind not only for the breath and wingbeats of kukinis but the footsteps of men. Before daybreak they came: a distant shushing through the snow, a steady hiss behind, as if from something dragging. Above it, he tried to make out whether the footsteps were of one or many, though, when he worked up the nerve to look, he saw, instead, coming across the snow, his middle sister, turned nine not long ago, pulling something behind her.

When she was close enough to hear, he whispered to her. She stopped, said his name. And then was nearly running, nearly into him. He stood outside into her hug, her holding to him as she had not since she was small and scared at night and in their shared bed would press close as if she might wear him like armor against her fears.

What are you doing? he asked.

She said, Bringing you that.

He looked behind her at the place in the dark where she'd let go the sledge.

From our mother, she told him. And then, still clinging to him, Will I see you again?

He managed not to cry till she left. But searching through what his mother sent undid him. His snowshoes, his father's cougar-skin wrap, his bow and quiver and knife of chipped obsidian, enough dried elk to last him long enough for what?

He cried then as he had not since he had been a little boy. In the hours after his father's death, he'd tried to be strong, to let his mother and sisters release his grief with their own wails, felt then the responsibility come upon him so suddenly, a weight so great it had stopped his tears, the way squeezing a cut can bind the flesh with blood. But he had failed—his mother, his sisters, his father's memory, his family—and in the failure felt the weight rip off him, the tears released.

Tomorrow would be his last day in the cleansing hut. But beyond the bark walls, back in the village, the home he'd grown up in was gone, even its ash erased by snow, his mother and sisters living in his uncle's hu, a home he knew could no longer include him. And who now would help him build his own? The way they had his father when his grandfather died. What family would let him take a daughter for a wife? What friends would still be willing to speak to him? Who in his whole village? In any village of the whole tribe in all the mountains? When they learned what he had done. Enough elk meat to last him maybe a week. To get him where? For what? And if he waited till morning to leave his hut? His mother had sent his sister without a torch, and he knew he should repack the sledge, leave his fire to deceive whoever might be coming, slip out in darkness, run. But he was weeping, weak with fear and grief, wanted suddenly only to sleep, to shut his eyes, to step away for a small time from what the world would be after that night, let the kukinis do their worst.

That night it came—at last his father's great kukini—lumbering into his being, head swinging with the massive weight of its huge skull, mawful of teeth and shag of hair, all swinging, sweeping, back and forth. All but its eyes, their deep-set stare unmoving, unblinking, on him. The panom coming into his dream, filling his mind, the hut, the air till there was nothing but its huffing, its sloshing gut, the gurgling beneath the fur that he could feel as the kukini smothered his body, its belly hair wet and its breath hot and the insides of the great bear reeking not of flesh or blood but of his father, the scent of his father fallen asleep beside his only son and, in the middle of the night, reaching to hold him, pull him tight, his eyes so close—even buried deep in that fur, Walloki knew them: his father's eyes, boring down into his own, the sound of the voice he'd known all his life and thought to never hear again suddenly there. Saying, Disgrace. Disgraced, it said. Said, Your father. Said, Yourself. Said, Us.

And his eyes snapped open. For the last time.

The fur was there, the hair and heat and teeth and mass of it so close above him, but the eyes were slits, and behind the teeth, there were another pair, not the bear's but a second set gleaming in the same firelight that showed a second face—not his father's—and he came fully awake. Just fast enough to see the slash, the flash of claw-sheen cutting the dark. Fast enough to see it, but not to stop it.

One must have ripped his eyebrow in half, another digging at the socket, gouging the cornea, crushing the ball, the others tearing into his cheek and through his scream. Maybe it was his flesh that snagged the claw, maybe the mess left of his eye that held it, sparing the other: whatever kept the panom priest who'd taken his place from pulling free was the thing that saved him, the yomi's yanking at last lurching away, sending him tumbling, Walloki scrambling backward across the fire, clothes catching, hands burning, head smashing into the bark wall, and then his shoulders were crashing out, his chest, his frantic body burst through into the snow. His legs kicked free and he was pushing, shattering the wall in an eruption he could not see—not the cedar slivers scattering, or slabs collapsing, or firelight burning through the hole he'd made—his remaining eye so smeared with blood and shredded skin he could not tell where sight ended and emptiness began, could only feel the snow exploding around him, the rage of the man in all his massive bearskin bulk smashing at the hole, at the poles that held him, trying to break out.

How the boy managed to scramble up, I do not know. Or how he knew which way to run. He must have fled the sound behind, wiped handfuls of freezing snow at the mess of his face, cleared his sight enough to make out the rush of trees, black gaps between their trunks. Or maybe he just felt them, one hand before him, the other pressed to the wreckage of his eye. How did he make it? On his bare feet. The elk robe back in the kapum hu, lost with all else his mother sent. How did he not freeze? Or faint? Or simply fail to flee fast enough to escape the other?

Your questions, your questions. Can you not keep them? Can I not stop them? Your asking, asking, always for more. Another story, you used to say. And I'd oblige you. But this is not one I would have told you. Would not have then. Would not now. If I did not know I had to.

There was a boy, I said. I said, a boy. And, saying it, did not mean you.

It was near the end of winter—o'mi hintsuli, the squint-rock time, shifting to ko'no, what you would know as March—when the owls stopped responding to my calls. One night, the saw-whet drawn by my whistling; the next, nothing. Same with the great horned the night before, its booming so distant I could barely tell it from the beating of my heart. A sound grown louder in the silence the woods sent back as, lying on my willow bed, I listened through the river's rushing for a rustling or clatter or clack of stones. But there was just my heart. The river. In the day, the crows rose in cawing flocks, startled sudden as from a gunshot. In the lack of it, their loud commenting to each other on something I could not see. But felt. The way the gray squirrels moved in the canopy, their fleeing branch to branch like some breeze rolling through the trees around my camp. The quail seemed to retreat to higher ridgeside trails. The doe disappeared.

And one morning, checking my traps, I knew that it was there. Following me along my route. Something staying just far enough away I couldn't see, could only feel its gaze on me each time I came to a coon, a fox. Watching as I delayed dispatching each, stood before a spitting fisher cat with my eyes shut, motionless as if my stillness could make its struggling disappear. Till I slashed out, slit its throat—my breath coming fast as the blood, my eyes clamping back shut—and in the quiet last kicking, felt it again: something taking in my tight-knit brow, my trembling knife, studying me.

Year after year it had grown harder. To come upon a coon with forepaw snared and search its face for a sign it wasn't the one that would pluck offerings from my palm. To find a caught fox panting in the sun and know it could be the same that nightly barked back at my attempts at singing. No way to know if the otter I'd seen playing on a slide of river-stone might be the one I later found gnawing through its own wrist, its frenzy surging at my approach, till with my knife I finished the task for it. Its lurching stumbling flight awful to see. Stones blood-smeared, water pink in its wake. Washed clear easier than I could do the same inside of me.

I would have stroked their throats, ears—the way, years back, I'd seen the Kushna hunter do with the dying deer—if they'd have let me close. Sometimes I tried, despite their teeth. Stood by their trembling, trying to suppress my own, waiting with drawn knife or heavy stone, speaking soothingly. Sometimes I hummed. What snippets of the hunter's tune I could recall. Though for me it only made it worse—the memory of Dutchman's muzzle brushing my fingers, my mother's rocking, my own singing to you—so over time, I set fewer and fewer traps, ever farther from my home, my need for skins dwindling each year, and still the plews brought to Kushna my only way to trade for all I couldn't make, the meat my only way to supplement what I could gather, sate my hunger. For hard as it was to slit a throat or smash a skull, I'd come to fear my musket worse, refused to use it, its boom breaking into the world I'd found as if fired from the one I'd left, blowing a hole in the river's sound, echoing inside my chest, heart, mind. Each time a reminder of what remained inside of me waiting to ignite. What standing there with my breath strained, knife bright with fisher blood, I knew with sudden certainty had found me.

But when my eyes snapped open, the woods were empty. As they would stay all day. And all the next. Till the squirrels calmed, the crows quit startling, one night an owl's screaming waking me out of a dream into the eerie feeling the past days had been just that. That morning there were deer prints beside the creek again, the doe down on the gravel bank browsing willow shoots, the heron flying upriver same as ever. As if nothing had changed.

Which should have been a sign. Would have been the first thing I learned about Walloki.

When at last I saw him it was only because he let me. As if he had decided I was ready. A bright clear day, sunlight slipping down the canyonside all morning, warm by the time it reached my cabin, halfway to noon before it touched the river. I liked to wait till it was on the rocks before setting my net—the water freezing, the wading numbing—the stones, when I'd climb out, waiting to thaw the ice out of my legs.

Ice in my legs, my chest, my heart: him there. On a boulder out in the river, crouched as if about to spring. But stilled, his eyes on me. In his hands a spear, a fish on its raised tip, the sun just touching it: a flash of silver. Behind him, the rapids splashing; below, the eddy's swirl. But his body—still dark with canyon shadow beneath the sun-sparked fish—unmoving as the stone. I could not quite make out his features—his ragged hair, his face somehow malformed—but I could feel his stare. Could feel it clear on me as the sun's heat.

I stood there nude as him, the fishnet heavy in my arms, its cording cutting my fingers, no more able to move than make sound pass through my throat. Stood there knowing that I should speak, send him away, at least find out his tribe. Hese be minki wak'? His village, his name. Hese yapebe mi? Did he not realize nobody came to this stretch of river? Had no one from wherever he'd come told him of the Honpetayim Woole?

I was still trying to make a sound when he lowered his spear, reached out, slid the fish free. Though instead of fleeing then or tossing it to me to show he didn't mean to steal, he simply set it on the rock. Set his hand over it. Pressed its flopping still.

And I could feel it—my need to speak receding, the tightness in my throat releasing, a stillness come over me—as if his hand pressed on my chest. Beneath his calm palm: the fish lifting its tail. Then not. Becoming still inside the stillness of his grip, his gaze.

We stayed that way so long the sunlight found his hair, forehead, finally the lump-scarred brow, gleam of one eye. The other was a mess of pulpy flesh, a sunken divot creased by a line curving along his cheek. His nose, below its broken bridge, was wide and strong, his mouth the same, making his chin seem strangely fragile, his neck too thin. Thin shoulders, chest: a boy.

The press of his palm, his stillness: suddenly it wasn't enough. I shut my eyes, fisted my fingers in the net, fought the urge to shout, demand he go. Down canyon or up, so long as it took him away from here. Go! I would have snapped—Kinap!—but when I opened my eyes again, he was not there.

Just the fish. Still shining in the sun. By the time I got to the rock, the light had spread over the smooth gray granite. On it, beside the fish: his footprints—the two wet ovals of his heels, the small dark spots of toes—evaporating as I watched.

I scanned the river—shadows, crevasses, willows unstirred—then, stepping to my stone jetty, began setting my net. In the pool below the breakwater I submerged the branches, propped the mouth, let the tail float out, settled in to wait. But that morning my muscles wouldn't ungrip, the eddy couldn't hold my gaze, my breath stayed shallow. Yanking the prop-stick, I let the net snap shut, lifted it dripping, rolled it back up. All the while, the fish he'd left me lying near enough I could have reached it without taking a step. But instead left it to rot. Or lure him back. For I was sure he'd remained near enough to watch.

Returning up the bank, I kept glancing behind me, catching only the streaks of finches, a lizard's twitchy push-ups on a rock. Across my creek, a gopher snake shivering away. In my camp, a covey of quail scattering. And in the mud before my hut, his footprints. It did not seem he had gone in, but they were so widespread around my territory he must have wandered it all the time I had been fishing. Tracks like my own but smaller, thinner. Exploring my washing spot beside the creek, my grinding stone and granaries and bark-walled storage hut, my drawbridge log strung from an oak above the bank, pulley-roped so it could be lowered or raised. Though he had lingered longest beneath another tree: an alder dripping catkins, each tied with a tiny feather, the wind scattering their shadows over his footprints. Around the mossy boulder I'd quilled with rodent bones, his tracks were even clearer, as if he'd circled it, close enough to touch the tiny spines, before he must have heard me coming. And disappeared. Into wherever he was out there.

The rasp of crickets. Rustle of some forest rat or vole. The *tsee tsee tsee* of a whole flock of waxwings filling the canopy. And all around me, the low roar of the river, shushing as if trying to soothe my mind, slow my heartbeat.

A crash, a jangling clang: before the river could swallow the sound, my own footsteps were covering it, as, breaking into a run, I listened for the thrashing, trying to recall which trap I'd set in that direction. One big enough to break his ankle? Mangle a foot? But when I struggled up the slope it was into the snarling of a snagged badger. Teeth bared, eyes frantic. I stood short of its lunging, hands on my knees, slowing my breathing, staring back. Till, spotting a stone big enough, I hauled it over, raised it above the badger's skull, and with all my strength, slammed it straight down. The crash of smashing bone broke my breath into a roar, a sound desperate and loud as I'd imagined might have come from the boy. From him caught here. Here.

I stood there bellowing, bits of brain and skull spattered across my shins, blood pooling at my bare feet. Stood there till my shouting dwindled to a sound that might have come from the crushed body. Then bent and heaved the stone off the smashed head, stepped on the springs, released the jaws, tried to steady myself with work.

At first, fleshing the pelt, I was able to find some comfort in the fact it hadn't been the boy caught in the trap, I hadn't had to help him out or stitch him up or splint his ankle or let him stay inside my camp, my hut, my life. But what about the other traps still out there? Still buried beneath leaves? Marked by signs known only to me?

By the time I'd stretched the badger's skin I was hearing the snaps, didn't even wait to wash the gore off my hands before going after the rest. At each, I cut a branch, tied them with the strips of handkerchief I'd used before—the all-but-bleached-out red just bright enough, I hoped, to warn him—was flagging my fourth or fifth before I found it. Another badger lying motionless as if blacked out from blood loss or pain. Slowly I approached, axe in one hand, stake in the other. But it was dead, stabbed through the nape, a gash severing the vertebrae that, kneeling to push aside the blood-soaked fur, I could see had been made with a spear. Leaving the carcass there, I carried on, planted three more stakes before I found the next. This time a martin, speared too. Had he not figured how to release the snapped-shut jaws? Or left me some and taken others? But I came upon no sprung traps emptied and, making my way one to another, I grew ever more sure he'd been dispatching them for me. Though it wasn't till I reached the last—a coon so freshly stabbed its blood was still spreading over the leaves—that I realized the entire time he'd been moving barely ahead of me. Lifting the still-dripping carcass then, I held it out, spoke to the woods: Take it. Take all of them, I told him, though I knew he could not understand. Then said it in Nisenan as best I could: Tooyee hede. Tooyee kaanteem. 'Uk'oy Tooyee. Away, I said. Away from here. From me. 'Esak 'im kani? Understand? And the woods said nothing back.

Because he was not there. Was in my camp instead.

When I returned, the second badger was already lying in the bloodied mud where I had skinned the other, its body left beside the fleshed plew like the ghost of the first. Which would have been better than the truth: that he had killed it and the coon and martin and fish because of what he'd witnessed—my shut eyes, my shaking and bellowing—the fact that, for however long he had been watching, he'd been learning me.

That same evening I set out to find him. Or more truly, to follow the trail he left me. Footprints and broken branches and strands of milkweed string snagged on a bramble like a blaze. Even the scent of smoke. The sight of it. Though by then I knew where he would be: a shallow cave a little higher up the canyon side that I had stumbled on some years ago, a low crevice just big enough for a bobcat, or lion, or boy.

Through the smoke haze screening the opening I tried to see him, shifted my musket into both hands, haloed him—Ho!—as boy—Laho!—and hearing only the ricochet of my own voice, hitched my musket against my shoulder, stared down the barrel at the dwindling smoke till it thinned enough to show me he was no longer there.

Inside the grotto: a circle of stones; still-burning coals; a bird's charred carcass, plucked feathers piled where the slanting ceiling met the back wall; skin sacks and strips of sinew and a thick pelt still smelling green; the spear I'd seen him with that morning; his fire-drill and twirling stick; and on a flat patch of wall, charcoaled circles, diamonds. Drawings. To decorate a home. Not a mile from my own. Not a five-minute run. Not even on the river's other side.

And I was shoveling it out—feathers and sacks and pelt and spear and drill and husks of nuts—sweeping them off the ledge onto the ground, about to lean in and rub the rock wall free of drawings when I sensed him, whipped around, my musket already shouldered, thumb cocking, eyes sweeping, seeing him, the circle closing, squeezing everything else out. All but the boy, standing as if just stepped through branches, gone still as he had been that morning. This time his hands empty. He did not move them, not to motion for me to stop or even show that he was friendly. Simply watched me. Watched me fighting the shrinking circle of my sight, the focusing of my mind beyond the ability to speak, and pulling back, pushing the ring around me wider, till I could take a breath, another, get enough sound out to tell him to go. Kinap, I said. He shook his head. Yes, I told him. Haan! Go to Kushna, 'Ustoma, Wokodot. With each village name I jerked my head in its direction. And at each one he shook his own. Haan! I said again.

And, reaching up, he drew a finger across his throat. Kushna, he said. 'Ustoma, Wokodot. Three times crossing his neck. Nisenan, he said. Did it again.

Nisenan wi? I asked.

Notong k'oyom maidum kak'as.

I gestured northeast, where I'd heard the tribe was from, said, Kinap! again. Added, Notong k'oyona.

And again he shook his head. Drew his finger over his throat.

He said something then I could not understand—though I caught the word for *you*—his way of speaking skewed from that I'd heard in Kushna, and when he tried again, he used only his hands: pressed one palm to his chest, while with the other he pushed away. As if, had I been nearer, he would have pressed it against me. Then drawing both hands together, he fit each palm into the other. "You," I caught again, and this time also what I thought was "me." Though whatever he added I could not decipher. Nor what he said when, turning his palms down, he seemed to press them toward the earth.

Whatever he meant I knew then I did not want it, not any part of anything that he might wish or need or try to get from me. Again I shook my head, patted my own palm at the ground. Said, Nik'i. Mine. Pointed to him. Shook my head again. K'olom mink'i. Not yours. I did not know the word for *home*. And so used hu. Nik hu, I told him. My home. Pointed at the cave behind him. Said again, K'olom mink'i. Not yours.

And when he did not seem to understand, I turned back to the grotto, climbed in again. How else to make him see except to continue what I'd started? Crouching, I smeared away the charcoaled drawings, crabbing ever deeper, hand raw from rubbing, till, reaching the far corner, I stopped. There in the dimness: a mass of leaves and hair and bits of hide that seemed like trash till I saw the leg, the other. The tiny body made of grass, its tiny arms and head: a doll. Again, I felt the shock I'd felt that morning—the boy too near a child—and then was seeing you, feeling your weight atop my chest, and coughing, I backed out through the charcoal dust, shoving away, till I was off of the ledge, standing, catching my breath, clearing my eyes. Beneath his stare.

You can't stay, I told him. Said it in English, my lungs squeezed out and my throat aching. Said it again: You can't stay.

But he did.

Mostly away from me. Sometimes I'd see no sign of him for days. And then, upriver, setting a snare, I'd sense a splash, glance over in time to catch a water basket dripping above a pool before it disappeared with him behind a boulder. Or I might hear a rustling and turn, expecting a wheeling deer. But he'd be there, just walking, just near enough for me to see the quail he carried, till he passed on, leaving only the shifting leaves.

He was not trying to hide from me. Instead, as days stretched into weeks, he came increasingly close to my camp. Would simply appear. Squatting beside the redbud blooming across my creek, motionless but for his hands picking through a pile of seeds, slowly filling a basket, staying just long enough I'd grow nearly inured to him, as if his body was just another bush. Till, chancing to glance over, I'd find him gone. Or on the river, leaching bitterness out of acorn meal, I'd look up from the sandpit while the water drained and see some willows shaking, leaves flipping silver to green, as if brushed by a gust. But it would be him, snapping new shoots one by one. And I'd pour more water over the meal, let it drain again, watch through the steam as he stripped the stalks, just far enough away I couldn't hear the scraping of his rock. But later I might see the shavings float by downriver, look up again, only to find the same absence of anyone that had marked my life till then. Sometimes I even sensed him outside my hut. At night, sitting inside eating my supper, might feel him on the other side of the log wall, might hear, between my own chewing and slurps, sounds too similar to be a coon. As if he'd brought his supper near simply so he wouldn't have to eat alone.

And I'd known that if I rose and went outside, he wouldn't run, no more than he'd have come in to join me. Would have just sat there, chewed, his stare on his food or turned away, but never on me.

Maybe that was partly why. The way he always kept the wrecked half of his face toward me, never watched back. As if he could mark me the way a squirrel or hare or deer would with its head turned to the side. Except his eye was gone. Maybe if it hadn't been, I would have felt his gaze—its press at me, his presence on my skin—instead of the way that, as the weeks went by and ko'no drifted into wi'nuti and the time of oak tassels came again, I felt it less and less. Till by the time the fiddleheads were sprouting, the slopes crowding with flowers, his presence in the woods around my home had come to feel little different from that of the doe who drank at the bank each morning, or the mink who used my granaries for hunting grounds, or the ravens who accompanied me upriver, or the heron gliding by each dawn, each dusk.

Each day the boy making my rounds from trap to trap before me, each fox or bobcat lying speared by the time I found the body. Never a belly slit, never a heart or liver missing. Though surely, without a bow, he must have been hungry for meat.

I waited till a day I knew that he'd be gone. That morning, I carried a string of traps nearly a mile below my camp, set them mostly in the hope of drawing him away, then, returning to my hut, unhooked the bow I'd bartered for with No Rope long ago but never learned to shoot with well enough, wiped off its dust, the cobwebs from its arrows, slung the quiver over my shoulder, made my way upriver to his cave.

A few days later he brought me the fore-half of a buck, ribs to rack, gutted and cleaned, left in my camp for me to find. A kind of meat I hadn't tasted in so long I could hardly keep from wolfing some down raw, spiked the tongue over the fire and, before it barely warmed, was feeding it into my maw. From the skin I sewed him moccasins, my needle making neater stitches, I believed, than any he'd have seen. Left them for him on a rock halfway along the path that had begun to form between our homes. Where, a few days later, I found a flute. Four holes bored in a branch. Tried, that night, to pick out a tune—"Early One Morning"; "The Rolling of the Stones"—but there were too few notes, too wrong. So I just played. Let the sound smother my memories. We exchanged seeds, passing a basket back and forth atop the rock, mine filled with the few kinds I knew to eat, his returned with ones for me to learn. And, once, just flower petals, blue as lupine, the basket heaped with hundreds. To eat? Steep? Grind into paint? All day I pondered it. Till at last I spotted him beside a mossy log covered in the remains of paintbrush blooms I'd spiked it with a fortnight back. The boy just standing there. Till he was sure I'd seen.

That day I started knotting milkweed fibers into tiny nets, see-through sacks small as my thumb, each filled with the petals he had left: half a hundred droplet-shaped pouches, blue as a child's idea of rain. But carried by me to my creek. The water that, a month earlier, had spilled over the rock-lip in a wide sheen was now a trickle narrowing toward the time when it would tell me to start upriver, and I moved along the cliff face tying the bright blue sacks to roots and stalks. Left them to dangle where the water had once rushed. Fifty droplets frozen mid-fall.

While I worked, I wondered if he would stay behind, see the summer dry the petals to dust. If by the time the rains returned to swell the creek and sweep away the sacks, he would be gone. Same as the hawk that once hunted the skies above me for a week, only to tilt in a wind one afternoon and arc forever from my sight; the weasel that had been my playmate for an entire winter, then, with warmer weather, disappeared.

Though it was only when, stepping from my hut to fill a waterpot one dawn, I saw him come unbidden out of the half dark into my camp and felt my heartbeat unchanged, my breath the same, that I realized he was less hawk or weasel than I. Knew then that he'd approached me from the start as one might an animal unused to man. That all these weeks he'd been teaching my body to grow used to him. That all this time he had been training me.

But not for this. Standing there, holding the pot in one hand, the door-flap in the other, I could make out no more of his face than sweat-sheen. But I could hear his breathing—loud and fast as if he'd been running—and then, beneath it, the others coming: a crashing in the steep woods above, growing louder, nearer, becoming flashes moving between shaking branches, and then men breaking out of the trees, suddenly cramming the clearing with sharp glints of arrows and spears. And the boy was wheeling, notching his own too late to stop them from ripping away his bow, wrenching his arms behind his back, his body bucking with his gasp as they began to beat him. Four men surrounding an almost-child going down beneath their fists and feet. While nearby three more stood watching. No Rope: In the half-light I could just make him out. Pumk'uk'mi! I shouted, his face turning at his name. But my eyes were snapped away by the flash of a stone blade and I was shouting Hey! Hey! Hey!, the English erupting from me maybe what checked the hatchet's swing, maybe the way I was already starting to hurl the iron cookpot, stopped only by No Rope's fist suddenly gripping my arm. Silas, he was saying, Silas. From behind him I heard the words *honpetayim woole* mixed with others I could make nothing of except their anger. Hatip! I shouted past No Rope to the men behind—Stop!—hoping I'd remembered the word right. But it was whatever No Rope called over his shoulder that slowed their beating, set them to hauling the boy's slumped body up, the speed with which they'd burst upon the clearing leaching away, leaving only the sound of all our breathing.

In the growing light I could see the boy was bleeding, his face a dark slick mess, hair pasted to his head. I searched for what few words I knew that might be of use, came up with nothing better than *what* and *this*. Hesebe hedem? I said.

No Rope shook his head. Said something back I thought contained the words for *boy* and *you*. Then, turning, spoke to the others. They jerked the boy around as if to take him with them and I reached out, grabbed No Rope's shoulder. He spun on me, face hard, voice fighting anger, words coming faster than I was used to: Notong k'oyom and Kushna and c'haim wak', a word I remembered meaning maybe trespassing. You, he said. And for a second I thought he meant my home. But no: he had said, *Yours*. Again, he shook his head. Not yours, he said.

Behind him, the boy began to talk, and, turning, No Rope

snapped something sharp enough to shut him up. Then they were taking him, leaving, the space between us widening, their presence in the clearing easing, and I could feel my body wanting it to empty, wishing simply to return to fetching water, to disappear inside again, but there was the blood-wet hair on the boy's head, his smaller shape among the men, and I called out once more: Wait! Said it in English. Watched them stop, as if they understood, look back.

Haan, I said. Yes. Nik'i, I said. Mine. Thumping my fingers against my chest. Then, pointing at the boy: Him. Muhe. I said No Rope's name then. Said, Wi and Kinap. Don't go. Looked him straight in the eyes and told him, This. Mine. Yes.

I meant that he'd been wrong—it *was* my business—though, soon as I'd said it, I could see it meant something different to them. The boy talking again and the men speaking over him and No Rope's voice rising, silencing them all. The quiet so sudden that when he turned to me he could speak low, slow and carefully as when we tried to understand each other during a trade. Muhe, he said, and, Minki. He yours?

Haan, I said. Yes.

He shook his head as if I could not mean it, stepped back toward me, said slowly again, Your. Followed by a word I didn't know. And seeing my failure to understand, he reached to his crotch, lifted the buckskin flap, gestured with his hand, drawing an arc through the air from there toward the boy. Said the word again: Te'e.

Son. I know it now though did not then, would not till it was over, not till much later when I would learn the rest: How they'd seen the boy out hunting, tracked him to his cave, a Notong k'oyom trespassing on their land. Just the fact he was of another tribe, had crossed into Kushna territory without permission, enough to warrant death. Though to be sure they'd sent runners to Wokodot, 'Ustoma, Tsekankan, as far upriver as Yamako. Where they'd heard the rumor passed from a village one river over, come from another on the borderland still farther north: word of a ba'api, the son of a yomkapa jomin who'd refused his father's spirits, fled before they'd been avenged. A boy of fourteen years, badly wounded around the face, unfound till now. Bringing the spurned kukinis' fury upon whoever sheltered him. Unless the people of Kushna killed him first, or brought him back to face the spirits' wrath in his own village, or simply made him flee again, away from them, from me, the Honpetayim Woole who the boy, hearing the words I spoke in my confusion, had, in his desperation, claimed was his father.

All then unknown to me, only able to see the boy was hurt, to hear how hard No Rope was trying to make me understand. Minte'e? he asked, curling his arms into a cradle. Minte'e? Placing his palm as if upon a child's head, raising it to show growing, saying, Minte'e? till, at last, he tried the word for juvenile, one I knew from trading furs: a young mink's paler pelt, a cougar cub's still-spotted one. B'et, he said, pointing at me. Buck. Then back at the boy: K'utim te'e. Fawn. And finally I understood.

The light had grown enough I could now see, in the mess of the boy's face, the flesh surrounding his remaining eye nearly as ragged as over his other, the skin already swelling shut. All but a slit. Through which I felt him watching me.

Minte'e? No Rope asked again. Your son?

And I said, Haan. Yes.

Kept saying it throughout his disbelieving questioning, his words thrown to the other men, the boy, as he tried to work out how, why, if I might mean something else. His eyes, when he turned back to me, pressing for another understanding. Te'e, I said, over and over, the new word I'd learned: Te'e. By then the boy's eye had swollen wholly shut and I could see the panic flood his face, feel the fear I'd feel losing my sight, can only tell you it was that that made me say, My son. Though I'd yet to even learn his name, thought it Ba'api, the word I heard from them over and over. Ba'api and Notong k'oyom, and I nodded my head. Said, Mother. Said, My son, again. Muna. Nikte'e. Felt something shift. In No Rope, the others. The way they held the boy a little farther from themselves, on their faces the same distaste I saw in No Rope's, as if he'd begun to believe the boy and me, our lies linking us in his disgust. So that, for the first time, I felt the full weight of what I'd done. Was doing.

Ba'api, I said, thinking it his name. Ba'api nikte'e.

And maybe it was my mistake that did it, convinced them with an unknowing admission of truth: that he was outcast, a disgrace, a ba'api. But one I would still claim.

Stepping away from me, No Rope turned to the others, and for a moment, there was just their talking, the boy still held, head turned to better hear them, blind beaten face to me. Then slowly swiveling as No Rope came back, began again trying to make his meaning clear. Though all I could see was the seriousness behind each word, the morning grown too bright to hide the sadness in his eyes as he spoke of me, the boy, the ground we stood on. Till he was done. Raising two fingers to my shoulder, he waited for me to do the same. Held his a second longer, another, before he let them fall. And with a few words to the boy—the boy's quiet Haan and Haan coming in answer—he turned and led his men away.

Slowly the river smothered their sounds till there was just its roar around us, the boy and me standing there long enough the quiet clicks and chucks of jays returned. Rustlings up in the trees. My forearm aching from the pot's weight. Across the clearing, his battered face seemed, with each second, to grow more strained. From worry? Fear? He did not call to me, did not extend a hand, just stood there blinded by his swollen eye, blood bright over the bottom of his face but thickening, no longer dripping from his chin, the only thing breaking the stillness between us his shivering. He'd fled his cave unclothed and I knew it would be hours before the sun reached us down in the canyon, knew I should reach to him, lead him to my hut, knew it and told myself to do it and could not, the thought straining something in me worse than my forearm's ache. I switched my hands. And saw him feel my movement or hear the pot's faint clank. His face shifting a bit toward me. On it, such relief. As if he'd begun to think I'd left.

By the time I reached him, the relief had changed, built into a pressure I could see him fighting to contain. As if he might cry. A hard thing to watch on such a mangled face, the pressed-lipped quaking of his blood-slick mouth, the shaking of an eyelash engulfed by swollen skin, the stillness of the missing eye still worse.

Ba'api, I said. He shook his head. Ba'api, I said again.

And he managed through his split lips to tell me, Walloki.

Walloki, I repeated.

Yapa mi nik, he said. My name.

Haan, I told him. And felt him waiting.

How many years since I had held another's hand? A feeling strange as touching some other creature's paw. And had he gripped mine back I would have dropped it. But he just let me guide his fingers to the handle of the pot, close them behind my own, lead him slowly across the clearing to my hut.

Inside, I settled him on my bed, covered him with my blanket, went out again and tore some moss off of an oak, filled the pot with cold creek water and, back in the cabin, dipped the soft swatch in, gave it to him to hold against his eye while I warmed up the rest. Till, with a bit of buckskin, I could wash the blood off of his face. See if he was missing teeth or needed stitching. And touching

touching

I would write gently touching

would write to you of gently touching him. With these same hands that last brushed your brow, touched your cheek, washed your face, held your fingers

My son, I'd told them. Told them, My son.

And can it matter that all day I kept repeating it, trying to commit the Nisenan to memory—son, te'e; son, te'e—a mantra I'd say a thousand times that day, working around my camp, washing the bloody rags, collecting milkweed and lucky break to ease the swelling, saying it over and over as if to make up for all the minutes, hours, days I'd gone without thinking of you.

Elisha. That evening, when I came in, he said, Elisha. I'd thought him asleep, was pulling bark tea off the fire, and turning so fast I splashed the coals, I heard him say your name again, ask what it meant. Elisha, hesebe yapaito? Squatting in the sizzling smoke, I knew he'd overheard me, faced for the first time how thin the line between my thoughts and speech must have become. A thing that would not have mattered, had not, till him.

Elisha, hesebe yapaito?

And does it matter that I didn't tell him? Dreamed that night only of you? Not as I saw you last but as you would have been. Ten or eleven or anyway a boy—manaa—a boy I'd never know. Your face that for so many years I'd had to merely imagine come to me inside my dream. So that I woke in tears, crying because I could no longer remember what you'd looked like in my sleep, because the more I tried the more I lost you, because by waking I'd abandoned you again. And in my head only the words remaining: Nikte'e, nikte'e, nikte'e. My son, my son, my son.

Who did not come that night, was not the one to cross the room in the pitch-black, in his own blindness, hidden by my own noise, his nearness unknown to me till I felt his fingers on mine. I'd thrown my skins upon the floor, been lying on my back, my arm flung out over the mat, my hand turned up, and he had touched it. Just my fingertips. With just the tips of his. Barely brushing. But there. In the long silence after my crying, staying just over mine. My own unmoving fingers staying, too.

It will not surprise you to learn that when I woke again, he was already gone. Inside my hut the dawn was just bright enough to see my bed was empty, the washrag folded over the water basket, the moss beside it. The swelling eased enough, I guessed, to let his eye open enough to go. Though when I went outside, I thought he was still there, perched on a rock far up the slope, looking down at me. But no, it was another, larger, who, when I hallooed him, stood and in silence started back up the ridge.

That day I brought the boy his bow, left it in his cave. Saw him later by the river soaking his face, raising it dripping. Both of us going our ways. Though the next day I brought him the healing tea and, coming back, saw the same man perched on the rock. This time got halfway to him before he disappeared. The third time I saw him I was with Walloki, and when I asked who it was, the boy told me, Kushna. Said, Watching. What? I asked. Us, Walloki said. Added, Here.

But it was beyond what language we shared for me to decipher why. If the man wanted us there or gone. I only knew I wanted to be away from him. And so that spring determined to head upriver early, gathered my traps, cleared out my cabin—furs, blankets, cookpots, tools—buried it all, concealed the cache, packed my rucksack with jirk and meal, slung on my possibles and powder horn, took up my musket, and left. Hopping rocks upcanyon, taking game trails I'd taken the year before and the year before that, heading ever higher. Only, this time, together.

The spring of '44. My third migration. Already I'd come to know the cascades and cliffs, big trees and boulders, markers for me along the river. Or for the river to mark my passing. Sometimes I felt it watching—the giant pillar peering down, the willows whispering, old oaks leaned out over the canyon, wondering at the figure they'd only ever known alone now with another—and each time I came to a rock bearing a hint of color, a ledge scattered with mica chips, a fringe of rawhide strips left fluttering from a limb, I felt ashamed. Not that Walloki might see them, but that they would see him. With me. As if by bringing another upriver I was betraying them.

Though mostly he stayed apart, a presence I'd glimpse far ahead as I clambered over a boulder or beside me ascending the other bank, the water rushing wide between us, its roar a wall of sound. Following game trails higher up, he'd be a flash of movement snatched through trees, a rippling of sunlight and shade, tumpline tight across his brow, basket on his back, bow and quiver over his shoulders, spear in his hand, traveling faster than I could on the river, soon gone again. Sometimes he took the throughways atop the ridge, remained away all day, returned to a fire already lit—his fist dangling a glint of fish, a couple quail—and without even a nod, we would begin preparing supper, our evenings together as free of speaking as our days apart, each existing in our own sounds beneath the roaring of the river rushing out of the ever-nearer peaks.

Even once we'd made the lakes, unearthed my summer cache—nets, sacks, skins, traps—even then, roaming each alone across that higher country, the night would bring the howls of wolves and screams of catamount, the chance a Chi'soo hunter or Monaa or even some Notong K'oyom wandering down the range's spine might glimpse our fire. So that each day, before the sky succumbed to stars, we would return in time to share a bite, unroll our bedskins by the fire, the nights mild enough Walloki could set his far enough away to stay hidden from me, bury his breathing beneath the crackling, our time together spent mostly sleeping.

Though in the morning he woke me with his rising, or I woke

him, till after a while, we simply woke at the same time, came closer to the fire, warming ourselves a bit before starting our separate preparations for the day. A time that, as the days went by, grew longer, my mixing lure to bait my traps, him melting pitch to secure an arrow point, or pounding vertebrae into the mush I'd wrap in leaves for us to bake, sit eating together, sun splintering around the eastern crest, the morning growing later, gradually our voices joining in.

Mine first. No more than the same mumbling I'd been making on my own for years, but now drawing a cautious questioning: Walloki wondering at the meaning of some word I hadn't known I'd spoken, a sound that for some reason he wished to say aloud—*breeze*, *cloud*, *mother*—none of which I wished to hear. Ceased to repeat them, refused to teach him. Though, increasingly, he taught me. His language near enough to what little I knew that, as weeks turned to months, we grew able to speak, ponder the time that might have passed since a buck scraped his antlers, compare bear sign, ask where he'd hurt his foot, why I seemed worried, what he knew of mending baskets, trapping quail, calling salmon upriver at the season's start.

That summer he taught me how to shoot, correcting what I'd learned in boyhood, turning the bow level to the earth, replacing my three-fingered draw with pointer and thumb. Stood behind me helping me sight. Set me practicing on squirrels till I could knock one off a branch. Till the hardest thing was his standing so close, touching my hand. Hard enough I wouldn't have continued if I wasn't so grateful to be freed from what gunblasts did to me. A gift he didn't even know he gave me.

Instead, when I'd learned well enough to take down a deer myself, he took my hatchet and, unknown to me, made a trip far downriver to where he found a stand of yew. Cut off a branch. Carried it back up.

Nik'beku, he had begun to call me. And when I asked him what it meant he would not say, his fingertips touching the bunched flesh over his bad eye the way they did when he was nervous. Though when I told him others called me Honpetayim Woole, he shook his head, would use only Nik'beku—Good morning, Nik'beku; Like this, Nik'beku—a word I grew to think was just a name he'd made up for me. Till I asked him how he'd come, at his young age, to know the way to make a bow.

I'd watched him shave the sapling, scrape it with the deer's hipbone till the yew tapered at either end, and now he took the strip of sinew that days ago he'd cut free and dried, stuffed one end into his mouth and chewed.

I was crouched over my cookpot, stirring the muck we'd scooped off salmon skin, watching it begin to boil, asked him again.

Through his chewing he said something that sounded like Nik'beku.

And I looked up, watched him instead.

His eyes were down, held to the sinew as he fed it through one side of his mouth and chewed, and worked the softened part out the other side, and fed himself the next.

Between his chewing he said, Niktc'e. Using the Nisenan word I knew. But a little later, telling me how his father taught him—the right size sapling, the way to scrape it, to harden then resoften sinew—he slipped up again, said, Nik'beku. Though this time I recognized the *nik* as *my*. Knew in Notong K'oyom weye, *beku* must be father.

Good night, Nik'beku, he'd said. Here, Nik'beku. For you, Nik'beku.

I stared at him. He had stopped chewing, his mouth gone still around the strip. Between us: the fire, the pot of boiling glue. Walloki, I said.

And he began chewing again, jaw working harder, eyes refusing to rise.

Walloki, I said again, you cannot call me that.

His furious chewing.

You know I'm not.

His hands feeding the sinew to his teeth.

Walloki, I said, you know you're not my son.

The sound of his spit working the dead dryness out.

You're not my son, I said again, loud enough I saw him jerk. But his eyes stayed down, his mouth working.

Through the steam I told him, Say my name. And when he would not even look I shouted it—My name!—and stood—Pe'ap yapem mi nik!—and then was reaching across the flames, snatching the sinew, the boy rearing away, my fist ripping the spit-slick strip out of his mouth with such force I saw him grip his face as if I'd torn loose his teeth. Then his hand fell away and his voice came like a spray of blood. That night he told me all that happened, from his father's death to his own flight, told it in one furious rush, as if all his silence of the past months had burst, the spit-slurred words too fast for me to make out more than half. Which was enough.

Your name, he said when he was done. You never told me your name.

In the firelight his face was terrible, his bad side bunched with anger, a flickering slipping over the hardened scars, his one eye glistening with hurt. You know what it means? he said. Honpetayim Woole? His fingers banged the side of his head. A sick man, he said. Sick here. Then, circling his face madly with his hand: A sick white man.

On my face: the fire's heat, the air brushed by his fingers. Then he was gone, out of the light, become just footsteps receding into the dark. Below me: the pop and spit of the salmon glue, the smell of it, the pile of scraped skins seeming to slither beside the fire. I shut my eyes, tried to feel the emptiness around me, the vast expanse of that high country. But there was only the distant sound—almost unhearable over the fire's crackle, almost hidden beneath my breathing—of muffled crying.

By the time I found him he'd quieted again, returned to stillness: a dark shape sitting on the fallen trunk of a moon-bleached pine. Even as I approached, he stayed turned away, staring north. We were too low in our lake bowl to see the massif in that direction—the range worn down to knolls but for a last cluster of peaks aglint with snow into midsummer—but I'd come upon him gazing at it often enough to know that even through the lake bowl's blackness, he was seeing the mountain. The same that, when we'd first ascended high enough to spy it, he'd said loomed over his people's summer home. A lake at its base, a village on its shore. That once contained all he had known. Where the entire world he'd grown up in remained.

I stood behind him. Somewhere an owl called, somewhere another answered. Far above, the pine tops stirred against the moon, swept through the stars. And when I looked down again his hand was there, palm up. Dark and still. But moonlit just enough for me to see his fingers. Curled upward too. Their tips to me. Where my fingertips found them when I reached down.

That slight touch—fingertips coming to rest on fingertips, so lightly they barely brushed, stayed still—for all the words he taught me, it would remain how we spoke best.

Whatever had happened to Walloki—what he'd told me, what he hadn't—I think what changed inside him most must have happened between his fleeing and his finding me. I mean whatever made him able to live beside me. I mean what made him the only other I was ever able to abide. Other than you. When you'd still been a child.

Sometimes amid Walloki's teaching me to speak, to spear a fish, weave a basket, I struggled to remember how we'd gotten here, how he'd managed to fit around me, found the place where I could touch the world beyond myself and simply stood there. Sometimes I struggled to remember that despite all that, he was still a child too.

The way he'd gorge on chokecherries, strip them straight into his mouth, the purple juice staining his grin. His whooping as we dragged torches through dry grass, circling fast as insects fled inside, till, running, we'd shut the flame-hoop around a thousand crickets springing into our pit. Walloki, unable to contain his whoops, jumping and jumping, torch roaring in his hand.

And, from above, a hawk watching, a flock of crows, a scout squirrel standing on his haunches to better see Walloki hurl a buckskin ball high into the sky. Beneath it, the boy's upturned face, his hands held out to catch. A chipmunk paused atop a log to watch him throw it to me, then. My startling. My awkward throw back.

That summer sometimes he'd toss pinecones into the lake, the two of us striving to sink them from the shore, throwing stone after stone into the other's splashes. The explosions muffling his laughter, mine. And there were nights I'd sit alone beside the fire, my eyes shut tight, trying, on the flute he made me, to find a tune. Alone but for Walloki, out in the dark, far enough away I wouldn't hear the footfalls of his dancing. Could nearly forget that he was there. Even on the evenings that I'd sing to him instead. A song he taught me, maybe a lullaby, because he only asked for it on nights he couldn't sleep, knew how hard it was on me to break the quiet with my voice. A thing I could barely make myself do. But did. *Kassam, kassam, lil hanpi.* Just loud enough to cover his shudder. *Bluejay, bluejay.* His muffled crying. *Gather the pine nuts . . .*

And you? Did you dance when you were still a child? Alone to music from the bar below? Or holding your mother? Learning to allemande? Did she teach you to catch? Throw? Or did my father? Or was there another? Who tickled you when you were younger, threw you over his shoulder, taught you to grapple, shoot, carried your first kill back, both of you beaming. And do you call him Dad? Or Sir? Or Father? Does he save you the best piece of meat? Collect your favorite berries? Sing you to sleep? Stay awake a little longer just to watch your breathing ease?

Some mornings we'd wade into the lake, shivering beside each other, waiting to see who would plunge first. But in the afternoons, if we returned from our days apart while it was light, we'd head for the river, a clear pool deep enough to dive. Would clamber out on separate rocks, lie in the sun, boulders hot beneath our bodies. His smaller, smoother, browner. Mine bigger, paler, furred. His wounded face, my tangled beard. So different from each other. But there.

The way we were when the Monaa found us. Two backlit men looking down from cliffs above, unknowable but for their bows. We sensed them at the same time, scrambled up before they could hallo us. Though too slow to stop them shooting us if they'd wanted. Instead, they showed with open palms they meant no harm. What I assumed they called down too. Walloki knew the tribe as Tsaisu, spoke their tongue enough to glean they were returning from delivering a daughter to her new husband, had come up high in hope of hunting mountain sheep, seen me instead—my beard and skin—showed themselves because they wished to ask me for a favor.

Though Walloki couldn't quite make out what it might be. Some sickness, I wondered, that they hoped I could cure? Maybe a blessing? But he insisted it was simpler, something they wanted me to fix, some tool. Though what he couldn't understand was why they seemed to think the thing had come from me. Then, no: from another like me.

What does that mean? I asked him.

A knife, he said.

No, I said. What does—

A knife that folds.

No, I said again, the word changed in its meaning by the time that it was out.

Yes, Walloki insisted. From another white.

That evening we followed them back over the pass I'd crossed four years before, down the eastern side, moonlight leading us at last into their camp. The barking of dogs, shouting of families, some dozen Monaa crowding round me with the same disgust and wonder I'd come to expect. Except it was true: once we were squatting by the fire the older hunter brought me the knife. A clasp knife, its blade snapped off just above three stamped initials: *JCF.*

Through Walloki I asked where he had gotten it. And when he answered from a man like me, it seemed my chest would squeeze too tight to let me speak. But I managed to ask, A white man gave you this? No, he told Walloki, he'd gotten it in a trade. Gave me back my breath. On this eastern side, they might have bartered with Shoshocos, the Shoshocos with the Crow, the knife traveled a thousand miles before it reached here.

From his new son-in-law, Walloki told me. Part of the dowry. A word it took him a while to make me understand, though by the time he had I didn't care. Because by then it had come clear the son-in-law had seen the whites.

Many. A large party. The other men all talking quickly now, Walloki's face more worried each time he turned to me. A party they insisted was many times the size of their whole camp. Mounted on horses, with guns and swords, bright woven blankets, strange small stones strung up like clamshell strings. They went on. Walloki went on. But I was no longer listening, was staring at the clasp knife, trying to make a *W* out of the *CF,* the *J* make it all right: surely it was the party Joe Walker led a decade back, surely the wonder of seeing that would still be fresh.

But when I interrupted to suggest it, Walloki shook his head. Last winter, he said.

Ko'meni? I repeated.

Bo'mhintsulim, he said. Meaning the time of squinting and snow, the darkest months of greatest cold. Which could not be. No, I said, not across the mountains—

But yes, they all chimed in to decry such foolishness, insist that their tribe had tried to warn them, disapproval shifting to disbelief as, wide-eyed, they relayed what they'd heard from the Chi'soo farther south. More horsemen seen early that spring, a band of whites that must have been the same, must have not only crossed the mountains but returned, this time heading east.

At least there was that. That they had not remained. I tried to get Walloki to confirm no others had been seen, but the women had begun to serve the soup, a pine-nut mush an older one dished into scoop-shaped baskets, a younger handing them out. A girl near enough Walloki's age to make him deaf to me, his gaze on the baskets in her hands as if he'd grown suddenly ravenous. Though when she at last passed him one, his eyes were on her face. Dropped just as quick. Only to keep returning while she served the rest. His fingers scooping soup same as the other men, women, me. Though when the girl brought a washing basket and I'd splashed my hands, she didn't move to him. Stayed before me as I dried my fingers, her eyes not on my face or hands but forearms. Before she spoke, I knew, told Walloki to tell her no. But he said yes. A Monaa word even I, by then, could understand. Gave her a smile as she touched my arm hair. Though, watching her fingers' brushing, his eye filled with something else. Longing? Jealousy? Maybe just the wish that she would touch him the same way. Because when, lifting her basket again, she came to him, his gaze stayed on her hands. His own remaining by his sides till she reminded him to wash. Dipping his fingers then, he spoke to her, fast. I do not know what words. Only that while he did, his brow lifted in an expression I knew well—a hopeful question—the skin of his gouged eye tugged upward, the wound pulling his cheek, wrinkling his nose, so that the girl turned quickly away and, sliding the basket out from under his hand, moved on.

Even so, I know he would have liked to stay the night, know the Monaa wanted us to. But I was already too sick with what I'd heard to do more than pretend to eat, already sweating from the press of others as if I sat too near the fire. Knew Walloki could feel it in me. And still, when I folded the knife into its clasp and held it out with its snapped blade and asked Walloki to tell them I couldn't fix it, still I felt from him a thing I never had in all the time I'd known him: a flash of annoyance or resentment, or maybe just the momentary wish that I was someone else.

That night we traveled under the long bright arc of a nearly full moon till it sank behind the crest ahead, then sought a level spot, spread out our skins. All summer we'd slowly moved closer together so that by late se'meni, nights cold enough to need a fire, we were accustomed to sleeping just across the flames. But that night the trees were unfamiliar, the territory unknown, and so we lay in darkness, back to back, wrapped in our robes, wind loud in the pines around us.

I tried to calm my breath, convince my mind to sleep, but I could not stop hearing them—clatter of hooves, creak of leather, English voices—could not stop seeing them along the route they'd found. On their way back. Which would bring others. Just as Walker had brought us. Me.

The wind roared through the trees. And I could feel the keelboat shift under my feet, the current sweeping it along, the way that—even as, day by day, the Ohio had flushed away the stench and slime of sewage, the murk from the eroded valley had cleared, the slash had grown up in scrub, the sounds of saw, mills, foundries, receded as forests reclaimed the banks—I could never escape the sense that all of it was coming in our wake, swelling like some inexorable wave, a flood of men, women, children surging endlessly out of the east. Were there still beavers in the Rockies? Buffaloe on the plains? Already, at that last rendezvous, talk had turned to ways of hunting them, men plotting around fires fueled by logs brought in by squaws from distant hills, the whole of that smoke-choked valley by then already hacked clear of trees.

Above me, the pine boughs shook. And on the breeze I smelled their fires, in the soughing heard their sounds, lying there beneath the shaking limbs could feel the presence of them all coming like a wind blowing west across the desert, onrushing relentlessly as the sky-smothering flocks of pigeons that once darkened the sun in hordes of millions. But humans.

At first I thought that I was shaking. But I was deadly still. The shaking coming from behind me. Walloki. Wrapped in his robe.

I lay in silence beside his rustling, a rhythmic brushing against the furs, remembering my brother creeping down the hall from his shared room, past the closet where I slept. Later, after I'd begun sleeping in the barn, the sight of him leaving the house, crossing the dark yard to a place behind the coop he must have thought private. His moonlit shoulders shaking. And I had seen one of the men at the asylum take out his stiff at suppers, lectures. Known trappers to bring along squaw-wives, make camp off to the side, though not so far we couldn't hear. Had gone with trading parties to visit Crow and Arapaho, slept in wickiups full of families bedded beside each other and, lying awake, fighting the need to flee all those bodies, listened to one couple come to completion, then another, as if inspired, starting up. Had known a bossloper who, each night before bed, stepped to the fire's edge, stroked himself empty. Regular as taking a piss. Known two old coons who liked to keep each other company while they finished, a thing they recommended to each greenhorn as if passing along some hard-earned wisdom. Had spent those nights across the fire from Fancher and JG.

And yet, as I lay beside Walloki, all those memories seemed a separate thing. From him lying beside me being a boy. My seeing again the girl turning away, easing the water basket from under his fingers. My trying to stay as still as sleep, to keep my body from turning away as well, the only way I knew to help.

The sole time my father talked to me of self-abasement I was less embarrassed than he. If more perplexed. Still not ten, I hadn't yet linked what I did to sin. Even to women, girls, men. Anything except a way to escape all of them, clear my mind of the crowding world, shake loose its grip. A sensation so strong that for a moment, it could shed the rest, release me into such peace sometimes I could slip straight to sleep.

I believe I would have never known it as anything else, even as I grew older, had it not been for that talk from my father. Later, the drawings I found inside a tin hidden in the chicken coop, my brother's skill at sketching dwarfed by his imagination, but sufficient to infect my own. And then, of course, your mother. Delia's small shoulders raised beneath the taut back of her dress, her silent laughter, her hair stark red amid the parakeet-green grass, her arms flung out to spare me their embrace, her fingers forced into fists, her eyes squeezed shut. As if she could already see how it would be, the years she'd pass deprived of such touch, the bathwater brushed by her hands above my chest the closest we'd come to it again.

And I can only hope that in the years after I fled, she found another. A husband who could hold her waist, take in her scent, let it do to him what it was meant to, a stepfather to show you as you grew, a man more suited to the world I left, able to mate as we were made to. For I have seen the horned lark's swooping display. Weasels clinging to each other, loath to separate. Seen them come together later the same day, do it again. Have heard the longing in lions' screams. Have lain beside a boy shaking with the same desperation and listened to him finish—his breathing after, the sorrow in his sigh—and known I was unable to help. Unfit to. As friend or father, or even just a man who once had been a boy like him. Have lain there silent in whatever quiet struggle he was going through. Silent as I have been through all the years of yours.

The next morning we made it back to camp before the sun melted the frost off of the rocks. Found it all there: fire circle, furs, cookpot, Walloki's deerskin ball rolled by the wind or some small creature down to the lake. He went to fetch it, I to check the traps. But each time I came to one it seemed set by another man, made me want to dig a pit, bury it chain and all. While, in between, I kept hearing footsteps of others, nickers on the breeze, kept stopping to stare off toward the east. And the next day went back. Just far enough to stand at the crest scanning the pass. Didn't return till dark, didn't tell Walloki where I'd been. Though I'd spent my last afternoon swimming with him, would not throw stones at pinecones or dry on sun-warm rocks again that year. Hardly even hunted. My routes, after that day, chosen more for views of terrain than game that I might shoot. My bow abandoned. Though I'd again begun bringing my musket.

Most days I saw nothing but deer and marmot, hawks riding the wind, a few times bruin browsing with an intensity come from the ever-colder weather. Once a lone hunter I thought was Walloki following me, then realized was not and dropped till he was gone. Once an elk cow so big that, for a second, I mistook it for a horse, had my musket up, was sighting down the barrel by the time I saw it better. Though mostly I saw nothing. Mostly I stayed still. Out at the edge of open chaparral or a wide tumble of scree or high on a cliff surrounded by sky. Listening.

Walloki waited till the first snow, weeks past when we should have already left, waited till we were huddled beneath a hastily made shelter, watching gusts swirl. He was chipping with a bone-flaker at a stone for a new knife. Said, between clacks, Uncle. The word he had begun to use, that I'd begun to answer to. Nik'bono, he said, it's time we went back down. I let the sound of his chipping continue. Till he spoke again, said I couldn't stand watch over all the mountains, the Lokum Yaman, the entire range.

No, I told him, just this pass.

Or even that, he said.

There was the clack, clack, clack of his chipping. Its stopping beneath my stare.

Not from down there, I said. And walked out into the snow.

We stayed another week. Another. The snow by then near two feet deep, thick enough I told him it would soon be too late for all but the most foolhardy to attempt a crossing. And if you see some? he asked me. Some other whites?

He made us snowshoes—branch hoops webbed with rawhide-wrapped sticks strapped to our knee-high moccasins—and while he tended camp and brought down game and kept us alive, I made my rounds the way I used to check my traps, only now lookout to lookout, my tracks wending behind me in the white. Easy to see by anyone who might track me. But I had ceased to care about anything but seeing them. The men who might yet appear, riding their horses, snow on their hats and beards, the sight augured by a musket crack, the clack of hooves, a shout.

Though when it came, the sound was something worse. I stood, stopped on the snow, telling myself the bellow could have been from a bull elk. Till it came again, deep and awful, blowing out of the distance: the lowing of an ox.

I ran, tripping on my hoops, skidding down the slope, ran till, still far away, I saw a sight strange as any I might have dreamed: a team of oxen longer than I'd ever seen, two lines of nine yoked side by side, struggling against some massive weight, the chain behind the wheel team cutting a line back through the snow only to disappear over a cliff, the oxen pulling as if the emptiness beyond was trying to draw them into it, their hooves slipping, bodies crashing, bellowing echoing around the canyon, cut by the cracks of whips. Wielded by women. I heard them now, their high shouts terrible as the sight of children with them. Children and women and, as I watched, something long and straight rising over the precipice: the tongue of a cart. The flapping top, rims of wheels, the whole thing groaning, as, dragged over the cliff, it became a wagon. And the women were cheering, the children whooping, the oxen gasping and, beneath it all, from somewhere far down behind the cliff, there came a sound like the mountain itself exhaling, low and gusting. The shouting men.

I do not know how long I watched, only that it was long enough for them to bring five wagons up, each time the women unhitching the team, backing it toward the cliff, hawing and geeing and, at some sign from below, driving them forward again. Long enough for me to sink into the snow. So slowly it seemed to fall instead around me, building over my ankles, shins, soaking my moccasins, freezing my feet.

Still I did not move. Not till I saw the men. The first tiny figures climbing through the pines lining the cliff. Two. Three. Inside me a trembling, as if my heart and lungs were shaking on their own, the rest of my body held in such stillness that, when I broke it, the movement was small as the specks of men: one hand opening my possibles, the other reaching in, finding a patch, a ball, wrapping it with a twist, starting another. The shaking had risen into my face. Seven men, eight. And still I kept preparing bullets till it seemed no more were coming—a dozen standing now around the carts, dividing oxen into teams—till the women and children were back beneath the canvass coverings, the men climbing onto bullwhacker seats, or reaching for the lead beast's lines, or starting to kick through the high snow as the wagon train slowly began to move.

And I was running—*Look*, my mother said—snow spraying against my chest—*Silas, look at yourself*—my musket pumping in my fist, the shaking breaking into the pounding of my legs, my snowshoes shoving so fast I'd begun gliding by the time it hit: a slam strong as a cougar crashing onto my back, smashing me into the snow, blurring my sight with icy grit, till, wrenching, kicking, I rolled over, punching upward, still half-blind, my fist gripping my knife before I saw it was Walloki. The boy sprawled over me, one hand trying to protect his face, the other groping for my wrist, what advantage he'd gained by surprise already turned to fear, in his eye a terror great as if he'd glimpsed the blood-smeared teeth, felt the flecks of spit, seen, in that second, the blurred reflection of what his nik'bono had been back in that world.

The words I bellowed at him were as much fury as English, and through their incomprehensibility he kept saying only his name—Walloki, Walloki—as if I didn't know, as if that wasn't what drove my anger. Though what caught it was the words I caught him saying after: They would hear. Hear us. Nisem nisee pinowowis.

I lay in the cloud of my loud breath, him still over me staring down through his.

Shoot you, he was saying. They will—

Me? I spat back. Shoot *me*?

But he was shaking his head. Uncle, he said, you do not even have enough—

I have—

Not for the women, the children.

I stared into our breath mixed white between us.

What would you do? he said. Kill all their men?

I could feel my fury building again.

Leave them alone?

His weight on me too great.

To die in the snow?

His presence smothering.

Or hunt them?

Get off, I told him.

One by one?

Get off.

With arrows?

And I was shoving up, sending him sprawling, shouting at his stumbling shape to get away—Away from me!—shouting into his face twisted with shouting back.

Here! He threw his bow so it cracked against my upraised hands. Here! Hurled his quiver clattering into me. Take them! he shouted, take them, then! Use my arrows on the women. My knife on the children.

He drew it out, threw it at my feet with all the rest. And I stood mute but for my breath, the arrows scattered in the snow around me, the bow half buried, the musket lying where it fell.

Or let them go, he said. Let them go to follow the others. Over the mountain. Out of here. Let them go till they are gone.

That night he tried to heal me. Back at our camp, buckskins drying before a fire, sheep plews wrapped round us both. Me sitting so near the flames I could feel my beard becoming kindling, my nostrils starting to burn. And still I sat, unstirring. While, across the fire, beneath the stars, Walloki danced, the glints of deer hooves clattering around him, a rattle that he'd lamented should be dangling cocoons instead. This kind all wrong, but all he had. Along with memories of his father's dance steps, snippets of chants. Not much. But enough for him to want to try.

Since we'd returned, I had not spoken, had hardly moved. Even as he'd stripped my clothes, urged me to eat, sleep. Had only sat staring at the fire, seeing them. And all the others who would come after. An endless line of wagons stretching over the pass, wheels groaning, oxen grunting, above it all the calls of humans, words from a world no longer mine, sounds that, inside my mind, I could already feel dragging me back.

While, before me, Walloki danced as if he thought that he could stop it, shook till he was sheened with sweat, his body steaming beyond the smoke. But my eyes were on the rising sparks glowing against the night, bright as the others' fires would be right then, out there, a handful of them, and then the sparks extinguished, and more rising again. And from the fire the bursting of a branch sending a hundred embers swirling up, blowing the emptiness out of the dark.

Sometime later he set his rattle down, took up the pipe No Rope had given me, packed pine needles into the bowl. Not drilled from stone or filled with tobacco, but good enough to draw enough he could blow smoke out of his mouth over my head. Shut your eyes, he said. And when I refused, he blew into them anyway, forcing them closed, between each breath saying, Be gone, go far away, leave him in peace. And with each breath I heard theirs instead—women, children, men, huffing as they broke snow—loud as if they were beside me. Over my head his hand hovered, hesitating, so that I knew he was supposed to touch me. But his fingers only floated above my hair. While he blew smoke and said his words. And only when the pipe was out did his voice stop, his hand go still. Still slightly shaking above my brow. His breath shaking a little too. I'm sorry, he said, and it was gone, his hand, his breath, his whole self seeming to withdraw. My father, he said. Said, Would have. Said, Can't. Said, Why I am a ba'api.

In the corner of my eye I saw him set down the pipe. Then just the pipe lying where he'd been. Heard the rustle of his bedskins, his broken breathing, quiet crying. And said nothing, did nothing. Just sat watching the fire die, slowly growing cold, knowing before morning I would be freezing, before then I would be gone, by the time dawn brightened enough for me to see our footprints I'd be following them back. Till I found the wagon tracks, started after them alone.

But when the sky had drained of all but its morning star, and I began to rise, I heard him stir as if he'd been watching me all night. His words, when they came, like he'd seen my thoughts too. That morning he convinced me to wait. One day. So we could pack up camp, cache our supplies, follow them together far as I wanted.

Though by the time we'd strapped on all we'd carry back, dismantled the lean-to, scattered our ashes, they'd come to us. Riders appearing over the eastern ridge as if they'd followed our tracks, horsemen dark against the sky and dropping down to cut their shapes into the snow, their hollers blowing over the water to where we stood watching the first oxen behind them break over the lake bowl's lip, the bellowing and whip-cracks and whoops of kids slip-running down the slope, all coming like the day before reloaded, exploded again. And maybe it was simply that, the sense that they were hunting me, the sight of Walloki turning to flee, his snowshoes sinking and wrenching free, the spray around his body a thing I could feel inside my own. Except his was taking him away. From them, from this. Where suddenly I needed to go.

Down from the lake, the tumbling creek, the steep escarpment, the swale deepening into a canyon, the roar distant but building, rising over the ever-fainter clamor of the others, till it drowned them out. My river. Our snowshoes clattering over its rocks, slipping, stopping. Leaving nothing but its sound. Filling my ears, my mind. Louder, wider, wilder as we made our way down. The canyon walls each day a little higher. Till, between them, the world that held us in that chasm began to seem separate even from the Lokum Yaman, hidden from the peaks and ridges, whatever happened up on the crest. Maybe Walloki was right, maybe they'd merely pass by, out of the mountains, through the foothills, into the valley. Where they surely meant to go. Would surely stay. A world almost as far away from mine as the one from which they came.

It was the latest I had ever stayed upriver. Cold and colder down in the canyon. The first few days it snowed, flakes swirling in gusts above rapids swirling below, the boundaries between air and water blurring. As, wrapped in our skins, we traversed through, dropped lower, the snow thinning hour by hour, rocks and trees re-emerging. Still, the boulders stayed slippery with ice all morning, the sunlight reaching too briefly into the canyon before receding again behind the ridge. Yet we stayed on the river, day after day, never straying far from the water, never climbing out of its sound. Sometimes Walloki left my sight as he'd done on the way up, but now unfailingly returned before much time had passed, always came back by dark. Though, as we drew within a day of our winter home, he stayed closer, left less, the silence between us thickened by a downpour pounding our buckskin slickers, beating a roaring off branches and stones, turning the air into a wall of sound. All that last day we traveled a few rods apart and yet completely separate, the two of us alone together, as we had grown to be over our months away.

More time than I'd spent gone from my home since the day I'd found it. And still, soon as we came around the bend into view of the effigy—its stacked-boulder face not merely watching back, but waiting—I knew something was wrong, swung my gaze across to the far bank. Through the rain-streaked blur: my drawbridge, down. For a second I stood confused, the deluge battering my buckskin cowl, trying to remember if for some reason we had lowered it. Turned to Walloki. Though by the time I met his eye I knew we'd gone up the far side, left the log raised, its rope tied round the oak. Slipped? Broken? I could see it dangling, the bank-lashed log driven downriver by the high water, jammed at a slant. Always in autumn I'd returned early enough the water was still low enough to let me wade across, but watching it foam between boulders and barrel through chutes, I set my pack down by Walloki, told him I'd cross first—find out what happened, come back for him—my words swallowed by the roar so that, seeing his face stiffly unchanged, I might have thought he hadn't heard. If, staring past me at my winter camp, he hadn't seemed merely wary, the way he'd been ever since entering Kushna territory, but scared. As if he knew what I would see when I got near: the rope not rotted through, but cut.

Then I was not thinking of him, was only leaping, crossing,

reaching my bank, my creek, till, climbing the ledge, I could take in the rest. My cabin door stripped of its hide, the window of its shade. Inside, the mats and grinding stone were gone, even the herbs. Even my granaries. Through the window, I could see where they had stood. And then was out, running again, across the muddy mess of others' footprints, down to my cache, clearing away its cover of branches and stones, till, crouched before the opening, my eyes adjusting to take in skins and sacks, tool heads and traps, my breath escaping with relief, I felt a sudden presence at my back. Whipped around, sprang to my feet, knife already out. Only to find nobody there. Just the giant effigy's unblinking stare. And, below it, across the river, still standing where I'd left him on the bank: Walloki.

I was still leaping across when he began to speak, his sound buried beneath the rain and river. Though I could see he was repeating something over and over, words that, landing on the beach, I at last heard: I'm sorry. As if he'd been beside me in the ransacked camp or somehow known what I would find. I'm sorry, he said, face stiff beneath my stare, eye refusing to rise. I'm sorry, Uncle. Words I wouldn't understand until we'd reached Kushna.

The rain drained away with the last light and, in the quiet of new-fallen dark, the dog barks came—too soon, too far ahead—as if someone had run to warn the village of our coming. Walloki had not wanted to, had seemed, as we'd climbed up the canyon, to grow ever younger, as if each step toward Kushna knocked him farther back into the boy now flinching beside me at each bark. Then the dogs were bursting out of the black, all snarls and streaks of teeth, snapping at Walloki's wildly stabbing spear, his body drawn so near my own I could feel the furs strapped to his back. Smacking my musket stock at muzzles, I cleared our path. To either side: women darting in to drag off curs, men emerging from surrounding hus, in their hands torches, clubs, the glints of spears. Though, as we neared, they stepped aside quick as if I'd swung my barrel at their shins instead of simply asking why they'd armed against us, stolen from us. Around my words their own rose in a rolling chatter that seemed less driven by what I said than that I was speaking. *Honpetayim*, I heard over and over. And the words *talk*, *son*, *ba'api*, *back*.

Then we were nearly to No Rope's hu and he was coming down its mounded roof into the torchlight, hand raised not in greeting but in a sign for us to stop.

I had begun to sweat, despite the cold, less from the torches' heat than the sight of all those holding them, their closeness filling my throat, swelling it shut.

Friend, I managed to say.

Before he cut me off: Why are you here?

At first I wasn't sure I understood, the language strange after my months learning it mixed with Walloki's, but near enough for me to glean what he had asked, see the strain on No Rope's face, know he had not wanted to. Or did not want to hear my answer. And so I told him, simply as I could, that we had come with furs from summer, to trade the same as every fall, searching with each word I spoke for how he would receive it.

With a smile, it seemed. Then seemed not. So, he said, you've learned to speak.

Yes, I told him. The boy has been teaching—

Notong k'oyom weye, he cut in. The words spit out as if they hurt his mouth.

Yes, I said again. But—

You say even *yes* strangely now.

Maybe, I told him, but you understand. And I understand enough to hear from you who came to my home, who stole from me, why you—

Honpetayim, he started.

And I told him, I know what that means too.

He glanced at Walloki then. And when I glanced over as well, the boy would look at me no more than him.

Silas, No Rope said, raising his hand as if he might reach to my shoulder. Instead, he gestured in a short sweep from me to him. Come, he said, come in.

Behind him, the low opening glowed with the fire inside. I had not entered a k'um since my first year, did not know if I could do it now, only that I could feel Walloki watching, all the others watching him. And so, trying to think only of escaping their stares, of the fewer people in there, I dropped to my hands and knees, and, pushing my pack before me, crawled slowly in.

The heat hit my face like all the torches outside suddenly shoved close, the fire's brightness bringing water to my eyes. Squinting, I could see women and children crowding against the walls, away from me, as, crawling in, I hauled my pack toward the center, where it was emptier. Though hotter. Sitting on my stack of furs, I tried to keep my eyes on the fire, my breathing even. Through it heard Walloki dragging his plews beside me. Though he stayed standing, a bit behind me, his hands gripping the packet's straps as if they were the only thing stopping him from fleeing.

When No Rope joined us, he sat on a log beside the fire. Close enough we wouldn't have to peer through smoke. Nearer to me. Though, when he spoke, it was to Walloki: You didn't tell him.

What? I said. Looked from him to the boy, back.

You didn't tell him, No Rope said again.

Tell me what? I said. Heard, from beside me, Walloki's soft, I'm sorry. Then was only looking at him.

They took your things, Walloki said.

I waited.

Because, he said, they did not think that you were coming back.

I could feel the others listening too. Could feel their stillness, smell their sweat. The same stench of smoke and roasted meat and acorn soup and drying leaves that was the scent of my own home. But a hundredfold stronger.

I was supposed to tell you, Walloki said. They told me to tell you.

And I could smell his sweat, see it. What? I said again.

I'll go, he said.

Across from us No Rope shook his head.

I'll go now, Walloki said. And not—

Tell him, No Rope said.

Walloki. The word was hard to get through my dry lips. Tell me what?

When it came it came on one long breath: When they agreed to let me stay with you, I was supposed to tell you it was only if we both went away.

We did, I said.

And didn't come back.

Watching his sweat, I felt my own, slick beneath my leggings, my shirt, the buckskin beginning to stick to my flesh, as if the presence of others all around me would solidify into a second hide. Ever? I said.

He sat there sweating, looking past me at No Rope, No Rope holding his stare.

And suddenly I had to get my shirt off, was struggling to wrench it over my head, arms, the leather peeling away as if taking my skin, then gone. And Walloki was saying to No Rope, Please, and, I'll go now, and how he would never return.

But No Rope only turned to me, spoke as if Walloki wasn't talking, not even there. That, he said, was what the boy was supposed to tell you. Though the agreement was not to let him stay. It was to let him live.

If we left? I said. If I left too?

And Walloki was saying sorry again and I was asking why again. Why, because he's Notong K'oyom?

Please, Walloki said, he doesn't know—

He told us, No Rope spoke over him, he was your son.

Walloki went silent then. I knew he must be as hot as me, his face streaming with sweat, but he sat as still as he was quiet.

You told us, No Rope said to me, he was your son.

And before I could speak, Walloki was saying, No. Then louder, again, though No Rope refused to look at him: No, my father was a jomin. Beneath his words, or above them, or from somewhere beyond the walls, there came a sound like moaning. A jomin, he said, his voice rising, of the Notong K'oyom, the moaning growing with his speaking so that, when Walloki said *spirit*, said *grizzly*, the sound was loud enough to make me look at the ceiling. Kukini! the boy said. Yomkapa! The words nearly drowned beneath the rattling that had begun to come from the open hole, as if the smoke that billowed out was causing it, Walloki having to shout over it now: A yomkapa jomin!

In the rising moaning and rattling, No Rope's voice was so quiet

I could barely hear it. Silas, he said, his eyes bringing mine back to his. You lied to us too.

And the moaning broke into a roar, so low and long it seemed like struggled breathing, some strange and thunderous retching, till it came again, again, and I could hear the word: Baa'aapiiii! The rattling loud as a downpour on the roof. Baa'aapiiii! And through the smoke: something huge, roiling as if with air blown upward from the fire, feathers billowing and fur bristling as it filled the hole and, rattling, roaring, descended toward where we sat staring up.

At the black-plumed cloak, the shaking rattle, the crown of raven feathers shivering with each step down the rungs. Then he leapt, the cloak floating around him, the headdress fluttering, the rattle filling the k'um over the thud of his landing, the hu'uku's long bony face staring through the smoke, lit by the fire, fierce as I'd ever seen Kushna's head priest. And all his fury focused on Walloki.

Ba'api, he said again, low and short and quiet and worse, the rattle seeming to shake the word, then smother it, and I could not stop staring at the thrashing of gleaming cocoons till there came another movement, even quicker, flicking from the hu'uku's other side, a jerk that jerked my body, flung out my hand, shot my palm to block Walloki's chest, and by the time I saw the flash streak through the firelight, the pain was already stabbing my flesh. The others jerked as if they felt it too. No Rope, Walloki, all the crowd. A shudder through the entire k'um. Except the hu'uku, his hand extended, his feathers settling, only his eyes shifting. From Walloki to me.

My hand was bleeding. I drew it back. All eyes but the hu'uku's following, the firelight glinting over the sela: a piece of bone, big as my little finger, one sharpened end stuck deep into the meat of my palm, the other faintly shaking. As, reaching with my other hand, I tugged it out.

A burble of blood. And with it the eruption of all the others in the k'um, their voices coming fast and loud, my own rising over their talking as I told No Rope he was wrong. Yes, I said, this is my blood—my hand held out, the rivulet bright red all down my wrist—not his. But where I come from that does not mean he cannot be my son.

Maybe, No Rope said, among your people—

He is my people.

He is Notong K'oyom, No Rope said.

And, as if loosed by the word, the hu'uku's voice broke through: Honpetayim Woole.

We are Nisenan, No Rope continued.

Honpetayim Woole, the hu'uku said again.

And you are, No Rope began.

But the hu'uku cut him off: Homamenmadap. It does not matter.

I started to reply: I am—

Dead, the hu'uku said. Honpetayim Woole, you are dead.

I held up the sela. Because of this?

You are dead, he repeated.

And I said, No. My fingers tight around the piece of bone, blood dripping off my elbow. No, I told him, because you are wrong too.

Behind him I could see the others. Their stares on him, on me. Made myself stare back over the flames, forced my gaze to move from eyes to eyes, felt all their pressure on my skin and breathed it in till it pressed inside my chest so hard it pushed my voice out loud enough to smother theirs. Neighbors, I said, I would ask you a question. Do you think that this was meant for me? In my fingers: the sela lit with firelight. Do you think your hu'uku meant it to kill me? They had become so quiet I could hear the fire's crackling, the boy's nervous breathing behind me, the silence coming off the hu'uku like a rattle in the air. Or do you think he missed? That I was quicker? My power greater? My spirit strong enough to stop the strongest jomin in Kushna?

Across the fire the hu'uku's face seemed to shiver, his stare to shake. But I knew it was the heated air, that behind it he stood so still not a feather of his crown shifted, not a plume of his cloak. As if he'd ceased to breathe. My own breath seemed to burn my throat, my sweat pure heat pushed through my skin. And how hot it must have been for him inside that mantle, his body baking. Yet his face was dry, his brow unbeaded, his sunken chest showing no sign of breath or beating, still as his stare on me. And staring back, I felt it too, a focus shoving away all else, my breath slowing, my sight become finite, a feeling nearly like that of a trigger beneath my finger.

When I spoke again it was to him. Or do you think, I said, it was the boy's spirit? Stronger than yours? That made my hand take your sela into my flesh? For him. Can you imagine what spirit would be strong enough to have stopped you? Because—holding up my hurt fist, I squeezed it till my fingers dripped—this is not his blood, but his father's. Who gave it to him. So he might take in the spirit of the grizzly.

Behind me I heard Walloki shift. But I would not break my stare. Not even when the hu'uku sent back a grunt of such disgust it broke his stillness—his arms flung out, cloak-feathers flapping, their wind shaking the flames—said, loud enough for all to hear, He *might* have taken in the spirit, but he refused. Filled it with fury. At him. At his village for letting him. At us! the hu'uku bellowed toward the crowd. If we do not—

Hu'uku! I made my voice meet his. How do you know?

Again he turned to me. How do I know? A ripple of nervous laughter passed through the crowd. For you to ask, he told me, shows only how little you know. Of us.

Then teach me, I said. How you know that he refused his father's spirit. How you're so sure the boy is a ba'api. Because you heard it from someone at Wokodot? Who heard it from a village farther up? Who heard it from the Notong K'oyom? Who now you trust?

Silas. It was No Rope speaking at last, his quiet voice silencing the rest. Silas, he said again, look at his face. On No Rope's own, a rueful smile, his open hands seeming to show nothing left to say. A rumble of agreement went through the crowd.

And for the first time since the hu'uku came down from the roof I turned to Walloki. He was standing as he had been, but instead of holding the packet's straps, he was holding his face, his hands over both his remaining eye and missing one. And turning to No Rope again, I lifted my own hand toward his shoulder, the way we used to, my fingers pointing to the scar I'd made. And this? I said. Does this mean you can't be headman of Kushna? I turned to the hu'uku. Your pressed-in chest, I said, where the spirits must have set their weight when you were born. Does it prove you are no priest? Or mean the opposite? To No Rope I said, Is it what made you hu'k? Of the hu'uku I asked, Is it how your father knew the spirits were strong inside you? Because, I said, pointing back at Walloki, his father's kukini might have tried to kill him—

Why? The hu'uku demanded.

Tried, I continued, but did not.

When No Rope spoke it was the hu'uku's name: Momhe'elimda, he said, is it not true the spirits always resist? Fight leaving the body of the jomin who they'd resided in for one they do not know? Have even been known to hurt the one who would try to receive them?

Haan, the hu'uku agreed. Then, in a voice as quiet as it was angry, asked me the same thing I'd asked him: How do you know? Honpetayim Woole, how do you know he has it in him? How do you know that he is *not* a ba'api?

I know, I said, because I have known him, listened to him. Behind me, Walloki had gone so still he seemed to have ceased breathing. Too Much Water, I said, speaking the hu'uku's name slowly, with respect, I know because he told me.

And behind me, I could feel Walloki's hands drop from his face. His stare.

But it was No Rope who spoke: Then let him tell us.

No, the hu'uku cut in. Let him show it. Then the priest was reaching across the fire, his cloak billowed with heat, his hand finding the sela in mine, pulling the bit of bone free, withdrawing through the smoke. From behind which his voice came again: Hold him. Then, as he started to come around the fire: Hold the ba'api.

Silas, No Rope said beside me, hold the boy still.

Walloki no longer covered his face. Nor looked at me. Not even as I stood and, stepping behind him, placed my hands on his—our fingertips just touching, hidden between us—my words so low, so close beside his ear, only he'd hear: Do you want me to? He didn't move. His eyes held on the nearing hu'uku. Do you know, I whispered, what he'll do? No nod, no word. Just his stare on the sela in the hu'uku's hand, the rattle the man began to shake, the rattling cocoons so near I could feel the shaking air. Or maybe it was the boy. Walloki? I said. And his hands clenched, grabbed my fingers, held tight inside mine holding back.

Before us, Too Much Water lifted the sharpened bone till his long fingers hovered an inch from Walloki's face, the hu'uku's stare searching boy's. Then sliding down below his eye, his scar. The jomin's hand holding the sela, waiting, his eyes shutting, lips starting to quiver, their humming mixing with his rattling. Till his lids snapped open and his hand moved: the sela shifted beneath Walloki's nose, the sharp tip touching the nostril of his wounded side, waiting just below the opening. Before the hu'uku, in one smooth sudden motion, shoved it in.

In my fists, Walloki's jerked. A jolt I felt go through his arms into his shoulders, shudder his body. Or maybe just mine. Because, before me, his head stayed still. A stillness greater against the flinch that went through all the others—the silent crowd, No Rope still sitting—all but the hu'uku, whose thumb stayed pressed to the bottom of Walloki's nostril, the sela's entire length buried inside. The jomin's own face frozen, the rattle silent. The air filled with the fire's crackle, pop of a log, the breathing of us all. From behind, I could see Walloki's nostril bulge, stretched out along his entire nose, up into the scar tissue of his wound, the lumped flesh lifted by the sela burrowed through his face, the skin forever shut over that eye seeming squeezed even more tight. But his other eye open, steady. As the hu'uku told him, Now pull it out.

Only later would I learn what it would mean. How much depended on those fingers that let go, tugged free, left me feeling only their sweat. His fingers that felt for the sela jutting from his nostril, tried a faint first pull, and slipped—something in the failure to grip releasing the hu'uku's breath—before, wiping his hand on the peltries beneath him, Walloki gripped the bone again, and, with an awful slowness, began dragging the spike back out, his stare, steady as his hand, on the hu'uku's eyes. Till the jomin could not keep his own from dropping to the sela, now half removed from the distended nostril, its tip still visible beneath the skin. And then a sound like something in Walloki breaking, and the bone coming free in a gush of blood.

And if his fingers had been too slippery, his nostril too tight, the bone too thick, the blood too much, the point too far inside, and he had needed help? From me or the hu'uku or anyone? If the spirits had refused to let the sela be removed by him alone?

But they had not. Which even then I knew was the sole reason we went free—our furs traded for granaries, mats, meal, No Rope's promise to send it all after us—knew the spirits had spoken through Walloki to the hu'uku. But had said what?

On the long walk back we talked of it in the way we had grown used to, scant speaking scattered among a wider silence, our footsteps and breath a rhythm beating for long stretches between the few notes of our words, the meaning of what happened coming clear. The test he'd passed a sign from the kukinis that should they choose to speak to him he would be fit to hear. No more than a first step on the path to being a jomin. But one he had before that night refused.

Why?

Ahead of us the light from our pine-knot torches lifted the path out of the dark, slid it beneath our feet, left it to the dark behind.

Because, he said, he'd been afraid.

The leaves above us showed faintly flickering against the blackness higher still.

Had known that he would fail.

And flickered out again.

And I said but he had not. And he agreed.

For a long time we walked in silence, thinking of what that would mean.

I fear it will not make much sense to you—to stake a boy's life on what we agreed to—that you'll hear *trial* and think *ruse*, hear *competition* and think us fools. That if I write it was tradition, held each year far back as any Nisenan recalled, you'll think it mere proof of their benighted nature. That when I tell you how the priests would gather, some dozen jomins drawn from all the villages around—how they'd spit blood, throw poison, blow breaths that carried crippling pains, would dance for hours till one succumbed to another's power, fell writhing to the ground, the others then, in a frenzy, sucking at his neck and face to draw the sickness out, how, if they failed, the weakened jomin was dragged away, the rest returning to their dancing till, near morning, when only a few were left, they'd let the fire die and, in the dark, the remaining priests would begin to glow, haloed by blue, as they tried to fill each other with enough pain to make the rest concede, or faint, or even die—I fear you'll think them savages. Will hear how if, in all this, someone drew blood with his own hands, so much as touched another, he'd be condemned to death, and think them barbarous. I fear that, when I tell you this was No Rope's reprieve—that if Walloki could outlast the rest, cast off the ba'api's curse, he'd be allowed to live—that when I tell you the hu'uku was the one to offer it, but I to accept, you'll think me bad as them. Or worse.

But, son, what is reason if not acceptance of the limits of the world you live in? What is delusion if not refusal to recognize its rules? Ours different now for many years. And is your world any less savage? Does it treat you with greater care? The one that gave you a mother who could not speak. That took her voice, her husband too. Your father who abandoned you. To a life I am already unable to imagine, cannot conceive of the choices you've already had to make.

They gave me a rope tied with fifteen knots. One of which I was to cut away each day till there were none. When I would know it was time to return. With him.

That night, when we at last reached our winter home, the moon was down, our torches out, the morning still hours away, my hut still stripped of everything from door to blankets. But still my hut. Still as far from his cave as it had been in spring. And stumbling down to the cache to get a fur to sleep in, I stood before the opening, unsure, so tired from all we had been through that when at last I reached in again to haul out a second plew, I could barely carry both back.

He had already made a fire in the hearth, his flamelit face showing his surprise, so that he didn't have to say he'd made the fire solely for me. No more than I had to explain the two fur blankets. Each of us in our accustomed silence taking up our own.

In the morning we would wake and cut off the first knot. I'd given the rope to him and he'd tied it around his neck and, lying there before we slept, I could feel the knots heavy on my own chest. Staring at the ceiling's shifting shadows I whispered his name, asked what had changed. Why, if before he'd been afraid he couldn't do it, did he think that he could now? I meant had now, had done it, the test he'd passed that night. But listening to his breathing I heard how it must have sounded to him, less question than expression of doubt. That he could do what he still had to. And, in his silence, I began to wonder if he'd even heard, or had already fallen asleep, or was still lying there as awake as me, just unable to speak. Or unwilling. Or too scared.

Once there was a boy who woke in a strange house. One unlike his own or any he'd ever known. Woke to the breathing of another man asleep. A man stranger even than the home, skin pink and wrinkled like a newborn mouse, face sheathed in fur streaked gold as a scout squirrel's back, brown as a fisher cat, a curling pelt rising and falling over the pale man's chest.

And there is the pattering of rain turning to drumming, becoming a thundering on the roof above, the man's eyes open now, watching him back.

That morning, the boy rose without speaking. Without dressing, stepped outside. Stood letting the downpour wash away the blood crusted below his nose. Came in wet and shivering to find the fire crackling again, the room bright. And still he said no word and none was said to him. Quiet as mornings had been these past months of his life. Though on this one, crouched before the flames, he reached to his neck, untied a rope and, with the strange bright blade the pale man offered him, cut off a knot. Then, fourteen left, tied it again around his neck.

That day he wouldn't eat. Stayed by the fire carving bird bones, each in his fingers a reflected sliver. In his memory: his family gathered around the stone circle in the center of their hu, feasting on salmon, his older sister's cheeks gleaming with grease as she smiled at him across the flames, his mother teaching her the dance she'd need when she became a woman, he still too young to do more than beat the wa'tdako rattle against his hand, its split willow clapping. An even older memory: his father wanting him to eat, playing a sapsucker drumming his nose against the center pole, wrestling out a grub, running around the room, arms flapping, stopping before his son, feigning spitting into the small boy's tight-clamped mouth. All of them laughing.

And who would make for him his red-feathered wand? His white? His mottled?

Later that morning, he went down to the river and, in the rain, cut three willow stalks long as his arm. Brought them back, peeled off their bark, hung ropes of woven milkweed from their tips and, all that day and all the next, hunted the wet woods and banks for birds. Hung a line across the river, dangling nooses over the water, each hoop held open by a thin of reed. Climbed trees where he'd seen woodpeckers feeding and set snares over the newer holes. Stalked hawks circling high above, loping for miles, trying to keep them in his sight. Finally, with a blunt arrow, knocking a red-tail down. Ending its whapping with a rock. So weak with lack of eating that by the time he brought the bird back he hardly had the strength to pluck the russet tail feathers out, tie them along one wand's dangling string, the woodpecker's crown feathers bunched at its end. The next wand strung with black ones from the woodpecker's tail, down from the hawk's dappled chest. The last yo'koli with only the long white wing feathers of a goose.

That night he took them with his fire-drill and awl and a small sack of beadlike stones and hummingbird skulls and the orange slivers of muskrat teeth he'd been gathering all summer, slung his skin-bag over his shoulder, carried the yo'koli to the hut's door, the feathers swinging in the last firelight, glinting, then gone. As, wrapped in his deerskin, he stepped out into the drizzle.

Maybe he'd left markers—notches in trees, stacked rocks—or maybe just in his body knew the way back, something inside drawing him ever higher and north. Maybe he followed the flight paths of birds, tracks of deer, maybe recalled the border markers chiseled and carved along the route of his fleeing nearly a year before. Maybe, in hunger and fatigue, he lay down and heard, beneath the ground, the rumbling of water tumbling through another gorge and, rising, went on, led by that, his feet keeping up their ceaseless running. Or perhaps he flew, a gust lifting his buckskin cloak, the yo'koli's feathers flapping, as it blew him all the way to a third tributary. Set him down on that northernmost fork. Beside rapids birthed by the snows of peaks that rose above his people's village, still much too distant for him to see, but the river he reached on that third day of fasting made of the meltwater that might have flowed over his mother's hands dipped down to drink, his younger sister's hair when his older washed it, the same rainwater that soaked the soil of his father's grave and ran down the steep sides of the canyon where, as the sun dropped behind the trees, he stopped. Stood in the exact spot he'd been in when its light left him. Beneath the sky's last glow, his breath still gusting, he set down his fire-drill, took out his twirling stick, began to whirl it between his palms, his blurred hands working down the spindle till the tinder around it smoked, caught. Then, in the leap of firelight, he did not eat or even warm himself but, without pausing, put it out. Got to his feet again, went on. His running become a half-falling scramble down to the water's edge. Where, beside the raging river, he did the same: cedar hearth and whirring stick and blooming flame and smothering it again.

Through the smoke he could see the place he'd come to. Where his father had come when he'd been young. The cave high in the cliff, nearly hidden by the dusk, but there: a black crack in the rock big enough for a boy to stand up in—*for you to stand up in*, his father had said—and though he'd never seen it he knew it was the same, the split-trunk oak growing out of the rock above, the ravine narrowing below, in the middle of the raging river the white-streaked boulder flat as if cleaved in half, the other half remaining leaning against its twin, slanted like a ramp.

On the bank, he blew the flames to life again, stripped off his cloak, loincloth, and moccasins, left them by his fire-drill and leather sack. Took out his awl, clenched it between his teeth. And with the willow wands bunched in one fist, began to leap from rock to rock till he reached the leaning boulder, jumped the chute, hauled himself up. On its twin's flat top, he set all three yo'koli down, strings dangling off the edge, their feathers blowing wildly. And kneeling, naked, shivering, pulled his earlobe taut, set the awl's sharp tip against his skin and stabbed, pushing through the blood and burning, widening the hole, till, yanking it out again, he turned to his other ear. When it was done, he stood, shouted to the kukinis that he had come, was here, waiting for them. Then stepped to the edge of the flat rock and jumped.

Before he hit, the spirits took him, took his sight—the world rushing at him and under and all around, wilding into a blurring—took his hearing with a crash that left him deaf to all but his own heartbeat, and took that too, the thudding of the kukinis' fists banging faster and faster in his chest, blood, breath, as he tried to dive—but the cold—to dive down after them as he knew he had to—but the cold—tried to follow them through the cold, away from his body's tumbling against the rocks, fought to push down, kick down, dive deep as his father must have before him, his grandfather before that, all the jomin who'd come here before they'd become jomin, when they were only themselves, and he dove through the cold into the thrusting dark that had been waiting for them all and felt the slippery, the soft, the entering his belly, blood, brain

When he came to, he was on the bank, his body a boulder, cold and immovable as rock, his head an icy stone, his heart stopped in the crushing grip of a kukini. Who, in a rush of blood, released it, pumping a spasm through the boy's limbs, snapping his eye open, his lungs sucking for breath.

They could have killed him then, kept the air from coming, the blood from moving, refused to forgive his fleeing. In their fury at his father for forcing them to leave his heart, at the boy for being too weak to take them in, they might have deemed him unworthy still and let him drown or freeze or simply expire on the rocks.

But there was his fire, still burning in the blackness of the bank. And there was the star-strewn sky without rain or snow to put it out. And there was his blood, still filling him, his heart still working, his body still able to roll onto its side, his arms to push him up, his hands and feet to crawl toward the nearing light, the heat.

All night he circled it, walking for hours without stopping, unceasing as if tracking an elk till it might tire, his body needing nothing but to keep moving, stooping only to stoke the flames, his breathing singing, his singing filling the circle he walked around the fire, mixing with its flickering. Songs to call the kukinis back. As if his circling was a burrowing ever deeper into their world. What did he see? What visions came? What waters shown to him by kukinis residing in them? The spirits of some stream or lake? Or of a cliff he'd never known? A high pine blowing in wind? Or of that wind? Of the hawk riding it away into a cloud that held its own spirit as well? A thunderhead? A doe, running, frightened by lightning? Everything the realm of a kukini, and each kukini made of the thing itself. The dawn that slowly showed the flat-topped boulder, the flapping feathers of the yo'koli, even the circle of earth his feet had pounded round the fire home to its own kukini. When it had grown light enough to see the world beyond its glow, he went quiet, stilled. Lay down. Shut his eye. Slept.

Woke to his name. Loud and sharp enough to break his sleep. Spoken not by a single voice but many, all at once. Walloki. His eye open to the copper light of not quite day. And all around him, mist. Rising off the river, rocks, trees. The voices seeming to come from it, speaking not to him, but of him. Swelling, sinking, laughing, muttering. He lay listening to them argue his history and promise, watching the rising mist mix with the thinning smoke till it seemed the voices came from above, where both dissolved into the air and the cliff face came clear, the black crack of the cave up there. He sat. Heard them louder. And standing then, stared up at the dark entrance, listening to their warped voices echo out. Their worry that the strongest among them might still refuse him. What it might do if, when it woke, it rose in anger. If his heart proved not to contain enough of his father's blood to tame it, soothe it, take it inside him.

Then he was climbing, hand over hand as the air around him cleared, the cliff cracks darkening, grass blades sharpening, even the voices growing louder, as if they had been muffled by the mist. Till he was there, hauling himself onto the ledge, the cave's black depth before him, the air in there strangely grayed, faintly curling. A sight unsettling enough to make him stop. The cliff face clear and the trees above it clear and the ledge he stood on crisp with morning air and, inside there, the blackness shifting with some held-over mist, or trapped bit of smoke, or breath.

The faintest heat. The scent of something living. Soon as he felt it, smelled it, he knew. And, knowing, heard them again, saying something he only understood was a command, coming not from inside the cave but from behind him, the sound not echoing out from the blackness but off the rocks that framed it. He turned his head, heard it become a word, suddenly clear as if spoken into his ear: Uyep. Come. Unidi uyep. Come here.

In all he stayed away six days, following the voices of kukinis from place to place. Voices that seemed to come from wherever the smoke of his fires blew, or drew the smoke to them. Ridgetops, swales, hidden ravines. Whichever place he reached, he would remove a smoldering coal from its leather wrap, rekindle his fire, watch the smoke, hear them again. And, pleading with them to wait, would leave before he'd warmed more than his hands, only his constant moving staving off freezing. Except at night when, unable to see the smoke, he'd sit in firelight and listen, waiting for them to tell him he could stop, that they would take him home. What can I say except that, when at last they did, it did not seem to me he could have found it on his own or discerned his own voice from others he heard. That when he stumbled back through the rain to me, he seemed not only a week without food, but without sleep. What can I say but that when he emerged from the mossy oaks, came into camp smelling of sweat and smoke, his yo'kolis shaking with each step, feathers hanging heavy in the heavy rain, the sight filled me with a relief such as I'd not felt at the sight of another in all my life. What can I say but that taking in his torn moccasins and battered cloak and bone-pierced ears, I knew the boy who had returned was not the same who'd left. What can I say but that seeing the harder gauntness of his face, the look in his remaining eye as he drew near, I was filled with a sadness nearly as great.

That evening, I tried to feed him. Smoked fish, roast meat. But he'd take neither. Nor tell me what he might. Just crouched at the clearing's edge, hunched in his deerskin, gaze on his feet. Made a few picking motions, fingers to mouth. Miming just enough. Though even after I'd brought a basket of piñon nuts, he would not follow back to my hut, took it instead away into the rain.

That night I ate alone again, again prepared to sleep alone. Only to lie awake feeling his absence. A missing strange in me as the change I'd seen in him. The fur he'd lain beneath that first night back from Kushna was bunched against the farthest wall, just visible in the dying firelight, and watching it fade into the dark, I lay in the hearth's last glow feeling him out there instead, knowing he was near, hearing him beneath the hearing of my ears, the drumming rain, when at last I rose, went out. Walked in the dark downpour toward his cave. Caught his fire's flicker through the wet trees, his wailing coming back to me. Not the soft crying of that night in the high country, not even sobbing, but the tremorous lament of pent-up sorrow that, each autumn, blew across the canyon rim from the burning ground where all of Kushna gathered for its great cries, hundreds of the bereaved grieving their dead together, all making that same sound.

I went just close enough to make him out, bent beneath the low stone ceiling, blurred by the smoke. But the fire bright enough to cast his shadow shaking over the grotto, rocking with his rocking as he let loose his grief or pain or fear. Or all of it. For between his wailing he would talk, loud and fast. To himself, the spirits. Or perhaps it was their words made in his throat—shouted, sung, broken by sobbing—as he threw offerings into the fire. The sack he'd carried: teeth, skulls, seeds popping and snapping. The yo'koli, their feathers flaring. Finally, the straw figure I'd once mistaken for a doll. That now I knew must be a likeness of his father. As, with shaking hands, he threw it in too.

I left him then, crept back through the downpour to my dark hut, my rabbit-skin blanket, my own breathing alone again inside my home comforting as the last heat in the hearthstones. Lay down beneath the rain drumming on the roof above me. Fell asleep grateful for the sound.

Woke to the quiet of night without it. The dripping hush. A scuff, so soft I wasn't sure I'd heard it. Then it was there again: a brushing at the wall or the new door-hide, barely a whisper on the flap's other side. Before a thump, a grunt.

Walloki? I said.

Beneath my voice the grunt coming again, lower, rougher, like something clearing its throat. Something bigger than him. I reached to the wall, felt for my musket.

Outside: a burst of low hard huffing.

The sky had cleared, and in the moonlight from the window, I could just see the skin-door shifting, bulging in.

Ha! I shouted, sharp and hard, at the same time banging the musket butt against the wall. Watched the door-flap swing back. Sat listening for the sound of the bruin moving away. But there was nothing. Then breathing. Ha! I shouted again and, as if my breath had reached the door, the hung skin buckled—blackness giving way to moonlight—and, in that bright second, I saw Walloki on all fours, a blur of movement hurled as, with a roar ripped from no human throat, he rushed my bed, so fast upon me that, though my mind had recognized his face, my finger might have jerked the trigger had I not heard, beneath his roaring, my own voice shouting his name. Then his hands were ripping at my chest, neck, his nails tearing my skin, and forcing the musket between his clawing and my face, I shoved up, slid down, rolled away, slammed to the mat and, still on my back, his nails now ripping at my hand, found the trigger again and pulled. The blast blew everything else out of the air, the muzzle thundering so near his ear it must have deafened him. Though, for a second, I thought my own hearing was gone. His roar cut short so suddenly, his weight frozen above me. Scrambling up, I shoved him over, saying his name again, again, till I'd used up my breath, and in the space left, he spoke. Nik'beku, he said, his voice small, scared. And when I repeated his name, he said Father again, his voice starting to shake. No, I told him. No, it was only me. Said it into his sudden, silent stillness. Uncle, he said. And in the word there was all his crying had contained before, only now crushed to a whisper.

That night I lay with him beside me. On the same buffaloe robe, beneath the same blanket of rabbit skins. Lay with my body bent round his, my arm over his shoulder, his head nested into my beard. Lay, but did not sleep. Lay breathing against his breathing, waiting for my fists to tighten, my arm to lift, my neck to arch away, my body to pull free. Lay feeling instead the stinging of the scratches on my face, the blood starting to dry, my chest filling against the easing of his back as he breathed out, emptying to accept the press as he drew in. Lay trying to keep the rest of me completely still, wanting to move nothing that might open my cuts, make the blood begin to flow again, to feel again like mine. My breath, my breath. My heartbeat, my heartbeat. Instead of the slow peaceful pulse of the man who lay feeling another's against his own and could still sleep. Did. As I had not been able to since I had last held you.

How long before I woke? An hour? A minute? Woke and felt him close and had to pull away. Climbed off my bed and crossed the room to his empty robe and rolled in it against the wall, lay listening to his sleep-breathing loud as if we had switched places and he was curled behind my back. The scratches reopened on my face. My blood my blood again.

In the morning we did not talk of it. Rose with dark's lifting and lit the fire and washed our faces and dressed and ate in the same silent way we always had. Though he still wouldn't eat meat or speak of what happened in his time away. Till, seeing the knotted string where I had hung it, he took it down, counted the knots left. Eight. The last of which he cut off with his knife.

I asked him then if he had found them—the spirits he had sought—and he told me of the ones who'd come, led him to them, lived deep in creek pools and beneath huge cellarskins, in the fast-beating hearts of frogs and the bright red crown of a small brown bird that fluttered round him in his dreaming, the kukini who'd accompanied his father and his father's father and his grandfather's mother before that. And with each one he spoke of that was not the one who had defined his father, the one he'd fled, I knew. Knew even before I asked if he was ready. There was the boy again. His hand reaching to brush his face where his lost eye had been.

He told me then how he had been refused, or called away, or maybe just too scared to go into the cave. A fear the kukini must have felt in him. The panom's spirit that had followed his weakness like a scent, found him last night and entered him and might never have released his mind, forever turned him mad, had I not—

But it came, I said.

He stopped. The rope he'd been running through his fingers slowing, stilling. Haan, he said, his nod so slight that, if the rest of him hadn't been so motionless, I might have missed it.

Would it come again? He didn't know. Would it accept him? He didn't know. His father could have told him, would have shown him how to summon it, hold it in him, bring it with him to Kushna. Instead of just asking him questions.

If he tried, he could remember his father chanting, see him engulfed in the great grizzly skin, the peltry shuddering with his dancing, the massive maw seeming to huff as the huge head swung back and forth. As it had done the night the new yomkapa jomin had come to kill him dressed in his father's furs, wielding his father's claws, wearing the sloshing baskets that had been left atop his father's grave, beside the wands and rattles and skins his father had meant for him. Mediums that once had drawn the great kukini into his father's body, given him the strength to survive the pains thrown at him by other yomis, to retain, year after year, the title of hu'uku.

There were two ways Walloki knew to kill a grizzly. Had as a child watched hunters practice the first. The dozen best bowmen and fastest runners taking their places behind rocks and root balls, thickets of brush. All but one who, dropping to all fours, began to play the bear. Another, chosen to creep up first, draw an imaginary string, loose an imaginary shaft and, with all the strength of true fear, begin to flee, the mock-bruin following at full speed, the shooter racing for a stump or boulder. From behind which a second hunter sprung, loosed his imaginary arrow, began his frantic run toward the third. Who, leaping out, feigning a shot, would whirl to speed toward the fourth. The grizzly actor following one after the other, their fresh legs keeping each tormentor just beyond his reach. Till all ten had mimed their shots and the mock bear lay dying, groaning, rolling on the ground. While all around the woods erupted into laughter, the watching children no longer able to hold their silence, the hunters fighting their own grins, making fierce faces as they pretended to fire shafts back at their brothers, sisters, daughters, sons.

Though Walloki's father had come only after practice was over, before they left for the real hunt, come calling the grizzly's spirit—pleading that it release its locum without too hard a fight, let the hunters return alive—had sung his chant, shaken his rattle, danced with the necklace of teeth slapping his chest, the claws strapped to his fists, the laughter silenced, the children watching with an awe Walloki remembered more than the chant. Though what most remained with him was the day after, when the hunters came back. One hunched beneath the massive bearskin, half the others carrying the butchered meat, the rest either too wounded to do more than drag their own bodies back or burthened with the corpses of the two who had been killed.

He could not command it, his father had said later that night. Told Walloki it was not his right or role or in his power. All he could do was ask, speak through the spirit of the bear that had chosen to live in him to the spirit of the one out there, try to show it how it might fit in the world of bears and men. Told his son, that night, that sometimes he'd fail, might manage to keep the village safe or warn an angry panom away or throw pains into an enemy or even kill another yomi, but to ask a kukini to bring about the death of its own locum was, of all the tasks he had, the hardest. For the same reason he wouldn't eat the bear meat shared at the next day's feast, couldn't join the hunt, not with arrows or spear or sela or song—why for him to kill the creature that had come to him in the dreams that had made him a jomin would be to kill himself.

A thing he told Walloki the same night he spoke of the second way to take a grizzly's life—a way none in the village had ever seen but him—the way his own grandmother had come to wear the panom yomi robe in the Hessi, its heavy hide flapping about her feet, its gaping jaws hiding her face. The same skin his grandmother had given his father, that he now wore in the same ceremony. That one day he'd give to Walloki. One winter, he said, when I was not much older than you, nik'kotom went out looking for a bear and found its cave, and there found a great panom asleep, and built a fire and filled the cave with smoke. And when the panom, breathing it, awoke, she spoke, told it who she was, why she had come, the reason she needed it to give up its life, the way her body would become a new home for its spirit, how well she would take care of it. Sang to it. Sang as it rose up before her. Sang a plea that it open its heart, give her its heart. Sang, Your heart, my heart, our heart. Sang the words I'll now teach you.

Did he remember?

Haan.

Did he think he could say them? That he could sing them?

Haan.

That they would work?

It took us the rest of that day and all the next and into a third to reach the cave. The rock a little yellower than that of my river, a bit more broken, come from a different vein of earth. Above it, the trees seemed smaller, the gorge steeper, the sky heavy with the same clouds that surely hung over my canyon, but the roar beneath only making me miss home more.

To another's ear it might have seemed the same, the way that Nisenan sounds much like Notong k'oyom weye to someone who knows neither, but ever since leaving my river I'd grown increasingly aware of how unknown the world beyond my own was to me. And I to it. To whoever made the trails we didn't take, the fires we gave wide berth, the boundary sign carved in a tree we passed before descending toward the cave, though it was down in the canyon that I was struck by how much more I knew of the world we'd come through than I ever could the one Walloki was about to enter.

In the quiet after he'd told his father's story, I'd wondered if it was true for him too, if to kill the animal of his kukini would be to kill himself. Beside him now I asked, the river so loud around us I wasn't sure he'd heard till I saw him nod. And when I asked then what he planned to do, he called back, Nik'us. My spirit. If it was strong enough the panom would feel it, honor it, give him its heart. He spoke the words as if part of a chant he was already singing—Minki honi nik mei—then shed his deerskin and, holding in one hand his bow, in his other his fire-kit, inside himself the knowledge of what he'd now be called upon to do, began to climb.

I'd brought my musket, last of my shot, near-empty horn. Now busied myself packing powder and ball so I wouldn't have to watch his ascent. He'd said he didn't want me with him, it was a thing he had to do himself. Though when I'd wondered then why he'd asked me to come, he said so someone would know. Should he fail and it be proved he didn't have in him what his grandmother had in her, his father too. Then if he was wounded, I could carry him to camp.

If he was killed, back to his village. And I'd told him I wouldn't come without my gun, said *set upon by sentries* and *surprised by the grizzly* and *in case it comes to me.* Instead of the truth. That I knew I couldn't stand there watching him disappear into that cave and not follow myself.

By the time I reached it, he was already so deep into the darkness I couldn't even see his movement. Stood on the ledge outside trying, with as little movement of my own, to bring my musket up, creep forward in a crouch. Beneath my feet: the crackling dirt. Around me: the river's roar. First echoing off walls, then a quieter washing in, then slowly swallowed by silence till I could hear a whispered breath. Walloki. I stopped, swiveled, the musket a sweep of gleam. Beyond it only darkness and my adjusting eyes sharpening his shape, his movement, into the sudden understanding it was not. The breath too slow, too deep, coming from too huge a body. That I could now see, just well enough to tell it had not been hidden by dark, but was the dark.

A snap. Loud as a gunshot ripping past, whipping my face toward it. Halfway back to the entrance the brightness outside was broken by Walloki's shape, his body bent to the ground, his breath blowing. Then in a glow: his face, close to the tinder, lit by a flame. The same that, when I glanced back, showed the bear: its rising and falling side, its muzzle tucked beneath a foreleg, paw big as my head, claw-tips four bright pricks slowly dulling as the air clouded with smoke.

Stinging my eyes, thick in my throat. I would have started backing out if the bear hadn't stirred first. A rippling running down its flank that seemed to roll its massive weight onto one side, the forepaw slipping down its nose, its eye exposed, still shut.

Glancing behind, I saw Walloki staring at me, through me, felt a thud, snapped my glance back in time to catch the huge head rise. A glint in the black: its open eye.

And from its body a sound like air stored in its lungs for months let out.

And from behind me Walloki starting to sing.

Words I did not know. Or try to hear. Was listening instead to the rumbling coming from the bear, seeming to rattle through its flesh, was seeing the long neck stretch, the huge maw gape, the hint of teeth. And Walloki was saying, Wake—tuichenop—Rise—otop—and as if listening, it did, a swelling of rippling fur and swinging head loosing such a roaring it blew me stumbling back into the brightness of the entrance suddenly around me again, the clearing air, and I'd just begun sucking a breath when I saw him. Passing me the other way. Moving in.

I could not keep from shouting. Though he gave no sign of hearing, only kept singing—minki honi cheti, minki honi nik meti, minki honi nik mei: show me your heart, open your heart, give me your heart—kept walking away from me, into the smoke, toward the bear.

Coughing, squinting, I tried to see. Could only make out Walloki in the rolling gray, bow in one hand, arrow in the other, arms lifted as if for an embrace. Singing, singing. I could see him shaking, his shape slowly coming more clear, though I didn't comprehend that he was backing toward me till I saw the bear. It formed out of the smoke, a boulder shown by blowing fog, its shoulders huge, head heavy, brow a shadowed ridge, eyes gleaming behind its steaming breath.

By then I was all the way out, onto the ledge, would have scrambled the rest of the way off but there was still Walloki, still facing the bear, still singing, his arms still lifted, his bow undrawn, his trembling shape backing toward me, breaking through the smoke, till his quivered arrows clattered against my chest, their fletchings catching my beard, the top of his head brushing the bottom of the musket barrel I held sighted on the bear. Its body unfolding out of the opening, a mountain of shag and muscle rearing so near I felt its roar on the air, heard it rip Walloki's singing from his throat, strip away the river's rumble, rid the canyon of all sound.

I must have shouted to him then—to notch his arrow, draw his bow—must have because I waited, knowing he'd want to, need to. Must have screamed to him to shoot. But the truth is I cannot remember, would not have heard my words or his, could only hear the roaring, only see the body reared hugely before my barrel, its great arms spread, the seconds passing, passing.

And what can I say but that it was not till after we'd sawed off the claws, hacked the hide free of the feet, stripped it over the massive skull, not till after I'd crouched by the carcass feeling with unsteady fingers for a bullet or hole, not till, finding no sign of any wound at all, I'd sliced down to the heart and hauled it out and seen it pristine, unscarred, not till, knowing beyond a doubt the shot I'd fired somehow had missed, was not till then that I no longer could deny what I had already known, known even as I'd pulled the trigger, known with a sureness clear as the bear's unmarked heart: that the great kapa had not reared up with rage but with impatience, that its kukini had never meant for it to strike at all. But had been waiting. Waiting for him.

He wore the bearskin into Kushna wet. We'd fleshed it as best we could beside that river beneath that cave, scraped it again when we got back, hung it by the hearth, but the rains returned and the wet crept in and the morning Walloki cut the last knot away the skin was still clammy, ripe. With rawhide strips we stitched the bruin's head into a hood, its forelegs into flaps to strap onto his arms, left what remained to hang as a great cape.

In the days since our return, he had prepared the rest, searched the canyon for the right clays, brought back wet clumps of rusty earth, chunks of grayish white, a bright red fungus he'd mashed with bear fat, and when he'd finished making the paint, he began hunting his pains: strangely shaped stones, threads plucked off the remains of JG's bandana, splinters of bone, all the si'lam itu'm with which he would attempt to pierce the other jomins' flesh, embed his chants inside their minds. Though I'd known he would not find the moth cocoons for the so'koti or have time to dry them, so made him a rattle of my own: a rusted cup crunched into a ball around some pebbles, a buckle cut off a rotted hackamore, a few tin buttons from Fancher's coat, glass shards saved from a busted bottle. Tied it all dangling from a handle I shaved smooth and gave to him on that last day. The grin he gave me in return a last glimpse of the boy he'd been breaking through his paint-smeared face, his teeth bright in the crimson paste covering his mouth and chin, his old scars slathered in rusty clay, the skin around his eye smeared white, his nose an unpainted stripe cleaving the colors down the center of his face, left bare for me to finish.

In the last hour, I sat beside the mortar he'd filled with charcoal and grease, accepted the sharp bone he handed me. And dipping it into the ink, began pricking his tattoo—a single line straight up his nose-bridge, root to brow, the mark worn by men of his village, given them by their fathers—watching, with each dot I made, what little remained of the boy inside him leave, the bone needle poking the charcoal into his skin, the blood beading, each stab sending a shiver through his face, followed by him forcing it still again. And through it all, his one eye open, staring at me. My face a foot from his, my hand dipping and stabbing, moving slowly toward his bunched and trembling brow, the fingers of my other hand smoothing it out, holding it taut, so I could stab him again. It was the closest I'd been to another person since I held you. Not our bodies' distance or my hands touching his face, but the making of him, the small last thing that would end who he had been, leave him the Walloki who would that night take up his jomin's rattle, throw on his kapa skin, bring his si'lam itu'm into battle. By the time I was done tears were welling beneath his eye, spilling down his cheek, streaking the clay. And my hand was cramped, my mouth clamped tight, my own eyes aching. But the line along his nose was straight. And with my fingers I wiped the blood away, dipped my thumb into the ink, rubbed the black in.

I went with him far as I could, carried his bear hide to save his strength. Walloki holding only his rattle, his sack of si'lam itu'm tied to his waist, new claw necklace knocking his chest. His body, painted in white spotted with red, bare to the cold but for a loincloth, moccasins. The rain had broken and the clouds had thinned, and from behind them, the setting sun cast a strange glow over the world we passed through.

The village was already lit. Not just with light leaked from each hu, but from torches carried between. The air eager with children's shouts, dog barks, sounds of a thousand strangers. Come from

Wokodot and 'Ustoma, Tsekankan, Pan'pakan, Yamako. Each village having received a string, each hu'uku cutting the knots away toward the day they'd all converge.

I had for hours been trying to steel myself—the crush of the crowd, the packed dance house, the drumming, singing, talking, breathing—but taking in the masses gathered around the village, I could feel the pressure building on my chest. So many kapum hus set up beneath the oaks, such a cacophony of human sound. I found myself breathing so hard Walloki began to watch me, his gaze only adding to the weight, my face sweat-beaded by the time he stopped.

Uncle, he said.

I kept walking ahead.

Nik'bono, he said again. And reaching out, he touched the fur strapped to my back, lightly as if he knew that even through the folded mass, I could not help but feel it. Though when he asked for the bearskin, said he'd carry it in, I shook my head.

Behind us, I could hear another party coming on the path, their footsteps and voices casting ahead to meet the sounds of all those already there, and caught between, I could do nothing but glance forward and back, my head jerking so nervously I heard the worry thicken in Walloki's voice when he said, Come.

He led me into the underbrush, the two of us slipping from sight, listening to the others pass by. And in our silence, Walloki began untying the bearskin from my back, pulled it free by the time the party had become part of the rest farther ahead.

Go, he whispered.

I turned to him, my back cold in the absence of the peltry, my body buoyant from its lifted weight, as if each step could take me twice as fast away. But I kept still.

Uncle, he said, what would you do in there? And on his face I could see he meant what could he do for me. Go home, he said, his voice almost too soft to hear. Or it was just that he'd already turned away, set down the skin, begun unfolding it over the mossy stones. And I stood watching his white-painted shape, his body scattered with red spots as if already shot with all the si'lam itu'm the jomins had brought from all around to prove he was not fit to live among them.

Walloki, I said, and when he turned, I asked if he could feel it in him—the panom kukini—if he thought that it would work.

Beneath the trees the dusk was dimmer, his mouth and chin and ruined cheek hidden by their dark paint. Only his eye, circled in white, looked back at me. His but no longer his. Well, Honpetayim Woole, he said, his voice no longer Walloki's either, now we will see.

How long would he have to withstand them? An hour? Two? All night? Till another dropped before him first? Or till each but the last had been dragged off? Or would he have to outlast them all? Past even the hu'uku?

I was almost back to the path when I turned once more, watched through the tangled brush as he lifted the bearskin over his head, the peltry falling over his shoulders, back, legs. Till he was just a dark-furred mass standing still, silent. Even the rattle in his hand. A patch of darkness waiting in the thickening dusk.

Son, do you know how much I feared for you when you were young? Would fill with certainty something awful would one day take you from me. A fist squeezing my heart. Even this long after I left, even though I now know the awful thing was me, I feel it still. The way, some nights, I'd lie awake unable to stop watching you. The way that night I stood there watching him.

For night had come. Drumming from the village, voices carried on excitement blowing back through the trees, stirring the brush, the canopy, his cloaked body. Barely the sense of him there in the dimness. But coming from within it, the rustle of leaves, the sharp sudden shake of his so'koti, its rattle shivering through the dark back to me.

That night I lay listening to the rain. A strange thing, rain at night. No way to tell time's passing—no moonlight through a window, no sliver slipping across the floor, no darkening again—just the blackness of the world outside the hut, the fire there then died, the embers' glow gone too, the same blackness inside. Beneath the drumming of the rain, the rain. Maybe it lightens, meaning nothing. Maybe falls harder, meaning nothing. And through its battering on the roof: nothing. Not the squeaking of bats at first dark, not the barking of a fox marking the middle of the night, not the calm that comes upon the canyon before dawn, oaks resting their limbs, cottonwoods stopping their rustling. As the sky above releases first light. The sky that in the rain stays dark, pours down only the sound of rain.

So I do not know how late it was when he came back. Only that the rain had not let up, that he must have been cold and wet. Though I couldn't even see that. Only knew he was there because I felt the door-flap open, the colder air, smelled wet fur and rank flesh and the fainter odor of smoke, clay, sweat, Walloki. The smell I'd come to know as him. His footsteps. I felt them. Through the ground, my bed, the buffaloe skin, my own. And then he was beside me. Standing. Saying nothing.

I could not even see enough to see how close—if he was hurt or whole, in his own skin or still inside the grizzly's—and then he touched me. His fingers, my forehead. His hand slowly spreading over my brow. Then gone. In its absence: the scent of something burning. As if a wind had gusted down the chimney, blown ash into the air. Though slowly I became aware the blowing was him, so close I felt it in my throat, my eyes, smoke thick and cleared and thick again, as if coming from some tinder lit inside him. And coughing, I would have tried to rise if, through the rain's drumming, I had not heard his breathing. Loud enough to reach me. Too loud, too heavy. Not his. The breath of something larger breaking into a low, chesty rumbling I knew. Not from the night he had attacked me, but the blackness of the cave. The way the grizzly sounded sleeping, the draw and moan that had shaken its massive weight, that now rose through the rain and over me and I could see the claws, see them coming for my eyes, threw my hand before my face, felt him grip my wrist, push back, his strength too great, the words, when they rumbled into the blackness, none that I knew—not in his voice, but in the kapa's—blowing over me like a roar, his weight holding me down, even as I felt his teeth. His mouth on my throat. Sucking at my neck as if to tear the skin. Till he released, his lips and teeth no longer there, and I would have called out if I could have made a sound, if he had not called out his own, words unknowable and sprayed with spit, and then was latched back on my throat, teeth raking again, releasing just long enough to spit more words before clamping onto my cheek, my forehead, gnawing at my scalp as if seeking my blood, sucking at my skull as if he'd break it with his lips. And all I could do was lie there, lie in the shock of understanding, feeling his furious determination. To find where the sela had burrowed, draw it out, and, spitting froth and blood, spew it into his hand so I could see. So he could know it. So knowing it, he could heal me.

And lying there, my arms splayed to either side, my fists clenched, body stripped, blood sucked to my skin, my breath coming as hard as his, I let him.

Till his mouth was on mine, forcing mine open, his lungs stripping my breath, drawing it up my throat so hard it seemed he'd take my insides with it, lift them out of my body into his. Then he was off me, his sucking suddenly a gurgling coughing choking that threw him from me, caught in his throat and left him retching. And then, as suddenly, he was done. I lay breathing. My fists still clenched, face wet with his spit, mouth tasting of blood. Lay listening through the still falling rain for what he would now say. The rain, the rain. Slowing lessening. Still nothing.

And in the quieter patter I became aware that he was moving through the dark hut—the sounds of fur and leather lifted, baskets shifted aside—though it was not till he was standing in the blackness before me again, gone still again, having gathered his bow or quiver or buckskin or whatever he had needed to take, was not till then I knew that he was leaving. Knew it because I felt it. Knew the feeling from leaving you.

Elisha, do you ever still feel me waiting? Outside your door? My ear to the wood, listening? Hoping to hear you? Your breath. A word. A sound that could yet draw me back. Or maybe let me loose. Give me a way to hear from you goodbye. Instead of the silence I took with me, the silence I left for you.

I could feel him standing there too. Next to my still-clenched hand. Could feel his hand come close, his fingers hover. Could see nothing and still I knew, knew they were there and what they meant, and I would not do it, kept my fist closed, my eyes staring straight up into the empty black, the silence of stopped rain, drops from the trees above, small and soft as heartbeats, coming close together, then farther apart, then only occasionally, the space between grown wide enough for me to hear his footsteps reach the door. Another drop. Another.

Uncle, he said.

And I wished he had said Father.

Uncle, he said, and I lay with fists clenched, stare held to the black above. And when the patter came, I thought it was the roof, the trees. Then heard the door-skin slap softly shut and knew it was the drops he'd shaken loose when he pushed through.

Can you see now why I did not want to tell you? Why I had to? If you were to know me, to recognize my heart, when it returns to you.

As one day soon it will to him as well. On its last journey. Following the map he made me, drawn in the mud outside my hut on that last day I knew him as a boy, before he'd left in search of the kukini he'd once fled, his small body bent to the ground showing me where he would go: the ridges, canyons, rivers north of my own, the boundary tree, the cave, the way that tributary came from the higher peaks I'd only ever seen in summer, the mark he made with the tip of his stick to show his home. A place I never thought I'd see. Though now I know will be one of the first stops my heart makes.

What was he to me? A companion? A friend? A boy? Not you, not you. But still. Someone I lived alongside for a year. Someone I could. Could have for another.

Why did he leave? I know I know, but I mean why could he. I mean the thing I asked him before the bear, before I knew what I was asking. How could he have been so scared, back when his father's kukinis were first left to him, and then not have been? I mean what changed. In him. What changed him. From the boy he'd been to the yomkapa jomin who could reach into a creature and convince it to open its heart.

What did he find in mine? That night he tried to draw away my pains. What did he suck from my insides that made him retch so horribly? That let me find, in the days and weeks and months to come, the thing that all my life eluded me. That, in the years after he left, would let me grind larkspurs or custard cups or twinberries to make my paint, and linger, staring at their blue and yellow and purple-black, just as I used to, but now lost in color instead of memory. That let me toss snowballs at watching birds and, in the silence after, feel no sinking hollowing my chest. That, when I touched the eyeball of a fish, left me feeling just the smooth wonder of it, same as once must have drawn you. That, after it was charred and I'd picked clean the bones, was digging out the eye, would leave my finger still my finger, the socket just a socket.

How can I say this?

Your terrible child's voice: How can you say this?

His voice lower, older, a wholly different language. Nothing like yours. Except in me, filled with the memories of you both.

Alone in my hut, playing the flute he made me, trying to pick out a tune I used to sing to you. My own breath touching my own fingers, stirring my own beard. And in summer I'd play the tunes I used to up in the high country while he'd danced out in the dark beyond the fire, dancing by myself instead. In the earth shaking beneath my feet, the tremoring of floorboards, your small weight jumping. Swimming alone in snowmelt pools, my splashing echoing off rocks, I'd climb a boulder, bake the cold out of my body, and when I rose off the warm stone, there'd be the dark wet print of me. I'd watch the sun dry it till it was gone. Floating pinecones in a lake, I'd sit on the bank trying to hit them with stones, making explosions with my mouth. The way you would have when you were three. The booms so silly in my ears I couldn't help but laugh. And the next winter, alone again in my hut's quiet, I dipped my needle in the ink he'd left and pricked my skin. Sat in the firelight again beneath the drumming rain, drawing a line up my own nose, my other hand held fingertip to forehead as a guide, my eyes squeezed shut against the pain, my fingers grown as slick with my own blood as they had been with his. Feeling again his skin over the hard line of his cartilage, his bone as I rubbed the ink in, kept on long after the ink was gone, after the pain should have been great enough to make me stop. And if you had been there, Elisha, I would have drawn one on you too.

Wiped your blood away, rubbed in the ink, filled the holes I made in you.

What was he to me? Everything. Everything you could not be. And you all he was not. No, it's true: he was not my son, was not. But it's true too that in the year I lived with him I was the nearest to a father I had been since I abandoned you.

AUTUMN, 1849

A dot and a dot and a dot. Pricked dark with ink. The pen nib stippling spot after spot, line after line: a river, another, a third—Nem Sew, Puunimbam Sew, Chapakakum Sew—their canyons winding west, combining at the map's edge. At the far corner, to the north and east: the last massif of the range, dark marks shaping its sudden jutting peaks, empty patches placing the snow, each crosshatched shadow hiding a cliff, a crag. Perhaps a mountain sheep. A crow. Holding in its beak an elderberry: makka, blue spot sparkling in the sun. Here is 'A'ak, swallowing, cawing, flapping away. Here is Na'w, crossing a slide of scree on his deft cleft hooves. Here is a mule—kawayu'—following a path far below. A man on its back, a woole, half his face wrapped in a cloth stiff with the gore it has absorbed day after day. Seven now since he was shot. Six since his escape downriver. Four since the doctor sewed him up. Three since the dawn he tailed the posse to the hut of the man who'd done it, dug up the canvas packet, found this map. Three days now he has been following it to here. Become another mark on the page. Same as the blind koto surrounded by the cradle-stakes: Each layi another dot. Each of their seed-beating mothers. Each dead dog and deer and horse and rider and fallen hunter. And all the living. Even each tree: Tc'a. Each stone: O'. Each grain of soil: K'aw. A dot and a dot and a dot until the page is wholly black. And Silas a spot inside it too. Stopped, standing, staring up.

A sight he has seen in his mind for years, suddenly there, startlingly near: the massif cloud-white beyond dark spikes of firs, its clustered peaks a grove of quartz and porphyry standing alone against the sky.

If he is the first of his kind to see it, the forest gives no indication that it knows, the crows no sign they care, the chipmunks disappearing same as they would from bobcat or fox, only the massif itself perhaps marking the meaning of a woole: its stone-faced stare, the glare sent off its snow. He has to blink the sting away. Even as he follows the grandmother's signs, his eyes keep lifting from the path, seeking the peaks, so it is not until he reaches the creek crossed by two rows of stones that he sees the tracks. The half-moon prints of horse or mule. His eyes snap up as if the rider might manifest before him. But there is just the wind shaking the aspens, and as if it pushes him too, he starts forward again, good hand on the revolver at his waist, gaze on the path ahead, until—just as the grandmother said—it splits. Rightward along the river. Left to the peak, the lake at its base, the village. The hoofprints heading that way.

Higher yet, she'd gestured—her arm snaking to show the switchbacks—and for the first time, he breaks with her directions, slips instead into the undergrowth, climbs straight up, leaving the big firs behind, hemlock and bitterbrush opening into yellowed swaths of Scouler's willows, broad mats of huckleberry oak, boulders protecting patches of first snow. Looking back, he can just see the trail below, too distant to make out the mule's tracks, but not to sense it—the way he might an elk or bear about to break out of the brush—and then it's there, a grayness ghosting through a grove of aspens, drifting behind the thin white trunks, the rider, when he breaks into the open, so small at such a distance his hatless head is just a raw red gleam, something glinting in his hands: a piece of tin or glass or paper. For a while Silas watches, waiting for him to begin switchbacking up, draw near enough to chance a shot, but the mule merely lumbers on, dwindling away toward the south. There, the sky is massed with rafts of clouds, their fast-blown shadow sweeping the earth below, and as it comes, catching the rider, snuffing the glint out of his hand, it seems the man might just pass on, already fading, the mule dimming, beneath a blur of snow that, falling over the trail below, erases both from Silas's sight.

Then it is on him, the first flakes swirling into his face, wind cutting through his buckskin, and standing up into the gust, long hair blowing at his beard, his ears and nose and remaining fingers stung by cold, Silas turns, begins climbing again.

The snow is coming harder by the time he spots the smoke and breaks into a stumbling run, his moss-stuffed moccasins huge on his feet, strips of gray meat flapping at his waist, his breath-wet beard shaking as, coming through a copse, he sees the village and stops.

Above Timseh-koyo the bluffs are disappeared in snow, but below, the lake is dark and still beneath the flakes, its shore dotted with wickiups, ropes of smoke strung from their cone-shaped roofs. Inside each hu: a fire, a family, the warmth of women, children, men. One of them perhaps Walloki. Silas stands there leaking heat, cold seeping into his body, watching distant figures darting between the homes, waiting for the faint voices that come now and again, as if he might hear one he knows. Might recognize a shape. Out on the littoral, free of the trees, a few small boys tilt their faces to the sky, mouths open for the falling snow. To catch a glimpse, a sound, see he had made it back. To know he was alive. It would be enough just to know that.

For a long time Silas stands, snow starting to coat his shoulders, his hair, his good hand wedged beneath an armpit, his wounded raised into his breath-steam, his body leaning a little forward, like it might break his stillness with a step, bring him a little nearer the scene below. And if he were to go down there? Find the old woman had been right? The one-eyed man not a different yomkapa jomin, but a once-was-boy who might recognize his once-was-Nik'beku, might leave his now-was-family—Mother? Wife? Daughter? Son?—come out of his warm, crowded hu and, finding the wounded woole wrapped in thin buckskin, the Honpetayim Woole he had not seen for five long years, try to lead him inside. With them.

Before his face, Silas's hand has begun to shake, the bandage trembling in his shivered breath. He clamps his teeth, but it leaks out his nose, clouding his sight. And if Walloki found him an empty hu? If he hid in it away from the rest, made a fire, slept, how long before the first shot woke him? The mule-rider likely already following his tracks in the new snow. He looks again at the village below, sees the slow movements quicken into panic, the shore boys running as they scream, the men emerging from their homes with bows, blood blooming on their breasts, exploding from their skulls, the shooter firing into women, children, skin door-flaps and thin walls, shouting down for them to give up him. Silas, still standing above the village now, listening to shouts, watching the running. Where are the boys? And then he sees the others coming and knows—the cries and gestures are aimed at him—he's stayed too long already, should not have come, not till he'd killed the mule-rider first. Knows—even as he turns, recedes into the trees—it is too late.

He goes as far from the village as he can, as far back down the slope, before he grows too cold. Stops at a cluster of pines dense enough to hide a fire, provide him shelter. Inside the grove, the wind is less and louder, the outer branches swaying, treetops soughing. But the deeper he goes, the stiller it gets, the ground a blanket of needles as yet untouched by snow. Over it, he moves near silently downslope, the storm's buffered roar broken only by his shivered breath, until a blast of cawing: ravens, their hollow *wonk wonk wonk* rattling down, their dark shapes shifting among the branches. Dropping his gaze again, he sees they're not alone. A shelter. The bark cone of a low kapum hu, the kind made by a girl gone off to bleed, a woman mourning a stillborn baby, anyone abstaining from others. With his good hand he draws the pepperbox and, watching for smoke or movement, creeps close. The patch of collapsed bark, the unscuffed opening: replacing the gun, he crouches to peer beneath the roof. Just a nest of nut hulls, a basket half decayed to dirt, ashes scattered and cold.

Downhill, the copse dwindles away, the sparser trunks dark bars against the white beyond. A view, he realizes, intended by whoever built the shelter. Realizes, too, any fire will be seen by anyone below, out in the open, climbing the slope. *Good,* he thinks, gathering his kindling, striking a spark, blowing the flame. Thinks, *Let him come.*

Though, later, lying beneath the shelter, the dog meat staked drying around the fire's other side, his body curled close to a blaze big enough to warm him into sleep, his last thought is of Walloki. That this must be much like the hut the boy slept in the night he fled, the night before the journey that led him down the mountain, across two canyons, all the way to a third river, the flight that had not stopped till him.

Three times Silas wakes to the fire near burned out, the cold climbing the damp shirt on his back, the wet ends of his hair, gripping his face, chest, arms tucked under his body, legs to his belly, the freezing clenching like some great talon cutting into his flesh: once while the snow still slants through daylight beyond the pines; once in the settling of dusk; another time at night, the shelter blacker than the sky, the circle of coals a hole burned through the clouds. And on a fourth, still before first light, he wakes instead to brighter flames, the fire—strangely, impossibly—leapt higher. A fire built up while he slept. His face hot, his beard baked. But it is the warmth on his back that stirs his reach, draws his good hand behind him in bewilderment. Feathers. On his fingers. His eyes are fully open then. But, still, he does not rise. Lies motionless on his side. Beneath the blanket.

A blanket of black feathers. Warp and weft woven of bird-skins—coot or cormorant or crow—so soft against his own bare flesh—his neck, his hand—so warm.

Around him, above: firelight shifting over the shelter's ceiling. Before him: the flames so bright they blind his eyes, blacken the opening, strip the woods of the needles and branches that he'd see lit faintly red if only he would shift his stare. Which he will not. Does not. Because, through the flames, across the fire, too far into the blackness of the night to be more than a sense, there is somebody. A thing he cannot see but knows. Knows clearly as he knows the feeling of that nearness, the feeling it brings up inside of him. Though he has not felt it for years.

For a long time he does not stir. Just lies there in the softness of the feathers, the warmth of the fire, the feeling of the other, near. If he shuts his eyes, he can almost hear the boy's breath. Slow and steady as his own. Almost as if, across the fire, he is lying beneath a blanket too. As if they might drift into sleep beside each other. So long as he does not rise or open his eyes or stir more than this: his hand, reaching slowly around the fire, as far as it will stretch into the dark, the bandaged knuckles resting on the mat of needles, his wrapped palm up, his three remaining fingers fallen open, waiting. The crackle of the flames. The shifting of their red light across the inside of his lids. The tightening of his shut eyes at the touch of another's fingertips.

The oaks were tasseled in new catkins the day I left to trade with No Rope for the last time. Brought nothing with me but a stone pipe. Long as my palm wide as my wrist. A smooth white oval that in the mnths since Walloki left I had drilled out with sand & antlers. Worn down the points of an entire rack pounding & grinding & now climbing twrd Kushna I passed its weight from hand to hand. All the way till still a ¼ hr from the village I came round a bend & stopped.

He stood there waiting. The grove still far bhind. The old gold oak we always met bneath not even close. Him waiting there in the path as if come out to meet me. Or stop me. Keep me away. I watched his face. His stillness. Even as I came close enough I cld have reached his shoulder. Or he mine. A heartbeat. Anothr. At last he raised his hand made his near touch. Withdrew again. Waited in silence for me to ready myself for speech. The old kindness. Or a new wariness. In his eyes a concern that cld have come from either.

Handing him the pipe I watched him turn it over. Take in the smooth sides. The tapering cylinder. Attempt to hand it back. I shook my head. Tried to speak. But Walloki had been gone near a ½ yr & all the mnths since I last spoke were massed too thick inside my throat. Instead I reached to his hand. Closed it round the stone. Gently pushed it back at him.

He nodded. Wld not thank me I knew till I had broken our silence first. A wind rose rustling through the leaves & I wanted to say that I was sorry & the wind passed by & the leaves stilled again &

I wanted to tell him I was still the same Honpetayim Woole who had lived nearby for yrs. The same Silas he had known as something like a friend. Wanted to ask cld we remain as we had been. But the words wld not come. Not till I shut my eyes & emptied the woods of him. Just wind. Squirrels. A raven croaking back at me as I spoke quietly to them: The boy is gone.

Haan, the woods said back as quietly. As if it was a thing already taken in & let go again. Though when I opened my eyes & took in his I knew it was only buried bneath anothr worry.

Beyond him I could make out others. Villagers gathered far back as if to watch. Their movements strange as their shapes. Odd upright gangly animals unsettling in their grouping. Boys who might have warned the village of my approach. Men who might have once hunted Walloki.

I managed to ask No Rope if we should go to our old tree. Talk there. And when he glanced around as if searching for some other spot where we could sit, I asked him why he had met me here. The question drew his eyes back to me.

I meant, he said, to come to your camp first.

The breeze again. This time bringing a murmur on it so quiet it might have been made by the trees. But that my body knew was not.

I said, Is it because of the hu'uku?

He shook his head. The hu'uku, he told me, is no longer the hu'uku.

Haan? In my word, all the unknowing of all that I had wondered since the night Walloki returned. But if he heard the question in my voice, he did not show it. Simply lowered himself to a crouch there on the trail. And as if his movement loosed their chatter, the sound of all those gathered at the grove's edge grew. Something in their closeness their loudness the sheer number of them changed. I crouched down too. The two of us squatting in the path as if across a fire. But nothing between us but our gaze. As he began to speak.

Of men. Bearded and pale as me. Seen riding the same tall, long-tailed beasts I and the other wooles had appeared on four years before. But more of them.

How many? I asked.

He held up all ten fingers. Shut his fists. Opened them again.

And I could feel the air stirred by the gesture strong as all the others' stares. Could hear beneath their chatter my own voice inside my head saying over and over *here*. No Rope speaking of riders—*here*—come from the valley—*here*—at the first snowmelt. Men passing through lands nearby—Wokodot, 'Ustoma, Tsekankan—trailed by trackers passing word village to village to here. He'd heard they'd gone up higher in the Lokum Yaman, come back down with more. Men, women, children. One so young it must have been born on the mountain. A thing No Rope knew only from the Nisenan at Yamako who'd heard it from the Monaa: how a band of wooles had been snowbound all winter, sheltered in homes on rolling hoops, roofs flapping in high winds like giant wings. How their beasts had moaned like bohemkulehs, their hunters' blasts shook avalanches loose, burst blood on game ten bowshots distant. How the Monaa had found an elk brought down by one small stone, shown the wound around, wondering at the strength that it would take to hurl a pebble so hard it reached the heart. The way, No Rope said, his own people once wondered at wounds in their own men, in his own shoulder. Before they'd come to know me, could tell the Monaa the magic lay not just in the shooting sticks, but powder. How they, stunned that he should know so much about the wooles, kept asking if he knew where they'd come from, where they were going. The ones caught in the snows, the ones who rescued them, the more than twoscore who'd returned toward the valley.

All this he told me in words coming so fast at my unpracticed ears they collapsed upon each other, the chatter behind them building as the crowd drew closer, drawn by something more than the intrigue my visits always stirred, something I couldn't discern before No Rope's words began again. He was talking of more wooles, another party, another time, rumors come from the Konim farther south, up through Molma and Hemhembe, villages he spoke of as if they lay at the world's edge. Now brought too near.

Where were they coming from? This even larger group of whites the Konim claimed appeared out of the eastern peaks in the dead of winter, crusted in snow, noses and lips blackened by cold, lowering their bony beasts down cliffs on ropes. The Konim had seen them mount again, ride till they disappeared out of the Konim world as well. Out of the world, No Rope said. Into another I did not know. One that, the more he spoke, I thought might mean the sea. Some endless water he seemed to believe surrounded us. The mountains, the valley, the world an island in its midst. Held steady by five ropes stretching in the five directions. Across which he wondered if they'd crossed. Same as the stories that long had been told by valley tribes: tales of strange beings come from the west pulling themselves along the ropes in boats big as the one that once must have held the creator. Beings who had two bodies and six legs, ran on four feet fleet as deer, and then would separate to stand on two, looking like men, but speaking words that made no sense, shouting at great herds of huge-horned beasts they drove before them, drumming thunder into the earth. Beings who made their own thunder with sticks that could spit fire, point at anything and kill it. Beings no one had ever seen but jomins in their dreams, children in nightmares, the lowland tribes in tales they passed into the hills. Beings who'd always stayed at the edge of the world. Till these.

Why had they come?

What could I say but that I did not know.

Why did you? he said.

I shook my head and his gaze held hard enough it stopped my shaking, and I said, To get away from them.

These men?

Their world.

The breeze was in the leaves again and their sound rose round us as if the roar of the river beyond the ridge was trying to reach me, and in it he squatted silently, turning the pipe I'd given him over and over in his hands, and beyond him I could see the children and women and men trying through the blowing branches to catch a better sight of us. With the same intensity as the first time they'd laid eyes on me. But with less fear. So that, as they crowded closer and the wind died down and the leaves stilled again, I could feel their presence growing heavier around me.

No Rope's voice thick with it when he said, What is it like?

I watched the pipe turn in his hands.

Beyond the mountains, he said.

I shook my head.

Over the great water.

I shook my head again.

Silas, he said.

And I told him, There is no water. East of the mountains there's just land. Flat and dry and—

Land? he said. Beneath the eastern rope?

And I could see the idea crush something inside him, could see in his eyes what that one thing I'd said had done.

Beyond the Lokum Yaman? he said. Beyond the Monaa?

I shut my eyes.

Over the tunnel the sun takes under the world back to the east?

Held my head still.

Beneath the rope it follows back to us each day? There is no water?

When I spoke, my voice was louder than I meant: What does it matter? What their world is like or how they got here or where they came from or where they're going. So long as they pass through. What does it matter—

Because, he said, they came back. The ones the Konim saw that winter. They had come back in spring. Come driving giant herds of horned beasts out of the stories. Into the mountains. As many, he said, as there were deer in all the Lokum Yaman. Crashing through trees and tearing up trails like a storm blown all the way up to the crest.

To graze? I said. Must have said it in English because he raised his eyebrows at me, his face waiting till, in Nisenan, I asked him if they'd stayed.

He didn't know. Knew only that the Konim who'd spoken of them had been wounded. Had seen the fire leap from the sticks, heard the thunder, left more than twenty of their own behind when they had fled. Been set upon the way my party had fought his tribe four years before. But so many more of them. Of us. Of you, he said. So many more of you.

In his hands the pipe was still. No Rope, I said, staring at it, I am not one of them.

No, he said, but they are of your world.

And I wished that I could tell him it was separate, that between the world I came from and the one he knew there was a sea as he believed. Wished the land we crouched on was an island instead of just a patch of a far larger rest. Wished I could take back even the little I had said. But I could feel it passed between us, real as if I'd given him a thing I'd sworn I never would: a knife, or buckle, or bit of cotton thread, or powder, or shot, or gun.

They have your skin, he said.

I haven't seen them.

They speak your tongue.

I haven't heard.

Silas, he said, the Konim's wounds were made the same way you made mine, inside their bodies stones the same as this. And reaching to his neck, he lifted the lead pendant off his chest.

As if the gesture loosed the voices of the crowd, the woods around me filled with the words by which they knew me: Honpetayim Woole, Honpetayim Woole.

What do they want? I asked. He looked at me, saying nothing, the two us squatting close to the ground close to each other. And I said, low and fast beneath the others' sounds, They came from the east. They went to the west. That's all I know.

And just as low, just as close, he said, Why? His face, his eyes, waiting for my answer. Why now? he said. We want to know why they came now.

I cannot say.

If they will come again.

I cannot say.

If next time they will come here. To us.

I cannot—

If you will bring them.

I told him then I didn't know them, they didn't know me. And he told me that wasn't what he'd asked. When I stood, he stood with me, as if my knees unbent his legs. Though I could see that, even after the long time squatting, his were still. Despite the shaking I felt in mine.

Between us, he held out the pipe. Thank you for this, he said. It's well made. Almost as well as if by one of us.

It's a gift, I said.

He shook his head. A gift, he said, is always a trade. And I am asking you for something else.

I'm sorry, I said.

And he said, We want to know if, when they come again, they will bring the things you did. The meal, the knives, the guns. He used the English word, a word I had forgotten I had taught him. We want to know if when they come, they'll bring to trade the things that you refused to. Things, he said, still holding out the pipe, we cannot make ourselves.

I looked at the stone in his outstretched hand and thought of the hours I'd spent making it, night after night inside my hut, pouring sand into the bore, grinding the horn, pouring in more. And I could feel the twist inside me, the grit against my skin, the antler's pounding, twisting, pounding again. Could smell the bone dust, see the shaking stone. There in his hand. Looked to his face. And it was shaking too. And the trees behind him shook, and the gathered faces shook. And I knew it was me. Managed to say once more to him, It is a gift. Before I turned to leave.

Behind me: a breath so sharp it turned me back. He'd bent his mouth to the pipe, blown a small white cloud over his palm. The last dust left inside. Through it, his eyes held mine, and before it cleared, he'd stepped close again, raised his two fingers, touched my shoulder. Spoke lower when he said, You'll go upriver?

Haan, I said.

Good, he said. His fingers still on my skin. Waiting for mine to touch him. He wore no shirt and I could see the scar. Made the same way the others made the wounds in the Konim.

Good, he said again. Softer still, still waiting.

Though, that evening when I got home, it was the hu'uku waiting for me. Inside my hut, holding my pistol. Outside, the light had already begun to blue and there was just its sheen on his thin cheekbone, his long-stretched earlobe, his eyes mere glints. He sat cross-legged, the pistol in his lap. Before him a basket filled with a small white mound, my powder horn emptied out.

I stood in the doorway, its flap hung up across my back, letting in just enough light to see the angle of the barrel, the sliver of trigger unblocked by the old man's finger, the movement of his drooping lip when he said my name.

I let the skin-flap drop, the dimness sweep back over my shape.

Silas, he said again, and it was strange to hear it in a voice other than No Rope's or Walloki's. Worse inside my hut.

What are you doing? I said, my eyes adjusting, my glance sliding around the room: some baskets moved, furs disturbed, my possibles bag lying a little distance from the powder horn. What are you doing, I said again, in my home?

His smile made him look more gaunt: his bunching skin, the blackness where there should have been teeth. He said, I came to help.

You came to steal.

The smile again. Why would I have sat here waiting with all this? As if to display it better, he unfolded his legs, began to stand, stiffly as if he'd sat for hours, or in the past months had grown old, his joints cracking, his skin loose on his chest, his hands cradling the gun as if he feared it might leap from them on its own.

Give me that, I said.

Honpetayim Woole, he said, you are a sick man.

Give me that and get out.

You are much hurt. Stepping around the shot and powder, he came slowly toward me, said, Let me help you. Let me heal you. Find your pains and—

You're too late, I told him. He stopped close enough that he could search my face, that I could see the feather stuck through his septum shiver with his breath.

The ba'api, he said.

The yomkapa jomin, I said. And reaching out, yanked the gun from his hands.

You think, he said, that I am done. You think because I'm no longer the hu'uku I can't be again. But in a year there will be another ceremony. Without him.

I wish you luck, I told him.

And in his eyes saw something flare that might have seemed like anger—Show me, he said, how to use this—might have seemed like strength, if he had not reached for the gun and touched it so haltingly, so timidly, his fingers hovering, just brushing mine. Did he heal you? he said. Are you not still even a little sick?

His breath stank of sour grubs and his skin was sour too and I could feel his body's heat, the pressure of him so near my own. Drawing away, I shoved his hand back with the gun butt, and then he was gripping my wrist, pulling me close again. Did he show it to you? he said. The pain? Did he tell you who put it in you?

Hu'uku, I said, hoping the title would pacify him.

But his voice rose: I can hurt them. Whoever did it, I can hurt them for you. Tell me and I'll find them, fill them with such pains they'll die before they can call another jomin. Tell me, Honpetayim Woole, is there nobody you would hurt? Nobody you'd wish me to keep from hurting you?

I would have ripped my wrist free, swung the gun to knock him back, had his eyes not been so huge, so close, so filled with desperation, the desperation of having had a place in the world and had it taken, a desperation to get it back, a thing I could feel inside of me as if it was a sela he'd slipped beneath my skin. Gently, I pried his fingers off my wrist, told him I was sorry. There was nobody. Not that he could reach.

And still he swore to me that if I would show him how to make the pistol spit fire, he would find them for me, find them and kill them.

And I told him that he could not.

Why? he demanded. Because they are like you?

No, I said.

And he told me he knew, knew I had lied. When, long ago, I'd told them the magic was not in the weapon but in my blood, told them making it work was a thing only my kind could do. Knew because the Konim had seen others who looked like them with the white men, seen them shooting too. And so he knew that I could teach him. The power not in my blood, he said, but here. His hand reaching as if to touch my head.

Then the pistol was between us, its barrel pressed to his chest, my head shaking a silent *no*.

Why? he said.

Because, I told him, if I were to put the power in his head it would kill him. Sure as if I shot him. Now go, I said, pushing slowly, steadily, almost tenderly, till he was backed away from me. Go before I do it with this instead.

There was the press of his chest against the muzzle, the swell and ebb of his breath sent through the metal into my hand, my arm, my shoulder, chest. Then just the air between the muzzle and his receding shape. The elk skin flapped back in place. The sound of his footsteps slowly sinking into the sound of the river. The pistol pointing at nothing then but the hut's emptiness. My hand still holding it. The gun growing heavy. The muzzle beginning to shake.

AUTUMN, 1849

He wakes to his hand tucked back against his chest, his body curled under the blanket, the feathers pulled over his face. And still all of him cold. Pushing the blanket off, he finds it frosted with his breath. The fire is out. The sky above the pines is already grayed enough to show the snow-bent boughs, black shapes of ravens. They rustle: a small flurry of flakes filtering down.

His hand hurts. The flesh that used to hold his fingers feels on fire, hot as the rest of him is cold, a stinging heat that ebbs and leaps as if the meat is being blackened, flames licking up his arm, into his elbow, the bone, the marrow. A tremor shakes him, and wrapping the blanket tight, he sits up inside the harbored dimness of the hut. Between it and the bright entrance the fire is a black circle flecked with last embers, and beyond it, there are the strips of dogmeat dangling from their stakes and, beneath them, a basket. Barely bigger than his fist. Reaching across the fire, he brings it back, holds it close enough to see its pattern of blackened pine root and pale willow, splints woven tight as if for water, but, inside, leaves. Dried gray and brittle but still long, felted, faintly redolent of pine, vinegar, soap: tarweed. His eyes lift, searching the opening, as if the boy, returned a second time to bring this while he'd slept, might still be there.

Crouching before the fire, wrapped in the feathers, he blows the embers into flame. And when he has it crackling, he uncovers his wound, carefully peeling away the stiffened leather, prying it free with his spud blade till he can see the mangled stubs, the sutures where the yarrow mash has flaked away, clumps still stuck to the lumped skin. But no purulent yellow liquid leaking out, no sign of infection. And when he's cleared the poultice off as best he can, he sticks the rest inside his mouth, gingerly shutting his lips around the stumps, letting his spit dissolve the blood and leaves, trying to keep his tongue from touching, even his breath from moving against the wound. Until, withdrawing it again, he takes a few tarweed leaves, stuffs them in his mouth and, same as he'd done with the yarrow, chews, drools the plant-paste into his good hand, packs it painfully over the other's stubs. Then, rewrapping the leather, pulling it tight, wincing at the press of the new poultice, he waits for the numbing to start, the pain to ease. Only then does he allow himself to stand, step out into the grove, around the fire, search the needle-smothered ground for signs. But he finds none. No bit of blanket-hair or hint of footprint. The snow caught by the branches above, all but a dusting blown in between the trunks at the grove's edge, the view beyond opening into a wide white slope. And in the newfallen snow a line of tracks.

Stepping through the drift, he squints into the blinding expanse, stands of pine and hemlock islanded like boulders in a frozen river, and between his grove and a higher other, footprints stretching across like a strung bridge. Clear as if the moccasins that made them had just then disappeared. Though when he senses movement it is not in the trees upslope, but down: a dark spot in the bright distance, so far away it's hard to tell if it is moving. Until it separates into two, becomes mule and rider slowly climbing, following no trail Silas can see. Unless it is marked by the smoke rising behind him, the flicker of his fire, his own figure.

Back in the copse, he lifts a piece of dogflesh from its stake, rips off a bite, plugs the basket with the half-dried rest, mashing it over the tarweed, throws the remaining strips of jirk into the musket's empty sheath, slings it across his shoulder, stands chewing hugely at the meat and gristle while he takes a long and spattering leak. Then, wrapping himself again inside the black feather blanket, walks back to the gap in the trees to take in the progress of the rider.

Still not close enough for him to shoot. Not with the sightless pepperbox. From behind the screen of snow-sagged branches, he watches the gray mule climb even more slowly than before, a dark gray blanket wrapping its rider like a shawl, hooding his face into near-blackness, a mass of gray and darker gray and darker yet advancing slowly up the slope.

There is something in the pace that makes it worse, and though Silas knows he should wait longer, he draws the pistol, checks all six caps, repacks each chamber, leans against the tree, props his forearm on a branch, stares down the barrel, breathes—the blanket shakes around the man's hunched shape, the mule steps another second closer—and fires.

The blast shakes snow off the branches above, drops a curtain over his sight, and in the seconds before it clears, he hears only the echo of the boom, the ravens' cries as they rise from the trees, and then the snowfall thins and there is the rider again, still mounted, still coming at the same pace, the only change the blanket now slipped to his shoulders, his head bared, his face—Silas resets his grip—his face—pulls the trigger just enough to turn the next barrel into place—the man's face—sights—is gone. Where before there'd been a rag now there is nothing. Nothing where his mouth should be, his chin, his jaw. Nothing but raw redness of meat, a wound like Silas's own blown fingers but wrecking the whole bottom half of the man's face. He is now close enough Silas can see the ragged mass of sagging flesh shiver with the mule's steps. The ravens' croaking: four big black birds flapping away against the bright gray sky. And still the man comes on, the reins still slack, rifle still a glint across his lap. And still squinting down the pistol barrel, Silas watches. The crows dwindling to distant specks, the man slowly closing enough Silas can see—both his eyes open, his face rising—the stars. Pale stars stitched on the blanket's corners. The blanket that once belonged to a different boy. Who he had shot. This man's dead son.

Slowly, he lets the pressure off the trigger, steps back into the grove, is halfway to the kapum hu when he sees how it will be: the rider crashing into the copse, coming upon the shelter made by someone from the nearby tribe, finding the warm ashes, the footprints leading back toward the peak, the lake beneath, the village on its shore.

Then he is running, his own body crashing through the copse, though, breaking out, he heads the other way, peak at his back, fleeing in a snow-stagger across the open slope, checking over his shoulder to make sure the boy's father had seen, again to mark the mule's change of course, the white puffs bursting around its steps coming slow as the same around his own. The way it will be for a strangely long time, one man wrapped in black feathers given him by a ghost, pushing toward the crest, chased by another, wrapped in the bedroll of his dead son. Behind them both, looming through the clearing clouds: the mountain, its cliffs seeming to grow out of the sky itself, peaks forming slow as the pursuit below, the huffing mule hardly gaining on the hard-breathing man, the span of snow between them closing over a quarter hour, another, until the clouds release the last of the sun-blasted massif and the gasping runner turns, stands, and, whole body heaving, stares back across his snow-blown tracks.

Through his own breath Silas watches the other come. The man's face breath-blurred too, though, as he closes, Silas can see the wound, the lower jaw reduced to loose flesh stitched over missing bone, the upper one still whole, the darkness between clouding and clearing where a mouth used to be. Now moving. Trying to speak. A garbled groaning coming with each mule-step, so for a second, Silas thinks it is just pain, waits for the man's rage, his lifting rifle, something that will make Silas aim his own gun, force him to shoot. But the muzzle stays across the saddle, the man holding tight to it as if it might keep him from falling. Again: his awful attempt at speech. And in the desperately repeated groan Silas thinks he hears *Where. Where* something. He is so close now Silas can see the wet flapping of his tongue. *Where is?* He's tied himself to the saddle, legs lashed to stirrups, rope wrapping his waist, body bound pommel to pommel. *Where is my boy*. That's what the man is saying. *Where is my boy? Where is my boy?*

A breeze. Fluttering the blanket around Silas's shoulders, brushing a shiver through the black feathers.

"Back on the river," Silas tells him.

When the father tries to speak, his tongue flails inside the wreckage of his face as if in desperate hope of landing on some piece of flesh that might replace his lower lip. A bad thing to watch. But necessary to figure out the words. *This River? Wish River?*

"Which River?" the man repeats.

"My river," Silas tells him. "The one—"

But the man cuts him off with a word he does not understand, hard as he tries, a single word spoken over and over with increasing urgency, till the spit in the man's mouth, or whatever other fluid might build up there, spills over his purpled flesh.

"I'm sorry," Silas says. And it is not until he looks into the father's eyes that he can hear it: *alive.* The man is asking if he had left the boy alive. And bad as his face is to see—the flesh all up one side swollen beneath jaundiced skin stretched to a sickly shine—bad as it is to see the swelling squeeze one of his eyes, the other held too wide, it is the hope in them that is the worst.

Of course: how would the man know? Of course: he had to. The boy's mule. The blanket. The gun in Silas's hand. And yet how could a father not hold to that hope?

When Silas answers him at last, it is the father who does not understand, Silas who says the word too quietly to let him. And so repeats it, louder: "No."

No, he was wrong: Worse than the hope is watching it go. Watching the man's eyes on him as it leaves. Then they are shut, the man's forehead bunching upon them, and worse than both is watching him cry. The way his face twists with the straining, the pain of tears streaking down into his wounds. The sounds. Bad enough to make the mule shift. Make Silas look away.

Out of the corner of his eye, he sees the man lift a hand, remembers the rifle—but it is just to wipe the snot, the tears, off of his face. The realization hitting Silas just before the man's hand touches his sutured flesh, the seizing of Silas's throat coming at the same time as the man's scream. A roar ripped from a face that hurts all the more for it. That leaves the father shaking, gripping the rifle before him with an intensity like he is being stitched up again. And when it's over he does not seem able to speak. Tries, and tries again, and then, instead, just lifts the gun.

In Silas's hand: the pistol rising as if drawn by the opposing end of the same string. For a moment, they stay like that, in a stillness so great not a feather of Silas's cloak shifts, not a ripple in the man's blanket, just their breath-clouds leaving their bodies, thinning to nothing beneath the bluing sky. And then the mule blows at the snow and shakes its head and Silas says, "If I was you, I'd kill me." Beneath his skin-shirt, the lead-ball pendant presses against his breastbone, eases, presses again, and through the sound of his own breathing, he hears the father say, *I was you.* Or *I want you.* Either way, followed by something Silas can make out even less. Until it comes again, something that sounds like a demand, that contains in it maybe the words *make me.*

I want you to make me.

No, there is more to it. The man says it again, and Silas hears—he's almost sure—the word *son* at the end.

But it is only the third time—the man's rifle still held at Silas's head, but the command shed from his voice, replaced by something more like a plea—that Silas understands, knows what the father is trying to tell him is that he wants to see his son, wants Silas to take him to the body.

Surely, if there is a journey between the worlds of the living and the dead, it looks like this. The new snow marked by sharp shadows thrown by the sun, the blue sky both close and fathomless, the black feathers of the cloak around the figure in the front shaking with his walking, the gray mule he leads blowing lung-heat out its nostrils, carrying a figure shrouded in a gray blanket marked by stars. A long-departed heart returned to lead one newly so, retracing the sun's path eastward to the face-washing gate that marks the valley of Ko'domyeponi. The archangel guiding a soul across the threshold of the darkly prowled world. Or maybe just a man whose world is coming to an end taking one of those who'd come to kill it back across the border, beyond the edge that once held those like him at bay, toward the world from which he'd come.

Maybe that is why Silas leads him over the pass, toward the east. Maybe he is only taking him away, far from his river. Maybe it is neither, not away or toward but just through time, step by step, minute by minute, aware of how few the half-faced man can now have left. The way the rider tips in his saddle, gun scabbarded so he can grip the pommel. The way he shakes, despite the sun, has begun to mumble to himself, call ahead to Silas—how far? how long?—asking again before a quarter hour has passed. Though the place he seeks is days away in the opposite direction. As if the man, in his delirium, can't see the sun, feel the earth's slant. And in the end won't it amount to much the same? Whether Silas takes him down to the river stones barrowing the boy, or east across the range, toward his memories? Either way, isn't he leading the father to meet the son? In body or heart? Isn't taking them out from the Lokum Yaman, leaving one less man in a world that asked for none, the least that he can do?

He has just brought them over the crest of folds and lakes into a rocky country of clenched hemlocks and wind-stunted pines, the snow barely a dusting on this drier side, when he hears the mule cough and choke, turns to see instead the man bent in the saddle, retching. They are midway across a creek, the mule trying to find its footing against the weight leaning over its side. The man seems as if, even bound to the saddle, he might fall off, and Silas crosses back, helps him upright. Already the current has swept most of the slick away, the creek clearing itself, the mule starting to drink. He asks the man if he is thirsty, unties a skin-bag from the saddle, carries it upstream to fill it. But, crouched over the clean, cold water, he cannot keep from thinking of the bits of sick that will now fleck stones farther down, gunk caught in moss, and when he glances back, there is the mud stirred by the mule's hooves, and he is filled with an urge to stand and shoot the rider in the head. The mule too. Instead, he brings the skin-bag back and, while the mouthless man does what he can to get some water in, looks past him, down at the creek, its surface spattered with all the rider spills, spreading out, swirling away.

Still, the man insists he does not need to stop. And not long after they have resumed, Silas hears the hoof clatter falter, looks back to see the rider collapsed. For a long minute he stands watching. The mule drifting, nuzzling scrub, the man fallen over its withers, one arm dangling, blanket starting to slip. The thought: if he was to keep walking, just wander on, the man would soon be dead, that that might be best for both of them. If not the mule. How long might it survive with a corpse strapped to its back? The scant forage, snow, cold, all only growing worse. Before a cougar found it, or a bear, or wolves, or someone from the village a half day back. And it is that—the idea of a big cat tasting horseflesh for the first time, a grizzly snuffling a white man's scent, wolves scattering bits of the blanket across unspoiled snow, the burdened mule and rotting man stumbling into an unexpecting village like some gruesome advance guard of the coming rest—that returns him to the mule, makes him shake the man, lift his wrist to feel the pulse, and, tying both hands around the mule's neck, secure the passed-out rider well enough to reach a hollow a hundred feet below, where an old rockslide has made a windbreak and a few patches of grass grow, where he unties the ropes, eases the man down.

He is still breathing, the infected side of his face still pulsing, and Silas drags him out of the shade, lays him in sunlight to warm, attends to the mule—loosening the halter, uncinching the saddle; it has been ridden padless, its back rubbed raw, sores on its withers, and he picks its burs out of its coat, then hobbles it to graze—before turning to their own trappings. The dead boy's blanket is wet and muddy, in places gunked with blood, and he drapes it over a bitterbrush, carefully spreads his feather robe out too, is finally tending to his own wound—cutting hunks of dogfat off the half-jirked strips, filling his tin cup with the chunks, setting it out in the sun to soften—when the man screams.

He is awake and clawing at his own face.

It happens too fast for Silas to reconsider: lunging over, he pins the struggling body, knees planted on either side, his good hand grabbing one of the man's and wrestling it back, but his mangled other struggling to grip so, for a second, their fists are interlocked and, in the surge of pain, Silas tries to wrench away, sees blood already seeping from his bandage, snaps his right hand off the other's wrist and, whipping out the pistol, jams its six barreled muzzle into the man's forehead, tells him, Let go. Says it again. A third time—tugging the trigger enough to lift the hammer, twist the brow-skin with the turning drum—before the man does. Lifting his freed hand over his head, letting the blood-pump ease, Silas kneels there, bandage pulled loose, palm held open above them both, as if administering a blessing. Both of them breathing. The man's breath reeking enough to make Silas sit back. Or maybe the stench is his face. The flesh bloated from cheek to temple, the swollen skin split, a fetid fluid leaking out. But his eyes are clear, more charged with life than Silas has yet seen them.

"My son," the man says, staring into Silas's own, "has a gun just like that."

It is the clearest thing he's said, and Silas, lifting the gun away, tells him, "Yes." Though it is not till the pistol is back beneath his belt that he catches the *has*.

"Who are you?" the man asks, and Silas is looking hard into the eyes again, trying to see if it is truly a question, when the man repeats it, the *who* like *huh*, the *are* a single vowel, the *you* a glottal sound pushed from the throat, but no way not to understand.

"Stay still," Silas says, and, rising, steps to the rock with the warming fat, brings back the cup, sets it down while he digs in his possibles, pulls out the basket.

Another question strung together from *Where* and *you* and *come.*

Scooping the half-melted fat into the dried tarweed, he begins to mash it with two fingers, tells the man it will be bad at first.

"Why?" the man asks.

"It'll help," he says, though he knows it is no answer, knows it and still the look that comes into the man's eyes at his words—had he said *I'll* instead?—the look in the man's eyes is so—*I'll help?*—in those eyes there is such gratitude. Relief. Belief. In him.

Looking away, he focuses on mixing the poultice. Until, scooping it out, pressing it gently—just enough to make it stay—he slowly covers the father's ruined face.

When he is done, the man opens his mouth as if to speak and Silas shakes his head—it will break the paste loose; it will be something he does not want to hear—but the father speaks anyway: "Thank you."

How near a thing forgetting is to forgiveness.

"Thank you," he says again.

For both the wrongdoer and the wronged.

For a while, then, Silas sits beside him, the poultice drying on the dying man's face, the paste cracking, fat glistening in the sun. Nearby, the mule grazes, shaking its head at flies. Sometimes one lands on the man's face and Silas reaches over, brushes it away.

When he is sure the man has drifted to sleep, he starts to rise.

"Friend," the man says, and either Silas is becoming better at deciphering the words or the herb's numbing is helping the father speak, because as unlikely a word as it is, it is the word. Followed by "favor."

Let, the man says, *Let* something, *Let her* . . .

"Letter," Silas says.

And the man nods, bits of dried tarweed falling from his face. Then he is reaching for something at his hip, digging into a pocket, drawing out a piece of paper, folded and filthy and shaking in his shaking hand as he hands it to Silas.

"Home," the man says, and Silas repeats the word to assure him he has heard it.

"Ohio," the man says.

"Ohio." It takes him longer to get the town's name, but when he does—"Marietta"—the man grins. A thing that seems to flood him with pain, leaves him breathing for a full minute to regain his strength.

In the sun, the paper is almost too bright to look at, and looking away, Silas sees again the gleam in the man's hand back when he'd been a distant speck far down the slope, and then he is squinting at the paper again, trying to make out the marks on the other side, within the fold. Too faint to tell anything except it is not writing. Not a letter at all. More like a drawing. Which, carefully, fold by fold, he opens up.

A map. Of here. Mountains and rivers, village and lake. Marks he knows as well as his own home. Where he had buried this beneath the floor, hidden by the dead boy's blanket now spread over the bitterbrush, bright in the sun, the stars embroidered in its corners more visible than before, the two stitched letters—*IS*?—red as blood.

The man's voice snaps Silas back. Two words. The first a single syllable, perhaps just *the*.

"Again," Silas says, and again he cannot catch the second. Nothing but that it begins with *s*. "I'm sorry," he says, and the man tries again, such desperation in his voice that Silas tells him, "Okay." Again he tries, anyway, as if to be sure, and maybe it is a surname, the Somethings, the key to the letter finding its way, and what does it matter? Silas turns the map over: the other side is blank. "Okay," he tells the man, "I understand."

And the man breathes. In, out, the exhale starting to shake. His voice, when he speaks again, shaking a little too: "My wife."

"Your wife," Silas says.

"And," the shaking growing worse so that Silas might not have understood if he did not already know what word would come, "my son."

That afternoon, while the man sleeps, Silas leans against the bleached trunk of a fallen pine, gazing at the map. Nearby, the scent of dogfat softening, the tang of tarweed on his hand, the deeper funk of a bear hide wet from fleshing, the earthy redolence of stones ground to powder for paint, soil wet from rain, loosed by a boy drawing with a stick in the mud outside his home. *Like a kaieskum*, Walloki had said, *fanning its crest*, and he was right: up close the massif looked less like the jagged teeth Silas had inked onto this map than the crest of a jay. Shutting his eyes, he sees it still: the lake bowl to the east, the rim where he had stood, the shore where a one-eyed jomin must have glanced up and glimpsed a distant figure turning away and somehow known. And come that night alone. *A lake*, the boy had said, scraping a circle in the mud, and for a moment Silas can hear his voice again—*its shape*—still a boy's—*like this*—still with him.

He is about to fold the map away, unlean his back from the bleached tree, when a breeze finds the paper, lifts. Not much, but enough to make him grip it a little tighter, keep him holding it a little longer.

The mule drifts a little farther. The sun shifts off the dead boy's father. The dying man sleeps on. Beneath the smell of warming dogfat there is a reek Silas thinks might be his hand before he realizes the breeze has shifted too, the stench of rot and suppuration coming from the father's face. He watches him for a few seconds—still breathing—then folds away the map, unsheathes his knife. In the late bough-splintered light he wanders among the pines until he finds one weeping, crouches, carves the sap free. By the time the sun has climbed into the treetops, he has gathered wood for a fire, and by the time the sun is off them, he has lit it, set the cup of dogfat close to the flames, filled it with sap and what tarweed remains, and in the last light he stirs it, blowing, letting the viscous pulp cool a bit, a little more, before he grips the stirring stick between his teeth and, shutting his eyes, plunges the stubs of his fingers in.

The stick still jutting past his cheeks, he paces while the pitch hardens into an opaque shell over his wounds, a russet glistening that, when it's cooled, he bandages again. And, feeling the coolness also come into the evening, he goes to the sleeping man, tries to shake him awake. Then to haul him nearer the fire. But the father resists, even asleep, crying out and flailing, so in the end he leaves him, goes to the blankets instead. The wool one is still wet and cold, so he lays the feathered instead over the father, drapes the other beside the fire, sits gnawing dogflesh, watching the wool steam, staring at the corner stars growing strangely whiter as the dusk deepens, at the stitched letters flickering with firelight—*I* and *S*—trying not to think of names.

The man is on him. Night, and the fire low, and in the near black the dead boy's father a presence too close, his weight too great, his hands pulling at the dried blanket Silas had wrapped around himself when he had gone to sleep.

"Son," the man says, "I'm dying."

And what can he say to that?

"Mother," the man is saying. Something about the boy's mother. Lifting one of the blanket corners close to his face, tracing his fingers over the star. "Mother," he says, and "made," and in the garbled rest, Silas thinks he makes out *stitch* and *this*, and then the man is pawing along the blanket, over Silas's body, asking about the letter.

"I'll send it," Silas says, but his words only lift the man's voice louder.

"Letters," the man nearly shouts. "Letters!" The mangled *s* drawn out and louder. And then he finds them, the dark red stitching inside the white embroidery, and squeezing the corner in his fist, says, "Forget." Something *forget.*

"I won't," Silas tells him.

"I," the man says, as if he would repeat it. But follows it with *s.*

And in the next breath Silas knows what he will say and with a rush of panic hushes it—"Shhhhhh"—loud enough to smother whatever word the man tries to make understood, tells him in the silence after, "Go back to sleep."

But the father stays, his weight hovering, his face too close when he makes the same sound in return: a hushing misshapen into a struggled blowing stripped of teeth or lips. He makes the sound again and Silas is about to shove him off him when he feels a hand. The man's. Touching his cheek. A soft and tender stroking. That terrible sound. And Silas shuts his eyes, squeezes them tight, stays still, and takes it, makes himself take it, takes it again, again, again.

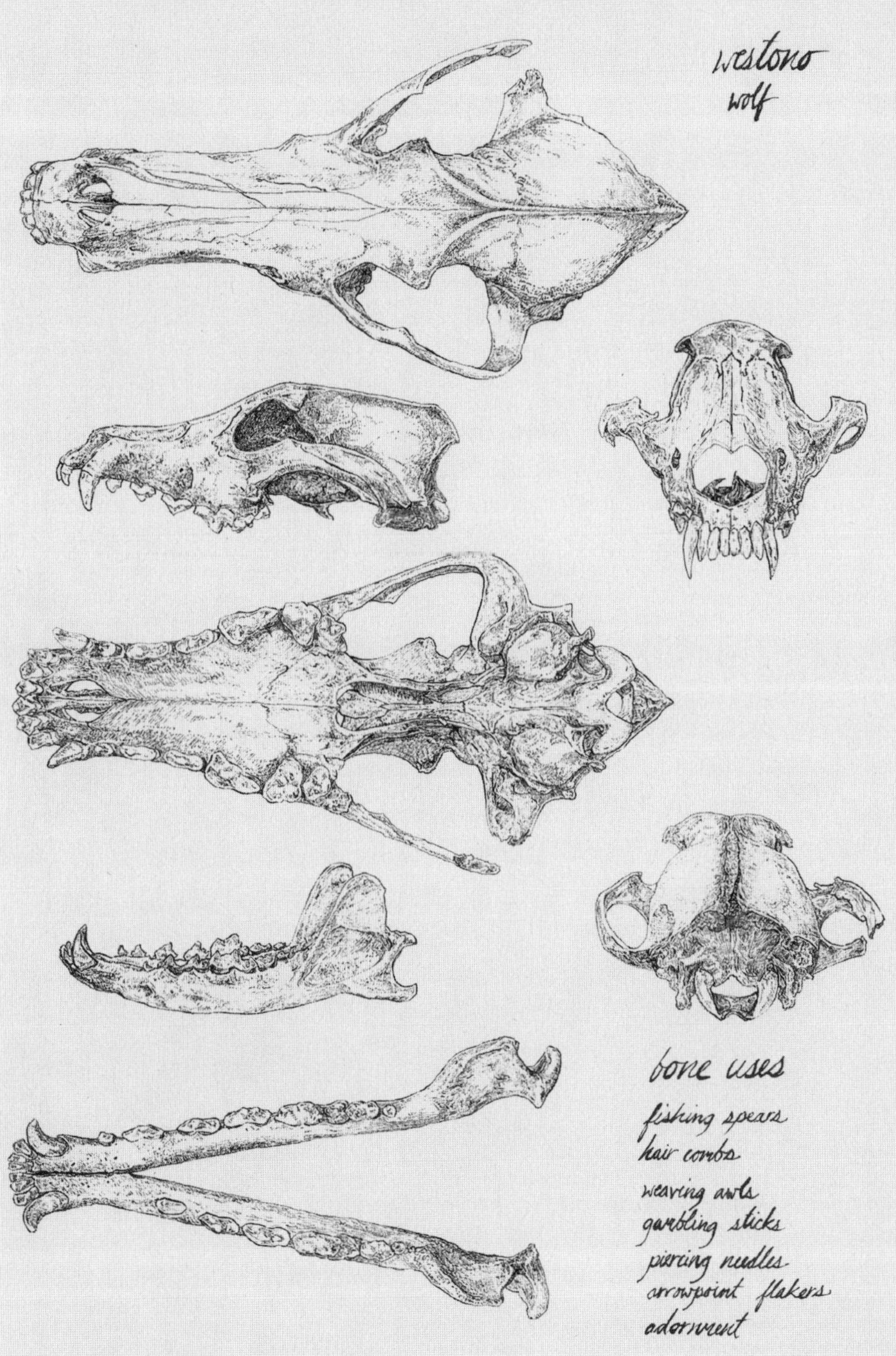
westono
wolf
bone uses
fishing spears
hair combs
weaving awls
gambling sticks
piercing needles
arrowpoint flakers
adornment

That wi'nuti I decamped for the high country free of a gun. My last shot back in the squint moon season at Walloki's grizzly. My musket ever since carried only as a caution. Agnst my fears. Though that spring standing down at the cache bfore departing holding the gun wrapped in a skin I was afraid to leave it. Made myself feel it. The way that fear welled up in me & fouled my mind the air even the river. Remembering how the blasts wld wreck even its sound. The scent sour the breeze. Let that give me the strength to shove the musket in & cover the cache & start upriver. My body with each bend moving a little faster. With each leap growing a little lighter.

You will disbelieve me when I tell you the canyon knew. But I cld feel it. The effigy watching as I passed. The heron appearing overhead & flying on & landing waiting lifting again staying all morning in my sight. The banks day aftr day remaining free of any sign of my own kind. No squaw soaking her splints. No hunter stalking game. Not in all the wks I made my way upriver. Climbing ever higher. No sign of what had come over the crest the yr bfore. No hint of what No Rope had heard. So that gradually my dread began to seem like something that belonged back in the world below. Of speech & stories & others. Outside of me.

A color. Blue. How cld something so small as a bit of blue undo all that? A glint flashing bneath the water. And I was splashing in reaching under knowing even bfore I brought it up. Glass. A small bottle of pale blue glass. An hr farther upriver I found a scrap of cloth. Fluttering frayed from a snag. Wld have ripped it free & buried it bside the bottle & too scared to see what had bcome of the camp up on the lake might have remained hunkered there on the river blinkered by its banks if round the next bend I had not found them wrecked.

A whole cliffside collapsed. The slope so torn apart it might have been the aftermath of massive floods but for the prints. Hoofprints. Oxen. Brought down to drink. Over and over. For long enough to leave such a slurry of scat I had mistaken it for mud. The snow and ice melted away to show the bootprints in it. Left by the men who must have herded them back up.

I stood on the sun-hardened muck feeling each print on my own flesh, the herd milling inside my chest wanting a gun a gun a gun. The need fierce in me as I had feared it would be. Stood fighting the tightening of my breath the tamping of my blood the ramrod of my pulse run through my veins and then was climbing fast as if fleeing the spark. Till cresting the bank I saw the stumps. Studding the wreckage of rutted earth. All round the clearing patches of snow stacked with discarded bones. Ox skulls and arcing ribs. Piles of ash. Half-rotted refuse. What trees remained were stripped of bark. Between their trunks the duff spattered with cowpies. Smaller heaps of human dung. The smell still strong enough to make me queasy. Get me moving. Following their wide-rucked track faster and faster down the mountain slope.

A day and a night and another before I came back up. Having tracked them far enough to be sure they veered farther away. Their route cutting across another part of the Lokum Yaman into another valley. Where they went then, I did not care. Only that there was no sign of their returning. That as I came again to the wreckage of their wintering and from there began retracing their trail eastward toward the crest, there was no indication of others come in their wake. So, traveling faster now that I knew the land, it was as if I made my way not just back east but back in time, the sight of them—that cart rising over the cliff, the women driving it, the men emerging from the snowy pines—increasingly climbing out of my memory till, reaching that ledge at last, I half expected to see it all again before me.

And still was not prepared for what I saw instead. Still farther east, beyond the cliff: a lake, a shore, and there on it, four wagons. Unhitched, unmoving. I scanned the land around them for shapes of oxen, the slow shifting of horses grazing. But all was still as the wagons themselves. The movement instead behind me.

A wolf. Less than a rod away, crouched in the dimness beneath a cedar's boughs, its eyes two glints in its raised head, its body staying strangely low. No sound. Not a snarl, not a breath. And then its head sank to its forepaws and, in the sudden sound of panting, I saw the chain.

The trap had caught her too high up for her to free herself by gnawing. Though, nearing, I could see she'd tried, her foreleg all mangled flesh and exposed bone, the ground beneath soaked dark. There was her snarl. Around her teeth the wet-clumped fur seemed to press the sound back down into a quivering of lips, her eyes on mine as I took in the rest. A hind-leg had been ripped open too, bitten deep enough to show the meat, the ground around her too scuffed from her own struggling for me to make out by who. Maybe coyotes. Some smaller prints mixed in. Though they could have been her young come back to keep her company, or to run off what had attacked her. Might have just then been frightened away by me.

I left her too—to them or to the other—making my way down toward the wagons, my bow unslung, an arrow notched, my eyes hunting each lake-glimpse for a sign of whoever set the trap, so that I nearly missed the crows, the raven warding them away—its croak clear as a word: *here*, *here*—the coyote I found nearby long dead. Little left but tufts of fur, its desiccated carcass just intact enough to make clear the waste. A thing that confused as much as angered me till I came upon a third, this time merely a skeleton scattered around the snapped-shut steel. So that, even before I found the next, I knew the traps had been set long ago and never checked.

I followed them the rest of the way down, a trail of bodies in different stages of decay. Some barely one week old, some more than a month. Crows and magpies marking my route, cawing and circling and flapping into trees, dropping down again behind me, till I stopped.

Beyond the wagons, half hidden in the woods: a cabin. The shade of the pines marked by lines straight as only made by men, the door a dark rectangle. I did not think they were still there. The pile of bones outside gone gray with age, the human scat half dissolved by rain, no laundry hanging, no stretched skins, no footprints. Till I went in.

The scent of rodent nests and fouling, dead flies and something larger moldering. Smells I recognized from my own yearly returns to my own home. Stood in the strange familiarity, adjusting to the windowless murk, the light splintered between the unchinked logs striping hearthstones too huge for a single man to move, stacks of more plates and bowls than a dozen could use, a single room stuffed full of bedding—quilts, blankets, furs—piled in every corner except the one containing a bed.

I took a step toward it, stopped. An ash-cloud billowing up from my moccasin, the hearth so full it overflowed onto the floor. In it: the tiny prints of mice, voles. Scattered round the larger prints of his. I stood looking down at the heel and ridge, the five small spots where his toes had touched, wondering what happened to him. The one bed and sole set of footprints and lone log stool and single plate lying face down, fork balanced on its back. I turned it over. Crusted remains of some last meal. Outside, I'd seen no graves, no markers. Yet there were so many bones thrown out the door, so many quilts and blankets, the four wagons waiting by the lake.

Crossing the ashes, careful to avoid his prints, I stood by the pallet trying to discern in the bunched blankets some hint of him. But there was just the faint impression where a peltry had been rubbed thin, no different than my own shape would have made. Above it hung a shirt. Red felt, tin buttons. I touched it, brushed it against my cheek, forehead, my eyes shutting beneath its softness as I drew it over my face. The plate, the fork. The blankets. Any bullets I might find. A powder horn. A sack of flour, coffee. Sugar. Salt. Maybe the man had had a pipe—tobacco saved for a last smoke—maybe a jaw harp, a fiddle. I opened my eyes, slung the shirt away. Would have retreated had I not seen the chest.

A small chest all but hidden by the blankets piled against it. As if it had served for a headboard. Thick leather handles, a locking top. Unlocked. I stood before it, trying to decide. Then in one sudden movement opened it up. Books. Their leather bindings laid side by side. I lifted the first one out. *Husbandry Spiritualized; or, The Heavenly Use of Earthly Things.* It had been so long since I had read a word that for a moment the *t* and *h* and *l* shoved all together threw me. Then I was opening the cover, flipping the first pages, reading: *Honored friends, it hath been long since observed, that the world below is a glass to discover the world above;* Seculum est speculum: *and although I am not of their opinion, that say, the Heathens may spell Christ out of the sun, moon, and stars; yet this I know.* Strange to hear another's words inside my mind. My thoughts commandeered. And yet, setting the volume down, I drew out another—*The Holiday Reward; or Tales to Instruct and Amuse Good Children*—read the first sentence of that too. *Shiver, shiver, shiver, stood little Henry Mendip, waiting till the servant opened the door.* I swallowed, wet my lips. Spoke the next aloud: "I am so glad to see the fire, dear mother," said the child, advancing to it. Stopping, I looked around. As if it might have been another who had spoken. As if the thoughts I'd given voice might have been made by him who'd lain there, the sense of someone else speaking the words so strong that by the time I finished the sentence I was sweating. My voice hung in the air, inside another's, inside my ears. Setting the second book down, I told myself to go. Said it in my own voice: Get out of here. Said it aloud: Silas, get out. And instead drew out a third. *American Medical Botany.* This time I merely flipped through the prints—lithographs of plants I had not seen in over a decade—paged through every plate and, when I was done, set it beside the other two and tried another, then another. Only after the entire chest was empty did I realize what I'd been hoping to find. Knew it by the hole that failing to had opened in me. If I had read it—*In my life's endeavor to comprehend the multifarious ailments*—had read his words—*that afflict the creatures God has given into our care*—would I have heard them in his voice? Would it have remained that way as long as I could speak? Had light to read? For a few minutes or an hour or the rest of the day or the rest of my life? Might he have been there again with me?

Maybe he was. Even without his words. Maybe his heart on its last journey paused there to watch. As I took in what lay at the bottom of the chest: a stiff packet of lacquered leather bound with a buckled cinch. Crouching, I opened it. Undid the clasp, unfolded the leather, breathed in. The scent of paper. A stack that seemed a thousand sheets. And beside where it had been: three tins. Their lids screwed almost too tight for me to twist them off. Though when at last I did, I lost my breath—all that powder waiting to be mixed back into ink—had to clap the top back on before I could breathe in. Last, there was a worn wood case. Inside, on velvet lining: two pens, spare nibs, a square of cloth streaked black where it had been used to wipe them clean.

For a long while I squatted there trying to not remove my rucksack, not open its top, not make space for the sheaf, the ink, the pens. And failed. Took all of them. Stood then, looking around the cabin, feeling the opening uncinched in my resolve. The flannel shirt, the hanging belt, the scissors glinting on an overturned basin. Knowing what each item must have meant to him. If he had lived alone with them. For a month? A winter? Long enough for buttons to become a comfort on his fingers, one missing a catastrophe. Long enough for the belt to become a hand on his back, the books his company, their voices friends. The way they would become for me. Watching the washbasin I could feel the fire-warmed water on my face, the scissors trimming my beard. To have an extra ladle, a new knife, needle, spool of thread.

Picking it up, I held it in my hand. Considered feeding it into the fireplace. And the shirt, books, belt, blankets. But it would take too long, make too much smoke. Worse to burn them outside in a pile, or to simply set the entire cabin alight. Either way sure to draw any nearby Monaa, bring them upon me while I was setting fire to the wagons. Or, hiding, watched them search the ashes for blackened blades, the buried glints of buttons, buckles, hinges.

I lugged the chest out first, full of its volumes, leaving a long drag mark down to the lake. Where, one by one, I threw the books far as I could, watched them splash and try to float and slowly sink. Before I went back in to get the rest.

All afternoon I worked, hauling out everything, hurling piece after piece into the water, hacking with an axe at crates, stripping my breeches off to splash in and shove barrels deeper. Climbing into the wagons, I threw all I could, carrying great armfuls of the rest into the lake. Then waded among the remains hacking with the axe, my chopping spraying, trying to make everything sink. Till the lake bottom grew so cluttered I'd trip splashing out, my body steaming, my legs freezing, finally flinging the axe as well. A last exploding splash. Followed by quiet. The ripples spreading, shaking all that still floated—blankets bulged with air, bits of wood and bobbing spools—a flotsam that, for a moment, seemed worse than if left in the cabin. Till, one by one, they sank, the air escaping pockets, the wood grown waterlogged, the spools simply drifting away, lost in the shimmer of the sun. The same that slowly dried my legs, my sweat, leaving only a tingling beneath the chilling air.

Behind me the cabin still stood, but it would not forever. Farther away: the wagons, one day to be just rusted hoops and collapsed heaps. The snows and rains and beating sun slowly reclaiming the shore, the lakes and mountains and canyons and rivers so much bigger than anything men could bring. My own body so small, standing beside the lake, it was impossible to imagine anyone could do more than pass through. My life among these mountains, along my river, one day reduced to bones. Before they were gone too. The way even the iron hoops would eventually rust back to earth, the cabin become a hillock of rotting logs hidden beneath new growing trees.

That night I retraced my path by moonlight. Trap to trap to trap. Each glint unnatural in the landscape. One by one depressed each spring, opened each jaw, unstaked each chain, and leaving the carcass where it lay, slung the trap onto my shoulder. By the time I'd climbed back to where the wolf had been, I was carrying enough weight, swaying chains clacking round me, to tilt my body, shorten my breath.

She was still there, still breathing. Though so weak she didn't even lift her head when I stepped near, couldn't manage a snarl, barely opened her eyes, two glints of moonlight amid the boughs, the rest so dark in there I couldn't see the trap. Felt for it with my feet till I stood on the springs, my moccasins six inches from her teeth. Under my weight, the trap released. But her paw stayed on the steel, the wolf too weak to draw it out. So, reaching down, I lifted her leg—the eye-glint growing wider—shook it free, snatched my hand back. But she didn't even have the strength to shut her jaws, the steel ones smacking closed instead, the sound somehow making her appear even more still. Her eyes again just slits. Her breathing shallow.

I'd dropped the other traps some steps away and, grabbing one of their stakes, I now began to dig, stabbing and scooping till I'd made a hole just big enough to dump them in. The clattering seemed to startle her—she shook, her breathing quickening—but she didn't open her eyes again. A quick knife-strike across her throat. I thought about it, thought about how she'd die if I did not—how long it might take to pass alone without her pack, how she'd look when it came at last: her breath gone, body still, life let out without my help, without another mark made by another woole's steel—then, shoveling the earth back till it buried the traps, I left.

And when first sunlight flared over the crest, splintering between the trees, I was still walking, heading west, back toward the lake I'd meant to reach a week ago. The cache Walloki and I'd left. By the time I reached it, it was near evening, and clearing away the cover, I could feel, in the late light finding my face, the fire's heat. Scraping away the moss, I felt his fingers hover. Rolling aside rocks, heard his hoof-rattle. Be gone, he'd said, go far away. I pried away the stones we'd placed, drew out the sheepskins, his fishing gig, his flute and rattle. Leave him alone, he'd said, leave him in peace. And in his echo, I held the sack of traps against my chest, heavy as the ones I'd buried across the crest. Then lowered them back in. Replaced the rocks. Unrolled my sheepskin. Slept.

I would not use the traps again. Nor those cached at my winter camp. Not that year or the next or the year after. No more than I would use the guns, or could have worn that felted shirt with its tin buttons, or taken the books and brought the thoughts of others into my own, their sounds into my river's. No more than I could have brought the scissors or axe or extra knife back to Kushna to trade. No more than I would have brought the whites. Or could any longer bring No Rope the peltries I no longer trapped, no longer needed, no more than I did the seeds or ropes or baskets I could now make or patch or do well enough without myself.

Myself.

What a strange animal is man. The way we use our hands, our tools, our minds. Sometimes that summer I'd catch a scout squirrel watching me smash pinecones with a rock, prying my knife at the hard scales, trying to pop free nuts. While he, a few feet away, stood on his haunches holding a cone big as himself, turning it round and round in his clawed paws, chewing free seed after seed with such speed and precision I paused to watch him back till he was done. Or one moonless winter night, awoken by a crash, I lit a pine stick against my blindness, stepped out of my hut to find the fish I had been drying scattered, the rack collapsed, the shine of eyes—startlingly bright, shockingly near—the big cat's stare there reflecting the flame, then gone, instantly beyond my ability to see. And setting nets in the eddy below my camp that spring, I'd come under the observance of otters: a family who, swooping on slides worn through the boulders, watched me—the father swimming up to inspect, the mother floating by, all four pups following, flipped on their backs, heads swiveling to watch me as they passed—while I crouched shivering in the cold water, pull-rope in my hand, waiting long enough to make them hungry. Because they would slip under, emerge downstream, silver flashes flapping in their mouths. While I, at last, might yank the rope, haul at the net, wrestle a single fish onto the rock beside me. The entire family staring as they chewed. As if I were a lesson for the pups in thankfulness that they weren't me.

Yes, a strange creature, man. Even stranger without another's company. Alone then in his two-legged tallness, his scant-haired skin, his whooping, laughing, shouting, crying, speaking. To himself or to the animals around him. Who cannot understand. Yes, a stranger creature than any one of them. And yet a creature still. Made to fill a space among the rest. What was it? That shape? What would it be to fit? Not into the space left for me by my kind, or even by the Nisenan—the hundreds in their villages, the thousands of their tribe—but to fit a space shaped for only me, between the shapes of other creatures. What would it be, then, to be a human? A human shaped by them?

The animals that, in the absence of my traps, slowly filled in around me. As if to show me. Clear as the loosening inside my chest, the lifting of my listening for distant snaps, a feeling as if I'd set the forest free. From me. From the last remnants of the man I'd brought from the world I'd fled. To this that I had thought I had sought out, found, cleared for my camp. Though I saw now it had merely accepted me, allowed me in, made me a place among the creatures already here. The coons whose eyes increasingly gleamed back at night. The foxes slipping by each dawn. The ringtail who seemed to have taken up residence in a corner of my hut. The catamount whose twisted leavings I found outside the shallow cave. Inside: the floor pressed flat by the lion's weight. I held my hand over the fur-brushed dirt, the fan-shape its tail had made in the old ashes. Then climbed in, curled up where it had lain. Where Walloki had once been.

Weeks earlier I'd returned from the high country, uncovered my winter cache, carried back to camp baskets his hands had mended, furs that had kept him warm, stood in the empty hut beneath the hanging tarweed he'd taught me could numb a wound, yarrow to stanch bleeding, crumbling the brittle leaves between my fingers, feeling a need such as hadn't come over me in years. Right then, I unpacked the papers, uncapped the powder, picked out a pen. Though when I'd mixed the ink, set out a page, sat at my table, I could do nothing but stare at the sheet. Till at last I dipped the nib, touched it to the white. A first small spot that, scratch by scratch, I shaped into a hut no bigger than a fingernail. Beside it: my river, my pen tracing its course east to the peaks, west to Kushna. My world in all its oxbows and lakes, ridge-trails and bluffs. Each village marked by a single k'um, their names like fencelines along the paper's left, guarding the southern border of all I knew. The Lokum Yaman's crest protecting the east. Everything west of Kushna cast off the bottom edge. Till only the part north of me was empty. Slowly I filled it in, trying to recall all Walloki told me, his marks in the mud outside my hut, the terrain we'd crossed to find the cave, the clustered peaks farther northeast that I'd only ever seen from far away, the lake he'd said lay to their east, a k'um along its shore, beneath it simply his name.

Maybe it was only this—what he'd removed from me—that left me at peace, let me leave behind my guns, find those wagon tracks and cabin and still not crack, not feel the flare of that old heat, or on the surface of the lake see that old face—its blood-smeared teeth and spit-flecked chin, head whipping to a blur—watching me back. Maybe what let me look away, wade out, return instead to this world waiting for me, was nothing that he sucked from my skin or drew from my breath, but simply him. Maybe, in the end, he'd had to remove only himself.

Maybe the self I became then was only what, shed of all other humans, I would always have been. Reshaped to fit beside a marmot so used to me he'd sun on the same rock, wake me with a warning bark, his eye on me for a split second beneath the shadow of a hawk before he slipped away, as if he'd stood watch for us both. A flock of crows I'd grown to know, each by their caws, their commentary as I picked berries, the game they made of swooping down to try to steal my basket, cackling at my cursing as if it was the most fun that they'd had in years. As raucous as the doe was quiet, her passing footsteps become such a marker of dawn I could tell when their gait changed, her weight increased, knew one day soon they'd be accompanied by smaller clatter. And I would blow the embers bright, knock another chip out of a half-made blade. While the ringtail slept through the day, slipped out at night, her huge eyes bright disks of moonlight I'd wake to in the predawn dark. The sound of her crunching on rodent bones. Sometimes silenced by a big cat's screams. Sometimes its scat left on the path back to the cave that it had claimed. Sometimes the remains of its prey: a breeze-stirred puff of squirrel tail, a gopher's skull scraped clean, a single scaup wing wholly intact.

For a while I'd tried to hunt them too—rodents, birds, sheep in high country, coon by my winter camp—but the anxiety that had accompanied my having to slit a throat or wring a neck had only grown. Where before I might have wondered if a trapped fox was one I knew, now the worry swelled to include all the world around me. The mind that let me snare a squirrel recalling, between bites of meat and piñon mash, the sight of the same nuts sprayed from its cheeks. The brain that knew to weave a net to catch a goose the same that, hearing honking overhead, stirred me to holler back. Gutting a buck, how could I know his offspring wasn't growing inside the doe?

Back in the Rockies I'd listened to old hiverannos speak of starving—winters when, waking to find a fellow trapper expired, they'd forced themselves to eat his flesh, fight the recoiling of their guts—believing, even as my gut clenched at the beaver meat we shared, that what they'd felt was surely worse. But now I was no longer sure. For how much more alike were we—the squirrels gathering mast beside my basket-filling self, the cougar stretching in the sun on the same boulder on which I'd warmed myself the day before, the geese whose calls each spring marked my migration—than I was to another human? Even the Nisenan, eating and dancing and gambling and grieving together, the families sharing their heat inside a single hu, the men who once a year might pass through my part of the canyon in a group, on their way toward another village teeming with yet more of the creature who'd come to feel less of my kind than any other.

My store of jirk lasted nearly a month. Filled out by fish that I still caught. Till even they came to feel too similar. Trout stirred to the surface with the same urgency that approaching rains would stir in me. Salmon rippling upriver, marking the changing season clear as the geese. Each fitting their own sliver of a world in which we—they and me—had been given our space to exist. A thing I found myself trying to do on bulbs and roots, roasted baynuts, boiled chokecherries, the winter berries of flock-hollies and cellarskins, mushrooms found during long mornings of hunched hunting, grass seeds gathered over stooped afternoons, my days increasingly spent wholly in the attempt to stave off hunger, my bow and quiver carried solely for protection, the way I'd once carried my guns. Though with the passing of another season I grew unsure I'd even have the strength to use them.

By that day that I climbed in the shallow cave where Walloki had once made his home, I'd grown so weak I could barely lift my body over the ledge, lay in the dirt, unable to make myself get up, breathing in the big cat's scent, my ear to the earth, hearing my own heart thump. Then gradually, beneath it, another pulsing coming from the woods: a rustling swelling and easing, almost a lapping. As if the water's sound was being dragged through the trees and let down and dragged again. Then I was up, whipping my bow off my shoulder, already reaching to my quiver by the time I saw her. She was hauling something heavy—neck straining, shoulders jerking—stopping just long enough to tilt her head, adjust her grip, give another wrench. Something that, as she broke out of the brush, I watched become the body of the doe. Its great swollen belly weight tugged, tugged. Till suddenly it stilled, dropped. The big cat seeing me.

I shot before I thought—the angle odd, the arrow rising, hitting too high—was notching the next, dropping my aim, loosing another, by the time the cougar charged. My thinking then only of the closing distance, the second shaft there on her neck, the need to aim still lower, twang of the string, the third hitting her chest. I shot two more after she was already stopped, though by the time I released the last I was shaking so badly the arrow clattered off into the trees.

After: silence. But for my breathing, my heartbeat hammering. Sitting, I let go the bow, my eyes on the cat but my mind caught in my slowing breath, my calming heart, the way it had leapt same as the doe's must have at the first strike, same as the cougar's must have making her kill. Same as it would in any animal. Before draining away. From the doe, had she escaped. From the lion, her prey's pulse ceasing beneath her teeth. From me.

That day I opened up the doe, reached in around her bulging womb to cut her liver out, removed the same from the catamount, and, sitting on the ledge again, slowly ate both. Taking small bites, wiping my face. Watching over the bodies while I chewed.

It would take the rest of the day to butcher them, pull out their innards, flesh the carcasses, wash the intestines and drain the bladders and cut the hearts free of their veins, to open the doe's distended womb and, with the two half-formed fawns, do much the same, pull their tiny teeth for beads, set aside their tongues to savor later. Another day to butcher and smoke the meat, boil the bones, strip the sinew, melt the fat for tallow, the hooves saved to make rattles, the scapulas for scrapers. Days after that to stretch the plews, clean and string the cougar's claws and teeth, cure her hide and stitch it into a cloak. Weeks till I'd be done.

Still, before I started, I went back to my hut, returned with paper and ink and pens. And, for a few hours, drew: the lines of their sinews, flow of their fur, lashes on the doe's eyes, pads of the cat's feet, the way the fawns' bodies were intertwined. Observed them same as I had the specimens my father brought me long ago, studied their faces the way I had the features of the deceased in parlors, committed their memories to paper: the muscling of the cat's neck making known its skill at hunting, the doe's teats swollen as if never recovered from the loss of her other fawns so long ago. Sketched them the way I would from then on draw each creature I killed—quail or coon or salmon or squirrel, with snare or net or spear or arrow—drew them so I could learn them well enough to do them right, take their fleeting lives and stand them still, saved on a page. Pages I began to gather so that, together, they might do the same for my entire world.

Their world, too. Though, in all of it, I was the only one among us who could do this. This that I would leave for you. So that one day you may know it as well.

And so know me. As I was meant to be.

See me, son, crouched on a stone smoothed by a thousand years of rushing water, still as the boulder, net in my hand, a shadow crossing my back, my face as I look up: the flap of wings, pale gray gliding away. See me kneeling between baskets of acorn meal before a shallow pit dug in the sand, lining it with leaves, packing them with the ground mast, covering that with cedar boughs, pouring boiling water over it all. See me running beneath a flock of waxwings just to hear their deafening trill, their shadows flitting over my skin, my arms flung wide and flapping as I'd not let them since I was young, my hands aflutter, my head thrown back, my face aswirl with sunlight and shade. No one to see me or hear my hooting or witness my happiness. But you. So long as I still hold this pen, writing these words. And see me drawing, too—the smooth nut of a buckeye, a cloudpine's huge cone, a lizard lowering and lifting its twitching body while it watches me back, a crow, a small dead bat—sitting cross-legged on a nearly black boulder, a beach of rounded stones, beside an emerald pool. Above: the oak catkins of spring. Behind: fall willows, yellowed and thinned. A red scattering of summer thimbleberries. Toyon clusters in winter. And on the page, a shadow passing. The flap of wings, gray gliding. See me slipping upcanyon too, passing back down. Spring my dawn, autumn my dusk. A year, a day. A day, a year. Another. And then another.

And never again would I leave my canyon. Not to trade or see No Rope. Nor saw him here. Went year after year without a visit to Kushna, keeping to my river even in summer, staying away from the high lakes, the peaks, the crest, the cabin. The chance of coming on new tracks. The urge to cross back east, take up a vigil.

You'll wonder if they came back, brought others in their wake. Or maybe you already know, heard long ago. All this having taken place halfway through a decade now coming to an end. Maybe even so far away, the news of the world is still your news, still reaches you. If so, then you know more than I of anything beyond what I could see. All I can say is if more came that fall they did not come over my ridge, into my river. That, as long as I stayed within my canyon, they stayed unknown to me.

Through '46, '47, '48. The years passing meaning nothing. The world up there moving in its unceasing march. Down here in its repeating circle.

While you, still in the world I'd left, were turning twelve, thirteen, fourteen. Becoming a man I will never see without losing the one I have become. Here. Apart from everyone. Even from you. Sometimes the truth is that simple and that terrible, both.

Maybe the Nisenan are right. Their world attached to whatever lies beyond it by five ropes splayed out in five directions. Maybe we did cross over one, Ballou and Fancher and JG and me. Maybe the others who came after followed the cord. Maybe the shaking I felt seeing them was the rope. Beneath their weight, beneath my own. Maybe all I'd done since I left you was walk. Far as I could go. Till at last I reached a place where I could stay. And, drawing my knife, cut the rest of the world away.

AUTUMN, 1849

In the morning, the man is dead. Lying beside Silas, his skin cold as the air, one edge of the wool blanket gripped in his fists. Silas wraps him in the rest. His own has blown into the bushes, hung up there, its coal-black feathers shaking in the cold wind of dawn. Fetching it, he cloaks himself again, stoops to the fire, blows till it grows crackling into the brightest thing in all the morning. Then sits beside it thinking what to do with the man's body. The only thing he knows is that he will not take it to his river. Probably the boy's remains are already no more than rags and bones scattered along the bank, the stones he'd piled enough to keep off coyotes, but not bear. And if he leaves the father here, it will just be the same. Unless his corpse is found instead by someone from the nearest village, Monaa or Notong K'oyom, maybe some wandering boys or a strayed hunter from Timseh-koyo who would bring back boots, buckle, a shirt with buttons, an ear or nose starting to decompose but still pale-skinned, or just a blanket woven from a fur they'd never felt, stitched with symbols they'd never seen. For a second, then, he wants to burn it, the body, everything. Staring into the fire, he hears how it would sound, the crackling hair and hissing skin, and then the last sound the man made is there again, the awful hushing, and he turns to see the rising sun. And knows. He will take the body east, as far down out of his world as he can go, back toward the one the man came from, leave him in the desert far below, far from these mountains, bury him facing Ohio.

All day then he rides down, toward the sun, and under it, and with the shadow of the range across his back, rides with the blanket-bundled man tied behind him on the mule, beds down that night in a high valley he has never seen before, but will leave before first light and ride all day again and the following night make camp farther down the eastern side than he has been in years, the shapes of the pinecones unfamiliar, the rocks unsettling, the sight of antelope fleeing far in the distance like something from another man's dream, the smell of salt and sage strong as his memories. Even the sound of an owl slides akilter from any he knows. But above, the stars are the same. As dense, as countless. The sky of home. Even if from inside his river canyon he could only ever see a sliver. The vast rest had always been there. Will be.

In the morning, he will ride a little farther down, leave the body propped to face the rising sun, then take the mule and rifle and map, the blanket of bird-skins, his knives and pistol and bag of possibles that has always been enough to get him through, and start again. Once more climb west, higher and higher, until he re-crests the mountain and can drop down the other side, into another canyon, follow another river, find another world a little north of the one he thought would hold him till he died. But the mountains are big, the sky wide, the Lokum Yaman wild enough to hide him from even a hundred miners, even a thousand, to let him make another home beneath another sliver of the same sky for another winter, another summer, maybe a year.

Before first light, he has bound the corpse back on the mule, mounted again, the moon gone from the sky, blocked by the bulwark of mountains behind, and in their regained blackness the stars burn bright, as if they know their time is short, can feel the coming thinning. All around him: the soughing of piñon pines blowing in a dry wind, the gusts catching his hair and beard, the feather cloak, a corner of the blanket holding the corpse lifting, flapping, stilling again. In the lulls he can hear wolves. Long arcing howls like the sound of dying stars. He lets the mule find its way down, following the trails of deer, coyote, maybe the wolves passing by in their midnight traversal, now the mule, its hoof clatter and snorts under the distant howls. Another gust blows both away, the slope opening up into sage and scree, the mule's gait increasing, as if it too is eager to unload the body, can feel the coming disburdening, the lightness upon them when they will turn and ascend again into the mountains. Beneath them, steepness slowly slips by, unseeable, and then must drop even more sharply because the mule balks, stops in a skiddering of rocks, their clacking scutter dwindling away under the wind. Listening to them, Silas can feel how far above the plain they must still be, and just catching the jut of an outcropping ahead, a promontory protruding into the sea of stars, he clucks the mule on, across the dark, till they are climbing solid ground again, rising up onto the ledge.

The wind. The stars. The fathomless expanse of emptiness beneath. Facing east, he can feel the drop, and beyond that, in the darkness, the distance. Farther still: the first faint flush of dawn. Way out on the eastern horizon, a breach between the darker land and a swath of sky already thinned of stars, so far over such a vast space he can just make out, in the delimitation between blackness and brightening, the curvature of earth. The wind abates. Out there, the wolves are a meteor shower. If he had his flute, he'd play it. Send back a sound. If he knew a song that could compare, he'd sing it. If he could simply wait there hearing them forever, he would.

There is the gust again. And in its silencing roar he sees a flicker. So distant and fleeting it could be the trace of a star. Then another. Another. All across the farthest stretches to the south: so many small glimmers so near the sky's edge he had mistaken them for its extremity. But they are on the earth, in the vast dark plain. Fires. Dozens of fires. More the more he looks, till he is seeing scores. He sits astride the windblown mule, staring, reins bowed with gusts, cloak rippling with the whiffling of a hundred birds, and by the time the dawn has carved his image from the scarp, the fires have begun to disappear, blinking out like a reflection of the dissolving stars, till both are gone. And in their place an even stranger sense: that the land where the fires had been is shifting, as if a strip of earth out there has broken loose, begun to drift.

Again, the wind abates. The wolves: he listens, listens—gone as the fires, the stars. And in their place, he thinks that he can hear whatever is happening on the eastward horizon, almost like a rockslide crumbling down some distant slope, or the rumble of thunder muffled by so many miles, or the roar of a river too far away to even see.

From where it comes: the first red sliver of the sun, an ember blown by the wind into a brightness such that he has to turn his stare away. And when he does, he sees the dust. A low long cloud clinging to the land, drifting in a wide line all the way across the plain back to the rising sun. As if it might be smoke blown from the fire of that great star. But is not. Is stirred off the ground, churned into air. By what? He cannot fathom. And turning south, starting again across the scarp, riding the mountain's eastern edge ever closer to the distant line of dust, he tells himself the fires must have been made by tribesmen, hunters driving a herd, funneling it into the strange procession stirring the cloud, tells himself it could be, could be, till he cannot.

His body knows—his gut gone sour, his breath chopped short, the ends of his blown fingers throbbing—before he hears it: the clanging, so faint it might have been the cries of a great flock of far-off birds, but isn't; the jangling, so distant it might have been the tail end of a rockslide, but isn't; the clatter and lowing and calls of men that could be nothing but what it cannot be, cannot—before he sees them: the specks too far away to tell they're horses except the way they move; the flitting glint that only spins off wheel spokes; the small white flecks, tiny as larvae carried by a swarm of ants, that are the canvas-covered wagons—before his mind can comprehend what he is witnessing and for a moment stops.

Maybe a second, maybe less. Maybe it is not unlike the hunter chosen to be a jomin collapsing upon hearing the voices of kukinis; maybe it is what comes upon old women in the great cry when they attempt to throw themselves into the fires; maybe what happens to a man's mind when entered by a bohemkuleh; maybe it is just the mountains giving him one more gift. Because when he comes back from it into himself, he knows it's gone: the mountains, the canyons, the rivers, his life.

Down there, where the world he'd fled abuts the one he'd found, where the world that hounded him borders his harbor, the line of carts and cattle and mules and horses and oxen and men goes on as far as he can see, the plain gouged with wagon tracks, beaten by hooves, littered with the leavings of all those who have already passed, their refuse and abandoned bones, broken parts and cast-off weight, and how many had he told himself he could withstand? A hundred? *Even a thousand.* How many times more than that are down there now. Even just the ones he sees in the second or minute or hour that he sits astride the mule watching them come.

Beneath him, the mule shifts, as if still impatient to be freed of its load, but now its head is lifted, neck high, ears cocked at the distance, and without his urging, it starts again toward them. The clatter of its hooves: as if the rest have been brought close. He winces, shuts his eyes, makes his mouth into the shape that should say *whoa*, but doesn't. The thought of his own voice too near the thought of theirs. Instead, he reins the mule to a stop. Drops the straps onto its neck. Lets himself down. The sound of his feet on the stones is nearly bad as the hooves. And then is gone and there is the distant din of all the others' footsteps and that is worse than both. Though the mule is stamping again, as if it would go to them, and looping the lead over a branch, he walks around it, tightening the ropes that hold the corpse, the rifle, cinching the buckles of saddlebags and waterskins, and when he's done, he stands, looks at the mule looking at him. As if it knows what he is going to do. Even before he draws the pistol. The whole time that he waits, staring down at the barrel, he can feel the mule wondering too, though it can't know the men down there are far too far and far too many, can't know the choices he is wrestling with, the possibilities, the potential, the power that is contained in such a small piece of wood and metal, how hard it is for him to give it up when, instead of lifting the muzzle to the mule's head or to his own, he shoves the gun beneath the blanket, wedges it under the ropes, returns it to its owner's father. Then he ties the lead into the reins, tucks up the stirrups and, stepping away, gives the mule a smack.

It jogs a few steps down the slope, the dead man juddering on its back, the shortened stirrups whacking its side, and by the time it stops to look, Silas is already climbing up toward the higher hills, his shoulders lit by the sun, his shadow slipping over the rocks before him as if to lead him back across the pass.

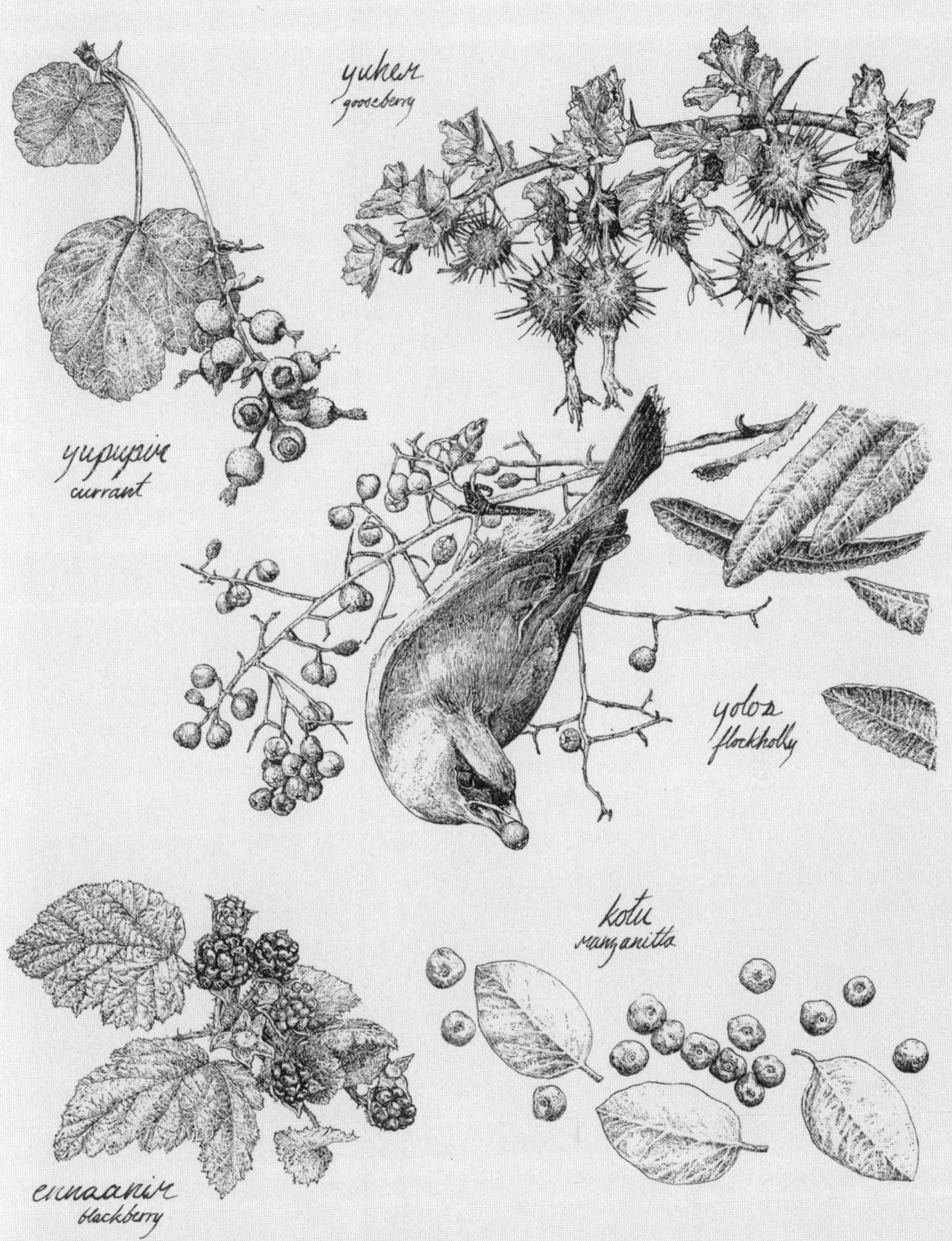
yuker
gooseberry
yupupire
currant
yolos
flockholly
kotu
manzanitta
ennaanir
blackberry

Sometimes I wonder if my heart has left alrdy. Might be alrdy retracing my life's steps. If it has visited the walnut grove outside of town. Found the ground littered with thrown stones bneath decades of leaves. Been in my mother's kitchen & smelled the warming butter. The ashes in the air. Seen her carry the bucket out & freeze in the old feeling of her son watching from somewhere near. If it has watched my father in the parlor lighting his pipe. Pulling a piece of kindling from the flames with his death-scented hands. Seen them shake. An old man's tremor. Sometimes I wonder if it has found your mother. In the same flat where I lived with her. Or if the flat now holds anothr family. How it then will find you. If when it does you somehow will know.

Sometimes it comes upon me you might no longer be there to find. Might have died bfore me & unknown to me & when it comes it comes crushing my chest & clamps my heart & the only way I know it cannot be is that it passes. That I can take a breath. Anothr.

Have you ever felt that? Thinking of anothr's dying? Perhaps your grandfather? Or your grandmother? Or your mother?

Maybe it is a thing only a parent can know for his child. A father. His boy.

See me I said. Begged you. See me. So how

How can I not

The boy the boy his father. To feel that clamp & crushing & inability to breathe & know it will not go away. Maybe it is just

I wish my heart had left already. Left the man I had bcome while I cld still be him. Instead of the one I am again. Maybe then I cld have ended this as I had meant to when I wrote the truth the truth the truth

The truth Elisha is as I sit here writing this I am surrounded by my traps. That I have set myself. The ones I buried dug up again. By me. For men.

'45 '46 '47 '48

The first ones must have come that summer. After I had already gone upriver. As if the world wanted to gift me one last season. Let me live a bit longer in peace. In my oblivion. Before that autumn. When I came back and found their cabin. Built right across my river beneath the effigy's blank stare. A cabin of new-cut logs spewing smoke teeming with men spreading their sounds and scents and presence all through the canyon to my home.

Six miners. Must have come from the confluence below Kushna. Worked their way up to my bend and stayed. Already they had wrecked the bar. Dug holes and trenches. And that first day back I crouched on my ledge watching them shovel and pan and shout and laugh and curse and fish and cook and drink and piss till it was dark and firelight was leaking through gaps in the cabin walls. Cracks in its chimney. The open door bleeding brightness into the ruined night.

I would like you to know I tried. That though each time they swung a pick or shoveled gravel I felt the iron hit my chest, the grit grind in my gut. Though I could hear my river's cries come from the cleaving bank. Feel the effigy's stacked boulders shiver. Still, I did not break. Shut my eyes against the slavered chin and bloody teeth of that blurred face. Refused to meet its stare. Would like you to know that though my home was back and high enough up off the bank to be hidden during the day, I knew to light a fire would bring them to me. Me upon them. And so did not. Despite the cold that night. The rain all the next day. The two three four that I stayed hunkered in my hut. Weeks eating only what meat I had, what plants I could quietly gather. Not even daring to grind my meal, fearing the sound would carry across the canyon to the men. And if they came across themselves? With the rains the river had begun to swell and so I did not think they would. Though I admit part of me wished it. Dreamed up the ways I might then rid the canyon of them. Instead, I left my musket cached, my bow and quiver hung. Might have gone upriver to hunt or made a fire far enough away or found another grinding place and eaten well—but to leave my hut empty? My clearing free? Abandon my river to them? For a day? An hour?

For a week already it had been rising, filling with fall rains same as each year, but if something in me knew it would find a way to free itself of them, it didn't speak till the first freeze. Cellarskins curling their leaves, juncos puffing tiny bodies to twice their size. That night it snowed. The next day the cold lifting just enough shift to a brittle rain. And I knew up higher it would be snowing still, drifts growing deeper, as the deluge down at my home lasted four days, five. A week of cold slanting sheets. Then, suddenly, the coldness easing, the rain coming as steady as before, but warm. So that I knew it would be raining higher up too.

All that snow amassed on frozen ground. All that meltwater with nowhere to go but to the river. All those days of deluge rushing the canyon all at once. All upstream from me, from them, from their cabin built just above the flat they'd worked, the holes and trenches that they'd dug already underwater.

From my bridge tree, I watched it happen. Woke in the night, broken from sleep by the shift in my river's sound, knew soon as I heard its deeper roar. By the time I climbed the tree the water was churning by their cabin, so close its current flashed with firelight from the open entrance. Then it was in, boiling over the floor. The light flickered, flickered out. That woke them. Though the river was too loud to hear their shouts, the night too black to see their fear, I could just catch their scrambling shapes splashing out into the surge, their cries as they were swept away, could watch their bodies pass by beneath me. Before the crash clapped me to the branch, a boom so loud I thought my tree had cracked. But it was the cabin, its logs collapsing into the flood.

By dawn it was gone. Roof and chimney and all four walls and everything they'd done to the bar and everything they'd used to do it. Maybe some lived. I do not know, did not go looking. Spent the day at home, making a fire, drying my hut, leaving only to bring back meat, eat in the peace of the floodwaters' thunder. Two days later it had eased, the river just low enough that, clambering along a toppled tree, I could just get across. The water was still rushing over the site they'd leveled, but I could make out the few things left: two hearthstones shoved down the bank, a spade snagged in an alder, cloth scraps tangling its leaves, a little up the slope the trash they'd thrown behind the building—tins, lids, shards of glass—downriver a half dozen hewn logs caught in a chute. I spent the day working them loose, shoving them into the rapids, watching them tumble away till they'd been carried far enough I wouldn't see them from my home. Rolled the hearthstones so their blackened sides were buried. Untangled the cloth, tugged down the spade, threw them on the trash. A pile that grew over the days as the sun returned and the river waned and I scoured the downstream banks for any sign that remained: the leather casing for a flask; a bit of wire screen; a small square paper, strangely thick and glistening, on which there was an image of a man seated beside a woman, a child standing between. Made with the grays of pencil but in a style nearer to painting. Though it was not. Not possible to paint or draw a likeness quite like that. Peering closer, I saw some of the softness was from the water, a bit like ink spreads when wet. But the child, the child between them: his face was dry. Yet blurred. As if whoever made it hadn't known how to do his features, had captured instead a sense of movement, of his moving, his being alive.

For a while I looked at it in wonder. Then tossed it on the pile and dug a pit and buried it with all the other evidence of them. Though it would be some time before I could quit thinking of the small metal pin I'd found attached to its clasp and spring, a thin circular band strangely elastic and strong, the changes taking place outside my canyon, the way they had one day simply appeared, the way some day ahead I might look up from laying my net or washing my knife and see another paper square floating downriver. Might turn then and see men coming up again.

And you will see me sitting here, still scribbling, surrounded by traps, hacking at trees while I wait for the rest to find me. Will see my white-streaked beard matted as if grown thick for winter, my mangled hand like a snared paw, two toes chewed off. Will think I could have gnawed through the rest and simply fled. Some other canyon, another river. But I have climbed a canyon and come to a tree-carved sign I could not read and felt the firmness of that boundary, have stood by another river and watched its mist swallow my shadow and known it wished to disappear the rest of me. For how could I abandon a world that had accepted me and then expect another to? Another where I'd be first of my kind again. Babies staring, their mothers screaming. Woole! Woole! Unless it was a place they didn't yet know the word. Which would be worse.

Was. Is. I hear you think it. No Rope and the hu'uku and Kushna. This canyon I came to, this river that took me in, this world that I refuse to leave: theirs long before I ever knew that it was here. All that its loss might mean to me multiplied a thousand times in them, again in all the villages nearby—Wokodot, 'Ustoma, C'hakankan—in all the other tribes—Notong K'oyom, Monaa—and in the bear and deer and fisher-cat and coon, salmon and heron, and all the trees and grasses too, mosses and lichens, and maybe the year that I came here I should have stayed camped down on the bar where the men who will come for me are camped now, maybe I should never have moved to higher ground, maybe the floods that came that winter just came too late.

If I could, I would tell the cedars and cottonwoods and boulders and bars and all that suffers me that I am sorry. If anything in all my canyon, my river, my world, would ever have had reason to even know that word. You will dismiss even the thought, but I have heard how my world speaks, heard it in the effigy watching over me year after year, in the way a cliffside once caught a posse so that I might escape, and in the boy that it once brought me, the miners it swept away along with every trace, then kept the rest at bay another k'ummen, yoomen, long enough to gift me one more summer, let me pack up my winter camp again, bury my cache, and leave.

How could I? How could I have felt it so strongly in my gut that that spring I took my musket upcountry for the first time in years.

To protect what, if not what I had left behind? How could I have covered that cache with extra care, recalling signs that, back in the Rockies, caught the eyes of men like me, and then abandoned my own home? How could I, a few days upriver, come upon some village women hunting morels, kicking wet leaves beneath a stand of cellarskins, and seen one in a skirt—red-checked cloth flapping before her scuffing feet—and not turned back?

Sitting here now inside my ransacked hut, the door-flap shot through with bullet holes, the river beyond rising again, its roar growing louder and louder, as if it wants an answer too, I have none. For it. Or you. Or me. Or the owls I once brought near my hut with hoots. Who now do not return my calls. The woodpecker whose knocking no longer echoes through my clearing. The heron who, in all the days since I came back, I have not seen. What would I say? To the cedars above me, the cottonwood whose golden leaves each autumn welcomed me home? My home, my river, my canyon? What can I tell them? Except I failed them. As I failed you.

But oh that summer! That one last summer. How could I give up summer high on the headwaters of my river, in my canyon, alone for one more season? One more 'okomen to myself. Myself. The self I was—I swear I was, son—before I failed him too.

AUTUMN, 1849

He climbs up the slope, away from the mule and the plain and the dust and the world in which it boils up beneath an inexorably rising sun, all around him the rocks and sage stained by its red light, his shape beneath the black-feathered cloak slipping up and up, over the land, like the shadow of some bird riding a gust blown off the scene below, the sounds it carries snapping at his heels, until he climbs over the rise and the ridge behind him blocks the wind and sun, and for a moment, there is only his breath and footsteps as he scrambles down into a shadowed swale still chilled with last night's air, as if it would resist the turning of the world. Then he is climbing again, back into sun and wind and sound. The way that it will be for miles, over ridges and up creeks and along the folds of foothills, until the Lokum Yaman can amass enough mountain between him and the world beyond to hide any last sign of what he'd seen.

By then it will be midday, noon of the next before he reaches the crest, crosses back to the western side, two days more before he makes the headwaters of his river. See him then beside the cataract that spills down from the lake, on a boulder above a pool just deep enough that he can leap, become a sliver slipping through emerald water, climb crashing out to lie flat in the sun, the freezing air, the last warmth in him lifting off his slowly drying shape like mist. See him turn over to dry his other side, one fist clenched, the other stiff in its wet bandage, his body wracked with shivering, but his face at peace.

Crossing the mountains he had been glad to find that, closer to home, the cold had come without the snow, the ground frozen just enough to hide his prints. Had kept clear of any other human sign, though there were times he thought he caught the distant glint of metal, nights when the wind brought whispers of what he knew was passing to the south, less sound than a disturbance in the atmosphere, so when at last he'd reached his river, had been about to crest the ridge, he'd paused, the canyon still out of sight, stood there, his feather cloak cowled against the cold, unable to take another step, afraid to see what might be inside those walls.

But there was only the river. Only the river and its roaring filling the air. Only the river and its roaring and the ever-taller canyonsides cut through a hundred feet of earth, then three, then half a thousand, barriers of stone and soil, trees leaning over the gorge as if they would protect it even more, catch anything beyond the ridges that might try to come down. But there is only the river and its roaring and the canyonsides and hawks riding the drafts as they have always done, showing no sign that they see anything but what has always been there. Only the river and its roaring and the canyon walls and the hawks and the clouds and the sky and the sunlight coming through the moss on the leaning oaks, and the otters stopped in its shimmer to watch, and the world as it was, the world and the shimmer and the roaring of the river and him.

And see him rising shivering on the rock, gathering his buckskins, leaping to the bank, emptying his tinder bag of a smoldering piece of punky wood, blowing it into a flame beneath a ledge blackened by all the other fires he has lit there before. See him by its light, reapplying the gleaming pitch, wrapping his wound. And on another night, over another fire, learning to use his remaining fingers and thumb well enough to carve a gig, pry pine nuts from a roasted cone. Again and again, a long line of fires flickering to life all down the length of Chapakakum Sew, from its source to his home, each one containing a little of the one before, so by the end his tinder bag holds inside it all of the river. And see him in the cold blue before the sun has reached into the canyon, moving through a shaking stand of manzanita, pausing his shucking of the rusty berries to blow gray breath over his hands. Hear the whoop he makes lifting a speared eel out of the eddy above a weir he built last spring, the hooting he sends back at an owl in the black of night, the booming *hoo hoo-hoo hoo hoo* of man and bird growing closer until they are beside each other, the owl in the tree above, continuing its calling while he falls asleep. Watch him return as if in dream along the track of his existence, rock by rock, rapid by rapid, memory by memory—old camps and oxbows and ancient oaks and stacks of boulders—as if he has already left his body, become his heart.

It is early November, the start of the long rains, the time of weeks of deluge between short breaks of sun, already past the point when the downpours should have begun. But the clouds roll on. The sky stays clear. The stars fill in above the canyon as if it is October, the water in the daylight limpid and jewel-like as September. Though at night it is so cold that were the rains to come they'd come as snow. Even as he works his way down to the lower elevations where it rarely falls. He wraps himself in the bird-skin cloak, sleeps near the fire, keeps fuel close. And in the morning smothers the flames, covers the coals, hiding each sign of his passing carefully as he would a cache.

Days, he moves downriver amid the sun-steamed frost, his footprints on the stones dark in the silver sheen, then fading as it lifts, gone as he moves on. Sometimes he comes across things that he'd left: a fringe of rawhide strips dangling from branches, the buckeyes he'd tied to each end long disappeared; the giant root ball of a toppled oak woven with redbud shoots into a huge maroon circle; a boulder spotted with chips chiseled all over its smooth sides. It takes him a long time to remove each strip of rawhide, cut the roots free of redbud shoots, and how many years will it take for rain and floods to wash the boulder smooth? A century? A millennium?

Under the snakeskin-dangling alder, there is enough frost that, sitting in the predawn dark, he can watch the moltings glow with both moonlight and its reflected gleam. Can, in first sun, sit among their strangely transparent shadows cast over the hoary ground. Then in the evaporating mist, walk beneath the branches cutting all the snakeskins down. Down at the river, he lets them go, one by one, into the current. The coming floods will wash away the white circle of quartz. Same with the barrow still mounded over the corpse. The boy's body as well. For a while Silas stands beside all that remains of the three wooles who came into his world three weeks ago. Then he bends down, begins rolling rock after rock away, till the hide-wrapped body lies reeking in the sun, ready for the rain. Later, far downriver, he will pass below the place where he had woken under the net-caught doves, his eyes searching the ridge as if he might yet see the speck of one last bird held still. But when it comes, it will be flying, a small dark spot flitting through, and then another, and then a third, appearing out of the unseen sky beyond the canyon's walls like emissaries from a still-turning world.

Tomorrow, and another day, month, year, and here, on this one bend of river, there will be a hundred men, in the camp a mile down a thousand, ten times that amassed along the entire Chapakakum Sew, climbing up every creek like some furious flood reversed. Except it will not ease, only grow worse. The clangs of spades broken by black-powder booms, their echoing subsumed by the thunder of water cannons blasting the banks, the canyonside cleaving away in sheets, crumbling down toward stamp mills standing like iron boulders, their massive maws smashing the rock into a slurry sent through sluices, those few riffles of quicksilver-sickened water all that will be left. The river gone. Its bed drained, its flow rerouted to fill the flumes instead, high troughs snaking along the canyon's contours like creeks suspended in midair, their scaffolding tall as the bridges that each year appear spanning another crossing. Behind them, the sky will never quite clear of smoke. As if, just out of sight, all the villages of all the tribes in all the Lokum Yaman have gathered for a great cry. But they will be gone too. The villages replaced by towns, the smoke come from the factories and mills and chimneys of all the engulfing mass of wooles who will overspill these hills, all the thousands of those others who lived here before soon sickened and starved and slaughtered down to a final few. Which will be more than the wolves or elk or mountain sheep, before long only their kukinis left to roam these ridges and ravines. Alongside the last of the grizzlies, a lone panom who will refuse to give up its heart to those who wrought this. Until, sometime after the turning of the century, they'll take it anyway.

But not its memory. Not from the massif at the crest, its clustered peaks still standing against the sky, or from the ancient pines high out of reach growing still older, or from the three stacked boulders still here beside the river, the effigy that has stood watching the turning of the world since it emerged from the receding sheets of ice, has seen the first appearance of elk and sheep, the changing shapes of wolves and bear, has watched the Lokum Yaman since before humans were here, will watch it still, waiting for their time to turn as well.

By dawn of the last day of Silas's long passage, the sky will have turned too, the strip above the canyon covered in clouds thin as his breath, glimmers of stars still showing through, though by the time they have faded away, the clouds will have begun to gather, massing all morning as if drawing on the breathing of all the beings below. Beneath their growing weight he moves through an increasing quietude—willows unstirred by any breeze, ghost pines motionless up on the ridges, birds withdrawn from sight—a stillness that with each hour closer to home seems stranger. Not just the lack of miners, but the absence of anyone, Nisenan or white. All the long journey it has seemed the river kept itself for him, as if it knew this would be their last trip together, though by the time his feet begin to know the rocks, his body the feel of home, he cannot but wonder if his solitude has not been caused by anything his world had wished, but what the miners downriver might have done to it.

There is the big pine still caught where it had crashed across last winter: his bridge. There is the bend of wider water, the willows and bit of beach. There, high above it, the three stacked boulders, looming huge as ever, the topmost seeming somehow heavier, as if filled with whatever it has seen since he's been gone, the sheer slab of its smooth face not merely facing upriver but watching, waiting, for him.

Hoofprints in the clearing. The paths he'd cut though the tall grass churned up. One of the granaries knocked on its side, its acorns spilled. Between them and the hut, the mound of dead men's things is scattered, picked through by the posse, or other miners after, or anybody from Kushna. It does not matter. Better little is left: a few playing cards (the boy's?), an empty tobacco tin (the father's?), a broken mouth harp (the man who he'd tried to warn first?), strewn like the leavings of some flood that had swept through. But for the scat of dogs, their pawprints in front of the hut's door. Holes shot in the elk-hide flaps. Inside: his hat lying blasted apart beneath the broken antler it once hung from, the wall behind it pocked and splintered, the floor strewn with baskets, skins. Between the blankets he'd laid over the mats, the bare place where the boy's blanket had been is littered with the dirt dug from the hole in which he'd hid the small tin box, the wooden case, the packet wrapped in canvas. Now lying beside the hole, unwrapped: the stack of paper slid sideways, pages scattered across the floor, his drawings—birds, plants, pieces of his world—lying there in attestation to a time that once had been, now stamped with signs of the same creatures they depict: mouse prints, piss stains, a few small pellets, some edges chewed. But there. To be gathered up again, flattened smooth, placed back in the stack of all the rest. All but one. Which he takes from his possibles, unfolds and sets on top. Where it had been. Rebinds the package, rewraps its canvas, sets it on the stretched-skin table beneath the small square window. Rights the toppled stool. Rehangs the hat.

It takes him longer with his half-hand, and by the time he has replaced the baskets and tools, refolded the skins, repaired his bed of branches and grass, is dragging the wool blankets out, the day is at least a couple hours later, whether before noon or after impossible to tell beneath a sky so dark there is not even a hint of sun, not even shadows thrown by canopy or hut or him as he works with an urgency odd under the stillness of the leaves, the air not even stirred by enough breeze to turn the blue-petaled pinecones hanging off branches by their peduncles, the feathers dangling from the driftwood tree. As if they all are rapt with watching as, searching the high grass, he gathers the scattered remnants of the other men, bundles them in the wool blankets, hauls each down to the rocks, uncovers his winter cache.

Across the river, high on the stack of boulders, the huge stone face stares down on the small figure crawling into a crack in the ground, dragging out the dark and heavy pelt cut from an animal many times his size. Though it is not until he's carried the buffalo robe back to his hut, the blanket of rabbit skins, his winter moccasins and good furs, cookpots, cups, the spade and splitter and felling axe, enough to almost cover up the sense of others; not until he has returned to shove the bundles of all their leavings into the cache; is only then—lifting a blanket, the scent of mule sweat bringing the memory of the father's hushing before he died—that Silas feels the gaze. Looks up at the great looming face. And hears the voice. There, in the still air, high enough above the river to just break through its roar. One single sound. A bellow, a shout, a whoop of joy. There and gone. Buried again beneath the stillness. Too brief to know more than that it came from a man. Somewhere downriver. And yet that close.

All afternoon he sets the traps—smooth jaws sized for beaver, bigger for wolves, a few huge enough to hold a bear, jagged with teeth—stands spread-legged over the springs and sets the dog, secures the chain, moves to the next. Each one he hides much as he might have done before, but with no lure. No musk and castor, no urine sprinkled beside the jaws. Just sets each in a place he would expect a man to step—the end of the stone path across his creek, the track to Walloki's cave, the first place a man would reach climbing the rockface up from the river—working outward into the woods, digging up old deer trails, burying traps in forest gaps wide enough to ride through on a horse, until he has surrounded his home with over a score of steel jaws gaping in wait.

Each place he flags with bits of fur, markers only someone who knew to look might see, is setting his last, up by the fallen pine he'd crossed that morning from the far bank, clearing his own prints away, when it begins to snow. A thing so seldom seen down at his winter home he would have thought the flakes bits of blown milkweed or even feathers, if they had not kept coming, melting into dark spots. He sits back, tilts his face up. Watches them fall from high over the canyon all the way to him, watches until it seems the sound of the river is the sound of them, then shuts his eyes, opens his mouth, feels their touch, cold and ethereal, on his brow, cheeks, lids, lips, as if they would keep on until they covered him in white, his crouched shape become part of the canyon. But when he opens his eyes, he is just wet, the stones just darker stones, the pine becoming the same wet-dark log last winter's floods brought down.

As if from nothing, he had said. And No Rope had shaken his head, said the rain, the cold, the snow high up, the wedge of bank come loose, the wall it made. *Blocking the river*, the hu'k told him. Damming the water above the downstream camp. *Until it broke.*

Then he is standing, turning, stones loud beneath his feet.

It takes him five minutes to come back with the axe. Thirty seconds to pick the tree. On the far bank: an alder, close enough to the water the fallen pine had sheared off a limb when crashing down, tall enough that it would reach all the way across the river when it falls.

The first whack cracks the snow-quiet, breaks over the canyon, echoes back to him, jaw clamped against the pain knocked though his wounded hand. And in the second of silence after, he breathes hard out his nose, grits his teeth, swings again. He holds the axe in his right fist, uses his left two fingers and thumb to grip the handle just enough to stop it flinging free, takes more swings than he would wish to notch the trunk. But does. Then steps around to the bank-facing side, sends another crack ricocheting down the canyon. Past his home. And in the last light of the fast-falling dusk, he stands there swinging the axe like the sharp cracks are the clangs of a bell, and he holding the hammer, ringing it. Crack: come! Crack: come!

When the hinge gives way, he steps back—the tree falling through its own thrashing to crash upon the rocks across the river—listens to the silence after. Nothing but the same rushing of water. Though not for long. He hears the thought as if the river says it. As if it is reminding him how late it is in fall, how soon the rains will come, how much louder it will rage then. And in its rush, he hears it speak to him again, turns back to the bank to cut another.

That night, he walks across on his own work. A tall ash, a thick cedar, the alder. All smashed together, pushed up against the pine, locking their branches into a wall, the water upriver churning against the jam, finding its way through, but deepening too, widening just a little, already starting to build.

A house of logs, he'd said to No Rope that night three weeks ago, *just like the one they're building on the bar now.*

Back at his clearing, he stands in the near dark, axe in one hand, the other throbbing, the snow become just a softness on his skin, a hush in the trees. Stilling his breath, he listens harder farther downriver—*Did you see their logs go past? Their bodies?*—but there is no sound except the rushing water, and letting himself breathe again, he listens to it a while longer—the heat of the chopping leaving his body, his hand on the axe handle growing cold—then turns and goes in through the elk-skin flap.

Inside, he unwraps the moldering chunk taken from the past night's fire, places it in the hearth, working by feel, carefully setting his tinder, bending to blow. When he has it caught, he adds some slightly larger sticks, unbinds his wound, sets the freshly bloodied bandage aside, spreads his fingers before the flames. Strange to see the silhouetted stubs: his hands like those of another creature. Or maybe just a man's made from a slightly marred mold. He reaches for a bigger piece of wood, places it on the flames, and with the bloom of firelight sees two bright eyes, huge and round in the effulgence, watching from the corner pantry.

Hello, he says—"Homaa kani"—a smile breaking over his face. Holds out his hands, unfolds his fingers, asks, "What do *you* think?"

The ringtail doesn't so much as blink. Or move when he gets up. Just watches him step to the table, retrieve the bear-fat lamp, as if it thinks it might be something to eat.

"Sorry," he tells it, and knows that he should get himself some sustenance, but simply stands, the unlit lamp in his hand, looking down at the table. The open pack of papers on it. The case of pens and tin of ink.

Lighting the lamp with a burning stick, he brings it back to the table, sits on the upturned log. The large flickering of the firelight around the hut, the small flickering of the lamp on the tin as he lifts off the top, pulls out a canister of powdered ink, taps a bit into the stone bowl beside it, mixes in a little water, a little more.

Reaching to the stack of papers with his hurt hand, he lifts the map he'd laid on top, as if he would set it aside, but sits there holding it, the lines of the three rivers catching the lamp's flicker so, for a moment, they almost look wet. The mountain peak. The creases make it fall over his fingers, and then again, so finally he turns it over as if he might find something different on the back. It is as blank as ever.

"Ohio," he says.

But when he dips the pen and writes, it is the word *Elisha.* Then *Hall.* Then *In the care of* and his father's name, his mother's. The town, the state, where he'd grown up.

Gently he blows over the words, beard hairs faintly fluttering. Blows until the ink is dry. Then lifts the page, sets it aside. Beneath it: a drawing of the ringtail.

"Look," he says, "it's you."

But the ringtail's eyes are gone. For a moment more he peers into the darkness where it had been. Then, drawing another page from the thick stack—six moths around a rattle made of their dried cocoons—turns the paper over and begins.

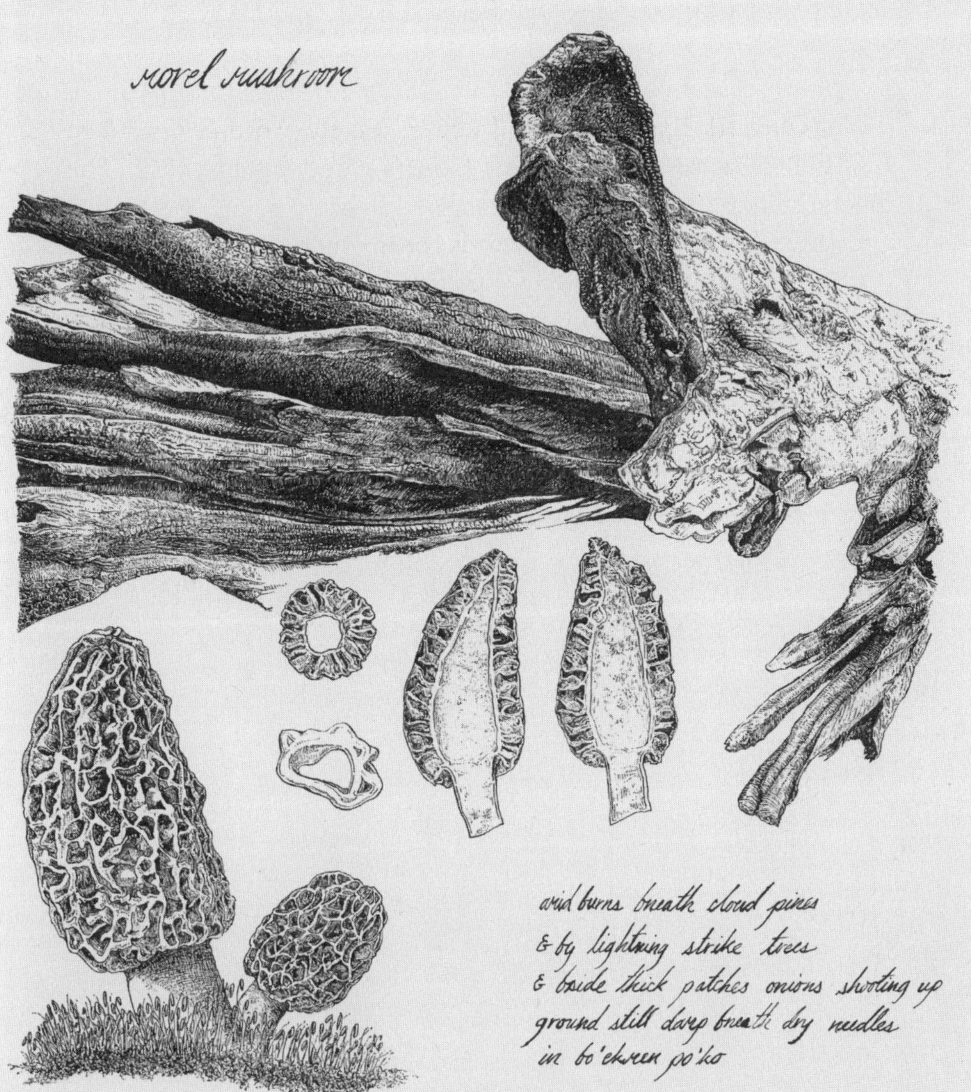
morel mushroom
arid burns bneath cloud pines
& by lightning strike trees
& bside thick patches onions shooting up
ground still damp bneath dry needles
in bo'ekwen po'ko

It has begun to rain again. Loud on the roof. Loud in the trees above. Loud on the ground. Bneath the farther loudness of my river. And through it I can still hear the other. The distant clanking coming from downstream that day. Now near a mnth ago. A sound unlike any that shld have been in that high country. A small sharp clanking over & over. Coming closer. Growing clearer. Till it was all that I cld hear.

A mule's bit? A metal tool tapping a stirrup?

Voices. Yes I still hear them too. 2 men. A boy.

Pa, he says. Says, Look Pa. Says, Pa you ever seen a place so pretty?

I have been thinking about what brought me. Not why I left but how it was that I came here. What made me cross the ohio. The missouri. The rockies. The great basin & salt sinks & sierra's crest. I have been wondering what drew me.

Do you remember the way Walloki ran through the woods? Stopping only long enough to light a fire to see which way the spirits blew the smoke? To hear them call him to each new place? Did you wonder how he knew where to find the bear? Or how it was he came to me? The people here say the kukinis live in lonely places. Caves & mountains & marshes & lakes. That when someone is meant to be a jomin the spirits draw him to them. That men have been known to walk into woods & disappear. Found days later face down in the duff bneath a giant pine. Or floating unconscious in a distant pond. Or sitting on a rock in the middle of a raging river unable to recall how they got there. And I cannot help but remember the fits I wld fall into when I was young. The rage that wld sweep over me. The flame agnst my skin. The blackness crashing down. The way I wld for hrs aftr remain unable to recall what I had done. Cld only see that frenzied face. Its stare on me. Wanting what? Telling me what? And once I ran down city streets at dawn only to wake in a deer bed inside a copse having slept ½ the day. And I have closed my eyes lying beneath a stone on the cold bottom of the ohio where I should have died and come to instead warmed by a fire on that river's western bank. And shot in the shoulder where did I blindly run to but here?

I am not saying I was called to be a jomin. Called to be anything. But me. The people here believe the kukinis have the ability to see into the distance. By which they mean the future and the past. But also simply far away. Beyond the edges of the world. Even as far as they would have had to see in order to see me. Standing outside our door. Listening for the flutter of a moth's wings. Before I lifted my head away and went down the stairs and walked out of the city and across the Monongahela and turned west.

Why do they call you? The spirits. Why do they draw you to their home? Why unless they need you. Unless there is something they need you to do.

And now you see it. The three figures standing in the roaring of my river staring across the darkness of the water hearing me scream. A sound I know you will hear too. Will now be for you the sound of me. Of your father coming apart. Again.

Could be a catamount, one says.

Another: Too low.

The boy: Think it's a man?

A boy. A boy about the same age as you.

It comes upon me, I said. Said, Crushing my chest, clamping my heart. The thought of you somehow already dead. And it is true. But true too, Shash, that when I feel it, I do not see you. But him. His face. Beneath the hole. The bullet hole. The bullet hole blown through his skull. By me.

Hey! his father calls across the river. Hey, you okay? You need help?

And I record his words with the same hand that pulled the trigger. That killed his son. And him. And the other.

The first night after they'd come, I sat under two dozen snakeskins strung from the branches of an alder, hunched and rocking as I hadn't done in years, hands pressed to my ears, trying to unhear the men, the boy, the mules' braying, the dog barking, the sounds of a language I hadn't heard since Ballou's last *Give me the gun*, trying to unfeel the pit they'd dug already in the gravel beach, the seep of water, the swirl of sand filling the hole, leaking through my stomach lining, grinding against my mind. Trying to keep it only on the moonlit moltings, their soothing swaying, the feeling of the breeze. Fighting to take that into me, make it calm me, keep from breaking. Fighting and failing.

And you will watch me crashing down the blackness of that bank, and hear my scream, and see it in my face—the bloodstained teeth, the spit-flecked cheeks, that rage-filled stare returned—and think all I've told you till now a waste. And maybe then it would be easier for you to understand what I would do, for me to tell you, if that was true. If you could replace the man writing to you with one you might remember, believe I succumbed to the same unsoundness that so long ago drove me away, in the end simply regressed into the self I'd been. Maybe then I could blame it on him too. That boy in the mirror come back out of the black to reclaim me after all. But the truth is, he did not. The truth is, I stopped. Still on my bank, still across the water from them. Stopped and stood there breathing, silent again. Still clear of mind. Still me.

That night I waited in the dark, listening to each burst of chatter break through the buffer of my river, each shard of laughter a stutter in its roar, till finally they settled down to sleep. For now. I crouched there in the absence of their sound, eyes shut tight against the light of their too-slowly fading fire, feeling the cold air blown off the water, the willows shifting with the breeze, the night shaping the canyon back into the canyon around me, the river the river, my world my world, as it would never be again. Unless

Last fall the river had disappeared the others, given us another year, and I listened for some hint that it might do the same again. But there was just the lower roar of it still waiting for the rains, just the feeling of the current passing, the sense of its unsettled surface listening back, the boulders watching, the willows stilled, the gaze of the stars. Clear as the one I'd known so long ago, inside the study where I'd sheltered as a child, the feeling come through the ceiling, in from the window, of the old elm.

Still, I tried. Though I knew to warn them would be to risk all the rest. To let them go would be to fail everything else. Still, I slit the dog's throat first. Though it was nearer the creatures of my world than were the men. Though stroking its side as it leaked its last life, my fingers shaking too much to safely clean my knife, I was sure it would have been easier for me to do to one of them. Though the next night, after they'd refused to heed my sign and I'd crept back into their camp, I'd find that I was wrong.

He came to me. The one who'd begun to leave, been drawn back by the others' shouts, who sat that night hunched by the fire on the last watch till, loosing the mules into the trees, I lured him out. He came cautiously along the bank, gripping a rifle tight, muttering something—it couldn't be, but was—in Nisenan. Some sounds wrong, words missing, but enough for me to recognize the chant I'd heard lone villagers intone against the presence of a bohemkule. Where had he learned it? This blackly mustached man, dark as a half-breed. The questions rising in me then, each shaping him differently, so that—holding their spade at the ready—I might not have managed to do what I had come to, might have stood still letting him pass, had he not sensed some glint or shiver in the black night beside him and looked at me.

The crack of the shovel-head against his skull—too loud—the clatter of his falling, starting to moan, the crunch of the steel spade slammed down again—too loud—his kicking boots, the gravel clacking, the shovel meeting his face again.

In the quiet after: a shout. One of the others, back at the fire.

Another, higher, the boy: What is it?

Get up: his father.

And, under the cover of their footsteps, I retreated into the trees, waited for them to pass, crossed back beneath the last of the night still hovering above the river.

No, not easier—the man's last mumbled prayer to ward off danger, the moan come from his smashed-in mouth, the sight of father and son finding the body, their faces wavery with torchlight, the boy turning away so fast his motion flutters the flame—but no harder either.

And you will think of Ballou, mark this my second murder, begin to count ahead—how many more to come—and I would only ask you count the others too, each otter and beaver, coon and quail, try to see me through the eyes of my own world, my life no more defined by the taking of others' lives than catamount or bear would define itself by the taking of mine. And yet a man, you'll say, a man. As if we weren't another animal. Though were you to sit here in my stead, feeling the throbbing in this hand, you couldn't help but see the similarity in blood, bones, flesh, breath, heart, mind, death, life. So why, then, should taking the life of our own kind be worse? Because we do not eat the meat? Cure the hide? Would it be better if I did? Or is it because I'm meant to recognize myself in other men? But if I do in a bear or bird instead? And still need to eat, defend my river, protect my canyon, preserve my home. No, surely if there's a wrong in taking a man's life, it's not in what is done to him but what the taking does to those he leaves behind. A wife? A mother? A mining partner? A boy seeing such a thing for the first time?

If only they had packed up and left, carried the warning with them downriver, perhaps held off the rest for one more winter. Or so I'd thought, hoped, while from the shadows of the far bank I watched them do neither.

That night the boy would see it again. Though this time his own father. Or so he believed. I do not think if he had known my shot had failed to kill the man, he would have chased after me. Would not have crossed the river, found the quartz circle bright with moonlight. Would not have been struck still by all those thousand glints. And I would not have seen him standing there, bent over what I'd made, his shoulders tight, face full of what? Wonder? Would not have caught in it the memory of another boy taking in his first sight of a drawing I'd done for him. For you. So much younger, so long ago. But something in the face the same.

Maybe I made a sound. Maybe when he looked at me, he saw only the man who'd killed his father. Maybe I would have already fired if, seeing his face, so close, so lit by moonlight, it had not hit me that he must be nearly the same age as you.

No, I do not think if he had known his father was still alive, he would have raised his gun, reached for his trigger. Do not think I would have pulled mine either. But I did.

What was it that I said? That if there is a wrong in taking another's life, it's not in what's done to him but what the taking does to those he leaves behind. I had been thinking of the boy's father. But he is now dead too. Instead, I should have been thinking of you. Of me.

And what then will this long missive do to you should you somehow receive it? Discover after a dozen years your father's specter speaking to his son again?

I think if the kukinis called me, it must have been because they knew. Knew I had once already left the thing I cared for most. I think they called me here because they knew I would not do it again.

And so I sit. Here in my home. Encircled by my own traps. Waiting for the drumming hooves, the thud of bootsteps running, a scream.

Upriver the trees are already booming, the crash of each one coming down shaking the ground all the way to here. To me. My pen. There. There again. Another laid across the river. Between the thunder of them falling, the ceaseless chopping. No Rope at last having gotten the tools he'd once wanted to get from me. How many axes had he traded for? From the sound, at least a dozen. A dozen Nisenan making short work of what I started a week ago. Maybe more since I began felling the trees, building my dam. Now No Rope's, too. This morning his men simply appeared, announced by their thwacks breaking between the rain, as if all week they'd watched me with my bad hand and single axe and at last determined it was too big a job for just one man. By dusk they will be done. Will leave the woods again to the rain's racket. Or perhaps the whisper of snow. Though nothing compared to what must be happening higher up.

It has been cold. Cold enough the past few nights the rain on the roof has changed to sleet. Cold enough farther upriver the ground will have become a sheet of ice, the snow above it begun to build.

There. See? Another boom. If you look closely, you can track them across the page. All the words between written to the sound of axes. Though, sitting here, listening to the hacking, I like to think instead it is the trees themselves, the old pines cracking their own hinges to crash across the water, the wind blowing their bodies where it wants them to lay, the canyon finishing for me what I had meant to do for it, the two of us now with nothing left to do but to wait. Wait for the river.

Though it will come too late for me. Surely the trees' thunder will draw the miners from their camp. To here. Here where I sit by the fire writing as I've done since I came back. Done little else. Eaten what I could find that I had left. Slept just enough to get up and write again. The only break my leaving to chop down a few more trees. Something that now for me is done.

How many days has it taken to write to here? Seven? Eight? I have lost track. How many years are in these pages? All you have lived? All that I have? When I was last up on the crest—found that cabin, followed those wagon tracks—it gave me peace to think they'd be mere hints in a few years, hardly visible in a few more, would eventually disappear. Now I know they'll be here long after me. But it gives me solace to know what a short time that is. To the mountains. The Lokum Yaman. The canyon. The river. The world. The world that for a short time made room for me.

A space, I said before. Between the shapes of other creatures. Not left by the Nisenan who live high up out of the canyon, but shaped only for me. Which I believe. Though it is true too that no matter whether it meant to draw me or I simply stumbled upon it, it was a different place before I came. That by stepping into the shape it left me I made a claim not so unlike the ones who stake theirs now. Except I was the first.

Of you, No Rope said. So many more of you.

And no matter how many rawhide strips I might untie, how many redbud shoots I cut away, how many snakeskins I feed to the current, how many corpses I uncover so vultures and wolverines can rid the river of the remains. No matter how soon the water might rise and sweep away the rest, erase the ashes of my fires, last of my footprints. Even if the felled trees hold and the dam fills, and when it breaks, the flood sweeps down, sudden and fierce as I hope, and smashes all below away. Even if, crashing down toward the miners' camp, it takes mine with it—these walls, this chimney, the stones of my hearth, every last sign of me—even then I cannot erase the fact that for all I've done, after all this world has done for me, I could not keep it safe. From what I know is now to come. Which for all the ways that I have failed is surely the worst.

Oh, if I were a jomin, if I was truly called by a kukini, if I had in me what this world would truly need, then I would sing—to all those like me, every miner in the camp or climbing higher or yet to come—would open their chests, chant to their hearts, leave their bodies collapsed on gravel, splayed on banks, scattered down the canyon by the hundreds, thousands, however many it might take. All of them, all of them. Including my own.

Instead I sit here, knowing soon I'll hear them come for me. The crashing clatter of men riding upriver. Their shouts and hollers. Yap of their dogs. All the wrongness of their presence here in my home, my world, even my thoughts, even this sentence.

How many more do I have left? How many hours or minutes or less before I lift this pen and dip it, only to find the time allotted me to speak to you is done. Not even enough left to finish a sentence. Or sign my name. Or say goodbye. Before they

I have just realized. Up at that cabin on the lake east of the crest? Why had I wondered what happened to the man who lived there? What could have happened but that he died? Had gone out hunting or to check his traps or just to get a little air, and not come back. Who would there be to bury him? To know?

If I had time, I'd mark my door black with a bit of coal, sit beside myself a while, try to draw my face. If I had time and a mirror. If

I had any idea anymore of what I look like. Any more than what you do.

Though the other night I could have sworn that you were here. Could feel it. Either in dream or after waking. It was not clear, I am not clear. Because if I was dreaming, I was able to see myself asleep, slumped over this stack of paper, cheek to the page. Beside me, the slush lamp burning low. Behind me: you. Though I could not see your body or face. Maybe refused to. Lay awake trying to make my breath steady and slow as sleep, knowing if I looked behind me, I'd find your heart had reached me first, that seeing it would make it true. Which I would not do—no matter how long you stared—would not turn and see the hoof-mark crushing your chest, your wet hair and iced-over eyes, the crow perched on your shoulder reaching its beak into the hole blown through your skull. A fluttering. I jerked up off the table, whipped around, found only the empty hut, the fire low, the slush lamp guttering, the door-skin settling. Or had it been already still? In the half-light I couldn't tell, could only know I'd felt a presence, the kind I have felt all my life, though this one did not spark or press or leave me with anything but the certainty it had been there. Watching, waiting. For what? Show me your heart, Walloki's grandmother had sung. Minki honi cheti. Open your heart, his father had taught him. Minki honi nik meti. Words I can still hear him chant watching the grizzly standing there spreading its arms, baring its chest.

Your heart, my heart, our hearts.

As if it was a thing unclaimed by either boy or bear. Belonging only to the world that they both shared.

Minki honi, niki honi, nisekim honi.

As if in death it could not be given any more than taken. Would just remain.

Watch me then. I would leave you this pendant. No Rope's gift to me to keep me safe. Which I no longer need. Will set it here, as if a paperweight, a gift to you should you come back. Or for whoever might find this letter. The lead ball and sinew atop the map. The address scrawled on back. The last of the mixed ink. The little powder I have left. The pens and the table of stretched skin, and this log seat, and all the baskets and nets and everything hanging from the antlers jammed in the walls, and the walls, and my hearth, and the fire. I would even give you the fire if I could. But it belongs to this world here as much as your father.

Shash, I hope you have another. I hope he calls you son. I hope he is a better man than I have been. Or at least good enough that when you were a little younger, he might have held you, brushed your hair, given you a hug. A good enough father that you might have wanted to hold him back.

Oh, go, go, heart. Go, I am already dead. Go now while you can still get out and find my boy and bring me something of him back. A word. A word in his voice. I do not care what one. The feeling of his hand when he holds it out to grip. The color of his beard if it has started to come. A bit of his heart. What it feels when he walks beneath a full moon in winter or dangles his feet in a creek in summer or sees a drawing that he likes or smells wet ink or horses put up in a barn at night or remembers me or hears a song that makes him want to hum along or anything, anything, anything he wants.

The boom, the boom, the rain, the river.

Can you hear it? The wind in the pines? The nearer rustle of oak leaves? The drizzle filling in between them both. The fire softer. The scratch of my pen.

This. This in the end is all I want. That this might reach you. That you might want it to. That

Here. Here I am.

kawatsu
cellarskin

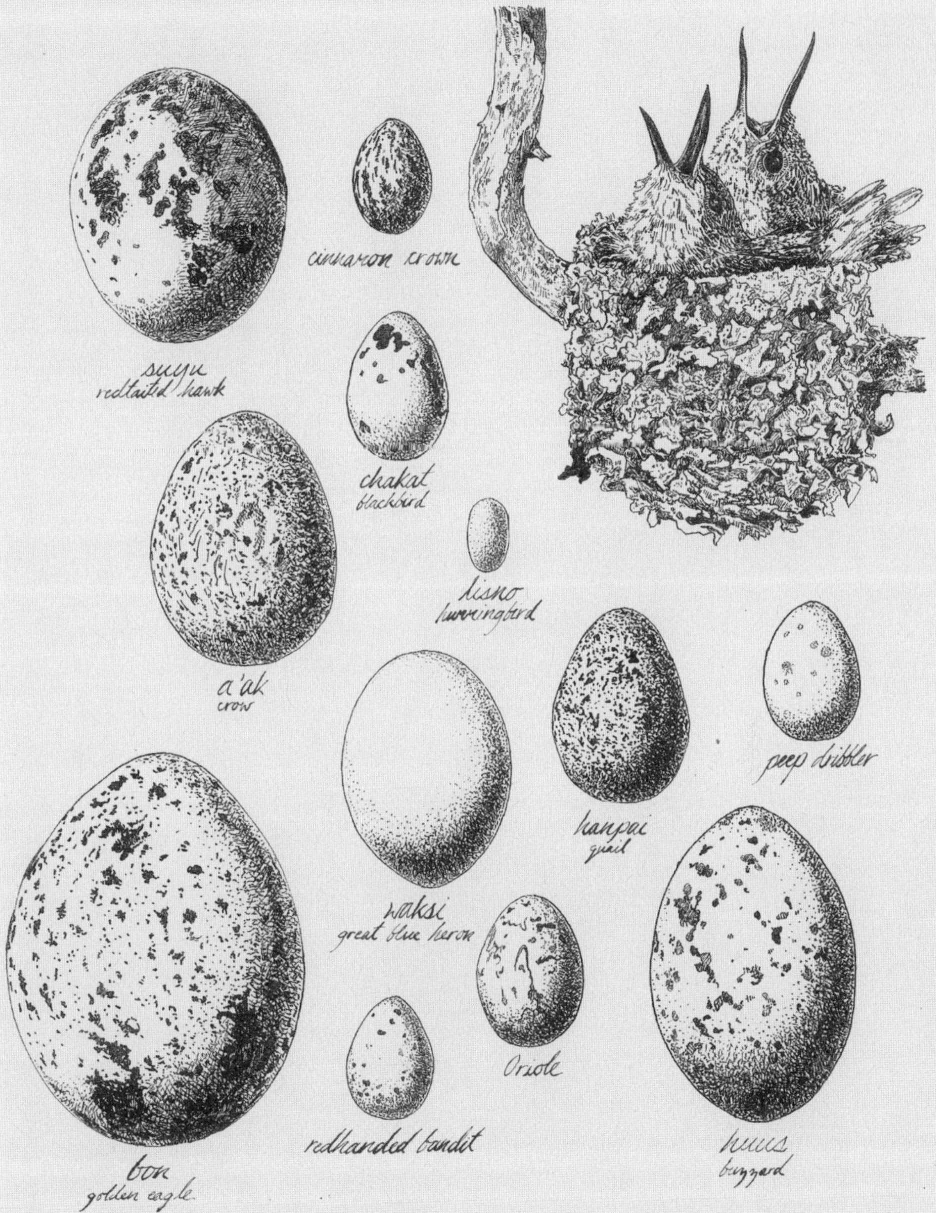

cinnaron crown
suyu
redtailed hawk
chakat
blackbird
lisno
hummingbird
a'ak
crow
peep dribbler
hanpai
quail
waksi
great blue heron
Oriole
redhanded bandit
bon
golden eagle
huus
buzzard

wibus at play
stoat

ACKNOWLEDGMENTS

Over all of American history I know of no greater ruination of the natural world in as compressed a time as what was wrought upon the Sierra Nevada during the California Gold Rush. In one year alone, an environment that had supported approximately fifty thousand indigenous people (plus a scant handful of non-native herders migrating seasonally up from the valley) found itself swamped by nearly twice that number: some ninety thousand new humans driven by the sole goal of ripping gold out of the land. The land itself was irrevocably altered, as were the lives of its inhabitants. None more so than the men, women, and children who already lived there.

Before the start of the nineteenth century there were thought to be as many as three hundred thousand Native Americans in what would become the state of California. By that century's end there would be just sixteen thousand. By some estimates, nearly one hundred thousand indigenous people died in the first decade of the Gold Rush. The Nisenan numbered around seven thousand in 1848; twenty years later fewer than five hundred survived. Now their descendants are fighting for federal recognition of the tribe, their government-granted status having been maliciously terminated (along with that of other California tribes) in the 1960s.

It is my great hope that this novel might help bring attention to their cause. But this is a work of fiction, written by a non-Nisenan, and so is in no way able to—or intended to—represent their culture. Still, I feel the weight of responsibility in my setting this story alongside a people's history so little written about and understood; I have tried to be as scrupulous and sensitive as possible in my depictions of tribal life.

I am indebted to Shelly Covert, Nevada City Rancheria Nisenan Tribal Spokesperson and executive director of the California Heritage Indigenous Research Project, or CHIRP, for meeting with me multiple times over the years as an invaluable guide and enthusiastic supporter of my research. For most of the Nisenan translations, I relied on the expertise of Sheri Jean Tatsch, PhD, author of *The Nisenan Dialects and Districts of a Speech Community*, and, later, additional assistance from CHIRP and the Nevada City Rancheria Nisenan Language Group, especially Andrew Eatough, who humored my follow-up questions and whose *Central Hill Nisenan Texts with Grammatical Sketch* was an important resource. For the Mountain Maidu (Notong k'oyom maidu) language, I drew primarily on Karen Lahaie Anderson's *Mountain Maidu Dictionary* and her generous assistance, as well as, to a lesser extent, William F. Shipley's *Maidu Texts and Dictionary*, among other resources. Each of the linguists I consulted used a different orthography and, in the interest of making the languages as phonetically accessible to the reader as possible, I've used a simplified approximation of sounds at the sacrifice of some accuracy. Any errors are my own.

As are any mistakes I may have made in my descriptions of geography or culture. Many of the names and exact locations of villages have been lost, and the effort to map them accurately is ongoing and evolving. I relied on CHIRP's most recent mapping project as my foundation and filled in what I could from elsewhere. The tribal borders are even more debated, though there is agreement that at each border there were wide swaths of less defined (and sometimes shared) land—especially in the higher regions of the Sierras, in which various tribes might reside during the summer. The Nisenan are part of a Maiduan language family that includes the Konkow, Mechoopda, and Mountain Maidu. For a long time, these tribes were erroneously grouped together. They are fully distinct peoples. However, their languages and cultures share many elements, and in the borderlands, especially, it was inevitable that there was some blending. So I have, on rare occasions, allowed for that in the fictional world of this book as well. For instance, where I couldn't find enough information on the Nisenan calendar, I used words for sections of the year from the Mountain Maidu one (a decision influenced by the fact that Silas learns Nisenan primarily from a Mountain Maidu character who speaks both and so speaks a combination himself). In some cases, such as with the Kuksu dances and ceremonies, where there were shared elements among tribes as far-flung as the Patwin, I turned to research on the Mountain Maidu or Konkow to fill out what I knew of Nisenan practices. In other cases (such as the kind of armor worn in warfare or the treatment of prisoners), I found contradictory accounts and had to choose (a decision bolstered by Shelly Covert's reminder that much variation between individuals, families, and communities exists in all cultures). As much as I could, though, I have stuck to what facts I found in the archives of the Foley Historical Library and the Searls Historical Library, and in so many books.

Most important to my understanding of the Nisenan and nearby tribes were Roland B. Dixon's *The Huntington California Expedition: The Northern Maidu*, A. L. Kroeber's *Handbook of the Indians of California*, Stephen Powers's *Tribes of California*, and *History of Us: Nisenan Tribe of the Nevada City Rancheria*, compiled by Tribal Chairman Richard B. Johnson. *Fur, Fortune, and Empire: The Epic History of the Fur Trade in America* by Eric Jay Dolin proved invaluable to my writing about the mountain men, as did *Firearms, Traps, and Tools of the Mountain Men* by Carl P. Russell and the website Malachite's Big Hole, maintained by Michael Schaubs. *Narrative of the Adventures of Zenas Leonard* by Zenas Leonard is referenced in the novel and was integral—along with other firsthand accounts by Jedidiah Smith, John C. Fremont, James Beckwourth, James Clyman, and others—to the chapters that take Silas west of Missouri and to the evolution of Silas's written voice. Among much research into the Gold Rush, I relied particularly on *The World Rushed In* by J. S. Holliday, *Gold Rush Stories* by Gary Noy, and the marvelous letters by Louise Amelia Knapp Smith Clappe—aka Dame Shirley—collected in *The Shirley Letters from California Mines.* Ted Steinberg's *Down to Earth: Nature's Role in American History*, Peter Matthiessen's *Wildlife in America*, and *First Along the River: A Brief History of the U.S. Environmental Movement* by Benjamin Kline gave me much insight into the changes in America's environment during the nineteenth century. Of all the sources I turned to for insight into neurodivergence, *Diary of a Young Naturalist* by Dara McAnulty helped shape my approach most. All of which is just the tip of the mountain of others' work that made this work possible.

I wrote this novel in an old camper-trailer set just downstream from land that, only recently, has been returned to the Nisenan tribe, on a neighboring property owned by my friends, Steve Rothert and Elizabeth Soderstrom. I cannot thank them enough for letting me perch there for the past decade. I owe great thanks also to my early readers—Shana Maziarz, Laura van den Berg, MLH—and Andrew Krivak, who later bolstered me when I needed it most. Thank you, too, to my agent, PJ Mark, my wise and trustworthy guide for nearly twenty years. And to my editor, Thomas Gebremedhin, who understood this book and worked with me to make it better in the way I'd always dreamed an editor would. To Johanna Zwirner, Pei Loi Koay, Oliver Munday, and the whole team at Doubleday. And, above all, to my family. My kids, Cody and Sadie, who always make returning from writing worth it. And to Jen, the love of my life, who, one winter morning when I was struggling, read through the first few pages of this book and walked down to my trailer beside the creek and told me to keep going and kissed me and freed me from doubt. Which made all the difference.

ABOUT THE AUTHOR

Josh Weil is the author of the novel *The Great Glass Sea*, the novella collection *The New Valley*, and the story collection *The Age of Perpetual Light.* A Fulbright fellow, he has been awarded the Dayton Literary Peace Prize, the Sue Kaufman Prize from the American Academy of Arts and Letters, a "5 Under 35" Award from the National Book Foundation, the California Book Award, and a Pushcart Prize. For the past dozen years he has called the Sierra Nevada of Northern California home.

A NOTE ON THE TYPE

This book was set in Janson, a typeface named for the Dutchman Anton Janson but actually the work of Nicholas Kis (1650–1702). The type is an excellent example of the influential and sturdy Dutch types that prevailed in England up to the time William Caslon (1692–1766) developed his own incomparable designs from them.